What readers and revie...

M.D. Kincaid has crafted ano... p knowledge of life in Alaska serves him well as he deftly maneuvers across Alaska—and beyond—bringing readers an exciting new adventure of courage, endurance, and love. From the very first page, he takes unsuspecting readers on a roller coaster of events based on his years of true experiences as an Alaska State Trooper. Even for those who are not "dreamers" of Alaska, this book is gold.—Nancy Owens Barnes, Idaho Writers League, author, *"South to Alaska."*

Mike builds the suspense, then takes you through the Blakes' adventures in great detail. He makes you feel like you are right there witnessing the action.— Bob Bell, Alaska Writers Guild member, author of *"Oh No, We're Gonna Die."*

Kincaid has captured Alaska as it actually exists. No "show boating" but the truth in daring-do and the hard choices faced by Alaskan Lawmen on any given day. As a former Alaskan Lawman, I highly recommend Trooper Jack Blake's and Jet's *"Alaska and Beyond."* It smacks of truth not often revealed in books of the 49th State.—Steve Knutson, Alaska Department of Public Safety, retired, author of *"It Takes One to Catch One,"* and *"Valley of the Shadow."*

Kincaid has brewed up an intriguing tale with all the essentials of a great story; good guys, bad guys, and airplanes.— Idaho State Trooper Kevin Murphy.

Mike Kincaid invests ALASKA & BEYOND with whirlwind cinematic pacing and the personal experience of real Alaskan law enforcement officer to make sure the adventures of Trooper Blake ring true. Strap on your snow shoes and rappelling gear: equal parts investigation and action, ALASKA & BEYOND is tons of fun—an exciting ride and a compelling mystery.—Randall D. Larson, veteran Public Safety Communications Supervisor and Editor, *9-1-1 Magazine.*

Kincaid reloads, adjusts his sights, and takes aim at more real life villains ripped from the pages of his case files. Always finding his mark, MDK points Trooper Blake in the right direction—square in front of the bad guys, and always armed with the skills & integrity to triumph over evil & skullduggery. You can't find a better read about the human wildlife found in Alaska, and running amok past its borders—it'll keep you on the edge of your seat and looking over your shoulder!" —David McRae, Alaska Bush Pilot & Commercial Fisherman.

ALASKA & BEYOND

A Novel By

M.D. Kincaid

The Sequel to *Alaska Justice*

Adventurous Books

Adventurous Books

Fairbanks/Coeur d'Alene

Adventurous Books,. LLC is a small press publisher based whose interests include Alaska stories and aviation-related works. We seek and find our own adventures for publishing, so please don't query.
WWW.AdventurousBooks.Com

Cover design: Tom Latham, Signal Point Design
Printer: Lightning Source, La Vergne, TN

Text © 2009 M.D. Kincaid

This book is a work of fiction. Any similarity to real persons, living or dead, is coincidental and not intended by the author. The author means no disrespect to any present or former Alaska State Trooper or Alaska State employee, who all seem to rise to the occasion when needed.

First Adventurous Books Edition: May 2009. ISBN 978-0-9796693-4-7
The Library of Congress has cataloged the paperback editions as: Kincaid, M.D. Alaska & Beyond.

To purchase books, visit the www.AdventurousBooks.com website, ask your favorite bookseller or contact your on-line vendor.

ATTENTION CORPORATIONS, ORGANIZATIONS & BOOK CLUBS: Adventurous Books publications are available for quantity discounts with bulk purchase for educational, business, or sales promotional use. Visit www.AdventurousBooks.com for information.

Acknowledgments

My deepest thanks to my dedicated and insightful editor, Kitty Fleischman, an award-winning editor and former Bush Alaska teacher. Kitty, publisher of *IDAHO Magazine*, has a better eye for boo boos than an eagle has for salmon. Technical Editor Forrest Schuck is not only a wordsmith, but knows every detail about things which fly and shoot, as well about the Northwest. Many thanks also to proofreaders Jill Kincaid (my own Jet), Nancy Owens Barnes, Ted Herlihy, Tedd Goth, and others who endured the process. Thanks for information provided by: the Alaska State Troopers, Stu Felberg, retired fish & wildlife trooper and herpetologist, Kevin Murphy, Idaho State Police, LAPD Detective Rick Jackson, Ret. LAPD Helicopter Pilot Larry Clark, LAPD Retired Lt. Kent Setty, Coeur d' Alene Police Department Sergeant Christie Woods, Coeur d' Alene Fire Department Deputy Chief Glen Lauper, Pilot/Attorney Chris Popov, Helicopter Pilot James Black, Kevin Purdy of Sky Dive Idaho, Sergio and Gary Planagan of Osprey Rafting Company, Jim Cullen/Softie Parachutes, Pilot and Forecaddie Sherry Stefani, Dr. Mark Manteuffel, Officer George Vrablik, Anchorage Police Department/SERT, Chef Alex, Bonnie Bassetti, Phoenix.

This work is dedicated to all the hardworking Troopers and support staff of the Alaska Department of Public Safety. Special dedication to the Alaska Troopers who made the ultimate sacrifice protecting the rest of us: Troy Duncan, Dennis Cronin, Larry Carr, Frank Rodman, Roland Chevalier, John Stimson, Robert Bittick, C.E. Swackhammer, Bruce Heck, David Churchill, and James Moen.

The main character is named for Jack Blake, my wife's father, whose final dog sledding race was his final day on earth.

"Show me an adventure and most times I'll show you a stupid mistake." —Former Alaska Governor Jay Hammond.

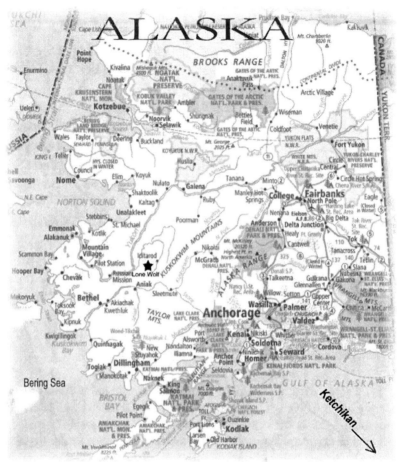

About the Author

Mike Kincaid survived an exciting career with the Alaska Department of Public Safety.
His adventures took him from Ketchikan to Barrow, with stopovers on Mt. McKinley and the deep Bush. Today, Mike pilots seaplanes for fun, writing when the weather grounds him.

Alaska & Beyond

Prologue

IT HAS BEEN JUST FOUR MONTHS since Alaska Trooper Jack Blake asked Wildlife Trooper Jet Torsen to marry him on the ice of this very remote, wind-blown lake. Only that day was darker. Darker and much colder. If it were not for Jet killing the man trying to take his life, Jack would not be here. And there would not be a wedding today.

The pastor is ready to join Jack and Jet in holy matrimony. The guests are already partying.

Suddenly, the ceremonies are interrupted by the familiar *WHOP, WHOP, WHOP,* of the Alaska State Trooper helicopter. The pilot pleads for help in stopping a killer who is holding hostages. There are only two troopers for the job. Their marriage ceremony will have to wait.

Ending the day for a crazed-killer is nothing compared to the challenges Jack and Jet face next.

Most people fear grizzly bears—with good reason. Jack Blake has spent enough time in the Bush that he is more comfortable hiking in bear country than wandering around a city with millions of people. Blake puts that aside to track what the Alaska attorney general suspects is a rogue fellow trooper on a killing-spree in the Lower 48. Jack meets people and sees things he never knew existed. But, when it comes down to the basics, he uses the same skills in L.A., Phoenix, Salt Lake City, and Idaho as he uses to survive in Alaska.

Jet has her own mission. Assigned to investigate the serial killings of young women by a Bush pilot/trophy hunter, Jet goes undercover. She purposely becomes the target.

Bush planes, guns, defensive tactics, and sheer willpower. Is that enough for the troopers to survive their intertwining investigations?

Alaska & Beyond

Part One

Chapter 1

MAN IN BLACK

DO I DESERVE WHAT I AM ABOUT TO GET? Probably not. But somehow, here I am. Shortly, a uniformed man will escort me—maybe even drag me—to stand in front of the Man in Black.

The lake is still frozen deeply, but the sun is bursting from the cobalt skies with enough power to warm the backs of the caribou trudging through the snowy Kilbuck Mountains. Layers of ice are still thick enough to support the fifteen Alaska State Trooper airplanes perched on their skis on this spring day. Thick enough to support the fifty-six lawmen and witnesses who would soon gather around the Man in Black. Thick enough to support the weight of fear I am hauling deep within.

I should not be afraid. It seems just yesterday when my patrol plane violently crashed onto the frozen tundra in the dead of winter. Badly wounded and without gear, I survived for an eternity in the harshest of Western Alaska weather. When rescue finally came, it came in the form of a madman who shot me—twice. Then, another would try to finish the job. Now that should have been fearful. But no, any fear I had that lifetime ago pales compared with the panic tumbling through my body at this moment.

Now's my chance to escape. The men are callously celebrating my fate with spirits. No one watches me. Maybe they will not notice my absence for a while. Ducking between the alder brush, I crash through the deep snow. My heart races and sweat drips from my temples. Legs pumping, I cover the fifty yards to the ridge that hangs over the lake. Stopping, catching my breath, I study the peaceful scene tucked in the Kilbuck Mountains. It is serene, beautiful, and as good a day as any for this. But I must continue my getaway.

Loosening the wool collar on the neck-choking jacket donned for the occasion, I keep moving. I need some distance. I need time to

3

think. More brush, more snow sneaking down into my boots, but now there is a trail. I break into a clearing, and then...

Crack! A gunshot. Probably a pistol. *Crack!* Another, then another.

Instinctively, I reach for my gun. It isn't there.

Crack! Another shot. Breaking through a clearing, I stop, sensing something—or someone—behind me. I turn slowly. A vision in white.

She's beautiful. Golden locks flowing onto the delicate shoulders of her blizzard-white dress. Pink cheeks glow through her olive complexion and that smile is enough to make my knees weak. She closes the gap between us quickly, wrapping her arms around me, immediately warming my core at least ten degrees.

She whispers into my ear "Jack, what are you doing back here? Don't you know the groom isn't supposed to see the bride in her dress before the wedding?"

Jet's ceremonial wedding dress, sewn by Village Police Officer Josh Luko's wife, is spectacular. The traditional Eskimo kuspuck is white, trimmed in teal that matches Jet's eyes. Wolverine fur adorns the hem and the cuff of the short dress. On her feet are mukluks, with sealskin soles, caribou uppers, wolf trim and colorful beads. We kiss, then she gives me her pouty look. She's wondering why I escaped from the makeshift bachelor party.

"Sorry Jet, I was just taking a breather when I heard the shots. Is everything okay?"

Jet locks her arm in mine, leading me into the clearing. An attractive, diminutive woman, flaming red hair flowing over the ruff of her parka and sporting stylish shooting glasses, grins at us. I recognize her immediately.

"Jack, meet Tinka Hines, my college roommate and now Governor Hines. She wanted to surprise you at the wedding."

"Pleasure to meet you, Jack. Congratulations on your wedding day. Care to join us for a little target practice?" The governor graciously makes me feel at ease. She holds a big, shiny revolver and a deck of cards.

"Thank you. It is an honor, Governor." The feisty leader has been making significant changes since she took office two years ago. Not just giving away oil money to the state's residents, but more importantly, overhauling Alaska's troubled justice system. I look at the deck of cards. An ace of spades is face up on top.

"Shooting is a great way to ease the nerves Jack. I see you're not packing a gun with that full dress trooper tunic. Here, take mine. I had it ported and I hand load my ammo."

The governor has read my mind. I'm still trying to shake off the fear of the pending ceremonies. I guess it shows.

"Jack, the game is to stick a playing card on that tree over there, step back fifty paces and rip the card in half with the fewest shots possible. Here, take a card and this clothespin. Clip the card to the nail in the tree and go for it." The governor nods to a spruce tree at the end of a well-packed snow trail.

It looks fun. The .44 Magnum is a powerful weapon, but the angry bucking it makes with each shot is another thing. Nice for protection. Not especially enjoyable for repetitive target practice.

I draw a deuce. Maybe I'm being set up, but I tromp to the distant tree. Pieces of playing cards are scattered around the trunk. I clip the clothespin on the nail, then attach the card in the pin's tip. Small target. Really small target at the distance, but I pace back to where the women are standing. I'm pretty certain I hear a muffled giggle from the governor as she questions whether I'm ready. Jet winks at me.

Confirming the .44 is loaded, I acknowledge the governor's warning that it shoots a little bit to the left, maneuver into the combat shooting position, and line up the heavy barrel with the card. The rubber Pachmayr grips feel good in my hand as I hold the big revolver firm. I take a deep breath, then with my lungs nearly full and the sight steady, I squeeze the trigger. The recoil isn't as bad as I expect. The boom is worse than I remember. The card blows into pieces.

"I can't believe you just did that Jack!" The governor shrieks. "We mortals face the whole card towards the shooter, not just the edge of the card! Where did you learn to shoot like that?"

The governor seems truly shocked. I'm embarrassed—I hadn't followed the rules of the game.

"Sorry, governor. Is that okay?" I stammer, trying to think of something to make up for my rule breaking. Their way was easier.

"You betcha, Jack. And I think you've earned the right to call me Tinka!"

Jet beams as she winks once more and covers for me. "You'll have to excuse my husband-to-be, Tinka. He was raised on guns." Then she delivers my fate: "It's about time for you to face the music, Jack. We'd better all head back to the lake."

IT'S TIME to meet the Man in Black.

Chapter 2

ABOUT TIME

THE TROOPER GUIDES ME to the front of the crowd. Ted Herlihy, also known as Titanium Ted because of his prosthetic hand, is my good friend. Together, we stand before former Alaska State Trooper Major Rich Emery, now Pastor Emery. He shakes off his parka to reveal the black cloth of the church. I turn to see the love of my life, Jessi Torsen—Jet to those who know and love her—being led down the snow path by Officer Josh Luko. Donning a brown parka, the Eskimo's grinning face makes him look even more like a big teddy bear.

Jet slides her hands into mine. I can now laugh at my earlier bout with pre-nuptial fear. T-Ted snorts and points to the heavens. A pair of bald eagles, their white heads and black bodies stark against the blue skies, is locked in a mating ritual, free falling towards earth. Maybe an omen. Maybe just a coincidence, but everything seems perfect.

Okay, not everything is perfect. The wedding cake is a mess. Trooper Ronnie Torgy tried his best to deliver it by dogsled. With Ronnie's usual luck, it didn't quite work out. The troubled, but happy trooper reported that the cake topper was lost, "somewhere between Bethel and the Kilbucks." The lead dog had bitten a chunk from the blueberry cake with white icing, but it's okay. Jet and I will finally be husband and wife.

I nod to the crowd of troopers, all dressed in sky-blue formal dress tunics and navy trousers with red and gold stripes. Ted Herlihy, all six feet-four of him, fixes his gray eyes on me, holding the ring box in his stainless steel prosthetic hand. He's taking his best man role seriously, focusing intently on me, making sure I don't miss a step. It's payback time, as I'd been his best man when he married a sweet, pretty auburn-haired lady named Anna who, like Jet, is of Norwegian

7

ancestry. I pull out the vows that Jet and I wrote together. This is actually going to happen. Nothing can ruin this day.

As my former trooper supervisor, Rich Emery had to judge my job performance. I now wonder if he's judging my dismal church attendance record. The pastor begins the ceremony with a personal note: "Someone here asked me just this morning how I know there is a God. I think of God as the father I never had, as my best friend, as my mentor, as my hero, as the One I can count on for everything else that is good. I talk to Him whenever I can, not just to ask for help when I need it, but to thank Him for all the good in my life. If that's not good enough for anybody, just look at the beauty surrounding us. Now to the task...no, to the honor at hand..."

"*WHOP, WHOP, WHOP.*" The sea of troopers turns, looking again to the sky. The department's "Helo One," piloted by Hayden Bensen, races toward the crowd. The troopers grab their Stetsons—except for Ronnie Torgy, who's always just a bit slow on the draw. His hat flies off, initiating a "Tour d' Nishlik Lake." As Ronnie begins his pursuit, the rest of us prepare for the blast from the helicopter's blades.

The sun glistens off the insignia on the blue and gold Eurocopter AS-350 "A-Star" as it settles onto the snow. Keeping the blades turning, Hayden points directly at me and briskly waves me towards the left door. My guess is that he's dropped in to give Jet and me his blessings. I guess wrong.

As I lean into the cockpit, Hayden yanks off his headset, yelling over the chopper noise. "Jack, we have a problem." I've heard those four words many times in my career. They never bring good news.

I crawl into the left seat, pulling on a headset. "Good to see you too, Hayden. What brings you here?"

"Jack, I'd really planned on coming for the wedding, but I've been tied up on an emergency. I need two troopers right now! A worker on a processor barge near Togiak went crazy and is shooting up the boat. At least three fatals so far and more hurting. I just hauled out Trooper Bell, who took a hit to his leg. You guys are the only troopers for several hundred miles. We gotta go. Now!"

Surveying the crowd of troopers, I can only find one who doesn't have a spirit of some sort in hand. The whole bunch is planning on making a party of this event, camping for the night on the lake. The only alcohol-free troopers are Jet and me.

"Hayden, I'll go with you. But I'm it. Everyone else is out of service." Just then, the back door of the helo opens. Jet crawls in, grabbing a headset.

Hayden smiles, nods at Jet, and continues. "Jack, this isn't a skiff we're talking about. The *Togiak Delight* is two hundred-seventy feet long and sixty feet wide, with plenty of places for a sniper to hide. There are sixty-five workers on board and all are in danger. I'd gladly take more than two troopers, but that's all I want to try to drop on the deck in the one-shot hover approach. Two are the minimum for safety. Isn't there one other sober trooper here?"

"Sure there is, Hayden. Standby, I'll be right back." Before I can protest, Jet bends under the blade wash and dashes to a Cessna ski plane. In a flash, she runs back to the chopper toting two gun belts with pistols, two assault rifles and a small pack. Even with that ungainly load, Jet somehow looks graceful jogging back to us.

I yank the back door open for Jet. We toss the gear and crawl back into our seats. The crowd waves, some with their drinks, as Hayden moves the control stick—or as he insists on calling it the "cyclic"—to the right, and we scoot sideways.

"Some wedding, huh? Sorry Jet. We were so close." I apologize to Jet through the intercom.

"Don't think you're getting out of our big day so easy, Jack Blake. Everyone said they will wait for us. Guess there is a downside in waiting to sip the bubbly! Where are you whisking us off to, Hayden?"

"I wish it was to someplace warm for your honeymoon, but we're headed to Togiak Bay. Some nutcase has been blasting away since last night. Sorry that it had to be you two. Well, honestly, there are no other troopers I'd rather have, but I do apologize for ruining your day." Hayden's bushy blonde mustache almost conceals his frown.

"It's okay, Hayden. We'll pick up where we left off." Jet speaks as she clips a magazine into a scoped-semiautomatic .223 caliber rifle. She looks gorgeous in her wedding dress. I just hope she doesn't get fish slime on it.

"Roger. We have about thirty minutes 'til we arrive. I'm going to go in as quietly as possible, but there are no guarantees that we won't take fire. What can I tell you?"

Glancing back at Jet, I marvel at how beautiful she is, even as she busily checks the magazine and sight on a .308 rifle.

"What kind of weapons does he have? And is he a good shot?" I ask Hayden.

"He's packing a large caliber hunting rifle with a scope. The vessel's skipper says it's carried for bear protection. I'm guessing it's for poaching walruses on Hagemeister Island, but no matter now. He also has a sidearm. Trooper Bell thinks it is a .357. He should know, since he was shot by it. Bell would probably say the guy is a darn good marksman, but then again, Bell is alive."

"Is he on his own?" Jet tenders that important question as she checks the .40 caliber pistols.

"Yep, he's a loner. Bell says he must have snuck some booze aboard. He got into a verbal confrontation with another slimer and it escalated. Next thing the captain knows the guy starts shooting." Hayden calmly answers as he pitches the helicopter to climb over a ridge, then forward to drop over Togiak Lake.

"How's Trooper Bell?" Jet asks Hayden over the intercom.

"He was hit just as he jumped out the helo door. You'd think he was a Hollywood stuntman the way he rolled across the deck and back on the skid as I hovered. He was hanging on for his life as I banked over the bay. He pulled himself into the cabin and I took him to the clinic in Dillingham. Thanks to all the meat he has on those gigantic thighs of his, once they find the bullet, he'll be fine. Let's talk about how we are going to make our approach."

Hayden details his plan as he guides the helicopter down a valley where we pick up a river leading to Twin Hills. The Eurocopter 350 is capable of flying at the altitudes of Mount Everest, but today we will be operating at sea level—although that doesn't make this mission any more friendly. "Let's hope the shooter is sleeping off his drunk, or otherwise occupied. These choppers are not exactly the most stealthy way to make an entrance. I'm going in fast, then hover over the deck. You'll need to exit quickly."

As Jet hands me a gun belt with a pistol, she makes a revelation. "Jack, I just realized that we don't have our flak vests. Let's have a rule—neither of us gets shot. Which rifle do you want?

"Good rule, but are you getting bossy now that we are almost married? Why don't you give me the .308? The .223 is more dainty." In the ship's close quarters, the light rifle will be better for Jet.

Jet slides the .308 over the seat to me. "You're right Jack, the .223 is exquisite, especially with this cute little knock-down scope." She hands me extra magazines for the rifle and for the Glock pistol from her pack. Then she pulls out two portable police radios, handing me one. "Let's do a radio check, Jack." She whispers intimately into the private airwaves.

"Roger, copy loud and clear. I love you too." I answer, smiling red-faced into the portable as we pop onto Togiak Bay.

The silver waters of the Alaskan bay look so peaceful—surrounded by rugged hills, dotted with islands, the herring fleet churning in circles—except for the threatening whitecaps

This one should go smoothly, I hope.

Chapter 3

ROUGH WATERS

"HANG ON, THIS IS GONNA BE A LITTLE ROUGH!" Hayden warns us, as his thousand-yard-stare—earned from years of flying in Alaska—grows even more intense. He fights with the complex controls to maintain command of the helicopter as we bang through the violent turbulence. What had looked like a peaceful bay transforms into a tumultuous torrent of air, as the craft is thrown about like a cork in a whitewater river. Jet grabs my seatback and I grasp what I can, as we dodge the flying debris in the cabin for the white-knuckle flight a thousand feet above the sea.

Bobbing in the waters, the herring fleet continues fishing, unaware of our battle in the air. Black nets drape from booms on boats as they pull gear from the water. Other boats race in circles, puffing clouds of dark smoke.

"There she is." Hayden points to the biggest boat in the bay. "It's too rough to do a recon, this approach is gonna be it."

Jet and I look at each other, shake our heads, and laugh. We aren't exactly dressed for the occasion. I'm sporting the trooper formal attire—dress tunic and wool pants with shiny black boots. Jet looks very bride-like in her white kuspuck and mukluks. At least the Eskimo-made dress is insulated with fur, so she will stay warm. The gun belt she grabbed at Nishlik Lake is big enough to wrap around her tiny waist a couple of times, but she made it work. Not the usual accessory for a wedding day, but the black leather gear—cradling the Glock .40 caliber—is practical for this mission.

Suddenly, Hayden yanks on the controls and banks hard to the right. Jerking my head to movement in my peripheral vision, a red and white blur rushes by the bubble window. The Super Cub is so close that the pilot's green David Clark headset is plainly visible, and the racing

Lycoming engine is audible. Lucky for all, the Cub pilot breaks to the left as we bank to the right.

"Herring spotters! They're everywhere out here, looking for those stinking fish!" Hayden wipes perspiration from his forehead and regains our course. Jet once told me that hordes of small planes spot herring for fishermen, with midair collisions being an accepted hazard. Looking up through the skylight, I now see a whole gaggle of Cubs, Cessnas, other small planes and helicopters swarming above us like bees over a hive. They have no clue what our mission is, nor do they care. They have their own missions.

The processing barge is huge with comparison to the little fishing boats. If it wasn't for the antennae, cranes, machinery, metal shacks and all the other equipment on the deck, it'd make a nice landing strip for a small Bush plane. Hayden points the helicopter between two of the tallest cranes. This is going to be close, especially in the rough air, but if anyone can get us on the deck, it's Hayden.

"Jet, since I have to jump out the left side, how 'bout you take the right? Then we can meet up once we hit the deck." Jet nods in agreement.

The helicopter pitches and twists. The booms look so close that it seems they can reach over and grab the spinning chopper's blades. I focus on the roof of the rusty white metal shack—the designated landing pad. Hayden doesn't broadcast as we drop closer. One hundred feet, seventy-five, fifty, now just twenty. I scan the deck. No one in sight. Is that good news or bad?

"Get ready to bail!" Somehow, Hayden deftly manipulates us below the overhanging cranes. He banks slightly to avoid dangling cables, while still fighting the turbulence. Two men are in the barge pilothouse. One is frantically waving us off. The other man is holding a pistol to the waver's head. I start to tell Jet, but Hayden blares over the headsets: "Jump!"

Jet and I fall several feet to the little shack's roof, rifles in hand. I slide to my knee on the wet surface, but Jet gracefully lands in a run.

We pile off opposite sides of the little building as the deafening helicopter rushes away.

I grab my radio, telling what I see. "Jet, two guys in the pilothouse. One with a gun."

"Saw them. I've got one dead over here."

The barge's deck is slippery, made so by seawater, herring slime and oils from the equipment. It smells of fish guts, diesel and sea air. The noise from the wind and the power plants will make it difficult to hear movement from the suspect, or much else.

The barge sways in the waves as we walk like drunken sailors to the bow, passing the body Jet had discovered. His eyes are open to the sky and there's a red spot on his sweatshirt. We pull ourselves on top of a shipping container to get an overview. Using the scope of my rifle, my scan finds the pilothouse now empty. Jet begins searching with her scope, but we're interrupted.

"*PING! PING! PING!*" The rifle shots tear into the metal roof, just a foot in front of where we lie. We spin off the container in unison.

"Jet, the shooter must be on the deck outside the pilothouse. How about you stay here and cover me and I'll try to sneak up on him." My voice cracks into the portable radio.

"I need to be closer, Jack. I can't get a visual from here. How about you take the port side and I take the starboard? I'll try to get a better vantage point."

What I really want is for Jet to stay put, behind the container. I don't want her in any more danger than she already is, but I know that won't fly with her.

"Okay, but stay low. Let's go." I reluctantly give in, like I have a choice. We start our approach.

Crouching along the side of the barge, I use the generators, equipment boxes, control units, and barrels as cover. Jet will be doing the same on her side. Only occasionally can I catch sight of her. That sight—her lithe body in the white dress with the flowing golden locks, and loaded for battle, is both humorous and sensual. It will be great when this part of the day is over and we can pick up on what we were doing less than an hour ago.

Movement to my right! Drawing the Glock, I swing the barrel toward the target.

"Meow." The barge cat. I sometimes think that it's the mission of felines to sneak up on us humans, often at the worst times. A dog would never do that. Maybe slop into you with his wet hide, demanding a toss of the stick, but not sneaky stuff like this. This is a friendly fella though, so I give him a quick pat on the head and read his tag: Skyler Edward King. "Hello, Sky King. Good to meet you," I offer. He stretches, and then jumps away. I take the break in concentration to call Jet on the radio.

"Jet, do you have anything yet? Nothing but a four-legged creature over here."

"Nothing yet. I think most of the crew must be below deck...wait. There's a lot of blood on the deck. More on the rail over here. Just a sec, I think I hear something. Up by the pilothouse. Standby, I'll check it out."

The pilothouse is about fifty feet from me. There is too much junk between my side of the barge and Jet's side for me to see her. I return to my crouching walk, then...

Scuffling, muffled voices, then a gunshot from Jet's side of the barge! Quickly, I scale the storage container separating us. What I see makes my heart sink and my blood pressure rocket.

The shooter has Jet! The burly, bearded wild man holds Jet in a headlock. She's facing my direction, her mukluks off the deck. She's struggling. Her martial arts skills are usually enough to get her out of almost any confrontation, but he has the drop on her and he's much larger. Plus, the revolver he's holding to her right temple gives him a distinct edge over her defensive tactics. He's roughly dragging her toward the pilothouse. I want to blast him out to sea, but I don't have a clean shot. Jet is being used for a shield and they are moving too fast. I need to get the advantage, and get it without delay.

My current position provides no cover, but there's a worse problem. Jet and her captor will soon be back in the high-perched pilot-house. From the roof I'm on, the trajectory is at too much of an angle for a clean shot, and there will only be one shot. I look skyward for inspiration. I find it.

Like a mast on a sailing ship, a large steel pole rises from the deck. Near the top of the pole is a crow's nest, surrounded by metal plates. Slinging the rifle over my shoulder, I begin climbing the slippery metal ladder on the pole. I get half way up before the first glitch.

"*PING!*" A shot hits the other side of the pole. I hear and feel it. The sniper has made me. Becoming as skinny as I can, I shinny up the pole with as much speed as I can muster. I dive into the crow's nest as the next shot hits the side plate. Above me, the yellow and black smiley face flag of the processing company flaps violently in the breeze.

"Jack, the captain's dead. Stay dow...!" Jet tries to warn me.

"Give me that!" The voice of what must the shooter's yells.

As calmly as I'm able, I speak into the portable radio.

"Sir, this is Trooper Jack Blake. Let's talk about this."

"What do you want to talk about, cop? It looks like I have the advantage here. I got me a cute little cop girl. Kinda reminds me of my ex-wife. I think we might retire to the captain's quarters. Guess he won't be needing his bed any longer, on account of the fact that he's dead and all."

The guy is a talker. That's good. Maybe I can keep him talking. Talking is better than him going on with his plans. I figure that he has locked the door to the pilothouse by now, so I can't rush him. Plus, there's no way for me to get to it without being in his line of fire. Me getting shot won't help Jet. My best bet is to keep him in the window. But Jet has a plan of her own.

The shooter's grimy hand, terminating in dirty, long fingernails, relaxes its grip on Jet's neck so he can continue his diatribe on the radio. Jet takes the chance. She slides a knife from the sheath of the trooper's belt and rams it into his leg. The force is so great that the blade breaks. So does the shooter's temper. Almost strangling Jet, he tenses his grip with the force of a grizzly. Exhaling with putrid whiskey breath, he screams into the radio.

"Forget what I said before, cop. This one reminds me a little *too* much of my ex. I'm just going to put her out of my misery right now, if you don't mind. Then we can continue our little chat." The killer puts the .357 revolver to Jet's temple as she prays silently.

"Hold on, hold on a minute. You don't want to do that." I need just a little more time.

Swaying in tempo with the seas, the crow's nest isn't the perfect shooting platform, but it will have to do. I poke the rifle barrel between the steel plates. Focusing on the pilothouse, I chat with the killer to keep him from killing again—to keep him from killing the reason for which I live.

"So, what's your name?"

"Call me 'Boss,' since I'm calling the shots. Now you go ahead and throw that rifle down. Then you can come up here and we can all have a nice talk."

"Okay. Boss it is. I'm Jack." Through the scope, the pilothouse comes into focus. It's tough to get a good visual. Each time the barge sways with a wave, the sun's glare blinds me. I have to get into the swing of things. Since I'm a lousy dancer, I decide to count. One as the shipped rolls up, two as it pitches down.

"Boss, how did this mess start?" One, two, one, two, one.

"Like they all say, cop, I'm innocent."

One, two, one... "I believe you, Boss, I believe you." One is now for the glare, as the barge pitches up. Two is now for the clearest shot. As a wave sinks I can see the killer holding the .357 to Jet's head. I can almost make out her beautiful eyes.

One, two, one, two. Steady on two.

"Excuse me a minute, cop. I've decided to go ahead and make my day." Boss mutters into the radio.

One, two... "Jet! DUCK!" One, two....

The bang is loud. The recoil is comforting. The broken pilot-house glass is reassuring. There is no movement from either of the heads that had been in my scope. The next words are pure joy.

"Jack, Jack. Are you on?" Jet questions over the portable radio. I can now exhale again.

"Yes, dear, did you need something?" I jubilantly answer.

"Yes, please, cleanup on aisle four!" Jet's sweet voice booms over the speaker mounted outside the pilothouse.

"You must be okay," I chuckle.

"I'm fine. Not the Boss, though. Nice shooting. Let's meet on the deck."

Climbing down the pole even faster than I had climbed up, I rush down the deck toward the pilothouse. Jet meets me halfway. I stop in my tracks, looking her up and down.

"Yeah, I know, I've made a mess out of my wedding dress. I used to get that same look from my father when I was kid, after a day of playing outside in Naknek."

Jet's beautiful white kuspuck is splattered with blood and other matter. So is her hair. She's in total disarray, but I've never been so happy to see her. We hug, but she winces in pain. I pull a small shard of glass from her forearm—her only injury.

Like fans exiting the Sullivan Arena in Anchorage after a big hockey game, processor workers swarm from the bowels of the barge. Some pat us on our backs, some clap, and others burst out crying. One young lady with big hair takes Jet to her quarters to "clean her up a bit." Returning shortly, Jet now wears new wedding day attire: a Dallas Cowboy's sweatshirt and a pink mini-skirt with white leggings. Her mukluks really set it off. Cute as ever.

"Jack. Jet. It's Hayden. Everything okay down there?" Hayden Bensen shouts over the police radio as he hovers above the barge. The blue, white and gold of the helicopter shines in the late afternoon sun.

"We're okay, but a couple of men need medical attention and there are at least two dead." I answer with the portable radio. Hayden acknowledges, then relays that he will drop off the investigative team he's carrying and then transport the injured to Dillingham.

Hayden promises to get us back to Nishlik Lake by dark. Hopefully in time to finish what we started—seemingly so long ago.

Chapter 4

MEANWHILE, BACK AT THE LAKE

"WHERE HAVE YOU TWO BEEN, CHEERLEADING CAMP?" Raising one eyebrow, Ted Herlihy addresses Jet's dramatic change of attire. She does look pretty darn cute in the mini-skirt outfit, now partially covered by a wolf parka a trooper loaned her. Ted's question draws laughs from the partygoers who have been celebrating our wedding for the past four hours—even though we hadn't had the chance to say the magic words yet.

"Something like that, Ted. Jack can fill you in later. We're ready to pick up where we left off," Jet offers.

Ted shrugs his broad shoulders. "That'd be great, but we have one little problem. Major Emery, I mean *Pastor* Emery, had to split. Seems that his new job requires him to be in church on Sundays. The air taxi guy flew in and told him if he wanted to get back tonight, they had to leave." Wisely, the pilot didn't want to fly through Merrill Pass in darkening skies. That narrow crag, dotted with airplane wrecks which are used as navigation aids, is scary enough during daylight. Guess they were all out of the good passes by the time it was Russ Merrill's turn to have one named after him. Ted had renewed his interest in flying, earning his trooper pilot wings two months ago. He'd made four trips through Merrill Pass since then. He almost got suckered into a wrong turn the first time—banking hard at the crashed Cessna 172 instead of at the crashed Cessna 170—nearly making his initial voyage into the pass his last. Two others were "near death experiences," because of low clouds and turbulence. The last flight earned him just a few new gray hairs, like most Alaska Bush pilots seem to have—probably in proportion to the flying hours in their logbooks.

Ted's right, it's Saturday night and Pastor Emery would certainly need to be in Anchorage for Sunday's service, especially since he would be delivering the sermon. I wish we could have said good-bye to him and thanked him for coming all the way to Nishlik Lake. I hope our paths cross again.

It's time to explore our options. Jet has been through enough today and I can see in her eyes that it's weighing on her. I feel the same way, but it looks like the wedding is a no-go. Suddenly, my old friend Ronnie Torgy bursts on the scene with a suggestion. Ronnie is one of those guys whose inner circuitry prevents him from realizing that some things are just impossible to fix. But just maybe one of his crazy, but genuinely well-intended notions, will work its way through his jumbled hard drive and provide some hope.

Stumbling through the crowd, Ronnie Torgy nearly falls face-first into the bonfire that has been providing both warmth and inspiration. As he extinguishes the smoke on the sole of his boot, the rotund Ronnie speaks: "Gentlemen, I say we break into groups, men in one group and women in the other. We can explore our options to get this wedding back on track. While we're at it, we can now resume Jack's bachelor party."

I'm not in the mood for a party with the guys, but we're out of ideas. I'm sure Jet is thinking the same. But, keeping up a good front, she and the other women trudge up to Josh's cabin. It's there that the governor set up a temporary post, conducting the state's business on a base radio system. The quarters are set on a little plateau above the lake, fitting for a remote Alaska governor's office. Last summer Josh had coated the logs with linseed oil and painted the trim a bright red. The sod roof, framed by tall spruce, is covered deep in the winter's snow and Josh's dog team is tied in front. The trapper's cabin looks as if it jumped from the pages of an Inside Passage cruise brochure. Not that a tourist actually ever ventures off the luxurious ship and into the Bush. More likely, the brochure is something to file away with snapshots after the trip, making them feel they had the peaceful Alaska experience. It would seem peaceful to me as well, if I hadn't once killed a man here.

The faces of thirty or so state troopers glow in the light of the fire pit. Most are edged with hard lines, earned by years of working in the Alaska Bush. Others host silly grins from a day of ice fishing and playing. Our little dilemma is nothing compared to the challenges and, in some cases, the horrors that they have seen on the job. It seems odd that they are now focusing their efforts on planning, or more precisely, saving a wedding. Nevertheless, we're a tight group and as day turns into evening, everyone wants to help. We have maybe two hours before the sun sinks behind the Kilbuck Mountains.

Dave Daniels, recently promoted to the supervising investigator position in Kodiak, speaks first. "Jack, I want to make a toast: Always remember the goal of marriage is to be happy. So, my advice for a happy marriage, from the husband's perspective—in my case, a husband for over twenty years—is that it's not our right to always be right. 'Yes dear' will serve you well. To Jet and Jack, may you live a happy life."

"To Jet and Jack!" the crowd choruses.

"It's okay to go to bed mad, but never go to sleep mad," comes another toast, followed by another round of drinks.

"It's okay to criticize your wife's driving, but never, NEVER, give her a ticket," shouts another trooper, who must be speaking from experience. The laugher and drinks continue to flow. I stick to my one Alaskan Amber limit, taking a swig for each toast and hoping the guys will quickly run out of their witticisms.

The usually reserved Josh Luko relates how his wife always seems to know how to put him in his place. "I once told my wife of an article I had read about a man who was a vegetarian, asking her if we should go on that kind of diet for our health. "Josh, she said, 'vegetarian' is just another word for 'bad hunter.'"

"Don't throw your red winter socks in with your wife's whites-only washer load...uh, never mind..." Ronnie tries to take his words back, but it is too late and the guys roar in laughter at what was more of a confession than a toast.

One trooper suggests using the governor's shortwave system to call Pastor Emery and have him perform the ceremony over the radio. A more sober trooper points out that it probably wouldn't be legal. "Just live in sin, like the rest of the world," another slurs.

"Nope, you can't live together in state housing unless you're married," argues someone.

"We could all just pile in the airplanes and fly to Bethel, where the Russian Orthodox pastor could hitch you guys," offers one pilot. That suggestion draws boos from the more sensible, but just as inebriated, men.

Rating the ideas from one to ten, I give them all zeroes. I'm about to admit defeat and accept that our wedding would have to wait another day. But then, the women reappear. All are glowing in that certain way women do when they have a secret.

"I think I can help. That is, if you don't mind." The voice comes from the back of the pack. Still packing the .44 Magnum on her hip, Governor Tinka Hine's brilliant red hair matches the brilliance of her beaming smile, but both pale in comparison to the brilliance of her suggestion.

"The ladies here presented the dire situation to me up in the cabin. That reminded me of the state law allowing the appointment by the court of a marriage commissioner to perform the ceremony. The appointment process usually takes at least a week, but my Chief of Staff made a call to a judge who I appointed to the bench. I'm now a marriage commissioner. Jack and Jet, if you'd like, I'd be glad to do the honors."

The women had apparently spent less time toasting and more time thinking than the men. But, they had done more than come up with the solution to the ceremony. Thanks to the governor giving up her bridesmaid attire and maid of honor Anna's resourcefulness, Jet's appearance has transformed from that of a beat up cheerleader to a magazine cover bride. Contrasting with Jet's ruined kuspuck, the governor's is teal, trimmed in white. It's really short on Jet since she is a good six inches taller than Tinka, but I think that makes it even better. Jet's hair is now full of curls, festooned with sky blue alpine forget-me-nots.

"Let's get this done, so we can get at those moose steaks!" Someone yells from the other side of the bonfire, anxious to complete the wedding and to begin the feasting. Jet and I join the governor on the makeshift stage. All my earlier shakes about the ceremony float away like embers rising from the bonfire.

The governor, clutching a Bible from Josh's cabin and notes she'd quickly scribbled, begins:

"Friends, out of affection for Jack and Jessie—who we all know as Jet—we gather together to witness and bless their mutual vows to unite them in marriage. They bring dreams which will bind them together. They bring a particular personality and spirit which is uniquely their own, and out of which will grow the reality of their life together.

"We rejoice with them as an outward symbol of an inward union of hearts. A union created by friendship, respect and—uniquely in Jet and Jack's situation—in having saved each other's lives. If that doesn't make for a strong bond, I don't know what does!" The crowd laughs as Jet squeezes my hand.

The governor continues, "Therefore, we are gathered together to unite Jack and Jessie in marriage, an institution the state may regulate and the church may sanction, but which only becomes reality in the lives of the two people involved. They ask for our support as they, together, begin the adventure of married life.

"A great person once said, 'don't just survive! Live!' And we say to both of you, 'don't just live, celebrate! And grow!' There will be rough experiences along life's journey, but remember, it's the journey, not the destination that will bring the most to one's soul."

The governor's bodyguard, a trooper sporting an "Alaskan Tuxedo"—a Filson wool jacket, Pendleton shirt, and gold nugget bolo tie under a parka—along with a stoic expression befitting his mission—whispers something in her ear.

"Oh, yes. Jack and Jet, do you have vows you'd like to say?"

Jet and I answer simultaneously that our vows are ready.

"Jack, you go first," the governor directs.

It takes what seems like a very long time until I remember that I'd stuffed my vows in the inside pocket of my tunic. I begin doubting if they make sense, but I read them anyway.

"Jessie, where there has been cold, you bring warmth. Where my life was dark, you bring light. Where there has been near-death, you bring full life. Jet, I pledge before this assembled company to be your husband from this day forward. Let us make of our two lives, one life. Let us always honor and respect each other, and cover each other's backs. Wherever the wind may carry me, I will stay by your side as your husband. Take this ring as a sign of my love, Jessie. I give myself to you, to be your wedded husband." Ted hands me the ivory band that had been carved by an Eskimo craftsman. I slip it on Jet's finger.

From her right mukluk, Jet removes a worn piece of paper and begins.

"Jack, I still remember the very first time I lost myself in your eyes. I knew then it was my future I was seeing. Since then, together we've danced under the Northern Lights on a mountain lake, mushed dogs across the Yukon, flown into the eye of a volcano, and stood side by side to fight for life. Love has given us wings, and our journey begins together. As freely as God has given me life and you have saved it, I join my life with yours. Wherever you go I will go, whatever you face, I will face. I will always back you up. Jack, I give myself to you, to be your wedded wife." Tears in her eyes, Jet places the ivory ring on my finger. This is finally happening.

"Jack and Jessie, by the authority vested in me by the State of Alaska, I hereby pronounce you husband and wife. Jack, you may kiss the bride." I kiss her. Then I kiss her again.

The crowd cheers as Stetsons fly skyward. Naturally, Ronnie's hat lands smack-dab in the middle of the bonfire. Troopers brought offerings from their posts around the state, making the wedding feast perfect. There are moose steaks from Glennallen, caribou ribs from the Alaska Peninsula, black bear ribs from Talkeetna, king crab legs from Kodiak, king salmon from Soldotna, halibut from Southeastern, and fresh vegetables from the Lower 48. Some is grilled over the fire, some are cooked in the coals, while others are roasted on sticks. Anna re-paired the wedding cake, so it appears almost as good as new. From kindling, Josh carved a new bride and groom statuette, replacing the one lost by Ronnie on the trail. It looks much more like Jet and me than the store-bought original. We rejoice with good food, cheap champagne, ridiculous dancing, toasts, and friendship.

The highlight of the festivity begins with a nod by the governor to her bodyguard. Within minutes of his transmitting on a portable radio, two Alaska National Guard C-17 Globemasters roar overhead. As they buzz us, the planes drop countermeasure flares, providing the most spectacular fireworks display one can imagine. The darkening skies light up and the flares crackle onto the lake ice. As the C-17s rumble down the valley, it's as if the lake is saluting the Guardsmen's service to our country with a series of pressure cracks, sounding like .50 caliber gunfire.

After toasting us, the governor motions to her pilot. He cranks up the Cessna 208 Caravan, then taxis around in a circle on the ice, towing a string of beer cans. After killing the engine, he holds the back door open, as if it's a stretch limousine. To a shower of dried Alaska wild rose petals, Jet and I walk among our friends to the governor's plane. Once we're buckled in, Tinka sticks her head in the cabin. "Royce is going to fly you up to my little cabin on the Tranquility River by Lone Wolf. It may not be the Juneau Baranof, but it's sure better than honeymooning here with a bunch of partying yahoos. Don't open this until tomorrow," she insists, handing me an envelope.

Chapter 5

FINALLY, THE HONEYMOON

THE FULL MOON GLOWS on the snow as we soar over the rock-crusted mountains. The purplish light is almost as bright—although with softer and more muted tones—as daylight. We pass over two small herds of caribou foraging for lichens. Otherwise there is no sign of life. Ten miles from the Lone Wolf airport, the pilot clicks the microphone switch, activating the runway lights to sparkle—seemingly out of nowhere in the mostly uninhabited valley. The plane's engine power is reduced for a straight–in approach to the unmanned village airport. We touch down softly, then taxi to the parking apron.

"That's the governor's house up there on the hill. Just follow the trail for about a mile with the snowmachine. The door is unlocked." The pilot wishes us well, climbs into the big Cessna, then flies into the moonlight as the runway lights dim quickly to dark.

The vintage yellow Ski Doo Alpine starts on the first pull. Jet wraps her arms around me and I point the "iron dog," onto the river. Using the lights from the cabin to guide us, we slowly bump across the rough, frozen surface. Stopping at the riverbank, Jet and I swing off the machine. Standing in the deep snow, arms around each other, we survey our honeymoon quarters.

Like a winter scene from a romantic oil painting, the cottage is comfortably tucked between towering evergreens on its own little hill. Warm, golden light flows from the windows onto the snow, illuminating what must be a full acre of forest. Built of hand-hewn logs with a massive rock fireplace occupying most of the left side, a country porch, and scrolled eaves, it is a fantasy come true. Searching up and down the river, we confirm there are no lights from any other habitation. Nor are there any sounds but our breathing. For the first time as husband and wife, we are totally alone. A frozen waterfall cascades from the little hill leading up to a creek that, in warmer weather, would come alive and flow into the main river. I hate to break the perfect silence, but I reluctantly yank on the starter rope once more to get us up the hill. We pass a little spot on the river below the cabin that is surrounded by glowing lanterns. It has been cleared for ice-skating. Hanging from log poles, more lanterns lead up the trail to the cabin.

Smoke from the woodstove drifts above the cabin, spewing the comforting scent of burning firewood. Two pairs of Nordic skis and two pairs of snowshoes lay on a handcrafted slat-wood porch swing. Stairs on the right side of the porch drop to a wood-fired hot tub. Pushing the massive split-log door open, I sweep Jet off her feet and carry her across the threshold into the scent of cinnamon and the melody of soft jazz. I lower Jet to the floor and we embrace for a long kiss.

A fire crackles invitingly within the river-rock fireplace that features a mantel crafted from a huge moose antler. The flames reflect onto the gleaming wood plank floors, covered only by a black bear hide in front of the hearth. A woodstove across the room provides more heat than the esthetically pleasing open fireplace. Enormous log beams cross the ceiling and rough milled posts accent the open floor plan that includes a great room, dining room and kitchen. The "Home Comfort" woodstove—painted gray with robin's egg blue trim and an old-fashioned perk-coffee pot on top—is the kitchen's focal point. Birchwood cabinets, slate countertops, copper pots hanging from a rack, and a view of the distant mountains from the window over the sink make it a dream kitchen.

A caribou antler chandelier graces a long plank dining table and moose babish chairs. The centerpiece is an Eskimo woven basket, cradling a bottle of champagne and fresh fruit. Jet picks up a note from the basket and reads it aloud, "Jet and Jack: Please enjoy the cabin and all that's in it. The hot tub should be warm for you. Use the skis and snowshoes to explore the trails (if you ever get out of the cabin). Don't open the envelope that I gave you at the lake until tomorrow! Love, Tinka."

"I'd forgotten about the envelope, Jack. Now I'll wonder about it until tomorrow—unless you can think of some way to make me forget it. Let's explore the rest of the house." She is like a village kid on her first trip to an Anchorage department store.

Jet grabs my arm and leads me down the hall. We pass a small bedroom decorated with fly-fishing gear and paintings of bears doing their own type of fishing. "Nope, that couldn't be it," Jet muses. Next is the bathroom, complete with a claw-foot tub and miniature woodstove.

"Here we are. Now we're talking!" Jet exclaims as we stop at the master bedroom. Rustic and cozy, the room features a big feather mattress bulging over a log bed. The fluffy sky-blue comforter is embroidered with the state flag of Alaska. Jet reads my mind, breaking my thought pattern with her words: "But not just yet, we need to finish the tour."

Reluctantly, I plod behind my touring wife as she gleefully exclaims over the great-room's down-filled leather furniture and expansive windows. A modest room behind the kitchen pantry holds only an antique roll top desk, a leather chair, and a rocker. That's all that will fit in the compact space, but it's all that's needed for the perfect office. Looking through the big picture window, I imagine what the river will look like in the summer—maybe with a floatplane tied to the dock. The cabin would be perfect for a combination home/trooper post. But Jet and I both know we'll be lucky to receive transfers from our current posts—me from Bethel and her from Dillingham—to serve together. If, and when that happens, it's likely the transfer will be to a big city post. We'll hate the city and that type of police work, but at least we'll be together. Until then, we accept that it will take at least a year of commuting for the occasional visits before we can share a home. And, it won't be a home like this. But, for a couple of days and nights, we can dream.

"Let's go for a ski!" Full of energy as always, Jet tosses me a pair of cross-country ski boots, somehow sized perfectly, as are the ones for her. We lace up the boots, grab the skis from the porch and slide down the hill to Tranquility River. After twenty minutes of heart-pounding aerobic exercise on the snow, we take a breather. Except for wolves howling in the distance, we are alone. Jet gives me a warm kiss, and then challenges, "Race you back!" Jet was a champion Nordic skier in college, so I know better than to try to beat her.

When I crest the hill at the cabin, my bride is nowhere in sight. However, being a trained investigator, I find it easy to follow her clues. First, there is one ski boot on the trail, then another. Then mittens, a ski jacket, nylon pants, a pair of fuzzy pink socks, a turtleneck, ski pants and finally, unmentionables. I track all the way to the hot tub.

"Well, don't just stand there, slowpoke, get undressed and get in here. The water's perfect." The steam rising from the wooden tub smells of lavender and Jet is a vision. She looks amazing. She was all made up for the wedding, but she is even more beautiful without make-up. Her curly locks shimmer in the moonlight. Her pink lips whisper, "I love you" as I float across the warm water to kiss her. Either the kissing, the hot water, or a combination of both, spikes our body temperatures and the cold air is now preferable to the feel of being boiled. We vote to make a run for it. Since I'd jumped in last, Jet feels obliged to get out first. Watching her bronzed body—I used to think it was from the sun, but seeing Jet now without any clothing—I realize that her incredible skin tone must be due to her Norwegian and Aleut heritage. I study— no, I gawk—at her athletic long legs, firm body and blonde hair as she pulls herself from the hot tub. I quickly follow and we race through the freezing night into the cabin.

We toss more logs on the fire, wrap ourselves in a quilt, and lay on the bear rug, feasting on grapes and champagne. When the bottle is drained and the grapes are only stems, Jet rises up, drops the quilt, and paddles barefoot down the hall to the feather bed.

I follow.

Chapter 6

THE OFFER

I SNEAK OUT of the comfortable bed after the best night of my life. As quietly as possible, I find my way to the kitchen and build a fire in the wood cook stove. Next, I stoke the woodstove in the great room to bring the cabin temperature up to human standards. Involuntarily, my face smiles as I reflect on last night.

While the coffee perks, I scavenge through the propane-fueled fridge, which is stocked full of food and beverages. Hands-on cooking with my uncle on his ranch in Idaho, followed by years of bachelorhood, taught me skills that are maybe close to that of a camp cook, but certainly not a gourmet chef. Today though, I'm going to step up my game and do my best to treat Jet to a decent breakfast in bed. After inventorying the supplies, I settle on a menu of omelets stuffed with smoked salmon, wild mushrooms, tomatoes, and leeks. I'm not sure what leeks are, but that's what the writing on the produce tag calls the onion-looking vegetables. I toast sourdough bread and grill caribou sausage on the stovetop. To top it off are blueberries and bananas, sliced into little bowls. Along with orange juice and fresh coffee, I load the feast onto a tray, then something else catches my eye—the envelope from the governor. I snatch it and put it under Jet's plate.

After quietly placing the tray on the table next to the fluffy bed, I bend over and kiss Jet.

"Good morning, Love. What smells so good?" Jet slowly opens her teal eyes, rising to return the kiss. "Are you kidding me? The world's greatest lover can also cook? I could get used to this!"

"You better not get too excited until you try my cooking, dear." I'm serious. I don't think a dogteam would put up with my standard fare. But, she doesn't choke on the first bite of the omelet. The morning is starting out perfectly. Then Jet sees the envelope.

31

"Jack, I'd forgotten all about that. I can't imagine how that's possible!" Jet giggles as she rips open the envelope. Her face quickly goes from her normal tan hue to bright pink. "You'd better read this, Jack." I cuddle up next to her in bed and we read it together.

"Dear Jack and Jet. Congratulations on becoming the Blakes. I hope your first night as a married couple was spectacular. You have my wishes and blessings for a wonderful life. I think there is something I can do for you to help make it so.

"As we all know, the Department of Public Safety has strict rules on how troopers can bid on posts. Plus, there is another issue of a married couple working at the same post. The one person who can cut through all the bureaucratic nonsense is the governor. However, these things must be handled very delicately. In order for an administrative waiver of the rules, there has to be good justification. This letter is about earning that justification. Justification that will serve all.

"First, all that I'm telling you is in the strictest confidence. You are not to share any of this with anyone. That includes your co-workers and supervisors. In cooperation with the attorney general's office, I'm forming a special task force for two very important investigative teams. My proposal is for each of you to lead the investigations on these separate, but equally critical cases. Neither is without consequences if they are not concluded satisfactorily. And neither is without danger. I believe you two are the best qualified, but if you don't want to take the risk, I'll understand.

"Now that you recognize there is peril, let me tell you about the rewards. I'm guessing that you are either in the feather bed or in front of the fire while you're reading this. I hope that you've found my Tranquility River cabin satisfactory as a home. Lone Wolf is a nice little town, but it's also about to change. The new gas pipeline route is within three miles of the airport. Undoubtedly, there will be a dramatic increase in the population. That unfortunately will result in an increase in general crime and poaching. We will need to establish a Lone Wolf trooper post. Jet, you'd be the wildlife trooper. Jack, you'd be the blue shirt trooper.

As much as I would like, I may never get back to my cabin, so I'd love you to live in it as long as you want.

"Make the cases, bring the guilty to justice, and you'll have the life you want. These are dangerous assignments, but I know that both of you can prevail. Think about the risks and the rewards. Call me when you get to a phone and let me know your decision. If you say 'yes,' we will meet with the attorney general and you'll learn more. Enjoy the rest of your honeymoon. Tinka."

Jet is so engrossed in the letter, that she let the covers she'd been modestly holding over her body drop. I notice. We have a lot of talking to do. Although the governor didn't give us many details to work with, we know we will have to put our lives on the line to get the future we want. Meanwhile, there's no need to waste a soft featherbed.

Chapter 7

DECISIONS IN THE SNOW

WE STRAP ON the Tubbs "Trapper" snowshoes and slough off into the woods behind the cabin. Snowshoeing is a great way to get our morning aerobics and clear our heads. Trying to be a gentleman, I take the first turn at breaking trail in the bottomless drifts. *Flump, flump, flump*...the music of the ash wood snowshoes breaking through a winter of untouched snow is the only sound in the spruce forest. Sagging from the weight of the snow, the giant spruce seem to beckon us deeper into the woods. We'll know the place when we find it—the place for us to dig deep into our faith and find the answers.

The "Church of the Woods." That's what we call our place of inspiration. Due to the nature of our work, Jet and I often find ourselves in places other than church on Sundays. We concluded however, that we don't need walls and a roof to express our faith or the seek inspiration.

It's thirty minutes into our trek when I decide to let Jet take a turn at leading our little expedition. She's been pelting me in the back with snowballs for the past ten minutes to make her point that she's ready to take the lead. I'm ready to give in. Then we see the packed trail.

"Looks like your turn to break trail came at just the right time." I nod toward the snowmachine tracks. In something between a skip and run in the snow, Jet rushes past me. The going becomes much easier, and contrary to mushers' saying, "Unless you're the lead dog, the scenery never changes," I enjoy my new position and the view of my bride. Suddenly, Jet stops.

"Jack, take a look at this," Jet kneels down into the snow.

"Moose tracks, a cow and a calf. And look...blood!" We begin following the moose blood trail. The blood spots become thicker and darker. The moose tracks are deeper and more erratic. "By the frost on the trail, it looks like these tracks are a day old, maybe more," Jet concludes, speaking as the experienced game warden and tracker she is.

After about a mile, the moose tracks end in a clearing. The snowmachine tracks break into trails, then converge at the opening. The first proof that Jet was right in her identification of the tracks is the freshly severed head of a cow moose. Scattered haphazardly are the guts, ribs, and the four quarters of the big animal.

"Watch your step, Jack. I'm betting there are traps around here." She's right. Breaking a branch from an alder bush, Jet springs a rusty metal trap that's secured to a stump with a short piece of chain. "A Manning Alaska Number 9. Very common and effective, made up in Fairbanks. Somebody poached this cow moose for wolf bait." We both quickly react to movement in the brush behind us. I involuntarily reach for my gun, then remember that neither of us is armed.

The yearling moose crashes through the brush, stopping ten feet from us. "*Ugher, Ugher!*" I don't speak moose, but I can tell the little critter is upset.

"That's her mom, all spread into pieces. She will have a tough time making it through the spring, but she looks healthy enough." Jet makes a quick assessment of the calf, which seems to be watching us with curiosity. We both decide it's not a threat and continue examining the scene. Using her pocketknife, Jet recovers a slug from the moose head. I find two Marlboro butts and a new hatchet sheath. We note the pattern of military bunny boots and the snowmachine tracks in the snow. We stick the evidence in our pockets, then spring five more traps. Jet snaps photos with her compact digital camera, then we agree to head into the town of Lone Wolf for answers. The return trip to the cabin is much easier with a broken trail. We grab our badges and pistol and jump on the Ski Doo, pulling in front of the Lone Wolf Trading Post and Café within an hour of discovering the kill site.

WALKING THROUGH THE DOOR of the trading post is like time-traveling back to the Alaska Gold Rush days. From the sawdust spread on the wooden floor, to trophies and furs from nearly every species of wild animal in Alaska, to the black potbelly stove, it's as if we happened into the pages of a Jack London adventure. The heavy air is sharp and pungent—a fragrance blended with the essences of leather, beaver hides, and wood. The pine shelving in the narrow aisles holds coffee, flour, sugar, candy, Pendleton blankets, tobacco, home remedies, pocketknives, lanterns, canned goods, and all the other staples needed for survival. Hardware, traps, antlers, and sled dog harnesses hang from the ceiling. Bins house fruit and vegetables and big jars protect candies from prying hands. A glass display case secures ammunition, ranging from .22 caliber to .358. An Alaska Department of Fish and Game poster announces that licenses and big game tags can be purchased. Taking up a good part of the counter top is an antique cash register, heavily engraved with intricate designs. "Lone Wolf Trading Post" is scrolled in big letters on the gold nameplate facing the customers. Thumb-sized buttons range in amounts from one cent to two dollars. Flags in the register window record the last sale: $2.05. Rifles and shotguns hang on the wall behind the counter and a few pistols are scattered inside the display case. So much stuff is crammed in the compact building, that it seems like absolutely nothing else could possibly fit. I'd bet an inventory has not been completed since statehood.

"James Stevens. I run this place. I'm guessing you are the Blakes. Tinka asked me to stock the cabin and warm things up a bit for you." The proprietor offers a firm handshake and half smile. Stevens, in his late thirties, stands about five-ten with a stocky build and shaved head, wearing a blue shop apron embroidered with a wolf. If Norman Rockwell had painted the interior of the Lone Wolf Trading Post, he would have put James Stevens behind the counter.

"I guess we kind of stick out. Thank you for all the work you did on the cabin for us." I say, returning Stevens' firm handshake.

"You're certainly welcome. Yeah, you guys look so happy together that you have to be newlyweds, so I knew who you were. Congratulations. Can I get you anything today?"

"Maybe just a little information, please," Jet asks with a smile. At that moment, what had looked like a fine specimen of an AKC-registered Golden Retriever lying in front of the woodstove, pulls himself up. Shockingly, it appears that he is equipped with the stubby legs of an English Bulldog. Carrying the unbalanced load of a normal-size retriever body and a big head with a toothy grin, the dog limps over to Jet wagging his tail, as if to say, "Hello, the boss is talking to you, so you must be okay." Jet kneels down and hugs him.

"That's Charlie. He's recovering from a mean trick a couple of the new lowlifes in town pulled on him. They poured water on the old boy when it was fifty below zero outside. He froze to the concrete. When we found him, his hind leg had severe frostbite. He never was much of a speedster with the body he was born with, but now he has to get around with only three little legs.

"I bet you want to know the flight schedule for the air taxi. That's an easy one, they come in once a day, about nine in the morning, unless the weather's bad, the pilot's sick, or the plane's down. Questions about hunting or fishing? I'm your man. I also run a guiding service."

"Thanks, we'll probably need to jump on a flight soon enough. And, I would sure like to hear about the local hunting and fishing, but right now, we have a more pressing matter. As the governor may have told you, Jack and I are state troopers. Today we came across a moose poaching. The carcass was being used for wolf bait. I thought you might have an idea who we should talk to." Jet wants to get to solving the case.

Stevens' face flushes red with anger. "I can guarantee you that none of the Indians around here would waste meat like that. That goes for any of the permanent residents."

"Who does that leave?" I ask.

"Well, as you may have heard, there's a natural gas pipeline coming through this way. I have nothing against developing our resources, so I'm all for the line. But, some of the characters it's bringing here are another thing. Seems like every week somebody associated with the gas line outfit rolls in here. Some think they can bring their booze and drugs into our nice little town. And they think they can just shoot any critter they see. Like they are above the law, just because they are from some big, Lower 48 city. It was a couple of them that froze ol'

Charlie to the sidewalk. I'd start by talking to them about the moose. Hey, you're in luck, that's them now."

Stevens nods toward the snowmachines that are racing toward the trading post. The machines abruptly turn, spraying snow onto the covered porch. Two men—one tall and thin, the other taller and more stoutly built—swing the door open with force. Both stop, glance at the three of us, then swagger through the store to the adjoining café. Charlie moans a low growl, then tucks his big red tail securely between his hind leg and stump, becoming even closer to the floor than usual.

"Thanks, we'll do that. Oh, and do you sell the hatchets that go with this sheath?" I show him what I'd recovered the poaching scene.

"You bet I do. Coincidentally, that tall guy bought one just a couple of days ago, along with some wolf traps."

"Were the traps Number 9 Mannings, by any chance?" Jet asks.

"Matter of fact, they were." Stevens sounds surprised, but doesn't pry.

I thank Stevens again, turning to follow Jet, who has already started toward the men. We enter the café together, which is easy to find by the smell of grilling meat, French-fried potatoes, and coffee.

"What can I get you folks?" A lady who looks just like Aunt Bee from the "Andy Griffith Show," turns from the sizzling grill and greets us. The eatery has a green counter top and six stools with red plastic seats. Four tables, covered with red and white checkered plastic tablecloths are lined up under windows that face the parking lot. Old black and white photos, mostly of gold miners, trappers with their furs, and hunters with their trophies, are arranged haphazardly on the walls, along with a hand-written, "PLEASE, NO SMOKING" request. There's one booth in a dark corner, illuminated only by a buzzing Pepsi Cola signboard. The suspects are sitting in the booth under the glow of the sign's blue light. Both are wearing white bunny boots. The extra tall one is smoking a Marlboro. He must not be able to read. The funny-looking white boots and the cigarette help tie them to the crime scene, but we need more.

"Not right now, thank you. We just need to visit with those men." Jet nods toward the booth. Aunt Bee frowns, shaking her head.

"Good morning gentlemen. We're with the state troopers. Mind if we talk to you?" I show them my badge. Jet does the same. The men remain seated, look at each other, then squint up at us with what I detect is disdain. I hate to start a conversation with disdain.

"What do you want?" Extra Tall asks the question with an attitude. Sidekick squints more. This isn't going to be a pleasant chat.

"We'd really like to ask you about those beautiful snowmachines. Would you please come out and show them to us?" Jet, knowing that most men love to show off their rides, asks with her most endearing smile, trying to break the ice a bit. It works. Extra Tall and Sidekick melt under her charm. At this point, I think they are so distracted, that they forget they were going to use the tough-guy approach with us.

"Sure, trooper. We'll be glad to show you our sleds." We follow the men outside. Outside is much better than inside. Stuff can get broken inside if things get rough. And, I have the feeling things will.

Jet and I look at each other, then nod toward the rifles in the scabbards on the snowmachines. I'm sure Jet also notes the snowmachine tracks and their similarity to those at the moose-poaching scene. The blood on the seats gives us even more probable cause.

"Nice machines. I bet that gets up and goes." Jet nods at the red one with yellow flames, getting them to feel at ease with some flattery. We are both in defensive stances, but continue the friendly chatter. At least for another couple of sentences.

"Yes, trooper, she's a mover. How 'bout I take you for a little ride?" Extra Tall offers. I don't like the look in his eyes when he talks to Jet.

"Oh, no thank you. I'm just wondering how it works in the deep stuff? Like across the river, up on the ridge." Jet isn't wasting any time.

"Across the river? I don't think we've been over there yet, have we partner?" Extra Tall looks at Sidekick for backup. Instead, he just gets an expression of puzzlement.

"Really, that's funny, being that the paddle tracks from these are the same as we saw over there." Jet points at the rubber tracks underneath the snowmachines.

"Probably lots of these machines around." Sidekick finally jumps into the conversation.

"That may be, but not many have fresh blood on them." I offer to help Sidekick understand.

"Also, that hatchet on your snowmachine seat fits in the sheath we found. Your boot tracks match those at the scene. The cigarette hanging from your mouth is the same brand that we recovered. Add that to the other evidence we've collected and the ballistics we'll soon have, and I'd say that we're talking to a couple of poachers. Wanton wasteful poachers, at that." Jet exchanges her charming demeanor for that of the investigator. An investigator intent on closing a case.

Extra Tall's face drops and his hand rises. He slips a pistol from his snowmachine suit. With my left hand, I chop his gun arm just inside his elbow. With my right hand, I grab the barrel of the pistol and shove it into his face. I kick his legs out from under him and he falls to the ground. Using the plastic zip ties Jet and I had found in the shed behind the cabin, I secure his arms behind him. Looking up from the ground, I see Jet holding Extra Tall's pistol on Sidekick, who had wisely raised his hands into the air.

Extra Tall turns his head from where it had made an indentation in the snow, and begins a philosophical discourse. "All this over a dumb animal? We just wanted to rid the country of some bloodthirsty wolves. You hicks had better get used to it. Things are going to change in this hillbilly town. You ain't seen nothing yet."

"KA-CLINK." We turn to the distinctive sound.

"Do you troopers need help?" James Stevens stands behind us on the porch holding a 12-gauge shotgun.

"Could you point me to a phone? First, we need to call the Bethel troopers to come up here and haul these guys to jail. Then we need to call the governor about a job. That is if you agree Jack, that Lone Wolf could use a couple of troopers." Jet awaits my response.

"I'm in if you are, Jet." We both know what that means. Today's events make clear what needs to be done.

Chapter 8

OUR ASSIGNMENTS

THE GOVERNOR'S OFFICE is plusher than we'd expected. I'd guess the one room takes up at least fifteen hundred square feet of Juneau real estate. Plus, there's a receptionist's office and two side rooms. I've seen photos of the president's Oval Office and it was impressive, but it has nothing on Alaska's chief official's workplace. A deep-blue rug, which would cover all the floors in our Lone Wolf dream house, is perfectly centered on the hardwood floors. The seal of the Great State of Alaska is loomed into the rug, just like the Presidential Seal at the White House. The ceilings, supported by massive white columns, and featuring gold medallions and white crown molding, are at least twenty feet high. Heavy blue and gold drapes hang from tall windows, which provide a view of the old mining town of Juneau. Two fabric couches, one dark blue and one gold, are gathered with two leather chairs around a coffee table. Overlooking this setting is the massive, slightly elevated, governor's desk. Crafted of sturdy Sitka spruce, the ivory-inlaid top could provide workspace for at least a dozen accountants.

The receptionist, a serious young man in a dark suit, white shirt, and red tie, shows us into the colossal office, then directs us to sit on the blue couch. The echo as we speak is intimidating. Even more so is the history. This is where mega deals have been made, where bills have been negotiated and signed, and where the government changed from managing a territory to administrating the 49th state—now home to North America's largest oil field. We pour water from the pitcher on the table, then whisper for five minutes. I don't know why people think they have to whisper in places like this. Maybe it's out of respect, or maybe because we think someone is listening.

Five minutes after our arrival, the door to the left side office squeaks open. Tinka Hines, dressed in a blue business suit, strides quickly across the room with her high heels clicking and her crimson hair bouncing. Jet and I stand up just in time for an impromptu group hug. I've never been much of a group-hugger, but it is Tinka, after all.

"I'm so glad to see you both. Welcome to Juneau," The governor speaks with enthusiasm as she breaks from the embrace. We thank her for the use of her Lone Wolf home, then exchange small talk for a few minutes. She then works herself around the intimidating desk, her small frame almost disappearing as she shrinks into the cushy leather chair. She pushes a button on a little box and asks the receptionist to send in the "A.G."

The attorney general looks like an FBI agent from the old days. Standing about my height of six feet with a slim frame and very pale complexion, he wears a simple gray suit, thin black tie and a white shirt. His flattop is a throw-back to the fifties and his serious face doesn't flicker. He sets his thick black briefcase on the coffee table and introduces himself.

"Cyrus Webster. The governor tells me we will be working together." Webster shakes our hands, then sits on the gold couch and snaps open the gold tabs on his briefcase. He removes two folders, handing Jet a blue one marked "Serial Pilot" and me a red one entitled, "Rogue."

"Before we begin, I want to reemphasize what Governor Hines has already told you. I understand that the governor trusts both of you completely, but some rules need to be discussed. The cases are to be investigated in total confidentiality. Communication is to be made directly with me. The chain of command is the governor, me, and you two. There are reasons that we need to do it this way, but none are of any concern to you, or to the investigation. You will naturally direct your teams, but they are to be told only what is necessary for them to carry out their assignments. Is that understood?" Webster speaks in monotones, but he's piqued our interest.

Jet and I both nod. The governor is taking notes, or doodling, I can't tell which.

"Okay, now that we are on the same page, let me provide synopses of the cases.

"Jet, you will be in charge of the team investigating a series of missing young women, probably homicides. The suspect, a white male adult, has an M.O. that I've never come across in my twenty years of prosecuting felons. Using a Bush plane, he drops in on various airports around the state and either by charm or by force, kidnaps young women. He then flies them out to a remote area and lets them go, only to hunt them down like big game animals. Our one and only surviving victim was taken from the village of Gold River. She agreed to go with the suspect for a promise of drugs. He flew her to a gravel bar where he yanked her out of the plane, then forced her to strip naked. After brutally raping her, he told her to make a run for it. Imagine the poor girl running through the woods stark naked, while shots are whizzing past her. Fortunately for the victim, she ran right into the camp of some riverrafters. Fortunately for the rafters, the suspect spilt in his plane without a confrontation. There is also a report from a wildlife trooper from Talkeetna who found bones and other evidence near a glacier airstrip. And a statement from a hunter who found more human bones near his sheep camp. In the file you will also find missing persons reports for more young women that are very likely related, plus a recent report from a woman who was accosted near Palmer. We need to stop this guy. *Now!* Any questions?"

"Just one, Mr. Webster. Why me?" Jet asks what I'm thinking.

"The governor trusts you, for one thing." Tinka's red head nods in agreement. "Also, we need a woman's perspective on this investigation. A woman pilot is even better. Plus, you know the mind of a big game hunter. The governor says you were the creative one in college, and God knows, we need some creativity about now to stop this killer. The investigation needs to be conducted in a manner so the suspect is not tipped—he needs to be caught red-handed. Well, 'red-handed' may not be the best term, but we need to make a case that will stick." Webster stares intently, sips from his water glass, then asks, "You okay with that, Jet? By the way, we all are going to be working together closely, so please call me Cyrus."

"I can work with that, Cyrus." Jet responds. I could hardly wait to hear her plan, but I'm worried about the obvious danger to her in dealing with this kind of maniac.

"Okay. Jack, let's talk about your case." Cyrus' steely blue eyes bore into mine. Neither of us blinks. "It appears we have a rogue trooper. So far, we don't even have a suspect. What we do have is a dead body in L.A. The only piece of evidence found near the body was an Alaska State Trooper Safety Bear pin. We have another dead guy in Phoenix. Same type of pin was found near that one, plus an Alaska State Trooper business card—well, part of a card. Everything was cut from the card but the Alaska State Trooper part. The only thing in common with either of these killings, besides the pins, is that both of the victims weren't nice people. One walked on a cop-murder case that he committed for certain. The other was a lowlife who scammed a family whose kid is dying of cancer. And, before you ask the same question as Jet, let me say that the governor trusts you equally. Also, like Jet, we need a pilot. Any questions?"

"I'm guessing that all of the known case details and any leads are in the folders?" It's all I can think of to ask, although I know Jet and I will bounce more questions off each other later.

"That's all we have at this point. I'll fill you in if anything comes across my desk, but I expect shortly you both will know a lot more than I do. Unless there's anything else, I've got to get to a meeting." Cyrus looks at the governor and gets her approval with a nod and thanks. He shakes our hands, then strides through the massive wooden doors.

Tinka leans over her desk and asks, "Well, guys, what do you think? Oh, wait, before you answer, let me add that James Stevens was impressed with both of you. He's pleading with me to transfer you both to Lone Wolf, which I hope to see done as soon as this is over. Also, I want to let you know that you can have whatever resources you need on these cases. Manpower, equipment, money, just let me know and I'll make sure you have it." I'm beginning to like this woman more each time I meet her.

"I like the sound of the 'Lone Wolf Trooper Post.' How about you Jack?" I concur with my bride. We have a deal.

Chapter 9

THE BEGINNING

I THINK IT WAS my wise Ol' Uncle J.D. who told me that it's always best to start at the beginning. The beginnings for Jet and me in our investigations are the police reports.

The timing is right for the covert investigations. Our friends will think that Jet and I are on an extended honeymoon, so we won't be missed. The next thing we need is a base where we have communications with the outside world, but where we won't be bothered. That place is Lone Wolf. Tinka's cabin will be perfect. It's warm and cozy and it's just across from the airport and trading post. And even though it's isolated, the cabin is now joined to the real world by telephone and Internet service.

We start at six in the morning by spreading the papers from the file folders in chronological order on the big dining table. The fire blazes across the room and steam flows from the kettle on the wood cook stove. We agree to analyze the documents as a team effort, then to bounce strategy off one another. Jet offers to make follow-up notes, as her handwriting is much more legible. We start with Jet's investigation, which contains reports beginning fifteen months prior to our meeting with Cyrus.

In February of last year, Anchorage Police Department Officer George Bradley was contacted by Candy Price about her friend, Karma Franks. The two women had been "working the bar" at the Big Fish Tavern on International Airport Drive. They were approached by a man described as about forty years old, five-feet-five to five-feet-seven, about one hundred-sixty pounds with black hair, black horn-rimmed glasses, and a pasty complexion. The man bragged that he was a pilot and a big game hunter. Price said that the man wore some sort of sheep head pin on his jacket. Franks was described as being about twenty-years old,

five-feet-two and one hundred ten pounds. Price said that Franks had
been wearing a blue mini skirt with a black blouse, and that she always
wore a pendant necklace with a photo of her boyfriend/pimp in it.
Franks was last seen by Price when she left the bar with the man. The
report was filed as a missing persons report and then closed.

Jet makes a note to find Candy and ask her: (1) whether she has
heard from Karma; (2) to get a photo of Karma; (3) whether she remembers more about the suspect; (4) whether the suspect said where he
hunts and what type of plane he has; and (5) to describe the necklace
and photo in the pendant.

The next incident is from March of last year. An Arctic Village
police officer called the Fairbanks State Troopers to report a missing
woman from his town. Betty Killdeer, a Gwitchin resident, reportedly
wandered off from a drinking party in town and "went missing."
Searchers on snowmachines and dogteams looked for her for two days
before the officer called the troopers. The troopers, the Civil Air Patrol,
and an unidentified white male in his personal airplane made at least
twenty sorties. Temperatures had dropped to forty below during the
search and no sign of her was found. The case was closed with the as-
sumption that Killdeer was deceased.

Jet makes a note in the margin of the report to call the village
police officer, to determine if the victim is still missing, to ask more
about the unidentified pilot, and to try to get a description of the airplane.

I throw another log on the fire and stand in front of the hearth.
The heat feels good and I sometimes think better while standing. "That
sheep pin is interesting," I offer. Jet agrees and makes a note.

After pouring scalding water from the kettle for tea, I call Jet to
the kitchen window to see a calf moose that is feeding on alder bushes
next to the hot tub. Since the yearling is alone, we assume that it's the
orphan of the cow moose that Extra Tall and Sidekick had poached for
wolf bait. Jet names the calf Annie, for the "Little Orphan Annie" character. I ask if we should feed it, but Jet explains that, since the little critter is eating bushes, it will be fine. Jet says people who think they are

helping wildlife by feeding them actually do more harm, as the animals become too dependent on humans. "They often end up getting poached, hit by a vehicle, or starving, because they lose their ability to forage for themselves," Jet says. And, I thought I was being nice.

The next report in sequence, taken early last June, is the one that Cyrus Webster briefed us about in Juneau. As the attorney general had reported, an eighteen-year old woman from the western Alaska village of Gold River had voluntarily taken a flight with an unknown white male in hopes of getting free drugs. Amanda Silverleaf reported that the pilot flew her to a remote area and raped her. He then shot at her with a rifle as she ran naked through the woods. Fortunately, for her, she happened into the camp of some river-rafters who helped her. The suspect flew away. The report had been taken by a trooper investigator from Anchorage, who, since there were no corroborating witnesses or evidence, filed it as closed. He was probably also a little put off by the facts that Silverleaf was a drug user, and that she waited two days to make the complaint. In the business of prioritizing cases to dedicate time and energy, this fell to the bottom of his pile.

After a discussion, a kiss for inspiration, and a few sips of cranberry-apple tea for energy, Jet makes the following notes for a call to the investigator: (1) Type of airplane? (2) Why did the victim wait two days to report? (3) What's the specific location? (4) Contact info for Silverleaf. (5) Name of pilot who picked her up? (6) Rafters' info? (7) Ask for a more detailed description of the suspect.

Next is a report taken by Sergeant Tom Crisp of the Fairbanks troopers, from last July. A complainant had appeared at the front counter of the troopers' office with a plastic trash bag of what appeared to be human bones and a skull. There was still some flesh on the bones. He reported finding them on a small airstrip at his sheep camp on Dall Creek, after he'd buzzed a grizzly bear off the strip with his airplane. He also turned in a woman's ring and a lapel pin that had the logo of a sheep and a bull's eye, which he found near the bones.

On her "to do" list, Jet notes to call Sergeant Crisp and ask him to ship the sheep pin to her in Lone Wolf. Also, she will confirm with him that the bones have been sent to the crime lab, and find if he has checked with the Arctic Village Police Officer to determine if the recovered ring was the missing woman's. That jogs my memory. I recall from flying in the Brooks Range that there was a Dall Creek west of Arctic Village. We check a topographical map and see the creek is only eighteen air miles from the village airport.

Just two weeks after the Fairbanks report, a wildlife trooper from Talkeetna recovered some bones during an aerial patrol on the Upper Susitna River, north of Anchorage. Trooper Gary Wickham had landed a department Robinson helicopter on a gravel bar to check what he thought, because of the foraging ravens and a fox, was the site of a moose killing. Instead, it turned out to be a scattering of human bones. The bones were sent to the state crime lab in Anchorage for analysis.

Jet makes notes to call Wickham and see if he will fly her back to the scene to look for additional evidence with a metal detector, and to call the crime lab for its report.

In August, the Glennallen state troopers filed a missing persons report on another young woman. The owner of a café in Copper Center reported that his waitress, Lucinda Bickel, had not reported to work for the past three days. He said that the twenty-two year old was sort of a hippie type, but that she had always been reliable. Trooper Wilkinson drove to Bickel's residence and found the door unlocked. A check inside showed no sign of a struggle. The bed had been made, and the jacket the complainant described as being worn by Bickel, along with her wallet, was gone. Bickel was known to take early morning walks on the ridge that borders the Copper Center airport. Trooper Wilkinson checked the unmanned airstrip and walked the trail from the airport to Bickel's house. Wilkinson contacted Copper Center resident Wilbur Hills on the trail. Hills reported that, while walking on the trail three days ago to check his fishwheel, he saw Lucinda Bickel. Hills said Bickel was talking to a white male adult at the airport, next to a white airplane. Hills said there did not appear to be any conflict between the two. He later heard the airplane take off and saw it fly up the Klutina River.

Jet makes notes to interview Hill and try to get better descriptions of the pilot and the airplane. She also plans to do a recon flight to locate possible landing areas west of Copper Center.

It's seven in the evening before we realize we've been at this for more than twelve hours. Annie is now camping on the cabin's deck. Jet and I throw together a quick meal of salad, biscuits and moose stew—with apologies to Annie—then continue mulling over the reports.

The most recent report came in early May, just two weeks before our wedding. Palmer Police Patrol Sergeant Audrey Hart took a complaint from a Nordic skier. Marie Hodge, a twenty-four year old female, had been skiing by herself at the base of Knik Glacier when an unidentified white male landed in his ski plane. The pilot engaged her in a friendly conversation, and then offered to give her "an aerial view of the glacier." When she declined, he grabbed her and tried to force her into the back of his two-seat airplane. Hodge struck the suspect in his face with the tip of her ski pole, drawing blood. Her husky/wolf dog began biting at the suspect until he climbed in his airplane and flew to the north. She described him as medium height, medium build, wearing aviator sunglasses, and a red cap with a sheep head on it. She remembers the airplane as being white with red trim, with numbers on the tail beginning as "N" and ending in "2" and that the skis were red. The sergeant referred the complainant to the state troopers, who had jurisdiction. Hodge never showed up at the Palmer trooper office.

This takes priority, as it's the freshest lead in the folder. Jet decides to put Sergeant Hart number one on her list to call to get contact information on Marie Hodge. She also makes a note to search FAA records for the partial airplane registration numbers. I suggest that she contact Jill, the administrative assistant to the Fairbanks investigative unit. Jill should be running the investigative outfit instead of doing the clerical work. She always knows how, and where, to find almost anything about anybody.

We enjoy glasses of Merlot, and then turn to my cases. My information is much easier to analyze, as I have nothing but what Cyrus Webster put in the folder. That folder contains requests from two police agencies—one in L.A. and the other in Phoenix—both asking for an investigator to contact them in person about cases with suspects who may be Alaska state troopers. I have to show up to get more. Showing up in a big city is my biggest fear.

With a little online research, we learn the population of L.A. County is almost ten million, or 2,344 persons per square mile. The Phoenix metro area shows a population of almost four million, or two hundred and fifty-five persons per square mile. With an estimated 683,478 citizens, Alaska's population density is only a little over one person per square mile, which is my kind of density. With the exception of switching planes in Seattle more than twenty years ago, I haven't been in a metropolitan area since I was a kid. But, that's where this investigation is going to take me and I'll approach it like any assignment. However, I'm much more comfortable facing a wounded grizzly bear than making my way through the streets of Los Angeles or Phoenix.

Jet and I kick around a couple of ideas until the featherbed beckons to us around midnight. What about the pilot's sheep pin? What trooper do we know who would commit murder? Maybe it's a former trooper. Maybe not a trooper at all. Of more immediate concern, what about the beautiful woman next to me?

After a restful night, we drain the water from the cabin's plumbing system so the pipes won't freeze, say goodbye to the constantly alder-munching Annie, and snowmachine across the rotting ice of Tranquility River. James Stevens agrees to keep an eye on the cabin and wishes us well. At 9:10 A.M., the chief pilot and C.E.O. of Greg's Alaska Airways, Greg Haerr, raises the gear of the King Air 200 and banks the plane toward Anchorage.

Chapter 10

BAR CANDY

"PICK ANYTHING YOU WANT." Hap Winston, the department's aircraft supervisor, waves his gloved hand at the Cessnas and Super Cubs tied down on the Lake Hood ramp in Anchorage. The governor had called the commissioner of the Department of Public Safety, and he called Hap. Neither were told the why, just the how. "I don't know what's going on, and I don't really care. All I know is that I'm supposed to let you take what you need, and that you're headed out in the morning. We also have a Cessna 208 coming in later today that's yours if you want it. Or how about a chopper?" Hap, with little white hair left on his sixty-year old head, runs the aircraft section like a military fleet, but is always affable and fair.

Jet and I go directly to our mounts of choice. I need something for speed. Jet needs something that will allow for operating in tight spots. Neither of us want to be conspicuous. I pop open the door of a white and red Cessna 185 on wheels. Cruising along at one hundred-sixty miles an hour, the four-seat Cessna will agreeably make the transition from Bush plane to commuter. Jet pries the clamshell door open on a white and green Super Cub sitting on oversized, Gumby-like tundra tires. Akin to an unmarked patrol car versus one with overhead lights and door badges, these "plain Jane" planes will blend in better than the rest of the badge-adorned blue, white and gold craft surrounding them.

The radio master switch brings the panel to life on the Cessna. It lights up like two color televisions surrounded by Las Vegas slot machines and computers. Pretty, very pretty, but there is no way I can learn to use all the state-of-the-art navigation equipment in time for tomorrow's departure. I grab the Garmin book for the glass cockpit from behind the seat and thumb through the pages. The phone book-sized manual will make good reading on the lengthy flight from Alaska to the Lower 48. Meanwhile, I scan the "Quick Start Guide," to get a handle on managing the communication radios. "Quick Start," is more like "Glass Cockpits for Dummies" to me.

Jet's choice is about as basic as they come. One radio, a GPS, and a standard panel. "Perfect," Jet says, as she pulls herself into the cockpit.

"These will be fine, Hap," I say, hopefully. He gives us each a paper to sign and promises both planes will be inspected and fueled by morning.

"I'm glad you got here today. That 185 is our test plane for the new avionics system. We were going to put on floats for water-testing tomorrow, so you're just in time. You can be the test pilot." Hap nods at Lake Hood, which had just made the transition from a ski airport to being what is the busiest seaplane base in the world. Hap intently watches a trooper Cessna seaplane as it's being launched from a trailer into the water.

"Taking delivery on these planes was easier than buying a new car, like a lot of couples would be doing after they just got married," Jet muses.

Hap turns his eyes from the launching operation, responding to Jet. "Yep, and cheaper, too. By the way, congratulations on your marriage. Where are you guys staying tonight?"

We hadn't made plans for accommodations yet, but answer that we have to be close, as we don't have a car.

"No problem. Just stash your bags in the hangar and take what you need for the night. I'll give you a ride over to the Alaskan Hotel. I need to take that floatplane for a check-out anyway."

Jet and I drag our big duffels to the hangar, then we each grab an overnight bag. The water taxi through the channel to Lake Spenard, where Hap beaches right in front of the four-story lodge, takes only a few minutes. "Tell them at the front desk that Hap said to give you the 'good guy discount,'" Hap shouts from the Cessna after we jump from the floats to the grass.

After winding our way through the lobby of stuffed critters—bears, sheep, moose, caribou, and an eagle statue, we learn that "Hap" is the magic word to the hotel desk clerk. We are awarded a spacious suite overlooking the lake, where seaplanes busily "splash and go" in a rush to start another season. After taking advantage of the hotel's steam bath, we wander into the dining room. The starched tablecloths, fancy silverware, and smartly dressed waiters make us feel out of place, but we give in to the pleasant aroma of good food. We feast on pan-roasted Alaskan halibut with Dungeness crab cakes in an orange sauce, while the "Blue Notes" jazz band plays in the background.

"Jack, since this is our one-week anniversary, and since we are heading in different directions tomorrow, let's make this a celebration," Jet offers, with a clink of our wine classes. "We just need to make a little detour first." Detours with Jet are usually fun, so I'm in.

THIS DETOUR REQUIRES a cab ride from the luxurious hotel to a seedy saloon. The Big Fish Bar is just a couple of miles from the hotel, but it might as well be across the world. The odor of cigarette smoke— and what is probably pot smoke—mixed with spilled beer, sweat, and vomit, whacks us in our faces as we push open the swinging door. Four men are torturing two guitars, a drum set, and a microphone. The stage is protected from the gyrating, screaming, beer bottle-throwing crowd by chain link fencing. A young woman dances naked on a corner ministage, swirling around a metal pole. We don't want a drink. We just want to get out of there fast. But first, we need to talk to a hooker.

At the end of the full bar, a cocktail waitress is slopping drinks onto a tray. She looks tired and disinterested, but she's our only hope.

"Is Candy here?" I yell. The waitress looks Jet and I up and down. Before her mind can develop the most perverse hypothesis, Jet jumps in.

"As you might have guessed, we're police officers, state troopers. Candy needs to talk to us about Karma," my bride explains. The waitress still looks tired, but now seems interested.

"You got anything new on Karma?" She asks the question while screaming a drink order to the bartender.

"Maybe, but we need to talk to Candy about it," Jet responds. The tired waitress again feigns disinterest, now by rolling her eyes, but she agrees to "fetch" Candy. She disappears into the pungent fog.

Candy doesn't look like a Candy. Candies should look sweet. This Candy looked sour. Sour like a woman who has heard every line every drunk could spew at her. Sour like a woman who'd become used to turning tricks for ten hours a night, then going home to a cheap apartment where she gets slapped around for her efforts.

"So you two is cops?" Candy asks, then sucks deeply on her skinny, brown cigarette. I bob to the right to avoid her exhale. She adjusts her red rayon mini-skirt and motions us to her private booth.

"Yes, state troopers. We just need to clarify a couple of things," Jet coughs.

We slide into the booth. Well, we don't exactly slide, since you can't slide on plastic that has been sliced and diced with knives. We sit around the sticky table, center-pieced with a white net-covered red goblet that protects a flickering candle. The candle is having trouble flickering to its fullest potential because of all the cigarette butts in the goblet. Candy sits on the outside, which helps the cigarette smoke drift onto the dance floor and away from us. She orders champagne in the house glass slipper. Jet and I don't want anything, but we order beers just so the tired waitress won't roll her eyes at us again.

"We have the report from the Anchorage Police Department about your friend, Karma Franks. Have you seen her since you made the complaint?" I ask, expecting the answer.

Candy leans over, her stainless-steel colored blouse flashing her cleavage to all. I don't want to look, but the little tattoo of a pirate on her right breast is intriguing. I wonder why someone would put that there. Jet gently kicks me under the table and I stop wondering. The light from the candle reveals Candy's hard face that she's tried to make softer with generous amounts of makeup. By her inch-long black roots, it looks like it'd been a while since she's had her hair dyed blonde. "Nope, have you?" Candy asks hopefully, probably knowing the answer.

"No, but we're working on a lead," Jet offers, not explaining that the lead doesn't have a happy ending. "Do you have a photo of Karma? Maybe also a photo of her boyfriend?"

Candy pulls a strip of photos from her orange pocketbook. They're the kind of photos that you get from one of those little walk-in boxes in a big-city mall. Candy lays the pictures on the sticky table, then maneuvers them over speed bumps of spilled booze and crumbs. She lines them up with a fake nail that is chipped and is only half covered with red polish.

"That's Tyrrell, Karma's boyfriend." She clicks a fingernail on his photo and takes another drag from her cigarette. "That's me." She clicks on a shot of her with blonder hair. "And that's Karma." Karma looks too innocent to fit with Candy and Tyrrell, except for the tongue piercing that she prominently displays for the camera.

"Okay, that's good, Candy. What can you tell me about the customer who Karma was last seen with?" Jet asks.

"I knew there was something weird about that dude! He went on and on about all the animals he's killed, grizzly bears, black bears, moose, caribou, bison, and sheep. Especially sheep, he even had this little pin on his jacket. Said that you can only get those if you belong to some club. He seemed a little scary to me, just weird, I tell you. I didn't want Karma to go with him, but she said that she always wanted to fly in a Bush plane." She begins what may be a sniffle, but, then again, it might be from the smoke.

Jet asks, "One more thing Candy, can you describe the locket that Karma was wearing?"

"Just a little heart-shaped silver locket on a snake chain. It's engraved on the outside with 'T.W. & K.F.,' for Tyrrell Washington and Karma Franks. There is a picture of Tyrrell inside of it."

We thank Candy and pay the tab, learning that drinks in glass slippers don't come cheap. Jet promises to let Candy know if she finds anything more on Karma. Ducking beer bottles flying toward the chain link fencing, we lock arms and weave through the rowdy crowd. The band keeps smashing away on their poor instruments, the guy with the microphone keeps screaming, and the skinny naked dancer keeps doing whatever she's been doing to the pole.

The cab drops us back at the hotel about 11 P.M. We wash and re-wash the bar from our bodies, then find the abandoned hotel sauna, hoping to deep clean more of the evening from our pores. Then we really celebrate our anniversary.

Aside from the detour, I can only hope that all of our anniversary celebrations go so well.

Chapter 11

ON THE MOVE

THE DAY STARTS with a quick run along Lake Hood in the crisp morning air. From Cubs and Cessnas to Otters, and a variety of vintage and other Bush aircraft in between, the planes hunker down on their floats at Lake Hood. The fleet is reminiscent of the penguin colony in the movie "March of the Penguins," in the scene where the birds huddle against the weather. Hundreds of Canada Geese, which have already taken up summer residence on Gull Island, honk constantly to call a mate, or to claim a nesting spot. Midair collisions between waterfowl and aircraft had become such a hazard that, after failing with conventional scare tactics, airport authorities came up with a great idea in the '90s. Pigs were set free to roam the two thousand foot-long island. It was a win-win-win solution: the swine ate duck, geese and seagull eggs, the collisions between birds and planes dropped significantly, and there was a big pig roast at the end of the season. Maybe it was due to the naming of three of the pigs Larry, Curley and Moe, but an animal-rights group objected, and the plan was scrapped about ten years ago. The birds have returned in record numbers.

After the passing the public safety hanger, we run into the Alaska Aviation Heritage Museum grounds. We jog among a PBY Catalina, a Goose, a Widgeon, a Waco, various Stinsons, and a Vietnam UH-1 helicopter. There's even an Alaska Airlines 737, on which Jet and I both think we have been passengers, probably when escorting prisoners. We run in place, promising each other to come back someday and explore inside the museum. We'd like to learn more about the pilots who opened aviation in Alaska, like Ben Eielson, Harold Gillam, Bob Reeve, Mudhole Smith, Don Sheldon, Russell Merrill, Noel Wien and the other great aviators. Jet leans in for a kiss to seal the promise, but we're interrupted.

"Hey, get a room!" Hap Winston waves us to his car as he waits for the electric gate of the public safety aircraft section to slide open. "Meet me at the hangar, a package came in after you left yesterday."

Besides State of Alaska credit cards, the package holds two marvels of modern technology from the governor's office. Resorting to my pocketknife, I recover two purple cell phone–looking devices from layers of cardboard, hard plastic, and bubble wrap. The color screens come alive with the power buttons. Message alerts beep from both of them and we push the corresponding buttons: "Greetings from Juneau, Jet and Jack. I hope all is well and that you have everything you need to begin your investigations. You're holding some of the latest technology in PDAs. These "Blueberries" take the Blackberry system a step further. They have Bluetooth and Wi-Fi connectivity, but since we can't always hit a cell phone tower in Alaska, they can also connect via satellite. This means you can make a phone call, send an email or fax, or access the Internet no matter where you are. Plus, you can immediately tap into the APSIN—the Alaska Public Safety Information Network for Alaska criminal justice research—as well as the FBI's National Crime Information Center, NCIC. Since you will be doing a lot of flying, both phones are loaded with the "Fly-Cast" real-time weather and flight-planning system. Speed dial buttons hold both Cyrus Webster's and my cell phone numbers."

Hap and Jet look over my shoulder while I push the Blueberry's touch screen airplane icon, which opens Fly-Cast weather briefing. "Which route do you suggest, Hap?" I've never flown out of Alaska, so I ask an expert.

The expert recommends flying the Inside Passage route. "You just follow the coastline and there are beaches to land on in an emergency. It's hard to get lost, unless the weather turns to crap. Plus, the scenery is incredible. I like following the Copper River to Cordova, then heading down the coast." I defer to Hap's experience. Too much of a hurry isn't good when you're flying in unfamiliar territory.

The weather graphics, satellite images, and text forecast all agree. I'd better get going now, as there is a big low-pressure system due to roll in within the next two days. Two days is all I need to reach Washington State. Jet has clear sailing for her planned Super Cub travels.

Borrowing Hap's car, I drive to the hotel and check out, while Jet stays behind to use the aircraft section's office to catch up on paperwork.

PARTING IS REALLY SWEET SORROW when you've only been a married couple for a week, but Jet and I say our goodbyes on the ramp. Jet slips an envelope into my hand with firm instructions to not open it until we've passed over Palmer—a half-hour flight from Anchorage. We climb into our planes and after giving each other the "thumbs up," start the engines and taxi to the Lake Hood strip, where the tower grants us a "flight of two" departure. Jet takes off first in the Super Cub, with me rolling down the runway just behind. At two thousand feet over Knik Arm, I pull alongside the Cub, throttling the faster Cessna back. Jet and I don't divert from our traffic scans to look at each other, as flying within the Anchorage traffic system is like playing a sinister video game to avoid sudden impact. Below us are three floatplanes, just above them is an Atlas Air 747 jumbo jet, two F-22 Raptors scream in front of us descending to Elmendorf Air Force Base, and we hear radio calls for an Piper Aztec headed to Merrill Field at our same altitude. I try, without success, to turn off the constantly screaming traffic alert system in the Cessna's avionics package.

Once we pass Goose Bay and are skimming over the mud flats of Knik Arm, we chatter on our "secret" radio frequency, telling each other how much we are going to miss being together. We make promises to email and call, and say sweet things to each other.

After crossing the flats to the Glenn Highway, we pass over the Alaska State Fair grounds, home to such midnight sun wonders as seventy-five pound cabbages. We switch radio frequencies to the Palmer Flight Service, then Jet breaks from our formation in a wingover. The green Super Cub shrinks smaller and smaller as it descends toward the airport. Increasing power in the Cessna, I glance back at the Cub. I feel an urgency to complete my investigation as soon possible, so we can be together again

Trimming the Cessna 185 for level flight, I enter the relatively wide Chickaloon Pass. I'm reminded of the time flying through here in a Super Cub, knowing for certain that the wings were going to fold as the little plane was battered by severe turbulence. The Cub was in a dive, then pointed to the sky, then inverted. I fought the auto-aerobatics, even harder when an ammo box flew from the baggage compartment and clobbered me in the back of my head. The little plane was so out of control that I was a passenger—and the only occupant. Whatever control inputs I made had little effect on improving the crisis.

"A DC-10 at Anchorage International reports momentary loss of control on final, due to severe turbulence." That was the only pilot report the flight service operator provided when I asked for help finding smoother air. That wasn't helpful, or encouraging, especially since the airliner outweighs a Cub by 427,000 pounds. Fortunately, I maneuvered to hard landing at Palmer, and neither the plane nor I received serious damage. Due to the un-forecasted windstorm, many airplanes on the ground were totaled, and a number of house trailers flipped over that day. I became more careful in weather briefings since that episode.

The air is smooth now as I view the Matanuska Glacier pouring from the mountains, said to be advancing a foot a day toward the highway. Dall sheep lift their heads from grazing to glance at the noisy Cessna, as I line up to zoom through the gun sight of Gunsight Mountain for old time's sake. Out the right side of the plane, the Chugach Range separates the Gulf of Alaska from the Copper Basin. Below me, the Sheep Mountain airport brings memories of a search and rescue from when I was stationed at the Glennallen Post. The pilot had dropped two hunters on a remote lake— without telling anyone where—then crashed on his way home. The crash site and the deceased pilot were easily located, but it took four days of hard flying to find the hunters. I finally lucked out, when on a night sortie in the Talkeetna Mountains, a campfire flickered on a lake. I'd become accustomed to night landings in floatplanes, so used the campfire's reflection on the water to guide me to an approach. The hunters hadn't heard the bad news, but were out of groceries and very happy to be rescued.

Passing over Eureka brings the vision of two bodies I pulled from the wreckage of a Maule airplane, on a minus fifty-two degree day. The poor guys, returning to the Lower 48 after their Alaska vacation, had tried to fly under the ice fog encasing the three-thousand-three-hundred foot Eureka summit. It took a lot of hacksaw cutting to free the frozen-in-place bodies.

Next, the rollercoaster dips of the Glenn Highway pass below, and my mind's eye flashes to the wreck of a Chevy Citation that left the road at high speed. The driver had been ejected through the rear glass. After following a trail of debris, I found his broken body on the tundra, two hundred feet from his car.

Flying past the Lake Louise cut off, I recall the sight of a wrecked Super Cub in the snow. Hunting wolves, the rear seat passenger had become a little too excited when they flew over a pack. As he was lifting his shotgun to blast away at the scattering wolves, the gun when off, removing the back of his pilot's head. The plane dove into the ground and both were killed. The wolves regrouped and continued on their way. Homicides, search and rescues, plane crashes, chases, car crashes, shootings, bear maulings—they are all replayed as I fly over the territory of my old post. In search of good memories, I make a straight cut to the Copper River, dropping low to fly over my old fishwheel site, envisioning the flopping salmon that were pulled from the fish box.

The silty Copper River, although not as expansive as the Yukon, is much more turbulent and dangerous. Flying low over the rapid waters reminds me of all the bodies that were flushed downstream and never found. Most were from accidental drownings, but some—like the murder victim whose body was zipped into an orange beanbag chair cover, then tossed into the river—met their end by other means.

To cleanse my brain, I think of Jet. As the plane sweeps between the canyon walls below Chitina, I remember the envelope she gave me in Anchorage. I pass over the ruins of the Copper River and Northwestern Railway, which hauled copper from the Kennicott mines near McCarthy to Cordova a hundred years ago. Between Childs Glacier and Miles Glacier, the Million Dollar Bridge—built in 1908 for the railroad, then used for vehicles until it was damaged by the 1964 earthquake—slips beneath me as I cut open the envelope. The contents are a pleasant surprise.

Spilling from the envelope is a binder full of typed pages and photographs. Jet's smiling face is under the title "A Guide for Your Trip to America." So that's what she was doing at the aircraft section, while I was checking out of the hotel!

Jet's hand-written note reads, "Jack, I'm glad you decided to take the scenic route. My dad and I twice flew to Seattle this way, and I've patrolled a few times in Southeast. Since you're flying the Copper River down to Cordova, my guide starts at the Copper River Delta. Enjoy, be safe, and know that I love you. Jet."

When I look up, I'm over the Delta. Jet's instructions begin, "From here to Yakutat is the easy part of the trip. You can land on most of those big beaches. Touch down just above the top of the wet sand, or you might get stuck. See that ridgeline to the southeast? When you get to the end of it you'll be over Katalla—a boomtown in 1900, and site of Alaska's first oil well in 1902. The harbor was destroyed by storms in 1907. If you look carefully, you still can see some of the shipwrecks in Controller Bay." Below me is what must be pieces of a ship. I flip to the next page as I turn to follow the wide, sandy beach.

Jet's narration continues. "After you pass the Bering River, look off your right wing and you'll see Kayak Island, a rugged piece of land pointing southwest in the Gulf. There's an abandoned Coast Guard station there. It's also where Captain Vitus Bering, a Danish sailor under the command of Russia's ruler, Peter the Great, landed in 1741." I'm betting the Bering River was named for Vitus.

"Cut across the lower edge of the Bering Glacier, the second largest glacier in North America. That's Vitus Lake at the foot of the glacier, which, due to the retreat of Bering Glacier, has expanded dramatically to become one of the largest freshwater lakes in Alaska.

"Next up is Cape Yakataga, where the Chugach Mountains drop down to meet the sea. That's not a bad airstrip down there, but make sure to land in the middle, as it has not been maintained since the seventies. If the weather is favorable, you can look out the left side of your plane and see Mount St. Elias as you cross Icy Bay. At just over eighteen thousand feet, it's the second tallest peak in the U.S." The white monster gleams in the distance.

"Get some altitude when crossing Icy Bay, as a sudden dip in that water wouldn't be anything like the hot tub on Tranquility River. That patch of ice is the Malaspina Glacier, which at forty miles wide and twenty-eight miles long, has the bragging rights as the largest piedmont glacier this far south in North America. 'Piedmont' is a fancy term for a glacier that's formed from where glaciers exit the mountains and meet flat ground. The glacier is named after the Italian explorer Alessandro Malaspina, who sailed into the region in 1791." I wonder how she knows all this stuff, but I'm impressed, and the trip is going quickly.

"If you have the ceiling, get up high to cross the fifteen miles of open water of Yakutat Bay. If not, follow the west side of the bay, adding ten miles to your trip." With lowering clouds over the bay, I take the mileage penalty. Gray whales are breaching just off shore.

"You may remember back in 1986 when Yakutat made the world news. Hubbard Glacier, up at the head of Yakutat Bay, began advancing quickly, forming a dam. Russell Fjord became Russell Lake and the dam eventually broke, dumping tons of water into the ocean. The five hundred people of Yakutat today live on one of the most geologically active sites in Alaska. By the way, did you know that those pretty beaches are a Mecca for surfers, because of the monster waves? I didn't think so." She's right, it's hard to envision surfers here.

"From Yakutat, it's about one-hundred-twenty miles to your next turn. You have a couple of choices, but I suggest taking a little detour to Glacier Bay. As you follow the coast, you will fly over six little airstrips that have Forest Service cabins—we should take a vacation at one someday. Get a weather briefing on the radio from here, as it's going to get lonely for a while. Follow the coastline while you look for those gigantic brown bears, and cross Dry Bay, where the Alsek River flows into the Gulf of Alaska. I know it seems tight in between the foot of the peaks and the ocean, but there are still some good beaches below you and it's just seventy-five more miles to Juneau. Soon the mountains merge with the shore, leaving just a narrow strip of land. Then the mountains rise more than ten thousand feet and that strip disappears entirely just past Icy Point.

"You will have seventeen miles of listening to every little sound your three hundred horsepower engine makes, but once you've passed a section of very harsh coastline, you will be at Cape Spencer, where you hang a sharp left." I ignore the imaginary engine sounds and, for the first time since I took off from Anchorage, I start a friendship with the glass cockpit. The GPS lights up with the airports of Gustavus, Hoonah and Juneau popping into view. I pass over the Cape Spencer Coast Guard station and head northwest towards Glacier Bay. One terrain alert after another warns of the rugged mountains surrounding the Inside Passage route.

"Keep Cross Sound on your right and work your way between the coast and those little islands through North Inian Pass. That's Glacier Bay on your left. Did you know that since Captain George Vancouver surveyed Southeast Alaska in 1794, this glacier has retreated sixty-five miles, making it the fastest glacial retreat on record? I looked that up for your trivial enjoyment. Okay, I know you well enough, Jack Blake, that you're going to skip the Glacier Bay tour on this trip. Like me, you're driven, and want to get the job at hand done before having fun. Just promise that we'll have a proper vacation, back into the ice age there someday." I promise.

"If you've had enough low-level sightseeing for a while, get some altitude for a direct route to Ketchikan, just two hundred more miles." My head was abuzz with the glaciers, bears, moose, deer, whales, mountains and the incredible scenery of Southeast. Now I'm ready to pick up some speed with a more direct route.

"Tinka would love to have you stay in the huge governor's mansion. You could stop by for a quick nap, or to grab a shower in one of the eleven bathrooms. I know you probably won't want to take the time to stop in Juneau, but you do have the option. I suggest flying over the gorgeous town of Petersburg, or 'Little Norway' as it's called. I know a wonderful spot up in the mountains called Swan Lake where the rainbows are plentiful, and the only sounds are waterfalls and jumping fish. There's a nice little cabin on the lake that we'll have to visit someday. Meanwhile, climb to five thousand feet, tune in the Level Island navigation radio on frequency 116.5, and then get on a highway in the sky, Vector 317. It will take you across Zarembo Island and down Clarence Strait to Ketchikan."

AFTER REFUELING IN KETCHIKAN, it's time to get a little exercise following eight hours in the cockpit. The walk along the flight line treats me to everything from Cubs to Learjets, with a beautiful blue and gold Grumman Goose in between. I pass the Alaska Airlines terminal, following a road that leads me to a gangplank connecting to a huge floatplane-filled dock.

"Looking for a scenic flight?" A man that I guess to be in his mid-70s seems to come out of nowhere. He's somewhat bent over, and since he looks like he started out at about five-foot-five, he appears close to the ground. He's wiry, very animated, and he talks at the level you'd expect from a fire chief at a four-alarmer. His blue cap, slightly tipped up and skewed to the right, screams "Catch-A-Can Seaplanes" in bold yellow print. Before I can answer, he continues up the ramp at a near run. "Bill's the name and seaplaning is the game. Let me show you my favorite bird." I have to pick up my pace as we race up the ramp.

"Jack Blake, and no sir, I'm not looking for a flight, but thank you. I just flew in, and I've had enough flying for the day."

"Oh, I bet that was you in the 185. Used to have one myself. No, I guess I've owned pret' near ten of them. Moved up to a Beaver back in '87. Funny, 'cause I'm eighty-seven myself now. Where you from?" I compliment Bill on his youthful appearance and his pretty Beaver, then tell him Lone Wolf. I'm already in the mindset of being formally *from* Bethel.

"Never heard of it, but I moved here from North Dakota in '45, right after the war, and started my air taxi. Never been north of Juneau since." Bill shows me his workhorse Beaver on EDO floats and delivers a history quick lesson: "Seaplanes brought aviation to this part of Alaska. In the 1920s, there were no landing fields in all of Southeast. Once the EDO float corporation began making sturdy, lightweight floats and bigger engines came out, things really opened up in this part of the world. By the way, did you know that 'EDO' stands for Earl D. Osborne, the company founder?" I didn't, but now I have something to add to my trivia vault.

I learn from Bill that Ketchikan is called "Alaska's First City" because it's the first city northbound from the Lower 48, and that the town started in 1887 around a fish cannery and copper mines. When I answer Bill's question about where I'm staying with, "in the back of the Cessna," he insists that I use the bunk and shower in his office.

Bill doesn't ask what I do for a living or where I'm headed. He just hands me the keys to his kingdom, with the words, "I'll see you in the morning, or maybe not." Bill's office features old photos of planes: a Lockheed Vega, a Fairchild, a Stinson SR, a Bellanca Pacemaker, a Junkers, a deHavilland Gypsy Moth and even the Ford Trimotor floatplane. Pilots, including Archie Satterfield, Bob Ellis, Shell Simmons, Clayton Scott, Joe Crosson and others stood proudly in front of their planes in the black and white reminders of those brave aviators who broke trail for aviation in Alaska. I fall asleep to rain pelting the metal roof of Bill's museum/office.

I'd slept like a baby, but I'm wide-awake by 4 A.M. I make coffee, munch on a food bar from my pack, then slog outside in the blowing rain to the 185. I grab my raingear and explore the airport, as the skies become light enough to reveal fog in all quadrants. By 6 A.M., the ceiling had lifted to a couple hundred feet, the visibility had improved a bit, and the wind was only twenty-two knots. I leave Bill a thank you note and climb into the Cessna. After obtaining a special clearance from a friendly flight service specialist, I initiate a scud-running journey down the Inside Passage.

The world looks much different today in the nasty stuff, than it did yesterday on the sunny leg to Ketchikan. The windows drip with condensation as I fly just a few feet above the raging sea. The rough air requires holding on to the wheel with both hands, and occasionally grabbing the overhead crossbars. Sightseeing is out, as I concentrate on keeping just under the fifty-foot ceiling and just above the waves. I now know what it must be like being inside a washing machine, as the rain and sea spray saturate the plane.

The color GPS helps—all I have to do is stay over the blue, and away from the green and red. I'm not an expert on the avionics package, but I know blue means water, green means terrain, and red means mountains. The system indicates a headwind of forty-eight knots, equating to much slower progress today than yesterday.

The governor's office had made arrangements with the Canadian Customs officials. Since they already know I'm a state trooper and carrying a sidearm, the check-in at Port Hardy is pleasant. The custom agent bids me a good day, a friendly fuel attendant tops off my tanks, and I'm back in the air in twenty minutes.

The weather breaks up as I continue south. Intrigued by the colorful little dots on the water surface between the rugged inlets far from civilization, curiosity gets the best of me and I descend for a closer look. The bright red, orange and blue objects turn out to be kayakers, exploring the Inside Passage in total peace. Passing over fishing boats, cruise ships and the famous Alaska Ferry System haulers, I take in the incredible beauty of the British Columbia and Washington coasts. It's easy to see why Captain George Vancouver spent so much time exploring this region and why the Inside Passage cruise is Alaska's number one tourist attraction.

Tuned to Vancouver approach control, the aircraft radio suddenly comes alive. Evasive action is necessary to avoid Vancouver's airspace, as the skyscrapers from British Columbia's largest city tower over the coastline. The mass of the municipality is intimidating, and I wonder how there could possibly be any metropolitan area larger than this one.

Part Two

Chapter 12

LIFE IN THE LOWER 48

I THINK THEY CAN TELL that I'm not from these parts. With the help of Victoria's flight controllers and the airspace depictions on the glass cockpit, I work my way through the dense air traffic to Bellingham, Washington. Two attractive young women in bright red shirts run out, chock my wheels, and ask if I need gas and customs. Not quite the same as getting gas in the Bush, where it often means hauling fuel to your airplane in jerry cans. I say 'yes' to both, and within a short time, I'm full of gas and paperwork. As I'm paying the tab, a guy who looks about fourteen, introduces himself as a flight instructor and asks if I just came down from Alaska. I confess and ask his suggestions to get through the air traffic in Seattle.

"I've always dreamed of going to Alaska to fly seaplanes, or to become a Bush pilot." The junior flight instructor wistfully comments as he pulls a chart from his bag. I encourage him to chase his dream and we study the chart together. "Just follow the west slope to the Cascades up here and you can skirt the Class B airspace in Seattle." I follow his finger, focusing on avoiding the big circle on the chart around Seattle, which means a lot of big planes. "You can cross over the mountains and take a peek down into Saint Helens, if you want." I had a thrilling close up look at an Alaska volcano with Jet a few years ago, but what the heck, I guess I'd rather fly over Saint Helens than Seattle. I thank him, shake his hand, and take off for the volcano.

The Cascades are friendly—smooth air and enough ceiling to skim over the mountaintops—but Seattle is the biggest city I've ever piloted near, and it gives me the chills. I'm startled by all the buildings, highways, and the hustle-bustle of activity in this metro area, boasting as many people as in the whole state of Alaska. I'd like to pick out the Space Needle in all the congestion, but I have a sudden urge to get out of here and into the backcountry. I know how a bear must feel when it bumbles into a town—nothing looks or feels right and the creatures don't speak your language. I was raised on a remote ranch in Idaho then shipped off to Southeast Asia. After that, I moved directly to the Alaska Bush. So, like the meandering bear, I'm out of my element.

The sheer devastation of the 1980 Mount Saint Helens eruption, with the force comparable to a hydrogen bomb, is still evident in the burned land and fallen trees. The explosion blew off thirteen hundred feet of the mountain's top and sent ash and debris more than twelve miles into the sky, covering three states—Washington, Oregon, and Idaho. Sixty-two people were killed, beautiful forests and lakes were destroyed, and there was three billion dollars worth of damage. Nearby Spirit Lake looks like it'd be nice for seaplanes—if it weren't for all the floating logs deposited during the eruption.

The weather forecast is for a system of low clouds and rain moving in from the coast, so I cross the Columbia River to follow the Deschutes River south, over Sun River and toward Klamath Valley. It's tempting to land at a little airstrip called Beaver Marsh, but I still have plenty of fuel, daylight, and energy, so I push on. A couple of F-15s give me a wake-up call, rushing past me near Klamath, at what must be at least Mach 1. The GPS confirms the military operations area, encouraging me to turn towards Mount Shasta's snow-capped peak in the distance. It looks like I can go "IFR,"—in this situation meaning, "I follow the river,"—the river being the Sacramento, leading to the town of Redding. That works until I get over Shasta Lake and the clouds sag down to the water. The conditions are still plenty high directly to the west, so I head to a place called Trinity Alps, hoping to pick my way down the river flowing out of Trinity Lake. The weather is even worse, so I decide to do a little sightseeing in hopes the clouds will lift in the meantime. This country reminds me of Kenai Lake and Moose Pass on Alaska's Kenai Peninsula. So does the current weather.

Bad news from Flight Service—the entire Sacramento Valley is socked in from a low-pressure system. Since it looks good to the east, I turn to intercept the Pit River, which takes me past the second military operations area of the day. Five-thousand-five-hundred feet gives good obstacle and cloud clearance, but turbulence is kicking in as I fly over ranches, dusty roads, and dry lakes dotting the high desert landscape.

The weather is dropping quickly and it's time to find an airport. The GPS shows that Reno is only sixty miles away, so I turn to the south and pick up a pass between "Totem Pole" and Mount Lola. Donner's Pass is a little more to the south, and I know from reading about the Donner Party that it's at even a higher elevation.

Snow! I can't believe there's snow at this time of the year, other than in Alaska! It's just spitting flakes now, but the wind is picking up and I'm racing the system to get out of the mountains. A glance outside brings more bad news—ice is forming on the wings. Here I am in the Sierra Nevadas, wandering around in unfamiliar territory, in lousy weather. I've become trapped by pushing it. Dumb mistake. I should have landed when I had the chance, but the only option now is to trudge on.

The snow is really coming down as I snake along a highway through another pass. The Cessna feels heavy, no doubt due to the layers of ice on the wings. An instrument approach to Reno is not an option, as that would require climbing into the clouds and loading up with even more heavy, and possibly deadly, ice. No, I need to keep over the road and use the truckers' lights to guide me. Right now I'd gladly switch places with any one of the men behind the wheel of an eighteen-wheeler. Twenty-two miles out of Reno, the visibility is down to a couple of miles and it's getting dark. The Reno air traffic controllers are swamped, mostly from dishing out holding patterns to jet traffic. Approach control confirms what I've already heard from the automatic weather reporting system: the airport is closed. The fuel gauges flicker between quarter tanks and nothing.

"Reno approach, Cessna November 98054." I report my position when the radio operator asks, admit that I'm not on an instrument flight plan, and tell that I'm just a little Cessna 185. He sounds surprised, but barks codes to punch into my transponder, so I can be indentified on his radar screen.

Blasting at the windscreen like asteroids, the snow reduces the visibility to less than a mile. The glass cockpit warns of the mountains all around me, that there are layers of planes above me, and that there are nasty weather systems everywhere. Reno approach asks my intentions. They want me out of their airspace. I agree.

"Reno, Cessna November five-four. Can you provide vectors to an airport with visual conditions?" I ask hopefully.

"Cessna five-four, advise when you are over Reno and I'll have vectors for you." Through the snow, I steal a veiled view of what must be Reno casinos. The needle on my panel swings when the navigation fix is crossed. The controller gives me a heading for a remote airstrip that's in visual conditions. I detect a snicker as he wishes me good luck.

Bouncing around in the rough winds, I focus again on a highway. It's too dark to see the snow piling up on the plane, which is probably good. Not seeing the snow load gives me one less thing to worry about. The road below is much smaller than the one coming into Reno, but I can now see a mile of truck lights, instead of just a quarter mile. The GPS points to a private airport eight miles off my nose. I drop another hundred feet. I'm staying low enough to see, but not so low as to snag a power line hidden by darkness and snow. The highway deteriorates into a country road, but there are lights ahead. I'm now in the midst of a serious blizzard. Just like home.

The plane feels like a rock, but the lights are getting closer and the GPS confirms they are by an airport. A quick pre–landing check sets me up for what I hope is a final approach. Now, at a hundred feet above the ground, I concentrate on the lights. This is not the time to worry about icing, turbulence, or low fuel. Just focus on the lights. The airspeed indictor shows eighty knots. I yank on two notches of flaps. Still no airport, but I continue to the lights. The mountain winds shove me across the road. I violently jerk the control wheel and cross over an eighteen–wheeler, setting up again for the lights. Then I pull the power back and push the propeller control in.

That's it! I'm over an airport. I don't know how long the runway is, or how much of it is remaining. I just want down, out of this mess. Yanking the throttle back more, I click another notch of flaps and flare. The plane bounces and slides sideways. The brakes are all the way to the firewall, but the Cessna keeps rolling on the snow-covered runway. The bright lights are getting closer. I raise the flaps and try to get more out of the brakes, but I begin to skid. I'm blinded as the plane slides toward the illumination.

Finally, the Cessna decides she's had enough fun with me, as we stop in a slush-pile of snow. The instrument gyros wind down with a mocking groan. A groan I deserve.

Several inches of ice have hitchhiked on the wings. The propeller's leading edge looks like an icicle. But the plane didn't fail me, in spite of me pushing it beyond normal limits.

The lights must either be a restaurant or a motel. I could use a shower to wash the stink of stupid off me. A hot meal would be a treat. A warm bed would be heaven. I push the heavy Cessna backwards through the sloppy snow, tie it down, grab my bag, and head for the lighted parking lot.

Wet snow pellets slap into my face as I bend over into the wind, trudging to the building. Snow has piled up on the roof, concealing the letters of the purple and pink neon sign. There are no cars in the parking lot, so I guess the highway is still clear enough for road travel. I don't see a "No Vacancy" sign, so I ring the doorbell on the crimson door. First there are footsteps, then a window curtain waves. The door opens slowly.

The motel manager is about forty, tall and slender, wearing a silky low-cut red dress. Her straight blonde hair is shoulder length, her lipstick is very red, and her perfume cuts into the snowy night. "Come on in out of the cold," she insists. I do.

This isn't like any motel I've seen before. I'm led directly to a bar, where the motel manager offers me a stool. She rattles off all kinds of exotic drink specialties, but I settle for an Alaska Husky draft.

"So, where are you from?" She asks while I sip my brew. I don't want to be rude, but I really would like to get a room key and clean up before dinner. I tell her that I just flew in from Alaska and introduce myself. She tells me her name is Bunny.

"Flying in this weather? Well Jack, that explains why you don't have a car in the parking lot. When we have one of these freak spring blizzards, business drops off to nothing." I tell her that surprises me, as I'd think that motorists would want to get off the road in the snowstorm. She tells me that most of their business is from tourists who are staying in Reno. I wonder why tourists staying in Reno would come way out here to another motel. It couldn't be for this little bar. A bar without a TV, just risqué paintings on the wall. But then again, I'm not from these parts.

Suddenly, six young women slip into the bar. Their attire surprises me. One wears a bikini, the others wear fancy pajama-type clothing. Some of it is see-through. I try not to notice.

"These are my girls," Bunny says proudly.

Funny, I think. Here's a woman out here on a lonely road with six daughters. She doesn't seem old enough to be the mother to all of them. Maybe they're adopted. Again, like the bear that wandered into town, I'm out of my element.

"Hi, Jack!" The girls respond in unison. Some giggle. One winks. One purses her lips.

I politely acknowledge the girls and return to my beer. They sit on the stools around me and Bunny retreats behind the bar.

"Would you like to buy any one of the girls a drink?" Bunny asks. I don't want to be rude, but first, being a married man, I don't think it's proper to have a drink with another woman. Plus, I feel I'd have to buy all them drinks, so as not to offend anyone. But, if it takes springing for drinks to get a room and a meal, I guess that's what has to be done.

"Sure, whatever you girls care for," I reluctantly offer.

"Wow, you Alaskans are quite the macho men!" Bunny gives the girls pink drinks. I blush, but I just want a room, and I think I've earned the right to ask now.

"Well, I don't know about that, but I sure could use a room," I plead.

"Sure, if you're ready. How about a shower and a hot tub first?"

Now she's talking. Nothing would be better than a shower and hot soak after ten hours in the cockpit fighting weather. I say that sounds great, but I ask for a menu first. I'm really hungry now.

"Okay, Jack, which girl would you like?" I'm focusing on the menu that Bunny is sliding across the bar, so I don't think I hear her properly. I apologize and ask her to repeat.

"Which girl? Choose anyone you want." Bunny waved at the girls sitting on each side of me. My mind races. Girl for what? To show me to my room? To the shower?

The menu opens in front of me. There isn't a hamburger, steak, curly fry, or chicken wing on it. Instead, it offers things other than food. Things that the girls provide in a private room and in the spa. I look around again. My environment now looks different. There's a reason these girls are wearing next to nothing, and that this is unlike any motel where I've stayed. Then I see the establishment's name listed at the top of the menu: WILD BUNNY INN.

Suddenly, I get it. Now I need to get out of it. *Fast!* I stand up and walk to the window. It's a total whiteout blizzard and the wind howls through the darkness. How naïve can a guy be? My uncle, who raised me on his ranch, obviously left a few things out when teaching me the ways of the world. I'd read about houses of ill repute in western novels, and even worked undercover on a prostitution case when I was rookie trooper, but I didn't know these places existed. In plain view, open to the world. I had good grades in college. I was at the top of my academy class. Now, I feel like a fool.

"Bunny, could I speak to you privately for a minute?" I nod to the entryway. Bunny follows.

"Jack, if you're going to ask for me, I'm flattered, but I'm just the madam these days."

"No, it's not that…" I start to explain, but Bunny interrupts.

"Well, then no worries. Whatever else you want goes. You're in charge!"

"I appreciate that, Bunny, I really do. But I'm a married man." I point to my new ring. Bunny giggles and shakes her head. I continue pleading my case.

"I'm a married man, very much in love with the woman I married only a week ago. I'd really just be happy to pay for a room for the night, to get out of this storm. I'm really sorry. I had no idea. I thought this was a motel. If I can't rent a room, is it okay if I camp in my plane?" Tilting her head in apparent disbelief, Bunny looks straight into my eyes, tears forming in hers.

"Jack, that is the about the dumbest, but also the sweetest thing I've ever heard. They don't have bordellos up in Alaska, huh?"

Before I can answer, Bunny locks her arm in mine and escorts me to the bar. "Ladies, I have an announcement to make. Jack here is a happily married man, been so for over a week. He needs a meal and a place to lay his head for the night. You will treat him like a brother, not a customer. Hands off!"

First the girls just stare. Maybe they are worried about losing the income. Then the mood changes. They all crowd around me. I get hugs, kisses on my cheeks, and a round of congratulations. Bunny has me follow her down a hallway and opens a door.

"This is the only room in the place without a theme of some sort. No leopard-skins or silk on the bed and no specialized chairs. It's yours for the night, Jack. Dinner's in twenty minutes. And you can call me Linda."

After a hot shower, I make my way back to the bar. The girls are all there, but they now are dressed in jeans and sweaters, or sweat shirts and pajama bottoms. There's a big table now in the middle of the bar and it's set for dinner. Linda turns out to be a great cook. And the ladies all share their stories—some sad, some amazing, some just like any other lost girl in this world.

I thank Linda and the girls for taking me in and sharing dinner. I assure them it's unlike any evening that I've had before. I pass on the community hot tub and lock the door to my room at 11 P.M. Then I remember the Blueberry. It lights up with an email from Jet.

Chapter 13

THE BIG CITY

"JACK, I HOPE you are being safe and behaving yourself." I can honestly answer yes to one of Jet's hopes. It's exciting to receive my first email on the Blueberry, especially since it's from my wife.

"Things are looking up on my case. Audrey Hart at the Palmer P.D. is a real sweetheart. She gave me a lift from the airport and we tracked down her complainant on the harassing pilot. Marie Hodge explained that she didn't want to report the incident to the troopers, as she had recently broken up with Talkeetna Fish and Wildlife Trooper Gary Wickham, and wanted to avoid running into him.

"Good news: Marie's ski pole—the one she stabbed the pilot with—still had a little blood smear on it. Using Audrey's evidence kit, I was able to swab a sample and will hopefully get some DNA, or at least the blood type. She remembers now that the sunglasses he was wearing were not aviator-style, but clip-ons over heavy black-framed glasses. She said that the cap he was wearing had the letters 'HOAR' under the sheep head. Maybe on one of those long flights, you can break the code for me." I'll work on that on a boring leg of the trip. Maybe "H" is for hunting, since we know the guy is a hunter. At least of women.

"Hodge, when I showed her a lineup of airplanes, identified the suspect's as a Super Cub. Even though there must be a thousand Cubs in Alaska, this narrows things down a bit. Plus, we have a partial registration number. Hodge is willing to cooperate with us as the case progresses, and says she will recognize the suspect if she sees him again.

"After Palmer, I flew up to Talkeetna where Trooper Wickham picked me up at the village airstrip and we had lunch at the Roadhouse. I told him about my meeting with Marie Hodge. He explained that they have an on-again-off-again relationship, this being their off month. Regardless, he feels she'd be a good witness. He's a very nice guy and a good trooper, although I had to remind him that I'm married. Gary sure can handle that Robinson chopper, and he took me right to the spot where he'd found the bones. The metal detector screamed as soon as I hovered the search coil over the hole. Gary dug about a foot deep, then pulled out the locket. It was just as Candy described, complete with the photos of her, Karma, and Tyrrell. The metal detector hit on something else, so Gary dug further and found what he says is probably tongue-piercing jewelry—I'll take his word for that. We also found a couple of teeth. Gary got me back to Talkeetna late in the afternoon and, after declining his invitation for dinner, I climbed back into the Cub and headed for Fairbanks.

"I set up at the Fairbanks airport campground—there's nothing like camping with your airplane, even if it's in town. I called the investigative section at the trooper office and your friend Jill answered, offering to come out and pick me up. Sgt. Crisp never got around to mailing me the pin that was recovered with the bones near Arctic Village, but I have it now. There's an image of a full-curl sheep on the pin, with the words "HOAR" under it. That's the same wording that Marie Hodge remembers. Jill and I had dinner together, and we had a fun time talking about you. She tells me that you are known in Fairbanks as 'Sundance,' and that she gave you that nickname saying you look like a young Robert Redford. But, it was actually to get you to start her car when it was sixty below. Well, now you're *my* Sundance! Now that she mentions it, I do see the resemblance. Anyway, Jill is terrific.

"Jill says that Sgt. Crisp is a little laid-back, so she took it upon herself to send the bones to the crime lab. She also called the Arctic Village officer and confirmed that the ring belongs to the missing girl. Jill also asked him about the white plane that the unidentified pilot was using to help in the search, and found that it was a white Super Cub on red skis. She offered to research the airplane numbers we have from Palmer, and to help in any way she can in the investigation. She's now on my Blueberry's speed dial! Oh yeah, here's a nice surprise! When Jill dropped me back at the airport, she handed me a wedding gift. It's a beautiful stained glass art piece she made, with *'1 Corinthians 13:4-8'* scrolled on the bottom. We will have to look that up. It will look wonderful in the Lone Wolf Cabin.

"I'm off to Glennallen tomorrow. Please email me or call, and let me know how it's going on your end. Love, Jet."

I call Jet on the Blueberry. She giggles about my stay at the "Inn," surprised at my lack of worldly ways. I promise to be safer in the rest of my flying. She promises to be safe as well. We ended the phone call with things newlyweds say.

AFTER A BREAKFAST of eggs hollandaise, fresh fruit and espresso, I try to settle my bill for my overnight stay. Linda refuses payment, saying that her renewed faith in married men is payment enough. It works out, as I leave a hundred dollar bill in the room. That way, I don't violate Alaska ethic laws by taking a gratuity, and I don't have to explain a charge from the Wild Bunny Inn on my state credit card account. Linda and her girls walk me to the plane, and after I do a pre-flight and climb inside, the fun begins. Singing "Happy Trails To You," the girls toss silver dollar-sized pancakes at the Cessna, while waving goodbye. There are strange customs in these parts.

Leaving a trail of flying mud, and an experience I won't share with my future grandchildren, I pop the 185 off the sloppy strip and head to the Reno airport for fuel and a weather briefing. It's more spring-like today, with clear skies and unlimited visibility. After a quick view of gorgeous Lake Tahoe, I head directly for the Sacramento Valley, then hug the foothills. Last night, Linda told me about a famous frog-jumping contest at a town named Calaveras, but I can't pick out that little hamlet below, much less the frogs. Continuing south, I peer into Yosemite Valley. Tiny, colorful dots must be climbers scaling the vertical rock face of the mountain they call Half Dome. Mount Whitney, the highest mountain in the Lower 48—a mere five thousand feet shorter than Denali—sticks out on my left. Little oil wells pumping away on the hillside of the town indicates where Bakersfield must be, but it's hidden by a brown cloud. The sky clears to the west, revealing a very blue Pacific ocean.

Rising out of the farmland is an expansive facility that, on closer inspection, I identify as a prison. Then it seems as if another prison passes below me every fifteen minutes. In Alaska, I'd count grizzly bears at the same rate.

Speaking of grizzly bears, my scariest wildlife encounter was with one of those fearsome beasts. Camping in a tent while I was building a log cabin in the wilds, I was awakened by a grunting noise from the vicinity of the cabin frame. That's where the dog food was stored, so I slid out of my tent to sneak up on my canine and catch him in the act of poaching kibbles. Slithering through the darkness, I made my way along the logs, homing in on the grunts. I was too close when I realized it wasn't my dog. The stink of his fur burned my nostrils and his hot breath panted on my head. We were close enough for an embrace and I was frozen in place with fear—fear that the bear could undoubtedly smell. Probably pondering whether he was going to eat me or the dog food first, the bear sized me up. If it wasn't for my dog suddenly bursting out of the tent and barking his lovely head off, it would have been the bear's call to make, not mine. Admittedly, I was scared then, really scared. I feel almost the same now, as I look at the sprawl of Southern California.

Acting on Hap Winton's suggestion—and from watching the movie *"One Six Right,"* about the history of the airport—I'd decided to land at the Van Nuys field. It's my best choice for avoiding Los Angeles International, an airport with more aircraft operations yearly than there are people in Alaska. A more tangible and immediate bonus is that I can get down out of this unbelievably congested and smoggy airspace sooner. The glass cockpit screams out the aircraft traffic in the sky, as I dodge through heavies and lightweights. Crossing over a mountain ridge I follow commands of the air traffic controller to land on one six right.

Ground control guides me past the Stearmans, P-51s, helicopters, business jets, and the fantastic static display of aeronautical eye candy—aircraft that I know exist only from photos. I think of the pilots who've touched down here, like Amelia Earhart after breaking the world speed record. Howard Hughes, Wallace Beery, Hoot Gibson, Cecil B.

DeMille, and Gene Autry used the airfield for their playground. I visualize the filming of the scene from Casablanca and see Laurel and Hardy clumsily climbing into a bi-wing for the movie Flying Deuces. I feel for Roscoe Turner's loss of his Sikorsky S-29-A, crashing near here while being filmed for "Hells Angels." I wonder how the local aviators manage to keep this historical airport open. Urban sprawl surrounds it, but for now, it appears pilots continue to enjoy recreational and business flying, as has been done for eighty years. As I shut down in front of Air Center Aviation, a man greets me on the ramp. He wears a blue Hawaiian shirt and jeans. He looks like he's been expecting me.

"Why in the heck would you leave Alaska to come down here? You going to Disneyland?" Hap had given me the name of a former sports car racing buddy who now has a hangar at Van Nuys. Duane, a stoutly built man in his seventies with swept-back gray hair and tinted glasses, leads me into the office. I tell him that I'm here to meet with the LAPD in Hollywood. Duane shakes his head.

"Let me show you something. That's Hap right there." Duane points to a much younger version of Hap standing next to a red Datsun Fairlady roadster. He shows me even younger versions of both of them with various old MGs and Triumphs in black and white photos. "Hap was a great driver, and he's probably an even better pilot." As I ponder the smallness of this world, Duane shows me the mismatched fleet inside his hangar: a military bi-plane that's in pieces, a Johnson Rocket, a Cessna 120, a Piper L-4, and a Learjet 24. "You can stick your 185 next to the L-4." Duane has a lineman tug the Cessna into the hangar, then hands me the keys to a subcompact rental.

"Hollywood is an experience you'll never forget. There are plenty of hotels right off Hollywood Boulevard, but you will probably find it a lot more peaceful back here in Van Nuys." I don't need another "experience" right now, but I plug the address for the Hollywood station into the GPS function of the Blueberry and head for Interstate 405.

What harm could come from just one night in Hollywood?

Chapter 14

HOLLY-WEIRD

I ONCE HEARD of a porcupine in Alaska that had two heads. That was strange, but it's nothing compared to the strange ways and strange people that I see today. Do motorists here have any clue that there are traffic laws? You'd think the speed limit on the freeway is a hundred miles an hour, not the posted seventy. Forget about tailgating and merging laws—it's every driver for himself as eye contact-avoiding drivers race into my lane, making me wish I'd opted for a bigger rental car. It is rude, maybe even uncivilized. But, if you want to see strange, just stroll down Hollywood Boulevard.

Before the setting sun sinks into the nearby Pacific Ocean, I want to do a quick recon to stake out an area for some urban hiking, find the police department, and check into a motel. From inside my rental car, Hollywood seems warm and clean. Palm trees grace the streets and the stucco architecture is refreshing. Reminding me of photos I've seen of Las Vegas at night, the buildings form a canopy over the street and the bright lights dance on the shiny hood of my rental. Pedestrians stroll like caribou munching on lichen—heads down, curiously examining the sidewalk. Some bend over and place their hands on the cement. The green, red and yellow lights of Grauman's Chinese Theater sparkle in the night as I pass by. It's the largest and most opulent structure I've ever seen. The Hollywood Wax Museum also catches my eye, as does the Space Needle-looking Capitol Records Building in the distance. The main drag also features eateries, fancy shops, big name retailers, cheesy tourist traps, porn shops, and tattoo parlors.

The Blueberry's GPS urges me to turn left onto Wilcox Street, directing me to LAPD's Hollywood station. There is nothing "Hollywood" about the one-level brick structure. Instead of palms, shade-producing trees loom over the front of the station. A fabric sign flaps in the wind, advertising for volunteer reserves. A white post states simply:

POLICE. I ask the Blueberry for a list of nearby accommodations and a dozen pop up. From drive-bys, the Renaissance, the Hollywood Roosevelt, and the Hollywood Celebrity Hotel all look above the budget of a state employee. My best option appears to be Bill's Hollywood Motel. From the street, Bill's looks like a clean establishment. Even though the stucco building is pink, it's designed like a fort. The motel courtyard is protected from the street by three walls. Guests drive into the parking area under the motel sign, passing the office which overlooks the courtyard like a prison guard shack.

A life-sized cardboard cutout of Shrek greets guests in the lobby. Behind what may be bulletproof glass, a dark-skinned man wearing a white turban looks up from a TV on which a game show blares. His nametag says "Badal" instead of Bill. I'm guessing that Badal is from India. "Do you want a room?" He asks in a heavily accented, not-too friendly tone. One hundred and twenty dollars a night seems high for quarters in the pink fort, but the Blueberry reports that's mid-range for Hollywood. I request a non-smoking room as Badal takes my credit card. Badal says all rooms are non-smoking, as he slides a key on a large rainbow-colored fob under the glass.

With the transaction complete, Badal offers a bit of friendly advice. "I suggest you visit Grauman's Chinese Theater. To visit Los Angeles and not see Grauman's and the Walk of Fame is like visiting China and not seeing the Great Wall. Make certain that you lock your room and your car." I thank Badal for his hospitality and advice. He's one of those guys who gets friendlier the longer he knows you.

The stairs squeak in protest as I climb to the second floor. It takes three tries to force the door open. Musty carpet and the lingering aroma of smoke greet me. I slide the window open, but a block in the frame only allows about an eight-inch gap. The orange and brown shag carpet appears to have been freshly vacuumed, which gives me hope. I pull down the well-worn bedspread to find clean sheets—another plus. The TV remote, which has been taped together, lies on the cigarette-burned bedside table. The table feels greasy, the type of grease that comes from cigarette smoke. Bill, or maybe Badal, must have converted this room to a non-smoking unit by removing the ashtrays just this morning. The white bath towels are tattered and thin, but the bathroom is clean. Bills' room will work for one night, but I'll search for better accommodations tomorrow. Meanwhile, it's time to explore Hollywood.

It's hard not have your head on a swivel as you weave along Hollywood Boulevard through a freak-show of street performers, musicians, druggies, homeless panhandlers, teenagers that look like runaways, celebrities, and wannabe celebrities. One man wears a Superman costume, another is Iron Man. A person, who I hope is a woman, is made up like Marilyn Monroe. Some guy, I guess to weigh a hundred and fifty pounds dripping wet, is in a giant Hulk costume, with his Hulk head under one arm and a bag from McDonalds under the other. A group sits in the shadows and stares at tourists who pass by. Their desperate faces are dirty and their hair is in dreadlocks. They look like they will kill for a fix of heroin, meth, crack, or whatever.

After grabbing a slice of pizza and a salad at a restaurant below the Kodak Theater—where, according to the waitress who wants to be an actress, the Academy Awards were held—I meander back to the boulevard. Shortly, a man with tattoos covering all of his visible skin tries to direct me into his parlor. Next, a woman attempts to coerce me into her store for a psychic reading. I pass on both, but now see why pedestrians are staring at the sidewalk. Trying not to step on Lucille Ball's star, I too now study the cement, passing over stars of Gregory Peck, Katharine Hepburn, Ronald Reagan, Andy Griffith, James Cagney and Dolly Parton. Nine blocks later, the stars end on Hollywood Boulevard with Paul Newman.

Enough of the tourist thing. It's a nice warm night, so I decide to take a run. The lights are dimmer as I continue onto side streets, deep into a seedy neighborhood. Tough-looking men drive by in big cars that have been modified to ride low to the ground. Other men and boys stare at them from trashed-out yards and porches of rundown houses. As I run further away from the Walk of Stars, the neighborhoods look tougher and the men look meaner. After thirty minutes, a convenience store beckons me in for a bottle of water.

As I approach the parking lot, two men come from the sha-dows. They wear baggy pants with their boxer shorts showing—a fa-shion statement that has yet to hit the Alaska Bush, probably due to the risk of frostbite in the winter and mosquito bites in the summer. Black tattoos cover both of their arms and their necks. Their black sleeveless shirts are emblazed with some sort of graffiti, maybe to honor their leader. Each carries something in his hand. They don't look friendly.

"Good evening," I offer.

"Give me your money," punctuated with an expletive, one screams his response.

"I don't think so," I counter.

The bigger of the two lurches forward. I guess him to be five-ten and two hundred and thirty pounds. He is swinging a short length of nasty-looking chain. He steps into my comfort zone. I glance at his partner and see a knife in his right hand.

Without discussing the proposed transaction any further, I throw a quick, hard punch under Chain Guy's nose. As blood gushes from his face, I borrow his chain. As Knife Guy lunges forward with his blade, I hastily side step and swing the chain over his forearm. The knife clangs onto the pavement. I whip his arm behind him, and using the chain for added support, anchor his arm into a lock. He screams in pain and becomes submissive. Chain Guy now has his shirt wadded over his nose, cussing as he tries to stop the bleeding. I order Knife Guy to grab onto the elastic on the back of the Chain Guy's boxer shorts and we march single file into the store.

The store clerk, maybe a relative of motel desk clerk Badal, rais-es his head from his TV on which the ending credits for a game show are rolling. When I ask him if he sells zip ties, he points me to the household section. With a little added twist to the chain, I encourage my new acquaintances to move down the aisle. I order Knife Guy to grab a bag of the large zip ties. There are four color varieties in the bag, so I ask my prisoners if they have a color preference. Knife Guy selects blue and Chain Guy chooses red. It appears they have worn similar restraints before, as they both ratchet them on without asking. I use a yellow one to fasten them together.

"Anything else?" The clerk asks as I pull out a five to pay.

"A bottle of water please. And could you call the police?"

The clerk rolls a bottle of water across the counter and nods his turban at the LAPD squad car that has pulled up in front of the store. "No charge. Those two have been harassing me for a long time," the clerk whispers so my prisoners can't hear. I want to pay him to avoid any conflict of interest, but the chain gang is in a hurry to get outside. I make a mental note to stop by later to settle the bill.

After I introduce myself and show my badge, the officers divulge the bad boys are well-known local criminals with outstanding arrest warrants. When I tell them I'm meeting with the homicide division tomorrow, they suggest I write a statement then. "Welcome me to Hollywood," one of the officers says as he climbs into the patrol car. With their police radio squawking, they race off with my new acquaintances caged in the back seat.

Back at Bill's motel, the clamor of the city intrudes through the window. Horns are blaring, engines are revving, tires are squealing, people are yelling, bottles are breaking, and sirens are wailing. It seems a perfect time to call Jet. She answers on the third ring, sounding so far away.

"Hi, lover! How are you? The ringtone on this thing startled me. It's so quiet out here." I think I hear a babbling creek in the background.

I lie and tell her that all is great. She laughs, detecting that it's not. Jet says she spent the day in Copper Center, where Trooper Wilkinson took her to the missing girl's house. The only thing of interest she found was the book, "*Alaska Bush Pilots*," making Jet think that Lucinda Bickel has an interest in flying. Jet also spoke to the man who saw Lucinda talking to a pilot. He said they were at a distance, but remembers the pilot was wearing a red cap. He recalled that the girl was wearing a yellow jacket and blue jeans. Jet showed the witness her photo line-up of airplanes and he picked out a Super Cub.

Trooper Wilkinson told Jet that two winters ago, he investigated the vandalizing of a remote cabin located eight miles west of Copper Center on Klutina Lake. One strange thing about the report is that the suspect had used a ski plane. The cabin was sprayed with bullets, which is commonly expected from mischievous kids on snowmachines, not a shooter with an expensive airplane. Wilkinson recovered two spent .223 shell casings and recorded measurements of the ski tracks.

As she speaks to me, Jet sits by a campfire next to the glacier-blue creek that runs alongside the Klutina Lake cabin. She plans to do more investigation tomorrow after a quiet night. I plan to do the same after the noisiest night of my life.

FOUR HOURS OF restless sleep is not bad, considering the action in the motel's neighborhood last night caused me to watch the day-glow numbers of the bedside clock march along to the sounds of the city. After a morning run in the still-sleeping "hood," I check out of Bill's, then drive the four blocks to the Hollywood police station. The station has its own "Walk of Fame," but this is much more significant than the one on Hollywood Boulevard. It recognizes the fallen Los Angeles police officers with the same star treatment in the cement.

Standing at the counter is a five-foot-eleven, ninety-pound woman with tall black hair. She wears a pink velvet mini-skirt, spiked heels, and black nylon stockings with runs in the back. She's making a complaint about getting ripped off by "a John." A clerk shows me the homicide section through a heavy metal door with wire-screen glass, pointing to a detective seated at a desk. The detective speaks before I can introduce myself.

"Sergeant Preston of the Yukon, I presume. I hear that you've been in town for less than twenty-four hours and you're already rounding up our criminals. I hope you didn't tie your dog team to the fire hydrant out front, or you'll get towed for sure." Detective Forrest Canon's sense of humor is as dry as the desert I flew over a couple of days ago, and I can't help but laugh. I like the supervisor of the Hollywood Homicide Division already. He's built like a Greco-Roman wrestler and I wonder if he competed in the 1984 summer Olympics in this city. He stands about six-four, with shiny black hair and matching mustache, and he looks like he pumps iron daily.

"Oops! Sorry, I'll go move them. I'll be right back," I retort. Stifling what might be a grin, the detective sticks out his meaty hand and introduces himself as Forrest. I return the handshake and take him up on his offer of a chair facing his cluttered desk. The wall behind is decorated with certificates of accomplishments from the LAPD, a graduation certificate from an FBI supervisory class, three shooting awards, and framed photos. There are pictures of Forrest reeling a large saltwater fish from the deck of a boat in blue seas, fly-fishing on a mountain stream, and standing on a mountain peak in climbing gear.

"It looks like you're an outdoorsman, detective. Have you ever been to Alaska?" I ask.

"No, but I sure want to get there someday." His face lights up and we are on common ground.

"I have an empty seat in a Cessna and you're welcome to ride back with me." I offer, knowing the improbability of that happening. He leans over his desk and smiles, congratulating me on busting the two guys last night. We then we talk for ten minutes about fishing and hunting in Alaska, with a few bear stories in between. I think Forrest is beginning to trust me, but first he wants to go through the male-bonding process.

"Let's get out of this stuffy joint. By the way, are you packing?" I have my Glock under my jacket and Forrest seems happy about it. Forrest whips his unmarked police sedan through the L.A. traffic like a wolf weaving through an alder patch after an arctic hare. In twenty minutes, we pull up to a building next to Dodger Stadium. We enter a high-tech indoor range, with targets that slide like clothing on racks at a dry cleaners. This sure beats plinking at silhouettes when it's twenty below zero. Forrest makes me bet lunch on a shooting contest.

Shooting comes natural to me, since my uncle made me practice almost every day at his Idaho ranch. I can't explain it, but whatever I point the barrel of a gun at, I hit. I don't say it to brag, it's just the way it is for me, like some people are good at dancing. I used to be concerned about being characterized as a gun nut, when I competed with other troopers in the required qualification exercises, but I got over it.

I win the bet.

Over lunch at Forrest's favorite Hollywood restaurant, he points out a few celebrities as we sit outside in the seventy-five degree sun. I have no clue who they are, but feign interest. I don't think he cares much either, but he's trying to be a good Hollywood host. He peppers me with more questions about Alaska, especially when I tell him about Jet's game warden work. Then he asks me the important question.

"So Jack, do you think you can arrest this guy? That is, if he is a trooper?"

I answer that it will be no problem. It could be tough if he turns out to be a friend, but murder tends to ruin friendships.

Forrest details the case over coffee. Two LAPD officers pulled over a car one night for a minor traffic violation. As the officers approached the vehicle, the driver jumped out with a nine millimeter semi-automatic pistol and began firing. Before the officers' guns cleared their leather, both were struck by bullets. The lead officer was shot in the neck. The second officer was hit in the forehead. Both lay on the ground as the suspect walked up and put a killing shot behind the ear of the lead officer. The second officer was unconscious and, with a gaping bullet hole just under his hairline, appeared dead. An eyewitness heard the man laugh as he climbed into his car and sped away.

The evidence was extensive. Dispatch had recorded the license plate number of the suspect's Survivor—the latest and greatest luxury SUV. The second officer eventually regained consciousness and returned to duty in a month. The officer made a positive identification of the shooter. The eyewitness, who was an off-duty EMT, provided first aid and testified in court against the suspect. The video camera in the squad car recorded everything.

"He was a big time rapper, going by the name of 'Daddy of Da Hood.' He even cut a rap song after the shooting, 'Capping Cops with My Nine.' He hired a team of high-powered attorneys who got him an

'O.J. Jury.' He had a great time in court, laughing and joking with his attorneys. Their only defense was that two officers, one white and one Hispanic, were just harassing him because he was black. The jury had lunch on the city, then acquitted him. The murdered officer left a wife and two kids."

I ask how Daddy of Da Hood met his death.

"Whoever killed him knew what he was doing. 'Hood' was found dead in his Survivor in the hills near here. The screen on his DVD player was flipped down from the car's ceiling and was probably the last thing he saw. The DVD was playing a continual loop of the news story about the shooting, and footage of Hood joking with his attorneys in court. His cop-killing rap song provided the audio track. He had a single gunshot wound to the head, nine millimeter. The weapon found next to him was the same one used to kill the officer. It was very poetic."

I ask about the evidence.

"No fingerprints. No strange fibers. No ballistics, except for the slug in Hood's head, which matched his own gun. The scene was discovered by a jogger the morning after the shooting. It happened in a fairly remote area, but we canvassed the nearest houses. The only thing we have to go on is the Safety Bear pin. What is a Safety Bear, anyway?"

I explain that the troopers use a silly-looking, but effective, bear costume for teaching safety to kids—precautions with firearms, bikes, lake and river ice, ATVs, and that sort of thing. It's a good program, and I'd once played straight man to another trooper wearing the bear suit in Bethel. Little plastic pins were given out to the kids as souvenirs.

"Maybe it was just dropped by someone who picked up a pin when he was a kid, but I'm betting it was a trooper, or ex-trooper who has sympathy for the LAPD's loss. Or for the families, or solely for justice and the American way. The American way as it once was, anyway. He'd be a hero in the Old West and John Wayne would have played him in a movie, but times are different now." Forrest shakes his head and sips the rest of his coffee.

I ask to see the scene where Daddy of Da Hood's body and car were found.

"We can do that and more. Meet me back at the station tonight at six and we'll do the grand tour."

Chapter 15

NIGHT LIFE

"SOMEWHERE BETWEEN A flying horse and a magic carpet." That's roughly what the famous aircraft designer Igor Sikorsky said of helicopters. The pilot of our flying horse is Officer Heather Husband of LAPD's Air Support Division. Her blonde hair flows from beneath the silver helmet onto the shoulders of a green fire-retardant flightsuit. The smoked glass visor covers her face, making her look more like a robot than the attractive woman she is. I have the seat next to her in the Eurocopter A-Star, where the tactical flight officer usually is stationed. Tonight's mission is not to support the hundreds of officers in their patrol cars who scramble from one call to the next. We've been allocated an hour for our investigation, as back-seater Forrest calls it, "show and tell." At least that's the plan.

The A-Star, painted in the same black and white scheme as the LAPD squad cars, rises up and away from the control tower. The bright lights of what is both the world's largest roof-top airport, and the world's busiest heliport, slowly fade below us. Heather's helmet is integrated with radio gear, which she now uses to communicate with dispatch. We begin our magic carpet ride between the skyscrapers of downtown L.A. and then we bank toward Hollywood.

Before the flight, Forrest and I had been briefed by Heather on the safety procedures with the A-Star, as well as the "what ifs" and the "don't touch this" warnings. She explained that the Air Support Unit flies backup on over seven thousand felony calls and helps the ground troops with over twelve thousand busts annually. The unit has seventy-seven sworn personnel and seventeen helicopters—twelve of which are A-Stars, like the one we are flying in—and two Beech King Air twin-engine planes, making LAPD's the largest municipal police aviation department in the world. "Our response time is from thirty seconds to one minute and thirty seconds," she proudly reported. Alaska only has a few hundred patrol troopers for a state that's almost four times bigger than California, making the job of a trooper tough. But, in what Forrest says is the lowest police-to-citizen ratio of any big city in the world, LAPD's seventy-six hundred officers have their hands full.

The city is a sea of lights—mostly gold and bright-white lights near the ground, while all the colors of the rainbow glow from the high-rise buildings. In ribbons of white and red, vehicles on the freeways come into and leave the city. Every square inch of real estate seems to be occupied by a person or thing. I don't see anywhere for an emergency landing, but one has to have faith that the mass of moving parts will stay together. It brings to mind the question posed by a wise thinker-aviator, "If helicopters are so safe, how come there are no vintage helicopter fly-ins?"

Between short conversations with dispatch, another patrol helicopter, a ground unit, and the FAA, Heather graciously points out touristy spots—Capitol Records, Hollywood and Vine, and the Walk of Fame that I strolled on last night. We hover over the famous "Hollywood" sign, then turn to follow a winding road into the hills.

Heather pushes a button on the GPS announcing, "Three miles to go." Before takeoff, she'd briefed me on operating the joystick-controlled FLIR infrared video-monitor-imager and the thirty million candlepower "Nightsun" searchlight. I'd used similar equipment in the Alaska trooper helicopter, so now it was just a matter of finding the right joystick and switches in a cockpit glowing with avionics. With Highway 101 on our right, we overfly a wooded area on the left and begin following the twisting road into the hills. The GPS labels the curvy line "Mulholland" as we pass over large homes on both sides of the road. The houses get larger and fewer, with wooded areas in between. Heather drops to two hundred feet, hovers over a hairpin turn in the road, and asks me to search the road with the FLIR. The device can detect temperature differentials to a tenth of a degree, so we easily pick up heat from the car's engine, then two bright white images inside. We've found some parkers, "probably teenagers," guesses Forrest through the intercom.

"Light it up," Heather orders. I activate the thirty million candlelight power Nightsun and, as promised, it's like night has instantly turned into day. Perhaps thinking that aliens are invading, the couple immediately breaks their embrace. In a cloud of dust, the car races away from the formerly romantic parking spot.

"This is where it went down." Forrest details where the Survivor SUV was found, explaining the difficulty in locating tire tracks of any value in the heavily-traveled area. Heather drops us lower, twisting the A-Star around as I flood the dirt with light. "We have no idea why the rapper would have stopped here. His house is less than half a mile up the road," Forrest adds.

We gain altitude and Forrest asks Heather to fly over a mansion. Responding to the joystick's commands, the FLIR finds twenty-six human glows around a huge pool behind the house, and approximately that many more inside. "That's the place 'Hood' was leasing. It looks like life goes on," Forrest quips from the back.

Suddenly, Heather raises her right hand—the universal signal for everyone in the cockpit, but the pilot, to shut up. I hear the last part of the dispatcher's calm transmission: "Suspect vehicle, a stolen Lincoln Navigator, LOJACK-equipped, is headed west on West Sunset Boulevard. Two male suspects, one has a rifle with banana clip."

LOJACK is a system that detects stolen cars that are equipped with special transmitters. This helicopter is equipped with a LOJACK-tracking device. With Heather at the controls, I like our odds.

"We're the closest unit." Heather dives the A-Star back toward the bright lights of Hollywood and hits the emergency trigger on the radio system to break into the chase conversation.

"There's the ground unit." She points at the distant emergency lights of a squad car. We hover while Heather pushes buttons. Suddenly, like an eagle spotting a fish surfacing, she picks out a car from the night traffic and dives at it. "That's our suspect, we have a positive with LOJACK," Heather exclaims.

We're now low enough for a visual on the black SUV. The driver must see us as well, as the vehicle makes a hard right turn and heads into the same hills we just left. The FLIR detects two persons in the front seats. The Nightsun lights up the stolen rig like a Las Vegas stage performer, but the driver continues his getaway, trying to sneak down a narrow road.

Heather directs the ground unit to "Greystone Park" and asks me to pick up the suspects on the FLIR. Two glowing figures race from the car and climb into a dumpster. At one time that would have been a good, although stinky, hiding spot. The technology at hand makes it an easy game of hide and seek, as we hover over the giant trash container and watch the human glows. With the helicopter's public address system, Heather orders the men to lift the lid and put their hands up. They don't respond.

"Try translation," Forrest suggests. Heather presses another button and her orders are converted into Spanish. Getting no response, she tries several more languages. That device would be handy in Alaska when we need to speak in Native dialects. Heather updates the ground unit, which has now pulled into the parking lot. A glowing figure races from the patrol car to the dumpster and jumps up and down, as if trying to get inside.

"There's the K-9 unit," Heather explains. The dog continues to leap in place as two officers approach. The officers empty the "trash" without further incident.

Our hour is up and we head back to the heliport. I'm impressed with not only the high-tech equipment of the evening, but with the precision teamwork of the L.A.P.D. The radio continues to bark with calls: "Code 415," "Robbery in progress," "Drive by shooting." As I look into the darkness below, I think of tonight like a movie, where the bad guys and good guys are down there fighting it out. Dispatch is directing the show and the helo crew's duty is to race in to give the good guys the edge. I hope for a happy ending.

Heather lowers the A-Star toward the football-field size rooftop landing pad. With surgical precision, she gently places the runners on her assigned spot in the string of lights. We invite her to join us for dinner, but the pilot's shift has just begun. I thank her and wish her luck

"Congratulations on the tough job you guys do." I salute Forrest and his department over the clink of beer glasses at the Smoke House restaurant in nearby Burbank.

"Thanks, but I can't imagine how you troopers do it up there. One riot, one trooper, I guess," Forrest offers. We agree that the job of a big city police officer is much different from that of a Bush trooper. Both have their unique challenges and only a cop can understand why there are those willing to do either job.

Chapter 16

SNAKES

THE CESSNA BUMPS comfortably through the light chop as Palm Springs and the Salton Sea slip thousands of feet beneath me. The plane hums in a symphony of spinning propeller blades, the powerful engine, the wind rushing over the wings, and the constant barking of the radios from other aircraft hidden in the skies. The "white noise" in the cockpit provides an excellent thinking environment, as my mind rehashes the rapper shooting. It's not so much a matter of inventorying the evidence in the 'Hood' case, as reviewing what we don't have. No fingerprints, no DNA, and other than the DVD, no evidence at the scene. Forrest will have a friend in the Hollywood movie business try to determine what software the suspect used to edit the movie—the short video, which so perfectly mocked the high-profile rapper—the last movie he ever watched. I get that the assassin knows something about modern technology, but I can't understand how he got Daddy of Da Hood to stop his vehicle.

"Jack, it was lovely laying out here under the stars last night with nothing but the sounds of the woods serenading me, but it makes me miss you even more. I hope you had an equally peaceful night in Hollywood." I don't even want to think about my last night in California. There was some sort of entertainment awards show in Hollywood. Every room in town was booked—at least that's what Badal told me. It was another almost sleepless night in the stinky, raucous motel.

Jet's email text has been converted to speech with the Blueberry's gadgetry, so I'm now listening to a synthetic excuse for her sweet voice though the aircraft's headset. It's not as good as talking to her, but it will keep me company on the two hour flight to Phoenix, giving me a pleasant break from over-analyzing the rapper shooting. The message was sent from somewhere in the wilds near Copper Center, then bounced off a satellite to me.

"This morning I was taking a hike on the ridge above Klutina Lake when a beautiful lynx trotted down the trail. It caught my scent, and all I could see were its giant paws as it turned and bolted. It's probably used to having this place all to itself, and here I come barging in. As I was returning to the cabin, I heard the unmistakable sound of a Super Cub in the distance. Soon, the blue plane was directly over me. After a couple of low passes, the Cub plopped onto the little beach in front of the cabin. The big tundra tires kept it from sinking up to its axles in the soft sand as it braked hard, coming to a stop just short of the water. Not knowing who was behind the stick of the plane, I approached cautiously, with my pistol at my side."

The turbulence kicks up as the Cessna descends into the desert valley. I cinch up my seatbelt as I pass over the Blythe airport, which looks like something kids had scooped out in a sandbox. The Colorado River is next, dividing California from Arizona and adding water to the otherwise parched wasteland. When it's dark and fifty degrees below zero at home, this part of the world would probably seem appealing. Right now, I miss the lakes, rivers, and mountains of Alaska. The Colorado disappears into the mountains to the north, then heads south to the border. I think about a kid who haphazardly floated this waterway from the Grand Canyon to Mexico, then got kicked back into our country to continue his adventure all the way to Alaska. The fun stopped in a remote area between Denali and Fairbanks, where he moved into an old school bus that hunters had dragged in during the winter. The troopers hauled his body out after he failed to survive living off the land.

I crank up the volume to hear more from my synthesized Jet. "Someone was struggling to get out of the rear seat of the Cub. I heard a yelp as a man became entangled in the door jamb and fell face-first into the sand. A hearty laugh came from the front seat as I walked closer. As he stood up, rubbing his forehead, the sand-covered passenger's identity became clear. Ronnie Torgy gave me his goofy grin and waved. Ted Herlihy climbed out of the front seat, his prosthetic hand gleaming in the sun. Help had arrived!

"Ted had flown to Glennallen to shoot in a firearms competition, with Ronnie along to officiate the match, when they heard I was in the area. They stumbled into becoming the first members of my task force, so now we have a team of three. I had to let them in on the investigation. With a metal detector, red evidence tags, and a human femur on the cabin's porch, it was apparent I wasn't on a fishing trip. The three of us spread out and found more bones and pieces that had been scattered by animals. Using scrap materials from the cabin, Ted built a little screening system to filter bone fragments from the dirt. We found a few teeth, then dug up the lower part of a skull that still had the teeth on one side. I'm hoping that a dentist will be able to match these to the dental records of Lucinda Bickel. With the metal detector, we located another sheep head pin. As soon as I get back to civilization, I'm going to find out the pedigree of those things. Three .223 casings were found in the woods behind the cabin, and I dug a bullet from the cabin wall. Also, clothing—which I think was Lucinda's—was neatly folded in a pile on the cabin floor. Included were a yellow jacket and blue jeans, just like Mr. Hills described. Also, in addition to a bra, there was a t-shirt with the name and a drawing of her workplace—the Copper Center Corner Café—on the front.

"Jill says 'hi' to 'Sundance.' She beamed me an email this morning with an update on the aircraft registration. She took the partial numbers we have from Palmer and ran them through the FAA aircraft registration system. There are thirty-three Piper Super Cubs registered in Alaska that are possible matches. If we eliminate the ones in Southeast Alaska, that leaves twenty-seven. My plan is to focus on the ones registered in the Anchorage and Fairbanks areas first. Twelve of the planes are registered to companies, so Jill is breaking that down. This is great news, unless the plane is registered in a state other than Alaska. Or, if the numbers are phony.

"I'm breaking camp soon. Ted is heading back to his bride in Aniak, and Ronnie will go home to Bethel. I'm going to Lone Wolf for the night—wish you were going to be there. I have some thoughts to run by James Stevens, then I will take off for Gold River to finally meet our only living victim. Have a smooth flight. Love you."

The bumpy flight continues over Arizona's Gila Bend Mountains in a direct route to Phoenix's Sky Harbor Airport. I'd prefer a smaller field, but Sky Harbor is near the Maricopa County Sheriff's office. Governor Hines paved the way for me by calling "America's Toughest Sheriff." She met Sheriff Joe Arpaio at a Republican conference a couple of years ago and they immediately hit it off. I've read some about Sheriff Arpaio and the third largest sheriff office in the U.S., with three thousand employees. I like the sheriff's attitude in handling the county's ten thousand prisoners, especially his famous "Tent City." Inmates are banned from smoking, coffee, movies, pornographic magazines, and unrestricted TV in all jails. At fifteen cents each, he has the cheapest meals in the U.S. and the prisoners are fed only twice daily. Reportedly, just not serving them salt and pepper saves taxpayers twenty thousand dollars a year. The mandatory pink boxer shorts for all prisoners is a nice touch. Today I have a meeting with one of his detectives.

A black Ford sedan rolls to a stop next to me at Sky Harbor Airport as I complete arrangements for refueling and parking of the Cessna. A young deputy, who could pass for a West Point Cadet, steps from a car that's emblazoned with gold graphics, stripes, badges, and "Sheriff" on both sides. He identifies himself as Deputy Clint Parnell and confirms with me that he has the right Alaskan trooper. I throw my bag in the backseat and he says we're going for a ride.

"Detective Sedillo is tied up in court this morning, so I'm supposed to show you around. If it's okay with you sir, I was thinking that we should go up to the crime scene first."

"That's fine with me, deputy, but please call me Jack."

"Yes sir, Jack it is. You can call me Clint, if you want." The deputy looks at me for approval. We are now on a first-name basis. Clint turns down Garth Brooks on the car's music system, then turns up the volume on his police radio to advise dispatch we are on the road. We head north with Garth once again belting out "If Tomorrow Never Comes."

Phoenix impresses me as orderly in its design. The streets are straight and long, taking advantage of the flat terrain. That changes as the Piestewa Freeway takes us through the Phoenix Mountains. Peaking out at around twenty-four hundred feet, these would be called hills in Alaska, but it gives Maricopa County some topographical relief. We wind through neighborhoods that seem to be segregated by the color of the stucco—first tan, then gray, then pink. Many homes have pools and all are clean and neat with pleasant curb appeal. Instead of grass, some of the single-level houses have colored stones for front lawns. Most are so close to their neighbors that one could easily traverse the subdivision walking from rooftop to rooftop.

I ask Clint what he knows about the case. "Hang on." The deputy reaches over and puts his index finger and thumb on the music system's volume control.

The deputy listens to the lyrics, *"Stick to your alibi! Don't try to deny it, when I reveal the truth!"* He then turns down the volume.

"Sorry, I just love Kristy Lee Cook, how about you?"

I've never heard of her, but agree it's a catchy tune. Maybe the deputy is trying to tell me something with his choice of songs. Maybe he thinks I'm the rogue trooper's friend and that I'm trying to help him. Maybe he just likes the song.

"I don't know a lot about the investigation sir, just that some scumbag got what was coming to him. I have to hand it to whoever did him in. Very creative and—if you ask me—very appropriate. I helped drag his stinking carcass from the car." I want to hear more about the creative aspects of his death and why the deputy hates the victim, but we've arrived at our destination.

The patrol car whips into a parking spot between two other cars, near where the paved road turns to dirt at a gate. "I have the gate key but, if you don't mind walking, I'd just as soon keep the dust off my patrol rig," the deputy says. I look forward to the exercise, and I understand how black vehicles attract dirt like no other color. Dispatch acknowledges the deputy's report of our location and we start our walk.

"RATTLESNAKES IN AREA, USE EXTREME CAUTION!" The warning sign ramps up my heart rate faster than if I just started a run. I'm glad I'm wearing hiking boots, but I'd rather see a sign warning about a wounded grizzly bear. At least you can see a grizzly, whereas a snake slithers along at ground level, camouflaged perfectly for the terrain.

Deputy Parnell shares his knowledge of the local flora and fauna as we head up to a little summit from the trailhead. A pleasant aroma greets us, which Clint says is mistletoe and lavender. A couple of little rodents, which he identifies as "antelope squirrels," dart toward us among the volcanic-looking rocks. They're probably looking for handouts, like the parka squirrels in Alaska's Denali Park.

Continuing up the trail, Clint identifies mockingbirds, hummingbirds, Gila woodpeckers, cottontails, and a red-tailed hawk that flies overhead. I tell him that I now see my first cactus, which he calls a "Teddy Bear Cholla." He says this is one of four varieties of cacti in the area, joking that it's not a Teddy Bear made for hugging. I'm surprised at the array, having been exposed to only one kind of cactus in "Road Runner" cartoons—the extent of my previous experience with these prickly plants.

Two rock wrens sing and bob as we pass by a huge water tower. "This is where the detectives think the victim and his killer first met. Some hikers saw two men talking here, from that trail over there." The deputy points to a trail about fifty yards away. "The witnesses heard the men yelling. After a minute or so, they saw the victim run back toward the parking lot. They said the other guy stayed behind, so they thought the conflict was over. They continued on the their hike and didn't report the incident until they read in the papers two days later about a dead guy being found in the parking lot."

I scan the area, trying to visualize the different parties, pondering what they were arguing about. We hike back to the parking lot, my eyes fixed on the ground looking for movement, while my ears listen for a rattling sound that I've heard only in cowboy movies.

"This is where the victim's car was parked. There were bites all over his body." Standing in an empty parking spot, the deputy points to his face, neck, arms, and legs, then waves over the rest of his torso. "They had to bring a snake guy up here from the Phoenix Zoo to get all the rattlers out of the car. He told me that rattlesnakes are in a class of snakes called pit vipers, and that they inject loads of venom with a very sophisticated system when they strike. The detectives would only go near the car after the zookeeper promised all the snakes were out. Smart guys. I guess that's why they made detective."

A shiver races up my spine, even though I'm sweating in the ninety-two degree desert heat. I ask for more details. Details I may never share with Jet, as she can't stand even seeing a picture of a snake. The facts of this murder scene would certainly give her nightmares. Heck, they might even give me nightmares, but I need all the information available. I am about to get all I want and more—in living color and with full audio.

Chapter 17

MID-DAY MATINEE

"THUMP. THUMP!" The patrol car rolls over a mini speed bump. Deputy Parnell slams on the brakes, pops the shift lever into reverse, and burns rubber. We "thump, thump" again.

"Here's your chance to see a rattlesnake up close." The deputy nods over his steering wheel at a mostly squished snake in the blacktop. "That looks like a six-footer. Would you like to take it back to Alaska with you?" I wouldn't, but it reminds me of a funny trick played on a Glennallen trapper years ago. A local man left the fifty-below cold of the Copper River Valley for a Hawaiian vacation. As he was driving to the Maui airport, he found a dead mongoose in the roadway. Unable to resist temptation, he packed the carcass in his luggage. When he got back to Glennallen, he flew the mongoose in a ski plane to a friend's trapline. He stuck the animal's leg in a wolf trap and flew home to await the news. Sure enough, a week later the trapper dragged the mongoose into the Alaska Department of Fish and Game. He was sure he'd found some exotic species that had somehow migrated into the Wrangell Mountains. The biologist was sure the trapper had been had. The trapper's bounty is still the source of good fodder for humor in Glennallen.

Deputy Parnell blasts 'Road Kill Bill" through the speakers. My listening enjoyment is interrupted by another song, "North to Alaska," —the ring tone on my Blueberry.

"Jack, Cyrus Webster here. Where are you now, and when can you be in Salt Lake City?"

"Phoenix," and "Tonight," I answer. Cyrus reports another murder, this time in Salt Lake City. Another Safety Bear pin was found. Cyrus promises to send me an email with full details, but wants to make sure I'll head to Salt Lake as soon as possible. I will, but first there's a movie to watch.

Detective George Sedillo is a happy guy. A smile comes over his mustachioed face as he sees Deputy Parnell escorting me across the squadroom. "Is Clint showing you the sights?" I note a slight Hispanic lilt to the likable fifty-year old detective's laughing words. I compliment the deputy for his local knowledge and hospitality. Sedillo knowingly smiles, then asks me to take the chair next to his cubicle. Both of us thank Parnell.

"First, I have to ask you a question, Trooper Blake. Are you going to bust your fellow trooper, or give him an award?" Sedillo laughs hardily. I assure him I'll do my job, wherever the investigation leads, and ask him to call me Jack.

"Good, that's good, Jack." Sedillo seems a little disappointed, but chuckles anyway as he pushes his gray-black hair off his forehead. Maybe he's feeling me out. I tell him about the call I just got from Alaska and that I have to be in Salt Lake tomorrow, in hopes we can move things along.

"Okay, here's the deal then. The boss has authorized me to give you everything we have on the investigation. I will give you the full report, but how about we watch a movie first?" I know the movie's genre, but I agree anyway. "This got 'two thumbs up' from the guys, so I think you'll enjoy it." The detective laughs so hard that he almost has me laughing. I'm used to the "cop humor" those of us in law enforcement sometimes use in dealing with grisly details. He spins his computer screen around so I have a clear view, then clicks the mouse a few times. A video begins rolling on the screen.

"Jack, I once heard a romantic comedy advertised as the 'feel-good movie of the year.' I think it may have some competition with the live video of this 'death-by-rattlesnakes' video. You did know there was a camcorder planted in the car that recorded everything, didn't you?" I didn't, but I know what today's matinee will be in Detective Sedillo's office.

Activating the fast forward control, the detective says there is no action during the first two minutes of the video. He slides a photo across the table of the exterior of an elegant red sports sedan, explaining, "The miniature video camera was mounted on the inside of the back window, with the lens pointing at the front seats." A teddy bear cactus can be seen through the front windshield, with a vista of the desert in the background. The action picks up in the third minute and Sedillo hits the play button, asking, "Hear that?"

The warning rattle of the Western Diamondback—the sound I'd feared hearing when Deputy Parnell and I walked the dusty trail an hour before—now vibrates through the computer speakers.

The camera focuses on the back of the white leather seats, the wood-grain dash, and the steering wheel. A car door opens. I almost want to warn the guy as his head slides into view. The next sound is of pants squashing onto a leather seat. Then the words, "Damn it's hot in here." Next is the *"CLICK, CLICK"* of automatic door locks activating. Then what sounds like a heater fan blowing. Then rattling in the background, which seems to encourage more rattling.

"What the hell!" A man screams. Hissing sounds and whipping sounds. The cadence of a door handle being worked, snapping back and forth. More rattling, then more, with the modulation increasing. More screams. What looks like a snake jumps into the frame, but it's too quick to know for sure. The man's hands jerk up to the right side of his face. More hissing sounds resonate. Sounds of thrashing in the leather seats, followed by the man's head thumping violently against the driver's side window.

"Please, help me, please!" More screams and violent working of the door handle. Now the man's legs are kicking at something in the front seat. More screaming, "Please, God, help me!" More rattling and hissing. A broad-headed snake slithers along the dash. Rattling. Clicking sounds. Another scream, followed by a painful moan, then a wail. Suddenly, the man slumps over in the front seat onto the steering wheel. No more movement, but continuous rattling. The heater fan goes off two minutes later.

"CLICK, CLICK," the door lock-controls again activate, probably unlocking. "The End" by The Doors plays over the car's entertainment system. More rattling. Another rattlesnake joins the one on the dashboard. The video ends with a total running time of 6:26.

After gulping from a bottle of water, I decline Detective Sedillo's offer to watch the recording again. One running of the video serves to permanently burn it into my brain.

"Isn't it amazing how people always seem to need God at the end, when it's too late? There were fourteen rattlesnakes in that car. The smallest was three feet, the largest six-feet-two-inches. The western diamondback kills more people in the USA than any other snake, and more people are bitten by the western than any other rattler. The coroner counted thirty-three bites on the victim, so this helps with the rattler stats." More cop humor and another hardy laugh from the detective.

The detective hands me enlarged color photos of the autopsy. Most of the victim's body is covered with puffy red, brown, and black welts. "Rattlesnake venom is highly toxic and destroys living tissue." I see what he means—the destruction of the victim's once-living tissue is grotesquely evident. I've seen bear-mauling victims who looked better than this corpse.

"What else do you have on the case?" I ask, having had enough of snakes for a while—better yet, forever. I put another check mark in the part of my brain detailing the benefits of living in Alaska: no snakes!

"Well, first of all, the video clip was emailed to us from an anonymous source. Our computer techs tracked it as far as they can, but it was a dead end. All the data on that is in the report, and I burned you a DVD. We do have a partial description of the suspect: About six-two, two hundred thirty pounds, muscular build, well-groomed dark hair and silver metal glasses. Not bad from fifty yards, but the witness was a bird watcher and had binoculars."

"How do you think the killer got the snakes and the camera into the car?" I ask.

"A witness reported seeing a box truck in the parking lot on the same day as the murder. It had the words 'Happy Rooter' on the side. We traced it to a plumbing company in Phoenix who reported it stolen the day before. It probably was used to haul the snakes. The zoo employee said the killer must be an expert to have handled that many snakes without being bitten. We checked the local hospitals, but no snakebite victims were treated that day. I'm sure you guys in Alaska have 'Slim Jims' to open locked vehicles, so I'm guessing that's how he got inside the car."

"What about cell phone records?" I ask.

"The victim used his phone four times from the area and the cell company provided us with fixes. The first call, to his office, was at 2:35 P.M., made from the hiking trail parking lot. His secretary/girlfriend said he'd called saying he was meeting with 'some rich hick' who wanted to look at view property. The next call was made twelve minutes later from the west side of the water tower. A trace of the call showed it was to a cell phone with a California number. The phone had been reported as 'lost or stolen' to the cell phone company the day before. Another call was made to his secretary/girlfriend nine minutes later, this time from the south side of the water tower. Fifteen minutes later, he made another call to the stolen cell phone from the north side of the tower. That's where the witnesses saw him talking to another man, who is now our suspect."

"Thirty-six minutes total. Probably enough time to get the snakes from the box van into the sedan," I think aloud. The detective nods in agreement, then guesses my next question.

"We searched the van. We found a long pole with a hook on the end of it, some large burlap bags, a pair of thick leather gloves, and these." Detective Sedillo hands me two plastic bags. One has a Safety Bear pin. The other has a torn business card, with only "ALASKA STATE TROOPERS" showing. He adds that there were no fingerprints recovered from the van or from the other items.

Anything else?" I'm wondering about the door locks jamming, the heater, and the music all operating with apparently no input from the victim.

"That's all we have. Here's your copy of our complete file on the case. How about lunch? I can fill you in on the killer's motive at a great Mexican restaurant near here."

Detective Sedillo was right, the restaurant is outstanding. He is friends with the owners, and says the authentic Sonoran cuisine is made-from-scratch. I have the swordfish tacos with spinach con queso, which is perfect, until I try one of the little green peppers on the side. My head feels like it's going to explode into a ball of fire! I drink maybe a gallon of water, but it's still burning. This is like the pepper-spray training all Alaska troopers are required to take. Some sadistic trainer thought it a good idea that, since we would be using the spray on criminals, we should know how it felt to be blasted in our faces by Oleoresin Capsicum—eyes wide open. The chemical compound—which causes sinuses to flow like the Yukon River, burning skin, pain, tears, and sometimes temporary blindness—must use peppers like the one I've just bitten. Seeing my perspiring face redden like a tomato, the waiter rushes me a Corona beer. It's tempting first aid, but I have to fly today, so I wave it off. The waiter then delivers a tall glass of milk, which I chug. The fat from the milk helps diminish the burning. I can at least listen to Sedillo as he explains, between bouts of laughter, the motive for the murder.

"The victim, Sal Palladino, owned a real estate company, but his license was pulled by the Arizona Department of Real Estate two years ago. To get around the suspension, he signed his girlfriend up for a course, so she could get her real estate sales license. Then he paid a retired broker to list his name on the company register, although the retiree never actually worked for him. Palladino was convicted of three felonies involving real estate fraud, and of two misdemeanor assaults in the past five years. He also is on the sheriff's 'Deadbeat Parents Hall of Shame' list. He liked to brag that he had Mafia connections back east, but that was just more of his bull.

"Palladino made the national news last year. Phoenix has one of the best children's cancer treatment hospitals in the country. A couple from New Mexico sold everything and quit their jobs to move a block from the hospital. They gave Palladino their life savings—thirty grand in cash—for a little house so they could be with their child every day. The problem is that Palladino didn't have any vested interest in the property—it was owned by someone who was out of town for the summer and had no intention of selling. The couple lost everything. They sued Palladino, but it will probably be tied up in the courts for a long time. Unfortunately, the district attorney says that it's a civil case, not criminal. The really sad news is that their little boy has taken a turn for the worse."

As I climb up into the skies in my "Cessna thinking chamber," I try to analyze Palladino. It's incomprehensible how someone could cheat good people like he did. It's understandable how he was selected as a victim. Now I just need to figure out the "how" and "who." I have three hours in the air to work on it.

Chapter 18

SKI DROP

I SET COURSE to the north. Since today's flight takes me over one of the world's seven natural wonders, I will study a chart of the Grand Canyon airspace. First, I must listen to two emails, which have been synthesized to voice on the Blueberry. First up is Cyrus Webster.

"Jack, as I mentioned in my phone message, we received another report of a death with which a trooper may be involved. An insurance investigator in Salt Lake City called the Anchorage troopers' headquarters. He has been investigating a fatal chairlift accident in which a skier was killed. The chair broke from the cable and fell a long distance into the rocks. It was being handled as an accident until a lab report showed traces of an explosive on the chair's cable-gripper. The chair seat has been stored outside for a month since the accident, and the snow has just melted from it, revealing a Safety Bear pin. The victim, Morgan Guda, was fairly well known in the media. He worked for B.B. Sipes, the seven-million-dollar-a-year baseball player. Guda and Sipes had recently been acquitted of a heinous crime. Sipes' ex-wife had been splashed with battery acid, then shot. Substantial evidence tied Sipes and Guda—Sipes' agent and close friend—to the scene, but their attorney pulled a fast one in court. A pair of boots that were recovered from Sipes' house had holes in them from the acid. The district attorney had him try them on in court and, like the gloves in the O.J. Simpson case, they were considerably too small. The prosecutor was banned from presenting evidence that anabolic steroid use by Sipes increased his shoe size from a ten to a thirteen, between the time of the murder and the trial, two years later. Since the men were being tried together, the jury acquitted both of them. Sipes was supposed to be on the chairlift with Guda, but he jumped off at the last minute to hit on a woman standing in the lift line. We need to get on this one, as Sipes is still a target. Good luck." Cyrus' email provides the address and phone number for Burt Gussell, the Salt Lake City insurance investigator.

Approaching the Grand Canyon from the east, I fly over the Little Colorado River Canyon at ten thousand feet, then follow the narrow canyon westbound. As the muddy Little Colorado flushes into the emerald green Colorado River, the awe-inspiring Grand Canyon fills my forward view. Climbing another five hundred feet, I cross the river as it cuts deep into the canyon that's colored in red, brown, green, blue and white. I thought the Grand Canyon was just a big ditch through the desert, but this is incredible! I wish Jet could be here. Avoiding the busy Grand Canyon airport, I climb another thousand feet and cross the canyon rim northbound. Passing over trails winding from the rim all the way down to the river, I spot what looks to be an old lodge among the pines. Surprisingly, a spectacular waterfall and a green oasis appear in the desert. My little tour ends where Havasu Creek meets the Colorado River and I program the GPS for Salt Lake City. I will have to push it to get to Salt Lake before dark.

"Jack, the nice thing about this time of the year in Alaska is the almost limitless daylight." Jet's voice pleasantly breaks the silence of the cockpit via the magic of the Blueberry. "I logged the evidence at the Anchorage crime lab, made a run to the grocery store, and landed at Lone Wolf around 11 P.M. I used Tinka's skiff to cross the Tranquility River, which is now totally clear of ice. Tomorrow I'm going to get with James Stevens and see if he has any ideas on the sheep pin. Then I'm headed up to Gold River to chase down our star witness. Right now, I'm going to build a fire and cozy-up to assess what I have so far in my investigation. I can't wait to get into that comfy feather bed. Wish you were here."

I'm glad to know that Jet is safe at home. Mentally reviewing my notes, I search for a common thread in the cases. In both L.A. and Phoenix, video systems were used. Both the vehicles were manufactured by the same company. Both were equipped with sophisticated electronic systems, which can be controlled remotely via satellite. The video from the Phoenix Survivor SUV gives an indication that the door locks activated, the heater came on, and the music system played, all controlled by an outside source. Sal was too busy—either fighting snakes or dying—to work the controls.

In L.A., I had trouble understanding why the rapper would stop his vehicle and pull off the road so close to home. Now I question if that was his choice, or if someone caused a malfunction in the car's electronic system. I quickly tap out emails to both Forrest Canon and George Sedillo, asking them to hold the vehicles in impound until I call with more information. I realize now that the suspect knows his way around electronics and snakes. I also have an idea what he looks like—at least from fifty yards away.

Air traffic control routes me around other airplanes in their system. First, I'm directed to report over the state prison, then I'm diverted toward the Great Salt Lake. The Kennecott Bingham Canyon Mine passes below—easy to pick out, as it's two and a half miles wide and three-quarters of a mile deep. Having produced more copper than any mine in history, the site brings back memories of a copper mine in Alaska by the same name. That's where a crazed man killed eight innocent residents, and where I had the pleasure of watching him fall to his own death at the bottom of deep glacial crevasse.

A cheery woman at a Salt Lake City airport flight school allows me to park the Cessna next to her training fleet and calls the gas truck. After arranging a rental car, I call Burt Gussell. His tone is blunt as he directs me to meet him at the Blue Iguana in an hour. He hangs up before I can ask him the "what" and the "where" of the Blue Iguana, but the Blueberry comes to the rescue again, identifying it as a Mexican restaurant in downtown Salt Lake City. Since we don't see much of this cuisine in the Bush, I can handle two Mexican meals on the same day, as long as they hold the hot peppers. Without the Blueberry, I'd be as lost as if flying over the tundra in a whiteout, especially now that it's dusk. Once you figure out the street layout in Salt Lake City, it probably makes sense, like a Rubik's Cube. However, for my quick visit, I'm glad a GPS is giving me turn-by-turn directions through the metropolis. As darkness falls, I find the Blue Iguana, then the neon lights of a motel draw me in like a moth. After checking in, I stroll down the street to the Iguana.

A hand waves to me from the upper deck of the Blue Iguana. Heavy post and beams, greenery, and Mariachi music gives a south-of-the-border feel to the rose-colored restaurant, bearing the motto: Mexican gastronomy at the highest of universal cuisine. The hand belongs to a chubby man who is about forty-five, has a full salt and pepper beard, bald-head, and bulky, gold-rimmed glasses.

"You must be Trooper Blake. I'm Burt Gussell, but call me Gus." I ask him to call me Jack.

"Alaska State Trooper, huh? That must be quite a job. How many miles per gallon do you get with your huskies?" I smile at the second corny sled dog joke of the past couple of days. He doesn't wait for the numbers.

"Have a seat." I take the one with my back to the door—a seat hated by most law enforcement personnel, but it's my only choice, and this looks like a friendly place. He orders us a pitcher of dark Mexican beer and "Killer Nachos."

"This is pretty good service by your department, sending a trooper all the way here to pick up a little pin." I tell Gus that I was in the neighborhood. Digging into the nachos, he explains he is an independent investigator, and that he works with a number of insurance companies.

After taking a sip of the frosty cold beer from a mug with condensation dripping down the sides, I ask Gus for details on the chair lift fatality.

"It started out simple." Hot sauce drips from the corner of Gus' mouth as he animatedly explains the case. "A chair fell from about twenty stories onto some rocks up at Von Huff's SnowHeap Resort. It's extremely rare that a chairlift fails. As a matter of fact, I've never even heard of one involving a death, so we sent all the parts to a metallurgy lab. They reported that the cable-catchers, the brittle bars, and the sheaves had shattered. They sent the parts to another lab, which found traces of Semtex. It's a plastic explosive, similar to C-4, that's easily malleable even in cold temperatures." He digs at the nachos while swigging more of the dark beer, causing foam to cover his mustache. "Terrorists love this stuff because, unlike other explosives, it's not required to have an embedded metallic code, making the origin almost impossible to trace. The only way it was identified was from the detection taggant that's added during production, which produces a distinctive vapor signature." I snag one nacho chip before Gus devours the rest, which he washes down with three mugs of beer.

"So, now we know it wasn't an accident. We don't think it was terrorism, as the focus was on only two men. In addition, those men had plenty of people who'd love to see them fall twenty stories. Those same people would have loved it even more if B.B. Sipes wouldn't have skipped the lift ride at the last second." Gus waves the waitress to our table and orders the Parillada, a grand feast of prawns, scallops, lobster, a tuna steak, served with drawn butter and pico de gallo. He asks for side orders of sliced steak and guacamole dip. He's ordered the priciest dinner on the menu, with options. I opt for the seafood enchiladas, without hot peppers.

"Any witnesses?" I ask.

"Some skiers saw the chair fall and crash into the rocks, but no other witnesses," he says.

"What about Sipes?" I watch as two waitresses pile dishes in front of my dinner companion. The food looks and smells superb. I suddenly realize how hungry I am.

"Yeah, that slimeball. He wouldn't talk to me, the police, or even the ski patrol. I called his team's headquarters and they say that he is on extended leave. I later learn that he's holding out for more money this season. Seven mil' a year for playing a kid's game must not be enough. Meanwhile, he's screwing off, playing golf with some other big-time celebrities." Gus digs into the steaming food like a wolf on a freshly killed moose. My appetite is diminishing.

"Any idea on other ways to reach Sipes?" I'd like to talk to the guy, even with his reputation.

"All I know is that he will be in Hawaii until June, then he is going to play in some big golf tournament in Coeur d'Alene." The lobster and steak are history.

"Where's Coeur d'Alene?" I ask, thinking it must be in France
or another French speaking country. The enchiladas melt in my mouth.

"It's a resort town in north Idaho, up by Spokane, Washington." My next destination has been established. Gus sops up the last of
the sauce from his meal with a tortilla and slurps his fourth beer.

As he picks salsa from his beard, Gus lays the Safety Bear pin
on the table. "I guess this is what you came for. The trooper who
dropped this is lucky he wasn't the one in the chair when it went
'boom!' These things must be worth a lot for you to come all the way to
Salt Lake City and buy me dinner." I've just realized that the investigator
has not considered a trooper as a suspect in his case. I also just realized
that I'm buying his dinner.

"Yes, Safety Bear will be happy to get his pin back, and just
hearing your story was worth the price of the meal," I stretch the truth,
as Gus orders a Herradura Silver Tequila Margarita for dessert and
hands me the lab reports. Along with the reports, I pick up the tab.

The motel room is large and clean, and the expansive windows
provide a nice view of Salt Lake City. The solitude makes me think of
Jet. The Blueberry follows my voice command and calls her. We exchange notes about our cases, discuss the sights we've seen and the
people we've met over the past couple of days. We say nice things to
each other, and promise to talk tomorrow. We're both lonesome for our
new-found intimacy, but we return to the quiet of our rooms thousands
of miles apart, and get back to work.

The Blueberry sends the email that I've just typed: "Jill, greetings from America. Thanks for the wedding gift and for being so hos-
pitable to Jet. She tells me you are being a big help. So, if I promise to
start your car for you the next cold day I'm in Fairbanks, could you help
me with a little research? This will take some digging into personnel
records, but it's very important. First, please check and see if you can
find any male troopers who took leave during the past thirty days. Also,
can you research the employee applications data base and see if there are
any male troopers with expertise in explosives and/or electronics? Also,
check to see if any have an educational background or experience in

herpetology. One more thing, could you find out if any troopers have been reprimanded during the past six months, and, for what? This is just between you and me. Thank you for your help. Sundance."

Fly-Cast opens in a window on the Blueberry so I can plan tomorrow's flight. The weather looks flyable, and the mileage is close to the leg that I just made. I should be in the town with the French-sounding name by noon tomorrow. Now, I vaguely remember hearing of Coeur d'Alene when I attended the University of Idaho, but it seemed so far away when I was stuck on campus without a car. At that time, sixty miles of winding road, with no Interstate highways nearby, might as well have been a thousand. I hope they speak English.

Chapter 19

HEART OF AN AWL

THERE'S NO PLACE like home. Even if it hasn't been home for many years, it is worth stopping by to see the old homestead. After navigating through the congested airspace of Salt Lake City, I head directly to the Sawtooth Mountains. Passing over terrain that challenges Alaska for its roughness and raw beauty, I pop into the Frank Church River of No Return Wilderness Area. Clearing a nine thousand foot mountain peak, I descend over the Salmon River. Slipping through Bear Trap Saddle, I then drop down to Rush Creek and set up for a landing. The grass airstrip, cut between canyon walls, looks much longer than when I first soloed a Super Cub from here many years ago. I think of the fright, the thrill, and the freedom I felt on that day. I remember it if it were yesterday, as I sit in the Cessna with the gyros winding down and the hot engine ticking.

The massive lodge is still here, its logs boldly standing tough against the harsh elements. This was my home when I was a kid. It's where my uncle taught me how to ride horses, how to shoot, how to fly Bush planes, how to defend myself, the value of an education, and how to be a man. It's where I learned to live, and it's where my uncle had willingly and honorably filled in for my father, who died in an airplane crash on this same airstrip. It's a place that I left for a good reason, although I didn't realize it at the time.

A man swaggers out of the lodge carrying a rifle. His cowboy hat isn't like the well-worn garb the people who work this land wear, but a "Crocodile Dundee" type as sold in tourist shops. His new designer jeans are sharply creased, breaking just right over highly polished dude-boots. The heavily engraved, scoped custom rifle in his manicured hands is probably worth at least twenty-thousand dollars, and his paisley western shirt completes the picture. I think he fits the description of "metro-sexual," although I've never actually seen one this close up. I want to take a look inside the lodge, to see if any of our old black and white photos still hang on the walls. I'd like to visit my old room, and to see the fireplace that my uncle and I sat in front of, as he told stories of the old days in this rugged country. It would be nice to step into the kitchen where my uncle flipped his famous—at least to me—huckleberry pancakes. But the city cowboy has other ideas.

"No trespassing," bellows the dude, with a jerk of his "Croc Hat" toward a big sign that backs him up. My uncle warned me of people who would someday come to these wilds with loads of cash. He said they believe their money gives them the right to prevent anyone else from enjoying the mountains, or from catching a fish in one of the clear streams. But, as my uncle also said, the mountains and the fish will be here long after the intruders are gone. I take another look at the lodge, and then I study the new owner once more. It was here that my uncle trained me extensively in martial arts. I consider stepping out of the plane and using that training to put the Holland & Holland rifle where it belongs, but I feel my uncle's presence. Following my urges would heap disgrace on all that he taught me.

Taxiing the wing over the sparkling-new luxury pickup, equipped with license plates from a state far away from Idaho, I line up at the end of the grass airstrip. Pouring power to the eager engine, I hear a little "ping" half way down the airstrip, but attribute it to a pebble a tire must have flung into the belly. The plane lifts off quickly, and like my uncle so eloquently quoted with a biblical reference years ago, I "fly upon the wings of the wind." Passing over the Pinnacle Mountains, I wave the wings at the ridge where my uncle's ashes had been spread, bidding farewell once more.

Passing over the town of Moscow, Idaho, I reflect on my short tenure there as a college student. I studied hard, but my heart was back at the ranch with my uncle. My plans were to get through college as quickly as possible, then return to the ranch for a life of guiding. But things change, and before I knew it, I was on the other side of the world, flying for "The Company." It was a good experience, but sadly, my uncle died while I was overseas. The lodge, which he'd put his dreams into, was sold to pay the medical bills for the cancer he was fighting—a battle which I didn't even know about until it had been lost. After the flying stint was over, I visited Alaska and took a "temporary" job. Many years later, it's still my home. A home I love, especially now that I have someone to share it with.

In ten years of living in Idaho, I had never traveled north of Moscow. Now, I look over the nose of the Cessna to see the crystal blue waters of an extensive lake with a French name. I enter Lake Coeur d'Alene in the research page on the Blueberry and learn that it was designated one of the world's most beautiful lakes by *Encyclopedia Britannica*. The length is given as twenty-five miles, with one hundred and thirty-five miles of shoreline. The lake breaks to my right where it winds into the hills, merging with the St. Joe River—listed as the highest navigable river in North America. To the east, snow-capped Silver Mountain sticks out among the Bitterroots. Sport fishing boats drift in the middle channel of the lake, while sailboats frolic in the white-capped waters of the north bays. Golfers are lined up to tee off on what the Blueberry calls the "World Famous Floating Green." I ask the Blueberry to guide me to other local golf courses, so I can get an idea where B.B. Sipes might play.

I've noted the oil pressure gauge drop a few pounds over the past hour. Now, the oil temperature is rising. That could mean a range of things—from a minor issue to a catastrophic one. I will keep an eye on the gauges and check the engine when I land.

The GPS guides me over the lake city of Coeur d'Alene, where a church steeple reaches out from the trees, and high-rise condos shade the historic houses. A hotel, which looks like photos I've seen of resorts in the Swiss Alps, overlooks Brooks Seaplane Base and the world's longest floating boardwalk. Classic wooden boats cruise in front of the town's sandy beaches and catamarans sail off the shore of the lakefront college campus.

I'm led over a heavily-treed public golf course that looks nice, but would probably not be suitable for a golf tournament meeting the demands of Sipes. I zigzag across the town to Hayden Lake and find two golf courses that are more beautiful. We don't see many two-toned shoes with spikes in the Alaska Bush, so I don't claim to have an understanding of the sport. However, from what I've seen, the Coeur d'Alene Resort's course would best live up to B.B. Sipes expectations.

Hayden Lake compares favorably with Lake Coeur d'Alene in beauty, although more secluded and more compact. A pretty yellow J-3 Cub floatplane is beached on the west end of the lake, and a stunning white and red Grumman Widgeon—an amphibian airplane that I've dreamed of flying—is taxiing in the crystal-clear waters. As I'm taking it all in, it happens.

It is subtle at first. A hot smell wafts into the cockpit, causing me to glance at the gauges. The oil temperature is dangerously high. The oil pressure is dropping and the cylinder head temperatures are rising. The engine could seize at any moment. I bank toward Coeur d'Alene airport—it's just four miles to the west, but with less than fifteen-hundred feet of air between me and the ground, I won't make it if the engine gives up. I consider setting down on a fairway of the golf course below, but the brightly-dressed people in their miniature cars would be endangered.

I broadcast my emergency on the uncontrolled Pappy Boyington Field's frequency. Smoke fills the cockpit, so I shove the side windows open. The airport is now in sight and I aim for the north end of the runway as the smoke increases. I expect the engine could erupt into flames at any moment. My mind flashes to a Cessna 170 in Alaska, on which a minor in-flight fire started at altitude. The plane burned into pieces before the pilot could descend to an emergency landing—a lesson in how fast aluminum melts. I glide at one hundred and five knots to starve the potential fire of oxygen. The smoke billows. I try one hundred and fifteen knots, then more, but the smoke increases. Popping the door open, I lean into the slipstream to see the runway. Suddenly, the propeller jerks to a stop. The only sounds are the wind and my fast-beating heart. The only sights are the flames and smoke. Slipping so the fire will diffuse away from the cockpit, I dive toward the runway. The wheels hit hard and the plane bounces twice. Skidding to a stop, I grab the on-board extinguisher, kick the door open, and jump from the cockpit as an airplane tug races over from a repair shop. A man jumps out, spraying inside the engine cowling with an industrial fire extinguisher. I do the same under the panel with the compact cockpit extinguisher.

"Is that how you always land?" The man with the fire extinguisher laughs, breaking the stress of the moment.

"I assumed it was required at an airport named after a famous World War II fighting ace," I shoot back. The windscreen is covered with hot, dripping oil. Black soot has darkened the cowling.

Jay introduces himself and hitches the Cessna's tail to his tug for a tow to Northern Sky Air Center, where we remove the cowling from the sizzling engine. "Looks like it's fried," Jay assesses with a glance at the mess of cooked wires and components. I describe the loss of oil pressure and high temperatures, recalling the dipstick showed full when I checked it this morning in Salt Lake.

"Could have been caused by an oil pump failure, bad bearings, or a variety of things. Where are you headed?" When I say Alaska, Jay laughs, "I hope you aren't in a hurry."

While making notes, Jay tells me that he spent time flying in the Alaska Range, and before that Hawaii. He tosses me the keys to the "Red Baron," a fifteen-year-old red Buick Skylark, and points me toward Highway 95. Jay says it will take a couple of hours to inspect the engine while I tour Coeur d'Alene. Chloe, his black lab, thinks that means she is going for a ride, but Jay throws a ball to distract the eager dog as I sneak out the front door.

Downtown Coeur d'Alene has the feel of a traditional small town, although the population is around fifty thousand. The Blueberry spits out factoids about the community, called "Cur Da Lane" by the locals. In the early 1800s, French-speaking Iroquois guided Northwest Fur Trading Company's David Thompson into the lands of the Schitsu'umsh. Probably due to their impressive trading skills, Thompson referred to the Indians in his journals as "pointed hearts," which is most likely a translation of French verbiage, "Coeur d'Alene." The name stuck and the Schitsu'umsh are now known as the Coeur d'Alene Tribe.

Centennial Park is the first landmark I pass, where crowds frolic in the shaded park, sun on the adjacent beach, and listen to musicians playing on a bandstand. Sherman Avenue, the town's main drag, was named for General William Tecumseh Sherman. The general camped on the lake in 1877 and was so impressed by the beauty that he recommended it to the government for a military installation. Fort Sherman was established and two years later a town was born. The timber and mining industries quickly flourished. Today, the downtown is a mixture of historic buildings and complementary architecture, most housing shops and eateries. I pass Hudson's Hamburgers, which boasts of having been in business for more than a century, then pull into a parking lot by the water. Finding the entrance to Tubb's Hill, I jog around the lakeside hiking trail featuring views of the lake and the surrounding mountains. There's nothing like exercise on terra firma to shake off a bad day in the air.

After learning firsthand why Hudson's has been in business for a hundred years, I drive to the golf course I'd flown over earlier; home of the world-famous Floating Green. The gate guard gives the Red Baron a double take, but after I show him my badge, he directs me to the clubhouse. I've noticed that when you flash a badge, few people look at the wording—which is good; otherwise, I have to explain why an Alaska state trooper is poking around an Idaho golf course. The fairways and rows of red geraniums I pass must require a considerable number of hours each day to keep in such immaculate condition. The club pro confirms a celebrity tournament will indeed be played here, and that B.B. Sipes will be teamed with a professional golfer. I enter the date in the Blueberry's calendar function and thank him.

A FOURSOME OF GOLFERS stands at the shoreline, facing the floating green. I decide this is my chance to learn about the game of golf, so I sip an iced tea from a patio overlooking the fourteenth hole and observe. A fellow dressed in yellow pleated shorts and a pink golf shirt stands over the little white ball, while the other three men watch him closely. He studies the ball, then the hole, then the ball some more. He wags his club in the air, and then shifts his hips like he is going to do a hula. He looks at the hole once more, then focuses intently on the ball. The club comes back high into the air, then he swings violently. "Ker-clunk," the face of the club meets the ball, causing it to fly into the air with so much force that it sails over the island into Lake Coeur d'Alene. The golfer hurls an obscenity, then looks at his club like it's the equipment's fault. He repeats the entire process, this time landing on the green. His co-players slap him on the back, then, with more studying, swaying, swinging, splashing, and cussing, they each land a ball on the island with second tries. Interesting sport. I visualize B.B. Sipes playing here and I try to predict how someone might try to kill him as he does.

It's funny how an idea which can change your whole course sometimes just pops up. As I drive north on Highway 95 towards Pappy Boyington's airport, I notice a Survivor dealership. I pull the Red Baron in between two brand-new Survivor EXT pickups and find the service counter. I ask if there is someone there who can discuss the company's electronic systems. I'm in luck.

The Survivor technician has just returned from a refresher course on diagnosing electronic equipment with sophisticated computers. Showing his pride in the product he services, he boasts that their systems have been very reliable. He concedes however, that just like with a desktop machine, it's not impossible that a tech-savvy person could hack into any car's computer, regardless of the brand. I thank the technician and head to the airport.

Jay has bad news for me. After wiping oil and soot from the cowling, he found a hole. That explains the nick on the engine mount and a wound to the engine block. A bullet, apparently fired from the ground, went through the cowling, then glanced off an engine mount. Some of its energy diffused, the bullet then ricocheted into the engine. A direct hit to the engine case would have resulted in a large hole and immediate oil loss. This shot caused a small fracture that was gradually enlarged by vibrations during the hour-and-a-half flight. All of the oil finally leaked out, causing the engine to seize. Jay hands me a spent bullet that he'd found in the bottom of the cowling.

I'll visit with the dude on my uncle's old airstrip another day. Meanwhile, the engine, some of the accessories, and much of the wiring needs to be replaced. Hap agrees to have all of the parts expedited, but, with shipping and labor, it will be a few days at best before the plane is ready to fly again.

Learning the next flight from Spokane to Anchorage is tomorrow morning, I find accommodations for the evening. The rustic A-frame cabin near Hayden Lake sits in the pines overlooking a meadow of grazing deer. Since the price is reasonable, it makes a fine base for the night. Photos on the walls brag of the huge trout that have been caught in the lake. From a flyer on the dining table, I learn the town was named for a farmer named Matt Heyden, who, in 1878 won the right to have the lake named for him—with a slight change in the spelling—in a card game. Before white men came, it was a hunting and fishing site for Indians. A few years later, a golf course was developed on the lake and still operates today. The flyer shows old photos of Bing Crosby, reporting he spent many summers here and that his family house still stands on the waterfront. I walk down to the beach as the little yellow Piper J-3 floatplane breaks free of the glassy water, rising up toward the mountains to the east. Strolling through the heavily treed neighborhoods, I happen upon a lodge-like log structure that would fit well in Lone Wolf. It's a restaurant called the Porch, and the menu features Idaho Ruby Red Trout and Alaskan Amber on tap. It confirms my earlier thinking that Hayden Lake seems a good compromise between Alaska and the real world.

Jet answers her Blueberry on the second ring. Despite the circumstances, she's happy when I tell her that I will be catching an Alaska Airlines flight north tomorrow. She offers to put off her trip to Gold River until I get back to Lone Wolf.

The flight from Spokane to Anchorage requires a two-hour layover in the Seattle-Tacoma airport. I don't know when everything changed, but the interior scenery is remindful that it's been a long time since I've been in a place with so many people. Many of those people have changed drastically in appearance since then. The common dress

code of the hip generation seems to consists mainly of flip flops and
wrinkled t shirts with images I don't understand, accented by tattoos
and baggy shorts. Their faces look pained as they drag their bodies along
the airport corridors. I stand in a long line to pay way too much for a
cup of coffee served by a young woman who sports so many facial
piercings that she reminds me of a salmon I caught downstream from an
Alaska snagging hole. Surviving assaults from fishermen, the fish had at
least ten lures stuck around its mouth and dorsal fin. How do the heavi-
ly-pierced whisk through security when my wallet badge sets off all
kinds of alarms? I admit to the culture shock and I'm glad my flight is
taking me home to Alaska.

The 737 lands in Anchorage at 6:10 P.M. An hour later, I'm piloting another Cessna 185 floatplane from the aircraft section's fleet. I
follow the sun west over Cook Inlet, a body of water where two of my
co-workers perished in separate aircraft accidents—one due to icing
conditions and the other because of a suspected engine failure.

I'm anxious to get to Lone Wolf for the surprise Jet promised
me during our phone call.

Chapter 20

KUSKOKWIM SPELUNKING

SUMMER HAS ARRIVED in Lone Wolf. I pass glaciers and snow-covered mountains on my trip from Anchorage, but my new home town radiates warmth. Not just in the midnight sun that glows over the village, nor from the birch trees that have burst out with bright green leaves, but from the person who awaits me. I glide the Cessna over the airport, splashing onto the waters of the Tranquility River. As I'd hoped, the dock in front of Tinka's cabin is perfect for a seaplane.

Jet rushes over to the Cessna and we embrace as my boots touch land. She has a friend with her. The friend is my surprise.

"Jack, I know it's only been a week, but it seems like an eternity since we flew our separate ways."

"I really missed you, Jet," I say, as we kiss.

"I missed you more," Jet says, then introduces me to her friend.

"Piper, meet Jack." Piper is black. Black with big brown eyes, a gray mustache, and a fluffy pile of hair on top of his head. He shakes my hand.

"Glad to meet you, Piper." I offer, then look at Jet for an explanation.

"Jack, I hope you don't mind, but Piper has been keeping me company for the past couple of days." I must look surprised. "When I first got back to the cabin, he was waiting for me, so I couldn't just run him off." Jet's eyes are pleading for my understanding, but I need more details.

Jet explains that the orphaned moose had taken up residence in the yard and was laying down when she got home. Jet went over to check on her and noticed something unusual, something she'd never seen in her years as a fish and wildlife trooper. A dog was curled up with the moose, a situation not common in critters of vastly different species. Upon seeing Jet, the mid-sized pooch stood up, wagged its tail, wiggling all the way to her. Jet says it seemed starved and quickly devoured a bowl of food. She had learned from James Stevens that a gas line worker had abandoned the dog to survive on its own when he left town, after being fired from his job.

"I named him Piper for my favorite airplane. What do you think, Jack? James said he will watch him when we travel." Now Jet and Piper both plead with their eyes.

I try to appear as though I'm deeply considering the issue. Truthfully, I love dogs and still miss the one we had on my uncle's ranch Piper looks like he will fit in well at the Lone Wolf cabin.

"Well, I guess we could give him a try," I offer.

Jet kisses me again, while Piper excitedly flaps his little batwing-style ears as if he's going to take off. We now have a mascot.

Maybe to sweeten the pot—in case I'd hesitated on accepting Piper into our household—Jet created a spectacular Tranquility River-themed dinner. The feast begins with a baby greens salad with fresh picked berry vinaigrette, luscious lobster mashed potatoes, and my favorite steamed and stuffed artichoke times two. Incredible meals in themselves, they are followed by Jet's amazing Tranquility River Trout crusted with macadamia nuts. Although I have no sense for these things, Jet says the award-winning bottle of Opulence Syrah I picked up from the Coeur d' Alene Wine Cellars goes perfectly with the incredible spread.

"Jack, this is the first real dinner I've been able to prepare since our marriage, and I wanted it be special." With a beautiful woman sitting across the candlelight-lit table, I find it more than special. The dinner conversation includes sharing our recent adventures, then discussing our plans after the cases are solved.

Piper stretches out in front of the blazing fireplace, and Annie the moose munches away at alder twigs in the back yard. Jet and I lay our investigative files on the dining table, agreeing to review our cases together, but not until morning.

The featherbed is a welcome change from the hard motel beds I've been tossing in. Jet is wonderful, and life is tranquil at Lone Wolf.

JET AND HER task force have made headway. Over morning coffee, we review the investigations while Piper romps with Annie in the yard—neither must realize dogs are related to wolves. Jet shows me Ted Herlihy's police report of a recently found-gravesite. This time it isn't just bones, but a woman's entire body. The coroner estimates the death occurred just before spring breakup. Since the body wasn't buried, just covered with brush, it is consistent with the ground still being frozen, and means that the airplane was probably on skis. Death was by a single gunshot to the back of the head, and injuries to the woman's wrists are consistent with restraints. The nude body has been identified as that of a missing exotic dancer from Anchorage. Interviews of the woman's friends, family and co-workers have not turned up any leads. Another sheep pin was found at the scene.

Ronnie Torgy has been busy driving around Anchorage, Birchwood, and the Matanuska Valley—in plain clothes and in an unmarked truck—photographing airplanes that meet the description of the killer's. He's located and photographed fourteen of the twenty-seven airplanes that Jill found in her computer searches. All are white and red, like the witness in Palmer reported, but that's a pretty common Super Cub color scheme. We pore over the photos, but nothing jumps out.

Dave Daniels agreed to be the third member of Jet's task force and he's now in Anchorage chasing down leads. Dave received a report through the Troopers' Crime Stoppers program, which gives him hope. The anonymous tipster says that he may have information about what he called "The Flying Killer." He doesn't elaborate, saying that he will email Dave more at a later date.

Working with a dentist who makes regular visits to Glennallen, Dave has him check the teeth from the jaw Jet found at Klutina Lake. They match the dental records of Lucinda Bickel. Dave says it will be at least another two weeks before the crime lab has test results on the other evidence.

A bright spot in Jet's investigation is a revelation about the sheep pin. James Stevens ran it by some of his guide friends, identifying it as the logo for a semi-secret group of hunters. They are known for taking only the biggest and best of all animal trophies. The only problem is that they hunt without regard to seasons, bag limits, or other hunting regulations. To earn membership, hunters must get a "hat trick" which, for them, is the taking of a trophy Dall sheep, a grizzly, and a moose, all in one year. Jet learned that one of the former members of the club was a prominent Anchorage doctor she had arrested ten years ago for illegally killing more than forty Alaska big game animals. Charges included hunting the same day as he flew, waste of meat, shooting bears and moose from an aircraft, taking over limits, and hunting game during closed seasons. Since the doctor liked to brag, he kept prodigious notes of his kills, as well as video and still photographs. Jet remembers one photo in which the doctor, still wearing his smock, held the head of a freshly-shot Dall sheep. One day late in the summer, he'd rushed from his office and flew his Super Cub to the mountains. He shot the sheep two weeks before the legal season, taking only the head. He entered the trophy in a contest, and won.

"I've always wondered if the psyche of a trophy hunter is the same as that of a serial killer," Jet says. She has a point, as both like to collect souvenirs from their victims. The doctor in question had since died in a plane crash, or he'd be on Jet's suspect list. Stevens also explained "HOAR"—the initials on the sheep pin stand for "Hunters of Alaska Rebel." Stevens said it was a group originally founded to oppose the federal takeover of Alaska hunting lands during the Carter administration, but that it had metamorphosed into the band of illegal hunters.

Jet charts the findings from my trip. The common threads she records are the manipulation of the vehicle's onboard computer systems and other high-tech aspects; the lack of fingerprints and the absence of other common evidence; the two videos; and the professionalism of the killer. She cringes when I tell the snake story, but agrees that the guy must know something about the animals she fears most, even more than grizzlies—although she and I once had the unpleasant task of recovering the remains of a young woman who had been mauled by one of those beasts. I tell her about the witness' description, the Safety Bear pins, and the trooper business card. We agree that we should be looking for a trooper that's gone off the deep end, and I tell her that Jill is researching some possibilities. It's funny that we just now think simultaneously and out loud. We comment on the similarity of our cases—both killers had left logo pins—one a sheep and the other a Safety Bear—at the scenes. We also agree that I should call Forrest Canon.

"I can do better than that, Jack." Detective Canon is enthusiastic when I ask him to check the Survivor's onboard computer system for evidence of tampering. "We have a guy at the motor pool who will hook up his computer to the SUV, as soon as I give him the go-ahead. His analysis will tell if the rapper's rig was messed with." I thank him and make the same call to Detective Sedillo in Phoenix, who happily agrees to arrange the same examination with the car from the snake case.

"When It's Springtime In Alaska, It's 40 Below." We just finish breakfast when Jet's Blueberry announces a call with the old song. During the phone conversation, I feed Piper on the front porch while the moose watches from her alder patch.

"Jack, we have a little mission before we can leave for Gold River," Jet says. I know by now how "little missions" can go in this business, but agree it must be done. Piper consents to watch the cabin for us, and we load our gear into the floatplane.

Our mission takes us forty miles down the Kuskokwim River from Bethel to recover the bodies of drowning victims. An Eskimo from a nearby village stands by an overturned skiff as we taxi the floatplane in the silty water. He waves us to a muddy point on the beach.

The villager claims to know the skiff belongs to the missing subsistence fishermen. We notice the low tide has exposed a cave in the riverbank. Due to some sort of superstition that we are not privy to, the witness says he cannot go into the cave, the most logical place for the subsistence fishermen—or their bodies—to be.

After removing my gun belt, I crawl into the culvert-sized cave. It smells of stale, wet, air, and of death. Jet is right behind me with a flashlight, not at all afraid since there are no snakes in Alaska. Ice-cold water drips down my collar as I feel my way through the confined tunnel. It's almost too narrow for my shoulders, and I can't raise my head more than a foot. I can't turn around to see Jet, whose flashlight illuminates the cave's ceiling. We soon realize that there's no reason for both of us to continue into the narrowing depths. The cave is too tight for both of us to work, and too confined if we must make a quick escape.

Jet agrees to hold her position as I scoot forward on my belly, reaching into the murk for the unknown. I can hardly move at all now. My shoulders scrape the walls and my head rubs the damp ceiling. What must be claustrophobia comes over me, something I've never experienced before. Using breathing techniques taught by my uncle, I mentally regroup and continue into the darkness. My hand contacts something other than mud and sand. Reaching further, I grab onto a rubber boot with my right hand. My left hand finds the other. My eyes have adjusted to the darkness and Jet's flashlight, although twenty feet away, reflects just enough light off the ceiling.

The backside of a man comes into focus. There's another body in front of his. I study them for a minute, wondering how they ended up in the back of this vault. Were they washed in tandem by the strong current of the Kuskokwim? Or, did they crawl in here for protection after their boat capsized? The second theory would explain why the bodies lay close together, but why are they face down?

After announcing my find to Jet, she crawls to me with a survival shovel she'd grabbed from the Cessna. I scoop mud from the man's boots, but the space is so tight that there's nowhere to toss the debris. I flip the mud onto the man's back and yank hard to break his boots from the suction of the muck. His body is much heavier because of water logging and the sand in his clothes. At least rigor mortis keeps his extremities close to his body, helping him clear the tunnel's walls. Progress is slow—crawling and yanking, crawling and yanking. Slow isn't good, as the Eskimo warns from outside that the tide is coming in. I pull harder, crawling with my grim cargo as I back toward light—light that I suddenly cherish, and wide-open space I crave. And, as if I've been submerged in water, I now need to surface to gasp oxygen. Finally, I reach the cave's mouth and Jet helps pull the body the rest of the way out. It took ten minutes of struggling to free the first man. It takes just thirty seconds to zip his heavy body into an orange post mortem bag.

We stretch the kinks from our backs and re-secure the float-plane, now bobbing on the rising tide. The water creeps even higher, trickling into the cave. Now we must make one more distasteful venture into the murky confines of the tube, crawling and squirming again into the darkness. Enough water has flowed into the cave—the tide comes fast from the Bering Sea—to require belly sliding in the Kuskokwim's frigid waters. The water has helped loosen the second victim, making it easier for me to yank him from the suction of the mud. The body almost skims over the cave's floor as I drag him from his temporary grave toward the light. Shivering, both Jet and I are muddy and stinky.

Spelunkers explore caves for fun, but hopefully their reward at the end of their crawl is always better than ours was.

The Eskimo witness turns his head as we close the zipper over the doughy face of the second man. He looks to the river, away from the orange bags, holding the floatplane door open. Struggling to lift the bloated bodies into the back of the plane—first hefting the upper torso in, then lifting with the straps on the bottom of the bags—Jet and I use leverage to shove them up and onto the floor. This plane is the newest 185 in the fleet and, until now, it was the prettiest—too pretty for trooper work. It was tagged with the name "Casper," due to its stark white exterior and matching Aerocet floats. Filling an immediate need to replace a plane that crashed, it was the only 185 the Cessna dealer had on hand. This deluxe model was intended for the sporting life, rather than becoming a Bush workhorse. The cockpit is now covered with mud and slime, and no longer smells of fresh leather.

After delivering the bodies to waiting troopers at Hangar Lake in Bethel, we head north to Lone Wolf. Piper cowers as he greets us with suspicion. Covered in mud and smelling of death, it seems the friendly pooch doesn't recognize us. That changes when Jet calls to him in her sweet voice.

Now in a rush to visit Gold River, we step into the shower together. After dressing quickly in clean uniforms, we grab some fruit to eat on the way and take off from Tranquility River. Piper contentedly rides in the back, intently studying Alaska from a perspective he's not seen before.

We are looking forward to a better rest of the day. Jet is anxious to finally meet the one surviving victim.

Chapter 21

GOLD STRIKE

"THE SHOOTING OF Dan McGrew" comes to mind, but the man who pulls our floats to the beach at Gold Lake doesn't look like he "stumbled fresh from the creeks, dog-dirty and loaded for bear…with a foot in the grave and scarcely the strength of a louse." Although Jet identifies him as such, he looks too unsoiled to fit my Robert Service-based criterion for a gold miner. Instead, Russ Harris is clean, healthy-looking, and unarmed. After he welcomes us to his mine and ties the Cessna next to his deHavilland Beaver, Jet introduces us.

"It's good to meet you both," Russ says with a firm handshake. He's tall, medium build, and clean-shaven, except for a perfectly trimmed gray mustache. He wears jeans, a chamois shirt, and a red cap embroidered with the outline of his airplane and "Gold River Mining." Russ asks if Piper, who now sits patiently in the plane, can join Moses for playtime. Moses is a big yellow lab carrying a stick in his mouth, which he drops to greet Piper. The dogs sniff one another, then begin gentle wrestling, while we tell Russ why we're here.

Russ knows the story of Amanda Silverleaf's abduction. "Amanda is one of our kids." He explains that he and his wife run a home for troubled children. Amanda was sent from another village by the state's health and social services department just two months prior to the incident. "Mining has provided us with a good living. For me, mining is not about finding the gold; it's about looking for the gold." He points to the mountains that surround this beautiful lake, telling us he has fifteen active claims. "It's there if I need it. Right now, we have God's work to do." Russ waves at children playing under a waterfall and to others paddling in bright red and yellow canoes. A silver and black horse sips from the lake.

"Kids Village cares for children who have been abused, neglected, are homeless, or are in severe family crisis. We do our best to provide a safe, loving, nurturing, and healing home for them. Amanda is

137

the oldest of the twenty-six children under our care. This lake is one of their playgrounds. Come on, I'll show you our headquarters."

Russ tells Moses to stay with the kids and their watchful lifeguard, then Jet, Piper, and I climb into a Jeep with him to head up a winding dirt road. We pass the Gold River airstrip where a Cessna 185 and a shiny Beech 18 are tied down. A general store, a school, a few log cabins, and a group of modern stick-built houses make up the town. We pull up to a log building that resembles my uncle's Idaho ranch house, only it's bigger. Russ' gracious wife, Barbara, welcomes us.

"Barbara is the nurse, bookkeeper, and one of the teachers. We have two other teachers, plus two staff members and four summer volunteers," Russ explains. The lodge sprawls on a hill overlooking Gold Lake. Windows across the front of the great-room provide a panoramic view of the lake and mountains. Through a telescope set up on the deck, I count six waterfalls cascading into the lake and a flock of Dall sheep grazing on a distant ridge. Accompanied by the aroma of freshly baked bread wafting from the kitchen, we walk down a hallway with children's bedrooms on either side. The hall ends in an "L," culminating in two large classrooms, a library, and a chapel. Russ leans into the library where three children quietly read and asks, "Amanda, could you please come with us? I'd like you to meet some nice people."

The eighteen-year-old Athabaskan girl rises from her study desk. Her gaze drops to the floor as Russ introduces us in a vacant classroom. Dressed in jeans and a sweatshirt, she doesn't look like a troublemaker. She couldn't weigh more than ninety pounds, she wears no makeup, and her glossy black hair is pulled back from her face. Amanda seems fearful and unsure at first, but her face lights up as Piper lays his chin on her knee and peers into her eyes. She pets his fuzzy head and finally looks up at Jet and me. Piper wags his tail.

"I did something really stupid and I'm very sorry." Tears dribble down Amanda's cheeks as she ruefully notes the events of her near-fatal escapade. "I didn't want drugs, I've never used drugs. My parents drink and use drugs and I never want to. I just wanted to see something different, and he seemed so nice. He said he'd give me some weed if I'd go flying with him, so I said okay. Not to get the dope, but for the flight. I didn't know what he was going to do to me." She begins to softly cry, but stops when Piper places his paws on her lap and leans in for a hug. She explains that, upon her return, she was too scared to tell anyone what happened. Amanda says she took a long shower to try and wash the shame from her body. She admits that she lied, until her conscience got the best of her. Jet reviews the facts from the case report, asking if there is anything Amanda can add. We almost fall off our chairs when we hear Amanda's next words.

"He put a big plastic tie on my wrists, really tight. They hurt badly and there was something else too." She continues to pet Piper. "There was a little thing attached that looked like a clock with a blinking light, but the numbers didn't tell time. The man looked at it, then checked something he had in his hand that looked like a little radio. Then he let me go. I ran as fast as I could into the woods and he started shooting at me. I was scared, but I ran right into those people's camp. I was so embarrassed that I wasn't wearing any clothes. They gave me a blanket and cut the plastic off my wrists with some fish pliers. Then they called a pilot with their satellite phone. He's the one who brought me home."

Russ explains the pilot who brought Amanda back is a friend and didn't know any of the details. Russ called the troopers as soon as she told him what had happened. Amanda's next words made our day.

"Do you want the little thing that was hooked onto the plastic tie?" We do, and now we have what appears to be a transmitter of some sort. Amanda says the light stopped blinking when the campers damaged the device while removing the zip tie from her wrists. She asks if we will bring Piper back to visit someday. We assure her we will.

On the way back down to the lake, Jet compliments Russ on the good work he and Barbara do at the village. "Thank you, but we just do what the Boss tells us to do. When I begin to worry about Amanda or the other kids, I think of a forty-five hundred year old Arabic saying that 'worry is an insult to God.' Amanda is a strong girl and will come out of this just fine. We are hoping to see her graduate from high school and go off to college next year. I pray you catch that guy before he hurts or kills someone else." We don't tell him that it's too late.

It's Jet's turn to drive. She pulls the Cessna off the glassy water by first raising the right-side float to break the surface tension. Once airborne, she banks and turns within the confines of the mountains around Gold Lake to gain altitude, then slices between two waterfalls before dropping over the Gold River. As we settle in at a cruising attitude of five hundred feet, I notice the flashing light on my Blueberry.

Played through the Cessna's headsets, the message is thirty minutes old and comes from Village Police Officer Josh Luko. "Trooper Blake, please come quick! We are downriver from Saint Marys and Trooper Torgy is in trouble."

Jet is already climbing and banking toward the Yukon as I call the number from the message. Ronnie Torgy answers.

"Jack, thank goodness. I got one of these Blueberry things because I'm on Jet's task force, and it sure came in handy. Josh and I are stranded on an island in the middle of the Yukon, just below Saint Marys. When can you get here?" Ronnie's voice is an octave above normal and he speaks so fast that he's hard to understand.

Jet has already entered Saint Marys as our destination in the GPS. Our estimated time of arrival is thirty-two minutes. "We should be there in a half an hour Ronnie. What happened?"

"Well, uh, I sort of messed up, I guess. I worked on Jet's case for half of the week, then came back to Bethel to see the family. A complaint about bootleggers running booze on the Yukon from Saint Marys came into the troopers, so Josh and I came up here. We borrowed the Saint Marys trooper's boat and found the guys just after they'd sold a bottle of whiskey for fifty dollars in Jacobs Slough. We caught up with them at a gravel bar. We made them both get out, but then I dropped my notebook in the river. While Josh and I are fishing for the notebook, one guy jumps back in their boat and the other one steals the trooper boat. If you see a red Lund skiff with a trooper decal on it, that's ours!" I try to calm Ronnie down as Jet drops over a ridge and picks up the Yukon River.

Eleven miles above the village of Saint Marys, two skiffs lunge against the waves of the Yukon. Jet drops the Cessna to about fifty feet above the water. One boat breaks away from the other. Jet dives at the one with the trooper decal.

"This place is oddly familiar." Jet refers to a spot on the river where she plucked me from the grasp of a killer, in what seems like a lifetime ago. Reducing power and pulling on flaps, Jet flies alongside the trooper boat. We are much faster than it is, and race past. The man refuses to acknowledge the plane and continues up the raging river.

"Guess we will have to play speedboat," Jet says as she sets up for a landing. She times it perfectly, touching the floats on the water adjacent to, and ten feet away from the skiff. She adjusts the power so we can act like a watercraft, keeping pace with the fleeing criminal. Like a motorcycle policeman, I wave the guy to pull over, but he ignores me. Jet eases in closer, taking care to keep the spinning propeller a safe distance away. We are five feet from the boat now, skimming on the floats' steps to keep up. Suddenly, the boater swerves and bangs hard into the float outboard of my seat. The Cessna jerks left, but Jet quickly gets us back on course. The boat comes in for another attack, but Jet anticipates and moves to the side. Jet advances the power to full, quickly lifting the plane into the air. "Sandbar," she yells into the headset. We zoom over an island that seems to have come from nowhere. Jet cranks the plane around for another landing.

"I have a plan," I say. Jet smiles—she knows what I'm thinking.

"Are you sure?" She asks.

"Why not?" I affirm by cracking the plane's door open. Jet again pulls up alongside the skiff. The boat operator bends over the steering console and pulls the hood of his jacket over him—as if he will somehow disappear if we can't see his face.

"Slower, just a bit slower now," I ask. Jet adjusts the power, adds full flaps, and paces with the skiff. She moves in as I push my door open into the wind.

"Okay, ease in closer." Sliding from my seat, I step out onto the float, securing the door behind me. Just as the float touches the skiff's gunwale, I jump onto the deck. Before the driver can react, I grab him in a chokehold with my right arm, yanking the boat's throttle closed with my left.

"Let go of me, cussack!" I haven't heard that derogatory term for a white man in a long time. With the boat slowing to a stop in the Yukon, I ratchet handcuffs onto the prisoner and ease him to the deck. Movement in the back of the skiff catches my eye, as a teenaged Native girl climbs out from under a tarp, also calling me a cussack. Jet stops the Cessna against the skiff and throws me her handcuffs as Piper pokes his head out of the plane's cockpit and growls. After attaching the cuffs to the girl, I sit her next to her thirty-five year old bootlegger boyfriend.

Jet takes off in the 185, returning shortly with Josh and Ronnie. Ronnie says he will charge the man with theft of the boat, bootlegging, eluding a law enforcement officer, and probably statutory rape, since Josh knows that the girl is only fourteen years old.

Shaking his wet notebook into the air, Ronnie promises Jet he will continue searching for the killer's plane tomorrow in Anchorage. Josh commits to catching the bootlegger's partner, adding that he's probably back in Saint Marys by now.

It's 11:15 P.M. when we get home. I fire up the hot tub for a well-deserved soak with my bride. It's been a long day, but we have come home with an important piece of evidence in the serial killer pilot case. When Jet mentions that obtaining the transmitter from Amanda was a stroke of luck, I quote something that I'd recently read by the famous U.S. Marine Corps General Victor Krulak, "The harder I work, the luckier I get." She smiles and tenderly embraces me.

Chapter 22

BIG BREAK

THE CURLY BLACK hair on Piper's neck stands straight up. A short window of opportunity allows an hour of relaxation after a couple of hectic days, so we'd left the cabin at 6:00 A.M. for a hike. Jet wants to check on the moose-poaching site, concerned that there may still be some traps under the snow. Piper, fifty feet ahead of us on the trail, stops and sniffs the air. He doesn't like what he smells.

Voicing a guttural sound something between a growl and a whine, Piper backs up on the trail, looking at us with his tail tucked between his legs. "Maybe a bear?" I ask Jet, wishing we are carrying something more powerful than our pistols. Jet suggests we find out.

Our first glimpse is dark brown fur. We advance cautiously, with Piper sticking close. The mystery animal faces away from us, not yet detecting our scent. We are not so deprived, as the odor from the Piper-sized animal reminds us unpleasantly of skunks I'd come across in the mountains of Idaho. It looks like a small bear, except for stripes of yellowish fur on its sides and its long tail.

"Wolverine!" Jet grasps Piper's collar as she identifies what she calls "Pound for pound, just about the meanest animal anywhere." We watch as this largest member of the land-dwelling weasel family lifts a moose leg bone with its sharp claws, then crunch it with its powerful jaws. Grinding the bone to extract marrow, this animal that fears no predators, suddenly detects our presence. Dropping its prize, the wolverine whips around and focuses on us. Growling, Piper lunges to our defense, but Jet grabs his collar. Together, the three of us back away slowly as the wolverine stands his ground—spitting, growling, and baring his sharp teeth.

As we weave through the forest, the spruce scent in the air reminds me of the value of these trees, apart from just the aesthetics. Sure, they make nice Christmas decorations, but they also are used to make everything from paper to violins. The Wright Brothers' first aircraft was largely built of spruce. The oils in the leaves and branches can be used to brew beer, and syrup can be made from the needles. Natives once used the roots for weaving baskets and for sewing birch bark onto canoe frames. Gum, made from the sap by Native Americans in New England, was the basis for the first commercial chewing gum. Vitamin rich tea I made from the needles once helped save my life in a winter survival crisis.

Back at the cabin, we find both of our Blueberries illuminating with messages.

Jet calls Dave Daniels while I return a call to Detective Forrest Canon.

"Jack, are you sitting down?" I'm not, but I do as Canon delivers the news.

"Our mechanic hooked up the diagnostic computer to the rapper's Survivor. Like you thought, it showed some unusual activity on the day of the murder. But there's more."

The detective reports the Survivor's Sat-Go "VCIM," or "Vehicle Comm and Interface Module" box, had been pried open. The mechanic guesses a "techy-type" figured out how to interface directly with the system. I don't understand all the jargon any more than Canon does, but the bottom line is someone figured how out to manipulate the SUV's system to control its electronic functions. The killer probably disabled the ignition, forcing the rapper to pull over.

I thank Canon, disconnect, and call Detective Sedillo in Phoenix. Sedillo reports a diagnosis similar to the LAPD's, finding abnormalities in the sedan's Sat-Go system on the day of the real estate agent's death. He will direct the mechanic to determine if the VCIM has been similarly broken into. The detective laughs when I decline his kind offer to ship me some fresh jalapeno peppers.

Jet's eyebrows rise as she speaks to Dave Daniels on her Blueberry. After she hangs up, she says simply, "How about a trip to Anchorage today for show and tell?" Jet promises to fill me in on details while in flight.

Piper isn't any more of the big city type that I am, so we take him to the trading post. James Stevens introduces Piper to Charlie, the golden retriever with the bulldog legs, and they immediately engage in the sniffing ritual. Who knows what dogs can tell about each other in that nose-to-tail dance, but Piper and Charlie seem to like each other. The sniffing turns into playing and James shows them the back door, offering, "Piper will be fine here, take as long as you need." Saying goodbyes is hard, even to a dog, so Jet and I make our escape out the front door and take the boat back to the floatplane dock. As we fly over Lone Wolf, we see Piper and Charlie romping behind the trading post.

It's one of those rare, turbulence-free, "bluebird" flying days, and we touch down on Lake Hood after two hours of soaring over stunning vistas of glaciers and mountain peaks.

We gather in a conference room at the Anchorage Trooper headquarters where Jet and Dave Daniels had agreed to call a meeting of the task force. Dave asked me to attend, saying he has someone that he wants to bring into the investigation who may be able to help with my case. Ronnie Torgy jumps out of his chair, banging his shin into the table as we enter the room, taking the role of note-keeper with a dry-erase board. Titanium Ted Herlihy stifles a laugh at Ronnie's typical antics and shakes my hand. Dave welcomes us both.

"Jet, if you agree, I think we should review what we have so far on your case. Then we can discuss Jack's investigation, if that's okay with you, Jack. Jet, when you told me about the transmitter being picked up in Gold River, I was reminded of Jack's email about the electronics in the victims' cars. We'll get to that in a bit. By the way, I'm pushing the lab guys as hard as I can, but some of these tests take a while. Your blood sample from the ski pole came back as Type A Positive, but we are still waiting for the DNA analysis."

Jet reviews what has been recovered from Talkeetna, Arctic Village, and Klutina Lake crime scenes, as well as from her interviews with witnesses. She shows everyone a photo of the sheep pin and tells of the transmitter we recovered from Amanda.

Ted presents the report detailing the match of the teeth found at Klutina Lake to Lucinda Bickel's dental records. He also reports on the body he recently recovered, including all the gruesome details. Graphic photos show the bullet hole in the back of her skull and the marks left by the restraints on her wrists.

I highlight what was just revealed by the diagnostic analyses of both the vehicles from the L.A. and Phoenix crime scenes. My summary concludes that the killer's skills include computers, electronic technology, explosives, and snake handling. I also inform the group that, since the attorney general believes this involves a rogue trooper, personnel files are being reviewed. Jet and I had listened to an email message from Jill over the airplane's headsets this morning on our flight to Anchorage, but I'm not ready to share the names of the possible suspects she suggests. Not just yet anyway.

Ronnie hurriedly records everything on the whiteboard, segregating information from each of us in individual columns, using a different color marker for each trooper.

Dave Daniels lifts his tall frame from his chair, walks to the front of the room, points at the board, and begins a summary. "So, in Jet's case, here's what we know about the suspect: he's a pilot, he has a thing for young women, he's an avid hunter who hunts the women as if they were wild game, and he restrains his victims with zip ties. The transmitter gives him a technological advantage when he tracks his prey. Similarly, he breaks the rules when he hunts, giving him an unfair edge in killing game.

"In Jack's case, the killer uses technology to break into the systems of the cars. Now bear with me, I've developed a theory." We bear.

Dave continues, "It started with an anonymous call to Crime Stoppers. The caller said he possibly had information on the pilot who is killing the girls. He claimed that he'd heard Trooper Torgy's radio conversation to another trooper about his search for an airplane involved in a homicide."

Ronnie studies the floor for a second, then says simply, "Oh no, I remember that. I transmitted on the scrambled frequency when I told a Palmer trooper what I was working on. Should have used my cell phone. Dang!!"

"No, you shouldn't have told anyone about the case, per our briefing!" Ted taps his prosthetic hand on the table and directs his steely gaze at Ronnie. Jet and I look at each other, wondering if the suspect has been tipped off and if her case is in the outhouse.

"As it turns out, it's all good. Ronnie's misspeak brought a witness that probably never would have come forward otherwise." Dave relieves the tension in the room and Ronnie exhales a sigh of relief.

Dave reports more good news. "Besides Ronnie's unintentional announcement on the radio, we haven't released anything. Of course things do leak out, no matter how careful we are, but I was curious about what the caller knew. He didn't want a return call. Instead, he left the web address of his blog, asking for an investigator to contact him with a coded message. We communicated for awhile in that fashion, then finally met in person. That meeting changed my outlook on the case.

"The informant's name is Dewey McDougall. Dewey reported he was air-boating up the Knik River last fall when he saw a white Super Cub flying low toward the glacier. At first, he thought the pilot was just a hunter. Later, when Dewey beached his boat on a sandbar, he saw the Cub land. Dewey is something of an airplane nut, so he decided to check out the Cub. As he walked toward the plane, he saw the pilot relieving himself. Then saw something else. There was a woman in the back seat of the plane with her head against the window. Dewey said she looked like she was asleep. When the pilot saw Dewey, he quickly climbed back into the cockpit and took off. Dewey didn't think much of it until he heard about our case."

"Did he get the numbers on the plane?" Jet asks.

"Not the numbers, but he took a photo with his cell phone camera. These have been digitally enhanced." Dave displays a photo on a wall screen using a computer projector. The image is grainy, but it's definitely a white and red Super Cub. A second slide enhances the registration number. It matches the partial number Jet has and gives her one more digit to work with. The next slide zooms in on the back window of the plane. A woman's face is clearly visible, but it's not enough for identification. The last slide shows the pilot, who wears a red cap and black-rimmed glasses.

"That's the best the lab can do with the photo," Dave explains.

"So what do we know about this Dewey guy?" Ted asks.

Dave smiles, shaking his head as he answers. "He's an interesting fellow. He has a master's degree in computer technology and builds custom computer systems, which he claims, are much sought-after from around the world. He was one of the consultants brought in by the department to redesign APSIN—the Alaska Public Safety Information Network—so he knows our system. For fun, he plays around with radio-controlled aircraft and develops inventions, like the decoding scanner he used to tap into Ronnie's radio conversation. His life's dream was to become an FBI or CIA agent, but he has a heart problem of some sort. The same condition keeps him from becoming a pilot, and that's why he flies RC aircraft. He says that's also his motivation for keeping himself in what he says is top physical condition. He lifts weights, runs, Nordic skis, and that sort of thing. He's a bit of a nerd, and his politics may be even more conservative than some of us in this room, if that's possible. When you get him going, he likes to talk nonstop. Bottom line is Dewey wants to help us. And I think he can."

"Do you think he might have a take on this?" Jet slides the transmitter across the table to Dave.

"How about you ask him yourself? He's just down the hall waiting to see me, like he has been every day for the past week. For what's it's worth, I've sworn him to secrecy." Dave nods toward the door.

Dewey McDougall struts into the room with the crispness of a Marine guarding the Tomb of the Unknown Soldier. Stopping curtly at the front of the room, he introduces himself and shakes everyone's hands. Strongly built, he stands a couple of inches taller than my six feet and outweighs me by at least fifty pounds. I guess him to be about thirty-five, by the gray flecks in his black hair and the crow's feet at his eyes.

"I'm pleased to meet all of you. First, I want to thank you for your service to Alaska. If there's anything I can do to help you in this case, just let me know. My specialties include computers and electronics, so I'd be glad to assist in those areas. I believe in justice and that criminals need to pay for their crimes. The pilot who has been killing those girls needs to be stopped." Dewey stands nearly at attention while he speaks, but almost seems to be talking down to us, as though we are his subordinates. My first impression is that he is a cop wannabe, possibly with an ulterior motive. I can deal with the first issue and will have to figure out the second.

"What do you know about one of these, Mr. McDougall?" Ronnie seems to be challenging the man who reported his radio indiscretions, as he hands McDougall the transmitter Jet had brought.

McDougall grins. "Please call me Dewey, I recognize your voice. Sergeant Torgy, correct?" Ronnie's face flushes, and he doesn't have to answer. He lights up though, when McDougall praises him for working the "hard duty" in the Bush.

Dewey pulls a pair of glasses from his pocket and pops open the transmitter's case. He makes a quick analysis. "Oh yes, a TLR CMV-M. This is a transmitter commonly used for wildlife tracking. It transmits on 140 to 250 megahertz. You just need a receiver and you can follow these anywhere."

No one else tosses Dewey another question, so I do. "What do you know about vehicle navigation systems, like the Sat-Go on the Survivor SUVs?"

"What do you want to know?" McDougall asks, somewhat smugly.

"Can they be hacked into?" I already know the answer, does he?

"No problem, if you know what you're doing. It's a cinch if you want to hook up to the GPS with a laptop and use it for navigation," McDougall answers.

"That sounds complicated. Why not just buy a hundred dollar GPS for your car?" I ask.

"Well now, that wouldn't be any fun, would it?" McDougall smiles like the clerk at the computer store when you ask a question like, "What's better a Mac or a PC?"

"Mr. McDougall, what else could you do if you hacked into the on-board system?" I want to see how good this guy is. He's anxious to show me.

"Call me Dewey, Trooper Blake. If a hacker knows what he's doing, I guess he could control almost everything on the car. You probably know that if you have the Sat-Go system on your car and you lose your key, you can call their toll-free number and they will unlock the door for you. Or, they can honk your horn so you can find your car in a parking lot." I nod.

"By hooking your car up to a shop computer, or remotely from their command center, they can tell how fast you've been going, when the car was last serviced, and much more they don't publicize. Their central command knows if you've had a crash and can dispatch emergency services. The possibilities are virtually endless if you figure out the VCIM codes." Dewey now speaks excitedly and with much animation.

Dewey knows his stuff, but I don't want to lay out any more details of my case to him just yet. He offers me his email address. Something about him makes me want to get to know him better before I feel he can be trusted, but I'll probably be emailing him with more questions soon.

"Well, if no one else has any more, let's break the meeting and get back to work." Dave suggests.

Ronnie approaches Jet and me in the hallway, offering an apology. "Guys I'm sorry about my slip-up on the radio." We both know Ronnie well enough to realize his heart is in the right place and that he's a hard worker, in spite of his continual little screw-ups. Some people learn from their mistakes, others just learn new ways to make mistakes.

"Ronnie, don't worry about it. It turned out to be a blessing in disguise." Jet puts her hand on Ronnie's shoulder as she consoles him.

"How about if you work with the additional number from the plane we just saw on the photo? We'll have a suspect when we find that Super Cub." Jet asks.

"Thanks, will do, Jet. Hey, I almost forgot to tell you, I'm taking flying lessons here in Anchorage." I know the thought of accident-prone Ronnie piloting an airplane concerns Jet as much as it does me, but we both give him encouragement.

"I'm going to be really careful. I even picked up some survival gear and a parachute!" Ronnie effuses his usual excitement in a new endeavor. A parachute? I consider the possibilities and don't like any of them.

Like always with Ronnie, I hope for the best, but fear the worst.

Chapter 23

FAIR CHASE

WE'RE OUT OF our comfort zones. Today we have to toil in Anchorage, which is difficult for a couple of troopers more comfortable flying across the ice floes of the Bering Sea than navigating the streets of a metropolis. But it's not just about location.

"Jack, that Dewey guy kinda creeps me out." Jet puts it simply, but it sums up my feeling about Dewey McDougall as well. However, he's deep enough into our investigation that we have to work with him.

Type A Positive is the second most common blood type, so even if a blood registry of all Alaskans was available, the test from the ski pole isn't a big help in narrowing down the population of Alaska males. DNA evidence is another thing. Those convicted of burglaries, sex offenses, and other crimes against persons, are required to submit samples for the state's DNA registry. If Jet's suspect is in the system for one of those offenses, we can move forward quickly, once the lab results are in. Meanwhile, we have some work to do in Alaska's biggest city.

While Jet digs through records at the wildlife investigations unit, I head downtown in an unmarked patrol car. My mission is to follow up on a possible suspect. I don't know any trooper who relishes the task of interviewing a fellow trooper about his involvement in a crime, especially murder, but that's what I'm about to do.

Anchorage has a population of nearly two hundred eighty thousand, almost half the total number of residents of the state. While waiting at one of the many traffic lights between trooper headquarters and downtown, the purple LED on my Blueberry flashes with an unexpected email. "Trooper Blake, it was good meeting you today. I just wanted to touch base so you will have my email address. I'm standing by to help you in your investigation, as well as in your lovely wife's. Don't be a stranger. Here's a thought for the day, by Aristotle: In justice is all virtues found in sum. Dewey." I've found that many people want to help law enforcement, but I'm puzzled how McDougall got my email address, which was set up on the new, highly restricted, Blueberry system. And, is it just a coincidence that we both favor Aristotle's take on justice?

The department's policy is to work with troopers who have personal issues. The goal is to get them back on track, but not to the point of sacrificing the department's integrity. Jill's email provided the names of three troopers with disciplinary actions against them in the past year, which resulted in suspensions. Three out of four hundred troopers isn't bad. However, it's always a disappointment that anyone who chooses this profession—then passes all the background checks and graduates from a demanding academy—falls down on the job. Sometimes they fall hard. One of the worst was my roommate at the academy who, after being fired from the troopers for his rough treatment of offenders, formed a bank robbery team. The team was quite successful for a while, with my former roommate piloting the getaway vehicle—a Bell helicopter. A saying goes that there is sometimes a fine line between the good guys and the bad—something that trooper proved.

The first suspect on Jill's list is a trooper in Glennallen who was suspended twice in the past six months—initially for a week, and again for two weeks. My guess is the third strike will earn him early retirement, without benefits. The trooper—who has a large family at home—had affairs with two witnesses. The last was the widow of a murder victim. Ted Herlihy agreed to interview him and see what shakes out. The second was a Bush trooper who had reported for duty twice while under the influence of alcohol. His job hangs in the balance, pending his successful completion of rehab. Dave Daniels is working on that lead. The third suspect trooper works in Anchorage and I'm on my way to meet him now.

Trooper Ace Trujillo moved to Alaska from the Dominican Republic. In his previous job, he piloted aircraft for the government while he was assigned to the National Investigative Directorate. He has been with the troopers for eight years, four of those in Fairbanks, three in Nome, and in Anchorage for the past year. He most likely would still be in Nome, but due to an "egregious violation of department policies" while transporting a prisoner, he was removed from flight status. Since his assignment required him to be a pilot, he no longer qualified for the Nome position. Trooper Trujillo now works with the department's judicial services unit, where he transports criminals locally, and occasionally to the Lower 48.

The clerk at the Judicial Services desk advises me that Trooper Trujillo had to make a quick run to the courthouse to help move an unruly prisoner. I take a seat in one of the green plastic chairs and grab today's copy of the *Anchorage Daily News*. Our landlord has made the front page with the headline, "Governor Hines Wants Overhaul of Welfare System." The article reports the governor is planning massive cutbacks in welfare benefits. She is quoted as saying, "We have programs which encourage our citizens not to work, taking care of them and their families when they are perfectly able to care for themselves. Welfare should be a temporary means to get through a crisis, not a lifestyle."

The governor went on to promote establishing the death sentence for child-killers. Tinka is my kind of governor, and I hope the voters see it that way during her reelection campaign next year. Paging through the first section, I find an ad for a big hunting show this weekend at the Alaska State Fairgrounds in Palmer. The event will feature big game trophies, hunting weapons and gear, and even a display of Bush planes. I tear the article out for Jet.

Trooper Trujillo whistles as he enters the office, checks in with the clerk, then turns to me. "Trooper Blake, it's good to meet you. There's an office we can use down the hall," he says in a heavy Spanish accent. Trujillo's uniform is sharply-pressed and his brass and shoes are highly-polished. He stands a little over six feet and probably weighs around two-twenty. He is dark-skinned, with wavy black hair and a thin mustache. I sit across from the walnut laminate top desk in the tiny quarters. I explain the focus of my investigation, then inquire how he got the name Ace, assuming it must be a nickname associated with his military-aviation background.

"Ace is a popular name in my country. It means 'unity.' Jack, I'm happy to do what I can to assist. I've heard good things about you."

I thank Ace for the compliment, and ask him to tell me about his background.

"I came here from the Dominican Republic to get away from the problems in my country. In my job, I was assigned to a special unit. Unfortunately, my home country is a transportation hub for the Colombian drug cartels, funneling almost ten per cent of all the cocaine that comes into the States. Our unit used a lot of boats and aircraft to seize drug shipments and bust those involved. I loved the work and all of the specialized training, but it got too hot for me. I was concerned for my family, so I followed my boyhood dream and came to Alaska." Ace pulls out a photo of his wife and two young boys.

I compliment Ace on his attractive family and then get to the important questions. "Sounds like exciting work. What kind of training did they give you?"

"Lots of pilot training, extensive firearms and defensive tactics work, electronic surveillance, that sort of thing. My unit was much like 'SWAT' in police departments, or the 'SERT' for the troopers. Ace doesn't flinch, and doesn't mention training with explosives or computers. But would he, if he knows about my investigation?

"What about explosives?" I ask, studying his face for expressions that he's lying.

"I learned about C-4 in a class from the bomb disposal team. They taught us just enough to make me want to stay far away from explosives." Ace looks me straight in my eyes and doesn't flinch. His heavy accent makes it hard to detect any inflections in his speech that might indicate he's hiding something.

"Ace, I know this may not seem like any of my business, but can you tell me about the incident which landed you in Anchorage?"

"Sure, no problem. When I first started flying in Nome, a trooper told me they never handcuff prisoners in state airplanes because it makes them nervous. I didn't approve, but since I was new to the Bush, I did what the senior trooper told me. I was flying a prisoner, not handcuffed of course, and somewhere in the skies between Teller and Nome, he goes loco. He grabs the controls and tries to crash the plane into the ground. I was able to regain control just before we hit. He smashed into the support bars over the panel, busting his head open. He was in the hospital for a week and sued the state. I couldn't believe that he could bring a court action, since he caused the crash. I've since learned that the justice system is much different in this country."

"Yes, sometimes real justice can be hard to achieve," I offer, then ask the important follow up question. "Do you have hard feelings about being transferred to this job?"

"Not at all, Jack. The city is a better life for my wife and kids. I'm learning much from this work. And I get to see new places."

"Where have you been able to travel?" I ask, hoping he doesn't say what I'm afraid he will.

"Well, I occasionally transport prisoners outside Alaska. Some go to prisons, and some are being extradited for court. So far, I've been to the SEA-TAC facility in Washington State twice, Lompoc in California, Leavenworth in Kansas, Salt Lake, Beaumont in Texas, and a desolate place way out in the Arizona desert. It's not the most fun way to travel, but it's my chance to see America." Ace seems excited about his sightseeing, and he moves up on my suspect list.

The clerk sticks her head in the door, telling Ace a prisoner needs to be moved from the jail to district court. "Thank you, I'll be right there. Jack I'm sorry, but can we continue this conversation at a later time?"

"Sure Ace, but I was wondering, since your home country is in a tropical climate, are there snakes in the Dominican Republic?"

Ace doesn't seemed bothered by the question, turning to answer as he stands in the doorway.

"The official word from the tourism department is there are no poisonous snakes in the Dominican Republic, but they do have beautiful sea snakes. My brothers and I used to grab them from the bottom of the ocean and play with them when we were kids. Then there is the Boa Hispaniola, which the country wants to protect to keep the rat population under control. Please call me if you need anything else." Ace and I exchange business cards and he quickly walks from the office.

Remaining seated, I study Ace's trooper business card. It has the same font color and style as the piece from the Phoenix crime scene, but so do probably eighty percent of all trooper cards. Ace has at least some of the skills used by the killer, and he certainly has the opportunity with his frequent flyer miles, but I don't see a strong motive. I find myself hoping that I don't find one, as Ace seems like a nice guy and a good trooper. But, since appearances can be deceiving, there needs to be follow-up.

JET MEETS ME back at trooper headquarters. She's been busy.

"How did your interview go, Jack?" Jet asks.

"Good and bad, how about your research?"

"Pretty fair. One of the wildlife investigators has a file on the HOAR group. The clerk ran their names, crossed-matching them with driver's license records. I now have twenty-six photos of HOAR members," Jet enthuses.

"Do any look familiar?" I ask.

"If I toss out the ones with light-colored or no hair, I still have nineteen. Fourteen of those require corrective lenses to drive, but none wears black-rimmed glasses in their driver's license photos. That isn't a deal-breaker, especially since FAA records show eleven hold pilot certificates. Of course, none of this is conclusive. We may not have all of the HOAR members in these records. But it's a shot—the only shot we have right now." Jet hands me the photos of the hunters, none of which jump out. If only one had a driver's license photo with him wearing a red cap, black rimmed glasses, and a sheep pin.

"How about a date to the fair tomorrow?" I ask, handing Jet the clipping from the newspaper.

"Think we could be that lucky? That our guy might actually show himself?" Jet asks, carefully studying the advertisement.

"Well if not, at least we will see some guns and planes," I say.

Agreeing that we need something a little less obvious than a Crown Vic with cheap hubcaps to fit in at the fairgrounds tomorrow, Jet says she will handle it. After a quick phone call, she is all smiles when reporting that the governor is offering her rig for our task. I'm a little hesitant, as I remember the governor's predecessor being driven around in a trooper-chauffeured Lincoln—not the ideal undercover vehicle for our needs. When Jet pulls up in a white Chevy Suburban, I remember that Tinka runs things a little differently than previous administrations.

After a succulent meal of fresh Copper River salmon—wrapped with a grape leaf fruit nut chutney—in the Alaskan Hotel's restaurant, Jet makes a phone call she has dreaded making for some time. Shouting over the background noise of the bar, Candy acknowledges Jet on the phone. She breaks down upon hearing the bad news about Karma. Jet has to say "no" when Candy asks if she can have the locket that was recovered with the bones. It's still needed for evidence.

WHAT SURPRISES ME most about the fairground's Raven Hall are the two Super Cubs inside. It must have taken some maneuvering, or even disassembly, to get them inside. One plane sits on 31-inch tundra tires, the other on brand new floats. Both appear to have every Bush option desired by Alaskan pilots. Jet and I mingle among the crowd of thousands, hoping to find a face that matches one from the drivers license photos. Taxidermy mounts from every Alaska big game species either stare at us from the wall, or stand in lifelike poses on the floor. From a twenty-seven foot twinjet riverboat, easily capable of running the Copper River's rapids, down to lightweight Kevlar Old Town canoes, watercraft vendors try to lure buyers to displays. Other dealers push airplane parts, camping gear, all-terrain vehicles, archery equipment, firearms, and all the other tools and toys hunters seek to get the edge over wild game. Booths sell everything from jerky to guide services, as videos flash on big screens around the building.

I once read about agoraphobia—the fear of being in crowded, public places. If disliking being bumped and stepped upon by throngs of people is a symptom, then maybe we've acquired it. Jet avoids the guides and hunters she knows—some through enforcement actions—as we weave through the crowd. Saturated with sights, sounds and minor bruises, we escape to solace with a small group sitting on a set of bleachers who are watching a demonstration of remote control helicopters. The maneuverability of the small choppers is impressive, but Jet and I wonder to each other how they relate to the hunting world. Suddenly, a hand touches my shoulder from behind.

"Fancy seeing you two here." Surprised, we exchange hellos with Dewey McDougall. Then we quickly ask him not to say anything that will identify us.

"No problem. I'm guessing you are here to look for our suspect. Me, I'm just enjoying the guns and the RC helicopter exhibit." Dewey points to a hovering camo green helicopter.

"See that baby?" We nod and Dewey elaborates. "That's the carbon-fiber 'Jolly Bean.' It can sling an impressive load, and has an onboard color video camera which transmits images to a base monitor. Costs about three grand. Hunters like them for spotting game."

"What's the range on one of those?" Jet asks, thinking of the possibilities for game violators.

"Out of the box, maybe a mile on a good day. I developed an application which uses a small Linux-based, single-board computer, replacing the standard radio controls in RC aircraft, maybe tripling the range. Dewey loses me with his computer-talk. Before I can ask more, the subject changes.

Dewey pulls a pair of miniature binoculars from his jacket pocket. "Like a boy scout, I always try to be prepared," he chuckles. "Well, what do we have here? Look at that guy in the red cap, over by the Survivor, Jack."

Taking the glasses from Dewey, I scan the room, easily finding the gargantuan, "tundra-red" 4X4 SUV. A model in a camouflaged halter top and matching cutoffs points out the vehicle's finer points. Standing next to the Survivor is a man wearing a red cap. I zoom in for a closer look and notice an insignia above the cap's bill. More importantly are the man's glasses—heavy, black-framed ones like once issued by the military.

"That looks like our suspect, the same pilot I saw up the Knik River with the girl in the Super Cub."

"Are you sure?" Jet asks as she peers through the binoculars.

"I'd say ninety per cent at this point. I need a closer look." Dewey replies.

It's hard to estimate how many people are stuffed into this twenty thousand square foot room, but a big chunk of them are between the suspect and us.

Jet and I jump down from the stands, trying in vain to scurry through the crowd. We get a glimpse of the red-capped man as he clears the front door, but the crowd blocks us from reaching him. Forfeiting our desires to be undercover, we yell, "state troopers," causing some to clear a path. Suddenly, the Survivor display lights up with an outrageous array of LED neon lights. Thumping rock music starts blasting, while the camouflaged model begins gyrating on the stage. The crowd freezes in front of the Survivor exhibit with their mouths agape. A human wall forms between the exit and us.

"*WHOOOP! WHOOOP! WHOOOP!*" The shriek of a police siren emits from my pocket, forcing me to grab my Blueberry. It's the first time I've heard that ring tone from my phone. The caller is Dewey.

"Jack, look up!" Dewey's voice blasts over the Blueberry.

The RC helicopter hovers above us, then races toward the big front doors, waiting for them to be opened. Jet and I push through the Survivor-gawkers, forcing our way to the exit. We are still fifty feet from the great outdoors as the tiny chopper maneuvers through the opening.

"I'm on him Jack! Stand by your phone! He's jogging toward a truck!" Dewey excitedly provides a play-by-play of his chase.

We're twenty feet away when the door closes. A robust security guard holds both door bars shut and tells the crowd to stand back, probably hoping to prevent the escape of any more aircraft.

"STATE TROOPERS! We need to get past!" Jet yells at the security guard, who demands to see our badges.

"Jack, he's in a blue extended cab pickup, in line to get out of the parking lot!" Dewey yells over the Blueberry.

We quickly flip open our badge cases and rush past the exasperated guard. Dewey gives us an update as we race toward the Suburban. "He's turning right on the Glenn Highway."

I jump behind the wheel of the Suburban as Jet flips on the grille-mounted red strobe lights. We force our way past cars exiting the fairgrounds and race onto the Glenn Highway.

"I've got you guys on camera now. He probably has a half mile on you, headed toward Palmer. This thing is about out of range, so I'm headed back to the barn. Good luck!"

I thank Dewey and we speed toward Palmer as Jet flicks off the strobes. We pull within ten car lengths of the blue pickup, then match our speed with the traffic, now in the surveillance mode.

There's not enough evidence at this point for an arrest, so we will just have to see where he takes us.

Chapter 24

MARMOT IN A BAR

STAKEOUTS CAN BE boring. This one is no exception, as we observe customers enter and leave the bar, while the suspect's vehicle remains parked. At least I have the stunning and sweet-scented Jet next to me, rather than a cigarette puffing, donut crunching, opinionated partner as usually depicted in cop movies. We had followed the blue pickup as it turned north to the Parks Highway. Allowing a car to pull between us and the suspect vehicle for a buffer, we watched it pull into the parking lot of the "Alaska Outfitters' Bar and Fine Dining," just north of Wasilla. We continued north on the Parks Highway as the suspect exited his truck and strode quickly toward the front door. Approximately a half mile down the road, I whipped the Suburban around on the four lane, and we now are cuddled up in the bar's parking lot with about thirty other vehicles.

Using our Blueberries to tap into state and federal databases, we find the truck is registered to Robin A. Homocker, a forty-six year old white male, who is listed as five-foot-ten inches, one hundred-seventy-five pounds, with black hair and corrective lenses. His address is 58 North Bear Cub Lake Road in Wasilla. His criminal record includes convictions for arson, driving while under the influence, misdemeanor assault, indecent exposure, as well as hunting and commercial fishing violations. Jet taps her Blueberry and pulls up FAA records. She finds that Homocker is a licensed private pilot, and that he owns a Piper Super Cub. The aircraft shows a recent change in registration numbers. The new numbers don't match what Jet has been working with and the old ones aren't listed in the FAA's computer files.

Next, we check our emails. Jet has a couple from Tinka, who asks if everything worked out with her car, and for an update on the cases. Jet responds with thanks for the car and gives a brief overview of our progress.

Ted's email relates he's convinced the Glennallen trooper is not our rogue trooper. He reviewed travel reports, and interviewed both the trooper and his supervisor. Even more important is the wife factor—the trooper's spouse has had what Ted calls an "extremely tight leash" on him since the affairs. The trooper has four children and is very active in a church that now requires him to attend weekly counseling sessions. Ted says if it was a serial-philander we were looking for, this would be our chief suspect, but he's not a murderer.

Dave Daniels also has emailed me. He found that the trooper who'd been suspended for alcohol issues has been remanded to an in-house rehabilitation program for the past month. A review of his leave and travel records prior to that showed nothing pointing to him as a suspect, nor is there an obvious motive. He prefers drinking to working, and the work of tracking victims, and then killing them, would not appeal to his fun-loving, dysfunctional nature. Dave also reports on my request to check with Ace Trujillo's supervisor in Judicial Services to learn more about what is now my only trooper/suspect in the Lower 48 killings. Ace's supervisor gives him high marks, saying that Ace is not only a good trooper, but also that he is their in-house expert on computers. Dave also sent an email to Ace's prior employer in the Dominican Republic to obtain information about his employment history there. That should answer all of my questions about Ace.

Four more carloads of either drinkers or fine-eating diners pile into the bar and we get back to the task. "I'm betting that Homocker is our man, what do you think?" I agree with Jet, then we discuss our next move.

"I'd like to get a look at his house and plane," I suggest. Jet comes up with a better plan.

"I can go in, sit at the bar, and order a glass of wine. I'll start immediately clicking away on my Blueberry, giving you a blow-by-blow of what I'm observing on our suspect. I'll take some photos of the place and of course, I'll 'accidently' get the suspect in one. If the bartender asks what I'm doing, I'll say I'm a freelance magazine writer, doing a story on life in Alaska. You know how men like to brag about their hunting escapades, and by the bar's name, I guessing there are some hunters hanging out in there." I'm concerned about Jet being too close to what is very possibly the killer of numerous women, but at least she won't be alone. The bar is crowded, I'll be just outside, and Jet can certainly handle herself.

"Hanna Beans, crack reporter!" Jet points her thumbs at her face. We kiss, then she slips out of the Suburban. Running up the establishment's stairs, she looks darn cute in her tight jeans and waist-length down jacket with a fur ruff. I can't help but worry, but I guess that's a normal feeling for a husband when seeing his wife run off to chat with what is probably a serial killer.

It's ten long minutes before Jet sends me the first text message. "Our man is sitting at the end of the bar, chatting it up with the bartender. I'm sipping on a glass of bad Merlot and watching him in the mirror from three barstools away. They are talking about hunting, or I should say that the suspect is bragging about his kills. They're laughing about Fish and Game and ragging on the regulations. Hang on, the bartender is coming over."

Two rowdy men stumble down the steps of the bar, then wait for a third, more sober man, to exit. The three drive off in a pickup. A family gets out of their new mini-van and walks up the stairs. The man of the family opens the door, turns back to his family, says something, and they all head back to the van. It must be not be family night at Outfitters. I check the clock on my Blueberry and it's been eighteen minutes since Jet's text message. Five more minutes and I'm going in.

The Blueberry beeps and Jet is back text-messaging. "I just had a nice talk with the bartender. He bought my Hanna Beans, reporter-extraordinaire story. He shared his expertise on the Matanuska-Susitna Valley, then boasted about his hunting quests. He claims to have the 'unofficial record' for the largest bull moose in Alaska. He nodded down the bar to our suspect and said that he's his pilot and has even more trophies. I think I'm about to meet him. I'm going to activate the Blueberry's video function and see what happens. Standby."

A video transmits onto the screen of my Blueberry. The bartender walks away from Jet. He's now talking to a guy at the end of the bar. It's too dark to identify him, but this must be the suspect. The bartender nods toward Jet and the men chuckle. After a minute or so, the suspect gets up and walks toward Jet. I hope she leaves the camera on.

I don't like my first close-up video of this guy. I imagine Jet senses worse. The Blueberry is lying on the bar, so the camera provides a strange angle shot, distorting the suspect's face. But, I can clearly see his black-rimmed glasses and red cap. And, even more clearly, I can hear his somewhat high-pitched voice as he speaks to Jet, "Hello little lady, I'm Rob. I understand you're a writer."

"Yes, I'm Hanna, good to meet you." I'm sure it's not, but Jet is good at her job.

"Well Hanna, Jimbo tells me you are writing about hunting. Is that right?"

"I'm actually doing a piece on Alaska for a tourism magazine. Hunting is just part of the article. But I find it positively intriguing how you Bush pilots fly into some of the most remote parts of the world. What kind of plane do you fly, a Cessna? And how scary is it to face one of those giant grizzly bears?" Jet is pouring it on.

"Well, Sugar, it is challenging, but once you know how to outsmart the wild animals, it's not that hard. And I fly a Super Cub, a true Bush plane." The man waves his hand at what must be the animal heads I'd seen in the early shot.

"Do you mind if I take notes on this little computer thing? I find this just fascinating!" Jet is on a roll.

"Why of course not, Sweetie, just spell my name right: Rob Smith, S-M-I-T-H."

A text message pops onto my screen: "What an ass! Smells like mold, looks like a marmot."

"Got it. Now, Mr. Smith, tell me, have you ever run across a bear as big as that one over by the pool table?"

"Sweet Cakes, my first reaction when I saw that little feller was, 'was the mother with it when it was shot?' Now you must call me Rob. Jimbo, bring the little lady another glass of wine."

"No thank you, Rob, I'm driving. One's my limit." Jet taps more into the Blueberry keypad, lighting up my screen.

"Okay, the marmot is now hitting on me. Is my makeup okay?" I smile at her message.

The bartender takes away Jet's half-full glass and replaces it with another.

"Well, thanks. Now Rob, please don't tell me that you've actually killed a bigger bear than that monster?" Jet sounds genuinely interested in the scumbag's hunting résumé.

"Several. Plus, caribou, moose, bison, sheep, goat, black bear, polar bear, walrus, you name it. All trophies, every one of them." Marmot chugs his beer.

"What do you have to do, go out in the woods and camp, then track the wild animal for days?" Jet takes a courtesy sip from the glass of wine.

"That's for tree-huggers. If you know how to do it, you don't even need a sleeping bag." Rob Smith/Homocker laughs.

Another text message comes on my screen. "If we don't get him for the murders, I'll get him for poaching!"

"Oh, Honey, don't write that down! That's off the record. How about you erase that and in turn, I'll take you up to my place and show you some real trophies?"

"I'd love to, but I've got to get over to the fairgrounds before they close. I'm including a little story on some show over there for the article." Jet thinks fast.

"Darn! I just came from there. How about I take you flying when I get back from Bristol Bay? I could show you some big bears and take you up on the glacier?"

"That'd be great! Here's my phone number. Do you hunt around Bristol Bay, too?" I can see Jet handing the suspect a piece of paper with what, knowing Jet, contains writing only legible to a med-school graduate.

"Commercial salmon fishing. I run a boat out of Naknek. I tuck my Super Cub into my hangar and go fishing for a couple of months, so I can hunt the rest of the year. Don't you want to finish your wine?" The man studies Jet while she types into her Blueberry.

"Coming out. You better duck, because I think he will watch me." I scroll down the screen to read Jet's message, then I lie over on the seat.

"Just a sip, then I've got to run." I can hear Jet sipping the wine.

"Okay, if you're sure you can't come up to my house now, let's get together as soon as I get back from the bay." Jet agrees.

I'm glad to see Jet's lovely face as she moves down the stairs. Even though she was so close, she seemed so far away. I'm not the jealous type, I'm just adverse to my wife being in the company of a serial killer. Jet pulls the driver's door open and slides onto the seat.

"I see him watching me. I can't wait to get out of here, Jack. I have the sudden urge for a long shower." Jet starts the Suburban and pulls onto the Parks Highway. Still lying on the seat, I congratulate her for a job well done.

"The bad news is that I know it's not the last time I will be seeing him. I'm just glad fishing will keep him busy for a while and away from his prey." Jet pulls over as soon as we turn onto the Glenn Highway and asks me to drive, saying she needs a short nap. She sleeps all the way to Anchorage, waking only long enough to get up to our motel room. Being with a creep must wear on a person. Especially knowing the creep is probably fantasizing about killing you.

JET SLEEPS UNTIL 7 A.M. "What the heck hit me?" Jet asks as I kiss her cheek. I tell her that she slept for more than twelve hours, handing her a cup of coffee.

"I don't ever remember sleeping that long. It must have been a more strenuous day than I thought. If I could brag about what sweet dreams I had, that would be one thing. Instead, I had nightmares about

Homocker, one after another." She kisses me, then gets up and takes her coffee into the bathroom and turns on the shower.

"Top of the morning, Jack! What's happening?" Ronnie Torgy answers his cell phone on the second ring. I ask him if he can rent the Cessna 150 from the school where he's taking lessons.

"Sure, Jack, but can't you get one of the state planes? If you need air support, why pay for it when you can fly for free?" I explain we have an undercover mission and need a plane different from what the public is used to seeing troopers fly.

"Standby, I'll give the school a call." Ronnie comes back on the phone in under a minute and reports that he's booked a trainer for 8 A.M. He gives me directions to the flight school and we agree to meet for a flight to the Matanuska Valley.

Jet comes from the bath wrapped in a towel and climbs back into bed. "Honey, if you don't mind, I want to snooze just a bit longer." I offer to get her breakfast, but she just wants to sleep, making me think that she may have picked up a bug of some sort. I kiss her forehead, telling her I'll be back as soon as I can.

Ronnie beams when we meet at the flight school on Merrill Field. He tosses his parachute in the back of the little Cessna trainer and hands me a cap emblazoned with the school's name. I praise Ronnie on that little touch, so now I can pose as his flight instructor. I just hope he doesn't put me through what he probably does his instructors on each lesson.

I've never flown a Cessna 150, but I keep a loose grip on the wheel as we break ground from Merrill Field, with Ronnie Torgy at the controls. We wallow through the air in the little plane. I handle the radio transmissions and remind Ronnie to hold a little right rudder, urging him to keep within a hundred feet of our planned altitude. After twenty-five minutes, we arrive at our destination.

"Jack, I have only ten flying hours and that strip looks way too short for me to attempt this landing." The paved runway next to Bear Cub Lake is eighteen hundred feet long, but it would seem short for a pilot who hasn't yet soloed.

We touch down on the threshold and taxi off the runway at midfield, following the Blueberry's directions to 58 North Bear Cub Lake Road. As we slowly roll by the vinyl-sided one story home, the door to the attached hangar lifts slowly. Just across the taxiway, a man struggles with a Super Cub.

"Play along, Ronnie. Don't say anything if you don't have to. That's our suspect." Ronnie's face flushes and he swallows hard. I pop the door open on the Cessna.

"Good morning. Do you mind if I show my student a real Alaskan Bush plane?" I speak to the suspect who now pushes his plane by the propeller hub.

"This is a private strip!" Homocker isn't happy to see us.

"Oh, I'm sorry. It's not marked as restricted, so we didn't know. We'll just get out of here then," I offer.

"Hell, now that you're here, both of you push on a wing strut and help me get this into my hangar. Then your student can get a close-up look at a Super Cub." Jet's right, he does look like a marmot.

The big tundra tires squeak as we turn and twist the plane to get it up the slight rise and into the hangar. I try not to stare at the marmot's red cap with a little sheep pin attached.

"Wow! So this is what a Bush plane looks like. I gotta get a photo." Ronnie speaks, then throws a quick glance at me for approval. I nod, but hope he doesn't say anything revealing. He clicks away with a compact digital camera.

"Damn right! But you gotta know how to fly one. It's not docile like that little dog you dropped out of the sky in," the marmot screeches.

I compliment him on the trophies in his hangar. One is an impressive moose head with pink panties hanging from an antler tine. The letters "HOAR" are stenciled above a sheep head. There's a full wolf mount standing on the floor with a blue mini-skirt wrapped around it. The suspect studies me, then Ronnie. "Glad you approve. I gotta go now." Marmot man taps the button to the big hangar door. It groans and churns to close, once again hiding his dirty secrets.

Chapter 25

MATRIX

SPINNING UNCONTROLLABLY TOWARD the ground is not my idea of fun. Ronnie Torgy prods me to show him how to stall an airplane, confessing that stalls "scare the heck" out of him. It seems that some instructors, either out of boredom, lack of real world flying hours, or maybe even because of sadistic tendencies, enjoy making this part of training a frightening experience instead of a learning opportunity. In real life, stalls—which occur when the airplane's wing loses lift—often happen when the pilot is trying to climb over an obstacle, such as a ridge, a tree, or even a cloud. Stall training should be taught to illustrate how to respond to the unexpected, not the obvious, like when the nose of the airplane is jerked violently to an extreme angle to the horizon.

Ronnie's hand shakes and he's apparently mouthing a prayer as I slow the Cessna, gradually raising the nose higher and reducing power. The stall warning horn buzzes, the plane shakes, then the nose drops. Lowering the nose just a bit more, the docile Cessna 150 picks up airspeed, recovers from the stall, and with full power and a flap reduction, we climb back up to altitude.

"Is that all there is to it? My instructor yanks the yoke back and points the nose to the sky when we do stalls! Can I try that?" Ronnie yells in excitement through the headsets.

Ronnie practices one stall and recovers nicely. Then he asks to try another. Now relaxed, I say, "Why not?" Big mistake.

It starts out well. Ronnie slows the plane, adds flaps, raises the nose, and waits for the stall as the warning horn screeches. Then, for some unknown reason, he slams his boot on the right rudder pedal, just as the plane breaks into a stall. Suddenly—violently—the Cessna's wing drops and we whip into a spin toward the tundra. The G forces pull the harness belts tight against us, as the earth seems to rotate out of control in the windscreen. Ronnie screams something about his parachute.

"I've got it!" I yell. By neutralizing the controls, tapping the left rudder, pulling the throttle to idle, and pitching the plane's nose down, we ease out of the spin.

Ronnie begs to go home now, but I don't want to waste a good teaching opportunity. That would only reinforce what was just an unpleasant experience. As gently as I'm able, I explain to Ronnie what caused the spin, specifically his heavy foot on the rudder pedal. We practice three more stalls. Ronnie is more careful with his footwork and I commend him for his perfect stall recoveries. Back at Merrill Field, Ronnie stumbles from the cockpit and kisses the tarmac, glad to be down in one piece.

Jet and I meet on the steps of the Alaskan Hotel. She wears a bright green cap over her blonde hair, shorts, a Naknek High School sweatshirt, and bright white running shoes. Her face is flushed and damp since she's just come back from a jog, but she looks wonderful.

"Morning, Jack, fancy meeting you here. Care to come up to my room?" I do care to.

Jet asks me for a detailed description of my morning with Ronnie. I tell of our meeting with marmot man, the panties on the moose antlers, the spin, and all the rest. She awoke only an hour ago and can't remember much since leaving the bar in Wasilla. We are both baffled by her deep and lengthy sleep. After a shower, Jet surprises me with new plans. She leads me down the hotel's hall to a small conference room overlooking Lake Spenard and the seaplanes in action. "Tinka called this morning, and after I updated her on the case, she insisted on buying the task force lunch. She arranged for this room and a catered meal which should arrive soon. The guys are on their way."

The room is set up with a laptop, LCD projector and a printer. Jet sits at the computer and shows me a spreadsheet she designed, at Dewey's request, for our two cases. One side of the spreadsheet is entitled "MARMOT," the other "SNAKE CHARMER," and the details are segregated with boxes. Both list all the information we have so far on Robert Homocker and the rogue trooper.

For spreadsheet evidence in the marmot man case, Jet adds what she found during her encounter with Homocker yesterday, and what Ronnie and I learned this morning. The evidence side of the spreadsheet is starting to look impressive. The side for "actions" simply has a question mark.

To the snake charmer's spreadsheet, Jet adds what was just reported in an email from Jill, our "go to" investigative assistant in Fairbanks. Jill apologizes for not knowing this sooner, but personnel rules kept the item under wraps until action by the trooper triggered its release. Jill reports that Tim Turbulenski of the Northway post tendered his resignation two days ago. This trooper was being investigated for numerous violations of department rules and he must have seen the writing on the wall, as he quit without notice. Jill spoke to Turbulenski's sergeant, learning that the trooper is a hothead, who feels that the department and the rest of the world are out to get him. The sergeant reports the trooper left the state two months ago—when the investigation started—and has been traveling throughout the western U.S. in a motorhome since. What's disturbing about this new suspect is that his background includes Special Forces training with the Army.

Next, Jet inputs the travel schedule for B.B. Sipes. I'd asked Alaska Attorney General Cyrus Webster to "lawyer-talk" with Sipes' attorneys to find out Sipes' travel plans. Webster said it took a lot of convincing, but the information was finally provided out of concern for Sipes' safety. He's in Hawaii for the next two days, and then he flies to Seattle. From there, he will drive with his bodyguards to a little town in Washington called Leavenworth. His next planned stop is Coeur d'Alene, Idaho for the celebrity golf tournament.

The conference room door suddenly swings open, and, like a moose in rut, Ronnie rushes in. "Did Jack tell you about the spin?" Ronnie doesn't wait for an answer. "It was amazing, we're spinning round and round, and Jack just gets us right out of it. I was sure we were going to auger into the ground!" I want to tell Ronnie that it wasn't due to any great aviator skills that we recovered from the spin—it's just I have a strong survival instinct—but he beams with excitement as he moves right into his next agenda item. "I hope it's okay to show some photos," Ronnie blurts, while plugging his camera into the projector.

Dave Daniels and Ted Herlihy come in next, followed closely by Dewey.

Two waitresses enter rolling a service cart. They unveil a spread of smoked halibut and pineapples on skewers, sandwiches, vegetables, fruit trays, and pastries. Like ravens on road kill, the assembled group digs in, even before the waitresses have a chance to put the pitchers of water and coffee on the table.

Dave, Ted and Ronnie grab sandwiches. Dewey layers his plate with veggies. Jet and I go for the halibut and pineapples—we don't see much halibut in our part of Alaska, even less tropical fruit.

"Gentlemen and lady, I'd like to start this meeting by showing some photos taken just this morning on a little jaunt Jack and I took." Ronnie wipes food off his mouth as he pushes a button on a remote control, activating the projector.

The first photo is of Ronnie's thumb, which he'd removed in time for the second shot, which is of his boots. The third photo is of Homocker's Super Cub, as are the next two. As we observed this morning in Wasilla, just a shadow of the registration numbers is visible on the fuselage where they'd been removed. The next two photos are of Homocker, providing a much better mug shot than his driver's license.

Next are photos of the moose antler/panty combo and the mini skirt on the wolf. I ask Ronnie to back up to the moose antler shot and to zoom in on the bench top. There it is—a clear plastic bag of heavy duty zip ties.

"Hold on! Trooper Torgy let me have the remote for a second." Dewey rises from his seat and takes the remote from Ronnie's hand. He adjusts the screen, then focuses on another area on the workbench. "Take a look at that." Dewey zooms in on a green object.

"Is that a canoe paddle?" Dave Daniels asks.

"No, that's a paddle antenna for a receiver that picks up signals from wildlife transmitters, like the one you showed me, Jet," explains Dewey. He then snaps a flash disc into the computer's USB port. The footage shot from the RC helicopter flashes on the screen. Everyone now gets to see action scenes of the suspect, a good view of his truck, as well as Dewey's RC piloting skills.

Jet adds "zip ties" and "receiver paddle" to the marmot man's spreadsheet.

Jet projects the investigative data on the wall. Listed are marmot man's alias of Rob Smith, his alleged hunting prowess, that he hangs out at the Outfitters Bar in Wasilla, that he will be commercial fishing for the next two months, and the details from Ronnie's and my visit this morning. Also listed are the registration numbers for his Bristol Bay boat, his confirmed membership in the HOAR group of hunting bandits, and his arrest record. She explains his uncanny resemblance to a marmot, when Dave asks about the heading on the spreadsheet.

As a boisterous Cessna 185 floatplane fights the friction from the lake water to get airborne, the group studies Homocker's spreadsheet. With a carrot stick hanging from his mouth like a cigar, Dewey educates us. "There's something about the marmot's record. The crime of arson is often tied to a person's need for control, as are rapes, kidnappings and murders. And the indecent exposure incident also could be significant." Dewey's criminology training is evident.

"It looks like we have enough for a search warrant on this dirtbag. I'd be glad to pick him up and throw his sorry carcass in jail. Or better yet, maybe I'll get lucky and he'll put up a fight," Ted offers between bites of a roast beef sandwich.

Dave lays down his ham on rye and responds, "Probably enough to get a search warrant and maybe an arrest warrant. But, then where do we go? We may end up with a lot of circumstantial evidence, however, we will need more to tie him to a specific killing and get a conviction. My opinion, since the suspect will be out of the picture for a while, is we keep at it and see what else we can dig up. Let's get the wildlife troopers in King Salmon to give us a heads-up when Homocker shows up for fishing. Then maybe we can work more on the bartender in Wasilla. Hopefully, the DNA test results will come in soon, which should tie him directly to the Palmer case.

"Good work on Homocker, everyone. We've come a long way in twenty-four hours. It sure looks like he is our man, and I'm sure we will eventually put him away. Let's turn now to Jack's case."

As I review my interview with Ace Trujillo, Jet enters "Travels to Lower 48, computer skills, defensive tactics and shooting, no strong motive" in the Ace-section of the snake charmer's spreadsheet.

We all stand up to watch a rumbling Beaver floatplane take off from the lake, then study the wall where the snake charmer's information is projected.

"Leavenworth? Isn't there a prison there?" Ronnie asks.

"Right name, wrong state. The prison is in Kansas, not Washington State," Ted explains.

"I went to Leavenworth with my family over Christmas once when I was a kid. It's a beautiful little town, but why would Sipes go there?" Jet asks.

Referring to the details of Sipes' itinerary, I explain that he is planning on whitewater rafting.

"Sounds like fun—do you think he can use a couple more bodyguards?" Jet asks.

"Probably a good idea, especially since his next stop is the golf tournament in Coeur d'Alene." I like Jet's thinking.

"Well, it looks like you only have one good suspect and he's roaming around in a motorhome," Ted says.

"Uh, that's not quite correct, Ted. We do have one more possibility." All heads turn to Dave. "Just before the meeting I got a call from Trujillo's sergeant. They had a last minute prisoner trip come up and Ace took it. He's escorting a felon down to Lompoc, California, then going on personal leave for a week. Says he wants to see the wine country, the Hearst Castle, drive through a giant redwood, and that sort of thing. I wish I could say that he has been eliminated from our suspect list, but I can't. Not yet. I've both called and emailed his former department in the Dominican Republic. So far, they aren't cooperating.

"Dewey, have you plugged any of the information on the rogue trooper, uh, I mean the 'snake charmer' into your 'matrix' yet?" Dave asks. Although I wonder what kind of matrix he's been playing with, I have to admit to myself that Dewey is growing on me.

"Yes I have, Dave. We're obviously looking for someone with high intelligence, and advanced technical skills, who is mobile. And he must believe as Cicero said, 'Justice renders to everyone his due.'"

"Don't forget his thing for snakes," Jet pleads, which gets chuckles from the guys.

"So do you think the killer is one of the two troopers?" Dave asks Dewey.

Dewey chomps down on a celery stick, then replies, "I'd hate to think one of our own would do such a thing."

"Our *own*," I ponder, silently questioning to myself, "when did he become 'Trooper' McDougall?"

"They each apparently have at least some of the skills demonstrated in the murders, and they both had the means and opportunity," Dave emphasizes.

"That's true. Sad, but true," Dewey says, as a Super Cub glides into view through the window behind him, landing on the lake.

"What next?" Ronnie asks no one in particular, stuffing down his second pastry.

The only sounds are the sipping of coffee, the projector's whining fan, and the floatplanes in the background.

I look over to Jet who busily clicks away on her Blueberry. "Taking notes, Jet?" I ask.

"Nope, making airline reservations," she says, smiling.

Chapter 26

FOX & GUNS

THERE'S SOMETHING MISSING at Lake Hood. We definitely remember tying Casper, the white Cessna 185 floatplane, to beach stakes in front of the state trooper hangar. We look up and down the row of planes bobbing in the water, but it's nowhere in sight. Adding to our frustration are two quacking, flapping, pooping mallards, seemingly to delight in our dilemma of not having transportation home.

"You kids looking for something?" Hap, the aircraft supervisor, joins the ducks in the fun.

Jet raises her hands, "I guess we are mistaken, but we are pretty sure we flew here. I know Jack and I would have remembered walking four hundred miles across the tundra."

Hap laughs, explaining that the Cessna floatplane was needed for a mission in Prince William Sound. The Cub Jet was using has been pressed into service by the wildlife troopers. Once we convince him we just need transportation for an overnight trip to Lone Wolf, he gives us the instant upgrade, handing us the keys to a new Cessna Caravan.

The turboprop Cessna 208 Caravan carries big loads and seats as many as fourteen. Today, with just Jet and me and a couple of bags, the 675 horsepower turboprop engine hurls the plane into the air after a ridiculously short ground run, climbing skyward like a rocket. As we leave the metropolis behind us, the pavement quickly turns to wilderness, reminding me of old saying, "Alaska is just a short plane ride from Anchorage."

Jet relates a sad story as we cross the Skwentna River. She tells of a trapper who lived on the river just below us who, on a cold winter day, found the battery dead on his Super Cub. The only way he could start the cold-soaked engine was to "hand-prop" it. This requires quickly swinging the long metal propeller by hand, a process similar to hand-cranking the engine of a Model T. The difference is, the worst that usually happens in cranking a car, is the engine backfires. This causes the crank to spin the wrong way, possibly breaking the cranker's arm. It's much more serious with an airplane. In the trapper's case, the ski-plane sat on icy snow and was not tied down. Standing in front of the plane, the trapper gave the propeller a hard swing. The engine immediately fired. The plane sped forward and the trapper couldn't get out of the way fast enough. He was decapitated as his horrified wife watched from the window of their cabin.

We climb over a wall of clouds and set the power for a cruise of almost two hundred miles per hour, touching down at the Lone Wolf airport in what is record time for us.

Piper just about turns himself inside out as he sees us through the window of the trading post. Even though he's only known Jet for a short time, and me less than that, it's like we've had him since he was a pup. Dogs are like that.

"Welcome home Strangers. It's a good thing Piper had Charlie to keep him company, because he really missed you guys," says James Stevens. Reluctantly, I share our quick turnaround plans with our store-keeper friend.

"Don't worry about Piper, he'll be fine here and I'm sure I'll ask you to watch Charlie for me someday. Oh, and Jet, your order came in."

"No peeking, Jack!" Jet takes the long package that's wrapped in brown paper and, with a knowing smile, thanks James. Piper excitedly joins us for the boat trip across the river to the cabin, almost leaping out once to mix it up with the waterfowl.

It's good to be home again, but we need to dedicate the night to preparing for our trip. I'm pleased that Jet can join me on the jaunt back to the Lower 48. I should drop marmot man a thank you note for commercial fishing, instead of killing young women. This gives Jet a break in her investigation so we can join forces. We'll have about three hours on our Alaska Airlines flight to Seattle tomorrow, to come up with a plan to stop whoever is trying to kill B.B. Sipes. Hopefully, we'll make an arrest in the process.

Annie, who is growing into her gangly moose legs at an impressive rate, turns to greet Piper nose to nose. The creek on the side of the cabin, which was no more than a trickle when we left a few days ago, now rushes into a waterfall as it flows over the bank, cascading into the Tranquility River.

Jet encourages me to open the mystery package which she says is a late wedding present. I'm surprised, but I'm prepared. At our wedding party, one of the long-married troopers told me to always be ready with a present when you're married. He called it a "get out jail" card with your wife. It just sounded like good planning to me. I excuse myself, dig into the back of the guest room closet, and retrieve a gift wrapped box.

Jet's gift to me is amazing. The matte-black .308 caliber Arma-Lite AR-10 Super SASS semi-automatic rifle nestles in my hands like it was made for me. It has all the goodies—bipod, Leupold scope, suppressor, and two twenty-round magazines. Both the stock and the checkpiece are adjustable to custom-fit the user. As if this isn't enough, Jet brings me my backpack, which she has modified with a padded side pouch to conceal the rifle. I'm so intrigued that I almost forget to give her my gift.

"Yippee!" By her shout, I'm guessing Jet likes her present almost as much as I cherish mine. I couldn't pass up Forrest Canon's offer in Los Angeles for a deal on the latest and coolest .40 caliber handgun. The textured handgrip of the Kahr Arms pistol fits Jet's delicate hands perfectly, and the lightweight and compact dimensions of the black polymer frame makes it easy to conceal.

"Let's take a hike and do some shooting," Jet says, as she slides a magazine into her new pistol and I carefully stash the rifle in my backpack. We hit the trail after breaking up Piper's and Annie's fun.

We decide to check the moose poaching site again. Hoping the wolverine has left for greener pastures, we want to search one more time for traps which may have been hidden by snow.

Piper leads the way as we again trek up the trail.

The scent greets us first, then we see them—the pink blossoms

of wild roses decorate the otherwise green landscape. Jet picks a couple
of buds and hands me one. "Try this—three hips have as much vitamin
C in them as one orange."

The rosebud is a little tart for my taste, but Jet tells me they are
used to garnish salads and omelets and to make tea. By his sudden halt
on the path, we can tell Piper's nose detects something more than roses.
Jet and I give each that "not again" look, guessing the wolverine is still
working on the moose remains. We sneak up on the kill-site, using the
alder bushes for cover.

This carnivore has a reddish coat, white-tipped tail, and black
stockings. The fox turns in our direction, sniffs the air, then struggles to
get away. It lunges and leaps, but seems to be limited to a radius of a few
feet. I grab Piper's collar while Jet advances.

"Trap! It's caught in a trap." Jet stands a few feet behind the
fox. The vixen glances at her intruders then looks away, as if she knows
it's no longer worth fighting. At Jet's request, I toss the package of parachute cord from my pack to her.

Maybe because they are both in the dog family, the fox seems
more curious about Piper than afraid of him. Jet asks me to move in
front of the fox while she unwinds the nylon cord.

"Keep him busy for a sec," Jet asks. Piper moves forward to
sniff, but I keep him restrained while the fifteen-pound fox cowers.

"Okay, she's secure," Jet says, after a rodeo-like maneuver with
the line. She tightens the tension on the cord and pulls the hind leg of
the fox toward her. The animal's body is now stretched its full four feet.
The front paw is still in the trap, and Jet has lassoed her hind leg. She
asks me to release the trap.

The excitement nearly kills Piper, but he obeys the command to
stay. I pry the trap open and free the bloody paw, then Jet slips the cord
from the hind leg. Holding Piper's collar, I anticipate the chase which
will undoubtedly ensue, but surprisingly, the fox doesn't bolt. As though
she can't believe her good fortune, the fox looks at all of us, then slowly
limps to the edge of the clearing. After standing for a quiet moment
next to a tree, she licks her paw, then vanishes into the woods.

Jet diagnoses the fox with a recoverable injury and puts a positive spin on the moose killing. "No thanks to the poachers, but at least the moose didn't go totally to waste—the carcass provided meals for a wolverine, a fox, as well as birds and smaller critters." We both decide that, by fate of circumstance, this spot has become the perfect place for our "Church of the Woods." If our lives turn out as we hope, we will return often.

Digging around, we find two more set traps, which we spring open and place in my backpack. While searching for a safe backdrop to begin our target practice, an obnoxious jingle fills the air.

Jet's Blueberry demands an answer. The Bethel troopers need "a quick favor." Since their post pilot is at his fish camp, they need us to fly downriver and quell what they describe as a minor disturbance. One of the town troublemakers is drunk and has been challenging others to fight. As do most of the male villagers, he has a rifle and is using it to shoot rounds into the air, and at an occasional inanimate object.

We jog back to the cabin, pull on our uniforms, and boat across the river to the airport. Piper insists on tagging along. Since this is supposed to be a quick mission, we allow him to jump into the big Cessna.

Nukluk's airstrip is covered with water, typical late spring conditions in the Yupik tundra villages. Mud splatters over the windshield, side glass, and the underside of the wings as we touch down at just above stall speed. It takes considerable power to keep from getting the tires buried in the muck, as we taxi off the runway to a little patch of gravel.

Nukluk seems like a ghost town today. No one greets us as we pass government-built frame houses in the rundown village. Only the sled dogs—tied on short chains next to some of the houses—seem to care. Their wolf-like howls are directed at Piper, probably challenging him to defend his honor. Piper ignores them as we continue past the twenty-three shabby abodes to a large, modern building centered at the end of the narrow dirt road. The stout metal door bangs to a close behind us, as we enter the polished linoleum corridor. We call out, but no one answers.

The "Molly Hootch" court case brought a massive school-building campaign to the Alaska Bush in the seventies. Until then, village high school students were sent away to boarding schools. The Nukluk school's multi-purpose room is big enough for concerts, basketball tournaments, or to facilitate a meeting of the entire community. The six classrooms are nicely equipped, and the principal/teacher has a glass-enclosed office. Teachers in the Lower 48 would love to have the teacher-to-student ratio here, as there are only eight children. A sudden desire to quench my thirst makes me realize all is not perfect as brown, foul-smelling water flows from the hall drinking fountain. I grab a bottle of water from my pack.

Satisfied the school is empty, we start down the wooden steps. "KA-BANG, KA-BANG!" Diving for cover, we know the shooter is nearby. Then we see him. A Yupik man sways as he struggles down the muddy road, sporadically firing his rifle into the air or at a piece of trash. The shooter is so drunk he doesn't see us weaving between the houses. Jet covers me with her pistol as I walk up behind him. He doesn't even flinch when I grab the rifle and leverage him to the ground.

"Oh, helloooo, Trooper. Why you come here?" Jet handcuffs him and I ask if anyone else is shooting with him.

"Nope, just me. I'm drunk. Name is Billy. What's yours, girl-trooper?" Being trained law enforcement officers, we'd already guessed he was drunk. The funny thing is, he doesn't smell like store-bought liquor, or of homebrew. Instead, his breath is pine-scented. We help him to his feet and Jet introduces us. Like zombies awakening from their graves, the townsfolk appear in doorways and curtains swish open in windows.

"Where do you live, Billy?" Jet asks. He offers to lead us to his cabin. With one of us on each of his arms and Piper heeling, we find Billy's house. When it was deeded to Billy twenty years ago by the federal government, it was as nice as the other twenty-two houses built for his neighbors. Today, the steps are rotten, the door hangs crooked on its hinges, and the two lower panes of the four-pane window are broken.

Little evidence is left that the house was once painted a cheery blue. We stumble among the clutter as Billy leads us through the mud room, or "arctic entryway," as it's called in the north. It's clogged with outdoor gear, rubber boots, and even two goose carcasses—stored for butchering later.

"Who's your bootlegger, Billy?" I've found that Yupiks are honest people and generally freely admit to their indiscretions, even if it means going to jail. I ask the question we always ask in the losing battle to fight booze-smuggling into the villages.

"Don't need a bootlegger. I don't drink liquor," Billy slurs.

"Well then, how did you get drunk?" I ask.

"I show you." We follow Billy into his kitchen. Dirty dishes and pans, part of a snow goose, bones, crumbs, and partially-consumed meals merge with litter. Although the kitchen looks like it has never been cleaned, it smells like a hospital.

"Here's my drink." Billy hands Jet a brown plastic bottle with a colorful yellow and red label and the brand, "Lysol" in blue. Below the name, red letters identify the contents as "Concentrate, makes nine gallons! Disinfects and deodorizes."

Billy must recognize our doubt, as he takes the extra effort to show us empty Lysol bottles lined up under the kitchen window, on the counters, and on the living room floor.

Jet reads some of the bottle's ingredients out loud: "Ethanol/SD alcohol, isopropyl alcohol, chloro-o-benzyl phenol, and potassium hydroxide."

"I'm going to check the rest of the house and make sure no one else is here," Jet says as she walks down the narrow hall.

"I can buy Lysol in the village store. It's much cheaper than liquor, and it's legal. I've come to like it better than bootlegger's whiskey or homebrew," Billy drools as he describes his party drink of choice.

Suddenly Piper growls, then barks as he trots to the front window of Billy's shack.

Eight young bucks from the village have congregated on the porch. Half of them carry rifles, one a 357 revolver. They push their way into the small living room.

"What are you doing with Billy?" One of the men screams.

"Taking him to Bethel to see the magistrate," I reply.

"You can't do that. We will take him to tribal court right here!" Another man yells.

Standing shoulder to shoulder with the angry men in the confined area, I try reasoning with them. "I understand about tribal court, and I know that works for you with some of your local issues. This time, Billy has broken the law by being drunk and shooting his rifle in town. He will most likely be home in a couple of days, but we have to let the court decide that."

One man raises his rifle, threatening, "We won't let you out of here with Billy! We have sovereignty!" The issue of sovereignty has been debated for years, but troopers still have their jobs to do. The impromptu meeting has deteriorated, highlighted by the racking of a shell into a shotgun by one of the protestors. Trapped in a position similar to one of Tinka's group hugs, even if I wanted to, I can't reach my sidearm.

"I think you might want to reconsider your plans, fellas." The men and I turn to see Jet standing in the kitchen with the present she gave me a couple of hours ago. Braced on the countertop, the bi-pod is extended, the flash suppressor muzzle is pointed at the crowd, and the scope-glass reflects the light of the room. These men know weapons, but I'm guessing they've never seen one as menacing-looking as the AR-10 sniper rifle. In quick succession, all of the villager's artillery thuds onto the wooden floor and eighteen hands rise into the air. I smile at my wife as she winks—we both know the impracticality of a long-range rifle in the tiny room, but appreciate the intimidation factor—then turn back to the crowd.

"Ok, boys, now all of you get to talk to the magistrate. Put your hands in front of you." Jet throws me a bag of temporary handcuffs, made of braided nylon with polycarbonate locks, and all nine are quickly restrained.

The trooper who meets us at the Bethel airport is surprised to see nine prisoners descending from the Caravan, especially when the group's leader thanks us. Jet had completed the police report en route from the village and, after getting the trooper's email address, hits the "send" button and our work is done.

Piper seems to forget all about Jet and me when we get back to the Lone Wolf Trading Post a little after 7:00 P.M.. He and Charlie romp in the back yard while Jet, James Stevens, and I enjoy salmon burgers prepared by Aunt Bee in the café.

Jet and I make quick work of packing for our trip, then hit the featherbed by ten. We have an early day tomorrow.

Part Three

Chapter 27

BAVARIA

"THE CONSTANT IS CHANGE." I don't know how many times I've heard that phrase, or who penned it, but it sure fits our investigations. During the first hour of our flight from Anchorage to Seattle, Jet and I rehash the "snake-charmer" case. We think we have a pretty good handle on it. There are two suspects—one a former trooper and one currently on the job—and we know the modus operandi. We also believe we know the next target. Combining all the factors, we have a constant. The email that just came up on my Blueberry brings the change.

"Jack, a detective with the Seattle Police Department will meet you when you get off the plane in Seattle. In response to a recent nationwide alert I posted on the rogue trooper's murders, the Seattle police just notified me of a homicide scene that you should see. Keep me posted. Cyrus." As with the killings in Los Angeles, Phoenix and Salt Lake, my role is simply to cooperate with the local departments and help in their investigations, since I'm out of my jurisdiction. Of course, the State of Alaska certainly has a vested interest.

Detective Jared Lund is a lanky man in his early thirties, wearing a blue blazer, gray slacks, white shirt, and blue-striped tie. He has close-cropped hair, needs a shave, and stands out from the airport terminal crowd. He looks like he is on a mission. We must look focused as well, because he walks right up to us, asking "Trooper Blake?" We introduce ourselves.

"My car is out front by the baggage area. We can head right to the scene, over in the Central District." The detective leads us to the curbside.

Jet and I are relieved that all our luggage makes it to Seattle, especially since my new rifle is in one bag, and our pistols in another.

We are lucky to have a local police officer navigating through the tangle of freeways in this busy metro area of over three million. Jet stares silently at the tall buildings, appearing to have the same difficulty as I in the transition from remote Lone Wolf to the twenty-fourth largest city in the United States.

Nervously tapping on the steering wheel, and occasionally making suggestions to rude motorists, the young detective tells us his first impression in this case. Initially he thought it was a killing by an "O.G."—the term given to the "original gangsters," who return to Seattle after serving hard time in prisons. This victim fits that profile. "Thirty to sixty gangs operate in Seattle, and they are always battling. When an 'O.G.' gets out of the big house after doing twenty years, he finds the young punks have taken over his turf. That's when the wars are waged. At first, we thought this was one of those wars.

"The deceased was being investigated for the drive-by shootings of a young black man and his three-year-old sister near a public housing project. The college student was visiting his family during a break from school. He was walking in his neighborhood with his sister when a black SUV drove slowly by, with guns blazing. The college student died instantly and the little girl is now lying unconscious in the hospital, with little chance of survival. We believe this was an unfortunate case of mistaken identity, and that the man and his sister were just in the wrong place at the wrong time."

Turning around from the front seat, Jet looks at me and we both wonder about what this travesty has to do with Alaska. The detective pulls in among the flashing lights of squad cars and a coroner's van in an alley. About ten feet away, a silver and black Survivor SUV is parked with the driver's door open.

"You're in luck, the stiff is still on the scene," the detective brakes hard and swings out of his unmarked Impala.

Jet and I stand with the detective, studying the blood-stained white sheet covering the body at our feet.

Detective Lund whips the sheet off the corpse. The man appears to have been about thirty-five years old. Blood drains from a gaping wound in his chest, and more flows from an exit hole in the back of his head. The detective grabs the dead man's right ear lobe.

"Look familiar?" Jet and I kneel down, instantly recognizing the man's ear jewelry. We confirm that it is a Safety Bear pin, fastened through his skin as if it was an earring.

"The sergeant told me about the other cases you've been working. Any suggestions?" The detective throws the sheet back over the victim.

"I'm guessing the scene was left pretty clean of evidence," I offer. Lund confirms my guess, adding that no spent cartridges or other physical clues were found at the scene.

The detective's interest is piqued when I tell him how the Sat-Go systems on the two other vehicles were hacked into. He takes notes on the M.O. of our suspect, saying he will have the Survivor inspected. "From what you tell me, I'd say the shooter knows how to make the punishment fit the crime," the detective deadpans. We agree, although this one seems to lack the creativity of the snake charmer's other killings. This looks like a hurry-up job. It's as if the killer knew we were coming to Seattle and wanted to do something to welcome us.

"Where are you guys headed next?" We tell the detective that we are planning on renting a car at the airport and leaving it in Coeur d'Alene, where we will pick up the trooper Cessna.

"I can do you better than that. A guy I went to the academy with runs a car rental agency in Beacon Hill. He's much better at renting cars than he was as a cop—he was fired for continually doing stupid things, usually breaking a law or two in the process. His rental office is always running rigs over to Spokane. He might be able to hook you up with a one-way rental with no drop off charge, if you're not picky." We're not, and the four-door pickup we draw suits us perfectly. The ex-cop/rental car agent suggests we take the scenic route to Leavenworth and gives us directions. The detective thanks us for the help and promises to keep us updated on his investigation.

The famous Seattle rain pelts hard on the windshield as we pass through the towns of Monroe, Sultan and Gold Bar. The urbanized areas turn to farmland as we follow a pretty little river called Skykomish to enter the wilderness. The Stevens Pass Corridor, designated as a National Scenic Byway, takes us through a valley into the striking Cascade Mountains. Navigating with the Blueberry's GPS, Jet suggests we pull over at Sultan's Bridge Crossing, where we take a short stroll in the light drizzle. The rushing wild and scenic river serenades us as we breathe the fresh country air.

"Do you see that guy? It's probably nothing, but he's been behind us for the past twenty miles." I nod at the silver SUV pulling over on the roadside about two hundred yards past us.

"Yes, I've been watching it as well. And, now that you're getting paranoid, I'll admit that I've been wanting to ask if you'd checkout the half dozen motorhomes we've seen since Seattle. I keep thinking one of them will have Tim Turbulenski, the ex-trooper, at the wheel. Hey, how about we call him 'Turbo,' that rolls off the tongue a bit easier."

"Fine, how about you look for Turbo and I'll keep an eye on our saddler?" I ask.

"Deal! This is more fun than the 'I Spy' game that I vaguely remembering playing on a car trip with my family—maybe on this very same road," Jet says excitedly.

The four-lane highway winds beneath the jagged peaks of the Cascades, and the gentle Skykomish turns to whitewater. Avalanche chutes, which we've also seen along Alaska's Seward Highway, are more frequent as we get closer to the Stevens Pass ski area. Jet studies the drivers of all class three motorhomes as we pass them, providing a running commentary: That's a woman, he's too old, that's a family with kids and dogs. The silver SUV has been reflecting in my mirror for the past fifteen minutes.

We notice the railway adjacent to our road has disappeared, so Jet hits a button on the Blueberry navigation system to find the tracks have slipped into a 7.8-mile long tunnel. The GPS's trivia feature tells us it's the second longest railroad tunnel in the Western Hemisphere. The trees change from Douglas fir and cedar to Ponderosa pine as we descend into the stunning Wenatchee River Valley, where the rain suddenly stops. We pass creeks named Stevens and Nason, then drive alongside the Wenatchee River as the flowing waters become rapids cutting through Tumwater Canyon.

IT LOOKS LIKE THE ALPS. It's almost as if we have taken a wrong turn as the winding road flows out of the Cascades and suddenly, what appears to be a quaint little German village appears. All of the structures in downtown Leavenworth are constructed in the Old World Bavarian architectural theme, with steep-pitched tile roofs and Baroque scrolling, set against the surrounding mountains. Bakeries, German restaurants, wine-tasting rooms, and even a cheesemonger dot the main street, along with the usual gift and tourist shops.

Being a man, I'd rather flounder around than ask for directions, but Jet gently suggests we stop and ask how to find the local rafting company. We climb a flight of stairs to the homey, heavily-stocked "A Book For All Seasons" bookstore. There are several river-running outfitters. The clerk suggests we start with the one his friend runs. He also gives Jet directions to all of the area RV parks, and sells us two audio books for the rest of our road trip.

"Welcome to Osprey Rafting." The attractive thirty-something woman greets us with a smile, introducing herself as Kristi Stewart. Jet explains that we are searching for the outfitter who has booked another group for rafting the Wenatchee River.

"There are several local outfitters, but give me the name of the party and I'll check." Kristi lifts a reservation book onto the counter.

"B.B. Sipes," I say.

Kristi slams the book closed. "No need to look up that name. Is he a friend of yours?" Her eyes glare across the counter, demanding an answer. I explain that we haven't actually met him yet, and that Jet—who again is posing as a magazine writer—is doing a story on Sipes' rafting experience.

"Good, because he's a jerk! His 'people' have changed his reservations with us twice and I've since learned that he was first booked with another outfitter who must have gotten tired of his antics. One of

Sipes' employees sounded totally exasperated when he told me that his boss decided the drive from Seattle to Leavenworth is too long. Now they are flying his Learjet to the Wenatchee airport tomorrow and are going to drive over from there. He sounds like a real prima donna. What is he a rock star or something?"

Kristi shakes her long brown hair when I tell her Sipes is a baseball player, saying "I should have known, one of those guys who gets paid millions to play a kid's game and still isn't happy. Well that does it, Sergio can take Sipes and his crew."

Agreeing to be our guide tomorrow, Kristi directs us to a nearby rental cabin, which she says offers a nice view of the Wenatchee River. First, we act on Jet's hunch and check all of the local campgrounds to search for the suspect motorhome. We find eight "Top Dog" motorhomes like Turbo is reportedly driving. We run all of the plates through the Blueberry, but none are registered to the ex-trooper. Of course, he could be using someone else's motorhome, or his could be licensed in another name. One of the thirty-two foot white and silver beasts tucked in among the pine trees has Alaska license plates. It's quickly eliminated when we see the octogenarian couple with two yapper-snapper, gray-bearded mini-dogs exiting the coach's door. Turbo is supposedly traveling solo and is only forty-one, and I can't see him choosing that breed of canine. He's seems more of pit bull kind of guy.

We decide a search for Turbo and Ace would be futile in this town full of tourists enjoying the eighty-degree summer day, and the festivities of the "Bavarian Bike and Brews Festival." The event features bicycles racing up and down local bike trails, and chugging ice cold beer at the finish line. Non-racers are welcome to just drink beer.

Kristi's directions lead us to a group of cabins which look as if they are from the Route 66-era. Tucked away just off the highway a couple of miles out of Leavenworth, the little "smurf" village offers solitude in the forest. Our cabin is simple and dated, but very clean. We find the best feature when we slide the big glass door open to a deck offering an unobstructed view of the Wenatchee River. The second best is that we are not attacked by a rush of mosquitoes like at home. Wearing little white shorts, a teal tank top which matches her eye color, and running shoes, Jet rests her hands on the deck rail and leans her small frame forward. Nodding down the rocky hill to turbulent waters, she observes, "This wouldn't be a bad place to pick off Sipes." We decide to explore that possibility further.

Hiking along a narrow road that parallels the river, we stop where the road ends. The water widens from a narrow stream, to rock-cluttered, turbulent mini-rapids. From across the river, a high-pitched sound competes with the riffles. An RC helicopter pops up from the trees, pitches its nose down, dives toward the water, then hovers. Next, it flies up and down the Wenatchee as if it's exploring every turn and rock in the river.

"Dewey would love that," Jet says. I agree, wondering if this little helicopter has a camera like the one which had helped us a few days earlier at the Palmer fairgrounds.

The sun sinks behind the Cascade Mountains as we enjoy pizza and German beer on the cabin deck. A small bird with a large, slate-blue colored head, long bill, blue wings, and a red band across its belly plunges headfirst into the river.

"That's a kingfisher. Unlike most birds, the female is more brightly colored than the male," Jet explains. I'm glad it's the same way with us.

We discuss scenarios on how someone might try to kill Sipes. A sniper could easily take him out at any number of places along the river we've seen today. The rafting trip tomorrow is sixteen miles long. We concur that the best we can do is to try and protect Sipes from our raft, by monitoring other watercraft and persons along the shore. If his bodyguards do the same from within his raft, he has a fair chance of getting through the rapids alive.

We click our frosted beer mugs together as the kingfisher enjoys a meal of fresh fish. It's quiet and peaceful so far from home, as the golden light on the river turns to darkness.

The perfect silence is only broken by a silver SUV slowly bumping over the dirt road in front of the cabins.

Chapter 28

WHITEWATER

"OURS ARE PADDLE RAFTS and the paddlers are the motor." Sergio of Osprey Rafting Company explains to B.B. Sipes and the rest of his party that they are expected to provide human power for their raft trip. The scowl-faced Sipes sports a large diamond stud in each ear and spiked-brown hair with yellow highlights. He has muscles on top of muscles bulging from his bright-yellow personal floatation device. He refuses to don the type of wetsuit his voluptuous and very blonde girlfriend, Destiny, and his twelve-year old son Zach are wearing. His two hefty Asian bodyguards also dress in the appropriate attire, though their wet suits bulge at the seams to contain their bulk.

"Sorry, but the water temperature hasn't reached fifty degrees yet, so wetsuits are required." Sergio isn't bending, as he knows the danger of being exposed to the early summer waters fed by snowmelt from the Cascade Mountains. The tradeoff for the colder water this time of the year is higher flows, meaning more exciting runs down the Wenatchee River.

"Damn! I have to drag myself down here at eight-thirty in the morning, now you tell me what to wear? Sipes isn't happy.

"Dad, chill out! Let's just go have fun," Zach, the good-looking twelve year old suggests.

"He's right honey, this is going to be a blast. Just relax," Destiny coos.

Sipes shoots Destiny a glare that discourages further cooing.

"Boss, we'll be glad to do the paddling," the bigger of the two Sumo bodyguards offers.

"It's about time you two earned your keep," Sipes' glower burns at the bodyguards.

"Mr. Sipes, could I speak to you privately for a minute?" I ask, as nicely as I can, considering what I've just witnessed. Fortunately, Sergio and our guide Kristi are busy getting the equipment ready, so they can't hear our conversation.

Sipes looks at me like I'm a baseball he's about to hit out of a park, sternly declaring, "No autographs."

"That won't be necessary, I believe you are expecting us," I nod at Jet.

"Oh yeah, the Alaskan cops. What happened, did your igloos melt up there with all this global warming?" Destiny studies her very long, red fingernails. The bodyguards glance nervously at each other.

"Yep, seems to happen this time every year," I reply. Zach chuckles. The bodyguards are also amused, but Sipes throws them another glare.

"I believe our participation in your current travels has been discussed between your attorneys and our attorney general. I understand you agreed," I say.

"The only reason I did agree is out of concern for my son. Personally, I don't think anyone could get past those goons, but I'm willing to play along if you keep out of our way." Sipes nods to the bodyguards, who raise their thumbs.

"Fine then. Jet and I will be in the raft in front of yours. The crew here thinks Jet is a writer doing a story on you, so I'd appreciate it if you don't say otherwise," I ask.

"I'd like her to do a story on me. Maybe we could have some time alone, for a real 'personal' piece." Sipes licks his lips as he scans Jet.

Jet laughs off Sipes' rudeness. Destiny looks away. The bodyguards shake their heads ever so slightly. I have the urge to punch Sipes' lights out. But Zach says it best, "Not cool, Dad, not cool."

"Okay, okay, do what you need to do," Sipes agrees.

During the brief mini-bus ride to the launching site, Sipes loudly expresses his desire to not get wet or get eaten by a bear. Sergio gently advises him that he will get wet, hence the wetsuit. He adds that no one has been devoured by a bear so far this week. Sipes is the only one in the bus who doesn't chuckle, and I expect the rest will pay for their indiscretions later. Two rafts are waiting for us on the river. Kristi directs Jet and me to the bright red one and Sergio guides Sipes and his crew to the blue one. That causes the first problem.

"I want the red one. See my son's cap? That's right, red! That's the color of my team's uniform. That is, unless they don't come up with my demands for this season." Kristi reacts to Sipes' words with a glance that makes me believe she shares my desire to throttle him. The raft switch is made anyway.

Our sky-blue raft has Kristi at the helm with Jet and me paddling off the sides. Behind us, Sergio patiently directs his crew from the stern. Seated just in front of Sergio are Bo and Jun. The bodyguards sit like Buddha statutes, but they turn out to be powerful paddlers. In front of them are Zach and Destiny, who act more like siblings than a child/adult relationship, as they laugh and slap their paddles to and fro in the river. Perched on the bow is the scowling B.B. Sipes. His paddle is held like a fishing rod and it's still dry. So much for teamwork. I don't know anything about professional baseball, but I have to wonder how that attitude works for him in his career.

Kristi instructs us on how to grip the paddles to get the best bang for our strokes. Bending forward at our waists, we dip the blades beneath the surface and draw the paddles toward us. The three of us develop an efficient rhythm. We have to slow our pace to keep from pulling away from the Sipes boat. They have more manpower, but the star of the show is so much dead weight.

The river begins with a gentle flow as we drift through the tall pines and cottonwoods, giving paddlers time to get used to controlling their craft. We've only floated for a few minutes when Jet alerts me to a light reflecting from a bridge. Using my waterproof binoculars, I find a man with something in his hands. Kristi detects our interest, saying, "You guys have good powers of observation. That's our photographer. He drives down the highway following our course, stopping at points along the way to take photos. You'll get to see the shots at the end of the trip."

Kristi points out birds representing the company's namesake, ospreys. With a "*cheep, cheep*" whistle, one of the extraordinary "seahawks" hovers above the river with its wings arched and talons outstretched. Suddenly, it dives into the water and comes out with a small fish.

"Cool!" Destiny and Zach yell simultaneously. Bo and Jun keep their heads down, intent on paddling. Sipes text-messages with his cell phone, while Jet and I scan our surroundings for anyone planning on harming him. My job requirements notwithstanding, I'd like to paint a target on his chest.

Canada geese scurry along with their newest family members—little yellow balls of waddling fuzz on the beaches—while green-headed mallards splash into the water. The town of Leavenworth slips past above us, then we drift through another calm forest. The water is cold, but the sun finds its way through the tree tops, warming the morning comfortably into the seventies. The air is moist and full of the scents of spring. Except for the birds and the rippling water, it's almost as quiet as home. That changes unexpectedly.

"What the hell are you talking about? I want twenty mil' a season, no less. You get me at least that, plus another ten in endorsements, or you're fired!" Birds flutter from their nests, and his son hunches his shoulders in shame. Sipes continues to scream his demands. Studying our surroundings, I find many good places for a gunman to pick off Sipes. So many that it's almost futile to search, especially with him adding sound effects to his already highly-visible red raft.

The yellow kayak streaks from snags of the shoreline. Jet sees him the same time I do.

"Kristi, we need to turn around, now!" Seeing the boat, Kristi back paddles as Jet and I do our best to coordinate a turn in the sluggish waters.

Bo and Jun see us turning, then they see the kayak. "Stay back!" Jun yells at the intruder.

Our raft bangs against Sipes' raft just in time to buffer the contact from the kayak. The paddler is enraged as he reaches for something in his boat. Having already slipped our .40 calibers from our waterproof camera bags, Jet and I now point them at the intruder's chest. Red dots from the laser sights on the bodyguards' Sig Sauers .45s bob around on his forehead. Sipes dives to the bottom of the raft.

With four weapons pointing at kill-zones, the kayaker's face turns from rage to fear. Both of his hands fly into the air. "DON'T SHOOT! Don't shoot! What's going on?" I ask him the same.

"Sorry, I'm sorry. My family and I are having a picnic and I hear some rude bastard, I mean I hear someone cussing. I came out to ask them to stop," the kayaker apologizes.

"What were you reaching for?" I ask.

"Just my video camera, I was going to record the jerk, I mean the offender." The kayaker had it right the first time.

Sipes raises his head saying, "This guy should be arrested!"

"Wait, is that B.B. Sipes, the wife-killer?" The kayaker now records Sipes on his camcorder.

Sipes orders his bodyguards to "Deal with the scum," but the kayaker already has turned back toward his camp as our rafts slowly resume their drift downstream. No one elects to chase him.

Kristi doesn't miss a beat, saying, "Nice cameras you guys have there. You don't really seem like a magazine writer, Jet."

Jet apologizes for our misrepresentation and explains that we are helping with Sipes' security detail as part of an investigation.

"I guess some parts of every job suck," Kristi says.

As we continue floating down the peaceful river, Jet and I search for the spot we'd walked to yesterday. We find where the road meets the river and where the remote control helicopter was flying. Almost simultaneously with our discovery, the gray RC helicopter races from downriver. We duck as it comes at us fast and low. It darts around us, then dodges at Sipes' raft. It hovers for a minute, dashes to the shore line, then climbs to tree-top level where it hovers again.

"Jack, do you see the camera?" There's a camera mounted on the helicopter, just like the one in Palmer. But I notice something else—the helicopter is carrying something beneath it. It drops down behind the trees before I can identify the cargo.

"A friend of yours?" Kristi asks.

"I was going to ask you the same thing. I thought it might be your photographer," I answer.

"Nope, his next vantage point is up there, from that bridge. We wouldn't use one of those detestable little things for our photography. Kind of messes with the whole 'peace and solitude thing,'" Kristi says, adding that this is the first time she has seen such an interloper on a raft trip.

The photographer snaps the photos of both rafts as we pass under the bridge. Destiny and Zach smile and wave with their paddles. Bo and Jun look up, seemingly to ensure the photographer means no harm, then continue churning the water. Sipes doesn't take his eyes from his cell phone.

After passing a little town called Peshastin, Kristi tells us to get ready for action. "Hang on, we're coming on to Sharks Tooth!" Jet and I paddle as directed, splashing through the white water with gusto. We're drenched, exhilarated, and since we have been out of the forest and in the hot sun for a while now, refreshed. By the commotion behind us, I'm guessing Sipes doesn't see it that way. Jet and I grin at each other.

"What the hell! You friggin' idiot! You made me drop my cell phone. Turn this thing around so you can get it for me," Sipes demands. We catch sight of the photographer snapping away from the shoreline, hoping he is recording Sipes' antics.

Kristi deadpans, "Now you see why I told you to hang on? I'm sure that Sergio told that fool the same thing. Now he's probably telling him, ever so nicely, that no one will be diving into the rapids for his phone."

Sipes continues to berate his guide and his bodyguards. He yells at Destiny for trying to calm him down. Meanwhile, Kristi warns us to get ready for Drunkard's Drop. If only it was named Jerk's Drop, Jet whispers.

It may be dangerous to take one's eyes off the task at hand, but I can't help looking over my shoulder. It's worth it to see Sipes being bounced up and down on the springy bow, screaming like a school girl. The rapids are unrelenting. Sipes looks like the prototypical drowned rat. Destiny and Zach laugh uncontrollably. Even Bo and Jun can't keep smiles from creeping onto their stoic faces. Sergio barks commands to keep the raft on course and for everyone to hold on.

Snow Blind is the next set of rapids. Sipes grabs both sides of the raft and cowers as we splash through the white water. I muse how lucky Jet and I are to be getting paid for this trip.

"Suffocator is coming up. It's a huge hole with an extremely powerful hydraulic," Kristi warns. Before I can grasp the meaning of a "powerful hydraulic," I hear what compares to the sound of being under a bridge when a locomotive passes over. We submerge almost totally, then come blasting out of the wave like a breaching whale. The three of us fight to keep the raft upright as we flop through the turbulent water, trying to balance, and hanging on to keep from being tossed into the whirlpool. The rapids are exhilarating, and if it were not for the skill of the guides, it would be extremely dangerous for rookies like us.

Suddenly, another scream comes from behind us. Not the type of scream associated with thrill, but one of fear. I turn around to see Sipes flailing in the water. His head goes under the current, but he pops back up and yells for help. Then he goes under again.

Kristi cranks our raft around in a pool just below the rapids. Instinctively, I dive into the river. The cold knifes through my body, then adrenaline takes over. Swimming hard across the river, I aim for the point where I last saw Sipes. Quickly, I tread to intercept it a flash of yellow in the white water. Sipes is unconscious, laying face up as I grab his floatation vest. Treading with one arm, I drag him to our raft where Jet and Kristi pull him aboard.

We stretch Sipes out on the rubber deck and turn his head to the side. Water drains from his mouth and nose, then Kristi turns his head back to the center. You'd almost think there'd be some hesitation—considering Sipes' murderous background and his behavior today—but Kristi immediately begins mouth-to-mouth resuscitation. She pinches his nose and strongly breathes four times into his mouth. That's all it takes—Sipes regains consciousness as he spits up water.

"What the hell happened?" Sipes chokes out the question.

"You went overboard and probably hit your head on a boulder. Now you see why we offer helmets, and how paddling helps keep you balanced. This is one sport where you need to keep focused and pay attention to your coach—in this case, your guide. We really should get you to the hospital to be checked. Head injuries shouldn't be taken lightly," Kristi urges.

"No hospital. Just get me off this damn river," Sipes chokes again, then glares at his crewmates, whose raft is now tied to ours.

Destiny and Zach ask Sipes if he's okay. "I'll live, but why didn't you two jump in for me instead of the trooper?" He demands of his bodyguards.

"Sorry boss, we can't swim," Bo answers.

"Oh, that's friggin' fantastic. Now's a great time to tell me that!" Sipes yells.

The rafts beach at what Kristi calls Huck's Hangout, where a barbeque awaits. After almost four hours of paddling, the lunch of grilled hamburgers, sautéed local mushrooms, fruit, and potato salad is welcome nourishment. Bo and Jun flop into hammocks while the rest of us gather around a large color monitor to review the shots taken by the company's photographer. The photos of the rafts in the rapids are spectacular. The one of a red raft deep in a blue and white wave is the crowd pleaser. In that photo, a body in a yellow vest is being tossed into the air. Another shot is of Sipes' raft in more tranquil waters—everyone is smiling, except Sipes, who appears to be engrossed in a cell phone conversation.

Sergio and Kristi congratulate all the crew members for their efforts in negotiating the rapids. We privately agree Sergio should get a medal, or at least a big tip, for putting up with Sipes.

A game of horseshoes is fun, until Sipes cries foul. Bo is blamed for causing a distraction by moving around behind him. Sipes claims that movement caused his errant toss of the horseshoe, resulting in him losing the game to his twelve-year old son. Zach agrees to concede the game.

During the van trip back to Leavenworth, Jet and I steadfastly decline Sipes' offer to have his bodyguards drive our rental truck to Coeur d'Alene, while we fly with him in his Learjet. We find it especially distasteful when Sipes loudly declares, "It would serve those goons right after that experience, plus I'd feel safer if you two accompanied me on this leg of the trip."

As I start to explain to Sipes why his wish won't be granted, Jet taps my shoulder, nodding at a vehicle passing us in the fast lane.

The familiar silver SUV will beat us to Leavenworth. Our plans change.

Chapter 29

SIDE TRIP

THE LEARJET SMELLS of new leather. The seating and the walls of the cabin are covered in soft pearl buckskin, blending harmoniously with luxurious pile carpet, exotic wood veneers, and fiber-optic lightning running along the ceiling. Jet sinks into the couch, stretching out her legs as if lying in front of the cabin's fireplace at Lone Wolf. Across the aisle I settle into a chair that resembles a La-Z-Boy recliner without the overstuffed arms. Sipes and Destiny occupy the king and queen thrones, which run the width of the rear of the aircraft. They're viewing highlights of Sipes' baseball games on a big screen. Two seats face them, but only one is occupied, and that's by Zach, who pecks rapidly at a hand-held video game.

A couple of days ago, the Cessna Caravan Jet and I took turns piloting felt like the ultimate go-fast machine. That plane now seems like a slug in comparison. The pilot pulls back on the control yoke and we are firmly pressed into our seat backs as the Lear 35 rockets skyward. Seemingly, as soon as we reach cruising altitude, the co-pilot advises us to prepare for landing. Shortly thereafter, the wheels kiss the runway in another state.

Rolling down the taxiway at the Coeur d'Alene airport, I point out the window at the trooper Cessna 185 on the ramp. "How about we break in the engine today?" Jet smiles her approval.

We accompany Sipes, Destiny, and Zach to the resort in downtown Coeur d'Alene, where a hotel representative dispenses with the normal requirement of checking in, instead directing us to an elevator. Jet and I are anxious to see what five thousand dollars a night buys in a hotel room—the price Sipes claims he's paying for the penthouse suite.

The bellman swings open the door to the resort's premier room. The entire front wall of the suite is windows, with a pop-out su-

203

nroom providing a dramatic view of Lake Coeur d'Alene. Decks on either side of the sunroom add more space from which to take in the incredible Northwest scenery. There are indoor and outdoor hot tubs, a fireplace, entertainment center, wet bar, and most amazingly, a swimming pool with a glass bottom for viewing from below. Destiny gives the bellman a wad of bills, then excuses herself, while we discuss a security plan with Sipes. Zach takes the opportunity to escape to his room.

"I'm going to stay right here until the golf tournament at 5 P.M. We'll order room service, as I know I'd be mobbed by fans if we go out," Sipes brags as he picks up the phone. His delusion—of thinking anyone in this resort town would know or care who he is—serves us well. Jet and I now feel comfortable leaving him alone until his bodyguards rejoin him later today. Sipes tells us to get a lay of the land from the deck, then begins barking at some unfortunate soul on the other end of the phone, including a complaint of his misadventures on the river and a "pounding headache."

The glass door opens to a deck overlooking Lake Coeur d'Alene. There's not a cloud in the blue sky and, with a temperature of about eighty degrees and a slight breeze, the day is perfect. Avoiding a racing speedboat pulling a rainbow-colored parasail, the Brooks Seaplanes' Beaver begins a gradual climb to the south for a sightseeing flight. As a classic wooden runabout burbles along in front of the boardwalk, the resort's drawbridge lifts to allow a sailboat to pass from the dockside mooring area. Kids splash in the water by the city beach, and hikers stroll along a path on a hill to our left. One of the resort's mahogany water taxis, used to ferry guests the three miles between the resort hotel and the golf course landing, scoots around an outcropping of rocks.

"I see why people choose north Idaho as their home. If we ever tire of fifty-below winters, right here would be on the top of my list," Jet says. Although I agree on the area's beauty, I know it's unlikely we will ever leave our beloved Alaska.

"Smart woman. Can I get you one of these?" Destiny clunks across the floor in high heels, tilting a drink bedecked with an umbrella. As when looking at the sun, I involuntarily glance at her tawdry, lime-green mini-bikini, and the tattooed "B.B." initials it reveals. Quickly, I turn my focus to the only woman I care to look at, as she responds to the offer.

"No thanks. We have to make a flight," Jet answers.

Destiny says she understands and hands us two crew passes for the golf tournament. She stretches out on a lounge chair, and we wish her a relaxing day—if that's possible with Sipes nearby.

At the Coeur d'Alene airport, Jay shows us the shiny new engine in the Cessna 185, calling it a "thing of beauty." Jet and I agree that, as far as engines go, it's impressive, but we're glad we're not paying the tab. Jay has flown the plane around the airport pattern to test the engine, but suggests we take it on a local cross-country trip before we set off on the long journey to Alaska.

"I have just the place, Jet. I'd like to show you where I grew up," I suggest.

"Sounds lovely, but isn't that the same place where this engine's predecessor was killed in action? Do you really want to go back to that shooting gallery"? Jet asks.

"Yes it is, and yes I do. I have a little unfinished business down there," I add.

Shrugging her shoulders, Jet smiles, saying, "Why not?"

Jet is enthralled by the flight south under the sunny skies. We first pass over Lake Coeur d'Alene, then the Palouse prairie, then on into the rugged mountains and over the grand Clearwater, Salmon and Snake Rivers. We cut across Rush Creek, as I point out to Jet where I learned to fly, rode horses, and hunted and fished in my youth.

We descend to inspect a cloud rising from a winding forest road—it's dust is being kicked up by a fancy blue pickup. Since there's not usually much traffic this far out, I'm betting it's the same truck that was on the airstrip during my last trip. I estimate he's about fifteen minutes away from the lodge.

Circling over the grass airstrip, I show Jet where I lifted off for my first solo flight, where I spent many happy hours at target practice and, sadly, where my father crashed to his death.

"Beautiful, just beautiful!" Jet says of the lodge after we touch down on the airstrip, agreeing that it looks like the Ponderosa ranch on the TV show, "Bonanza."

Strolling toward the lodge with Jet, I notice something that I didn't see last time I was here. A camera facing the airstrip is mounted on a pole. Several more cameras monitor the grass strip, and two more are under the eaves of the lodge.

Although I'm sure the lodge owner—the same man who I need to talk to about the hole in the airplane's engine— is currently absent, I bang on the door. A slightly-built brown-haired young woman answers.

"May I help you?" She asks with a tremor in her voice. I notice bruises on her cheek and what appear to be burns on both of her arms. She must weigh no more than eighty-five pounds. Her unwashed hair is pulled back from her tear-stained face. I guess her age at seventeen. Her hazel eyes look older.

I explain my need to talk to the owner. She answers that he had to go to McCall for supplies and should be back soon. She confirms he's driving the blue pickup.

"May we come in and talk to you?" Jet senses there is something wrong.

"I… I guess. Do you have business with Clancy?"

Jet explains that we are troopers and need to talk to the owner, who we now know as Clancy. I scan the room. It doesn't look, feel, or smell the same as when I stood on this rough-hewn wood floor to gaze at the mountains and wildlife. It was here by the river rock fireplace where I first learned the enjoyment of reading good books, and where I sat spellbound listening to my uncle's stories for hours. All of the old photographs are now gone. This grand lodge, where I learned about ethics and morals from my beloved uncle, is now decorated with animal heads and gaudy furniture. A painting hangs over the fireplace in the likeness of the man who shot at my plane. He cradles a fancy rifle and his boot rests on the shoulder of a freshly-killed bull elk.

"Oh, thank goodness. Could you please take me out of here?" The girl pleads.

"Why, is there a problem?" Jet asks.

"Clancy could be here any minute, so I'll tell you the short version. I hired on with him to cook for lodge customers. He brought me here from my home town, Sacramento. My mother didn't want me to come, but Clancy promised good wages, and I need money for college. There were supposed to be lots of customers for his dude ranch operation, but he ran the first group off with his pure meanness. Word got out and the rest cancelled. He took his business problems out on me and now won't let me leave." She trembles, then breaks into tears.

"He beats me. He burns my arms with a branding iron." She sticks both arms out to show us the fresh burns. "He rapes me over and over. He makes me do things, bad things." She breaks into wracking sobs.

"Jet, you stay with her. I think I hear a vehicle," I say.

The blue pickup skids to a stop in a cloud of dust. The driver is the same man who ordered me to get off his property once before. The same man who took a shot at my airplane, not caring about the consequences. Swinging out of his truck, he slams the door shut and glances at the Cessna while swaggering toward me.

"Didn't I tell you to get the hell off my property once already?" He demands an answer.

"I believe you did. And I left. There was no need to make your point any clearer by shooting at my airplane. The bill for the new engine is thirty thousand dollars," I answer.

"You can't prove that I shot at you," he bellows.

"Don't count on that. I have the spent bullet that will match your Holland & Holland rifle. Plus, I'm sure it was recorded on one of your cameras here," I nod at the camera on the pole.

"Who the hell are you, anyway," he demands.

"Jack Blake, Alaska State Trooper."

"A little out of your jurisdiction, aren't you, Blake?"

"There's no jurisdiction for justice," I firmly reply.

"Justice is for the poor. Something I'm not," he sneers.

"Justice binds society together. Not just with laws, but with morals, ethics, fairness, and equity. It's what keeps the world from blowing up into a big ball of fire." I answer, focusing on his darting eyes as he continues his rant.

"You're a dreamer. But, let's say I shot your plane and I'm just sorry it didn't crash at the end of the strip, like I hear some fool did many years ago. What the hell are you going to do about it?"

That "fool" was my father. This conversation is taking an unfortunate turn.

"What I'm going to do is make a citizen's arrest and ask you nicely to accompany me to the Idaho State Police regional headquarters in Coeur d'Alene. They also will want to talk to you about that little lady up in the lodge. I nod toward his captive, who now stands on the porch with Jet.

"That worthless little bitch? Sounds like you've been sticking your nose where it doesn't belong. It looks like I now have two bitches to serve me. The new one looks kinda cute and I have a thing for blondes." He scowls and starts toward me.

The man stands a few inches taller than me, but a couple of those inches are probably due to the heels on his crocodile boots, decorated with Egyptian god inlays. His massive belt buckle, big enough to cook a stir-fry meal over a campfire, glistens in the sun. He reaches for something at the small of his back.

Clancy levels the heavily-engraved .45-caliber derringer at my chest, firmly holding onto the ivory grip. It's a little late to remember I'd removed my pistol when piloting the Cessna. The side-holster interferes with operating the plane's flap handle.

"Kinda funny that an Alaskan trooper has to come all the way down here to get himself shot, but so be it. I'll just tell them you were trespassing," Clancy snarls.

First impressions are all-important. When I first met this man, my gut feeling was that the only way to deal with him was physically. I didn't think my uncle—whose presence is still felt right here, where he taught me the art of self defense—would approve. Now I know he'd be disappointed if I don't react to this man's disrespect for justice and for human life.

Moving into a defensive stance, my right leg slides back to support most of my weight, while my left leg moves forward. This provides the balance needed for effective kicking in martial arts. My uncle would string a stick between two posts and have me dislodge it, over and over, with kicks.

Clancy takes two steps toward me as he pulls the hammer back on the derringer.

"Like I said before, 'no trespassing,'" Clancy barks, as his finger tightens on the trigger.

With a snap kick, the right instep of my boot meets his gun hand. The derringer sails into the dirt. The incidental report of the .45 round echoes across the airstrip and surprises me. Following the sound, my eyes leave my assailant for a second. That second is all Clancy needs to throw a punch. My head jerks to the right and my jaw immediately throbs. I have to admit that this dude has some power in his fist. I also have to admit getting punched in the jaw sets off a rage inside me, further fueled by my extreme loathing of this man.

In the heat of battle, I don't think about any particular martial arts move that my uncle taught me. It's all just reaction. Somehow all my training merges into a flurry of punches and kicks. Clancy now lies before me in a heap. He starts to rise, but I discourage him with another hard punch to the side of his face. Maybe it's due to my anger over what he did to the girl, or him shooting the airplane. Maybe it's his disrespect for this land, or for justice, or all combined, that makes me want to punch him more, but I force myself to stop.

Jet grabs Clancy's wrists and ties them with rope. We hoist him, half-unconscious, into the back of the Cessna 185, securing him with more rope to the cargo rings in the floorboard. Jet sits next to him and the girl rides in front with me. As we are taxiing out for takeoff, Clancy awakens.

"You bastard, I'll sue you for this!" Clancy yells from the back, while he stomps and twists against the confining the ropes.

"Sir, I have to inform you. If you try anything to disrupt our flight, it will be considered a hijacking attempt. As an officer of the law, I will stop the hijacking attempt with a bullet between your eyes. Thank you for your cooperation." Jet's safety briefing to Clancy has an immediate calming effect. Like the smoothly running new engine, our prisoner cooperates on the flight home.

Waiting for us at the Coeur d'Alene Airport is a trooper from the Idaho State Police, who helps Clancy from the Cessna and into the back seat of his patrol car. Clancy will be spending some time in a windowless cell with three other inmates—quarters more suited to him than the beauty of the lodge. The felony charges should keep him away from the ranch for a long time. Hopefully forever.

Jay smiles when we tell him how well the engine performs. I relate the story of the battered girl, who now stands near Jet petting Chloe the black lab. Jay insists on driving her to the Spokane International Airport where she will fly home to her mother.

Right now, Jet and I need to prepare for a golf tournament.

Chapter 30

HOLE IN ONE

"AMERICA'S GREATEST GOLF EXPERIENCE," Jet reads from the brochure we picked up at the Coeur d'Alene Resort as we ride with bodyguards Bo and Jun from the airport in our rental pickup. Neither have hard feelings about being bumped from their boss's Learjet. Bo says it was a good chance to see this part of the country and Jun says it was a nice break from Sipes. After pulling up in front of the massive revolving door of the resort, Bo and Jun reluctantly exit the truck, in no hurry to return for more abuse from their boss. We agree to meet them later at the golf tournament and wish them the best of luck with Sipes. Meanwhile, Jet and I want to do some reconnoitering.

The gate guard confirms our names are on his list, makes a radio call to announce us, and then allows us to pass. Jet's relates from her brochure that the resort course is ranked number one in the category of "Beauty and Esthetics" by *Golf Digest*.

"Wow! This must be how golf is in heaven!" Jet exclaims as she views the lush carpets of deep-green grass cut in decorative patterns. Surrounding us are beds of brilliant red geraniums, pine trees, a trickling creek, white sand, quaint red-roofed buildings, and, of course, Lake Coeur d'Alene and the world-famous Floating Green.

Heath, the club pro, briefs us on the tournament which begins in three hours. After we explain the security concerns for B.B. Sipes, Heath agrees to assist. He points out some of the course's features from the windows of the pro shop, then displays a virtual tour on a TV monitor, explaining the challenges for each of the eighteen holes. Jet and I concentrate on the areas providing the best cover for an assailant. Even though we know nothing about the sport, we find the course remarkable. Everything is first class, from the little golf carts with chrome rims and heated seats, to what Heath calls "the signature hole"—where the distance from the tee box to the floating green is varied periodically, in moving the island by computer-control. After landing their balls onto the green, golfers are transported from the tee box to the island by an electric-powered boat. As we kick around a few ideas for providing extra security without being too conspicuous, Jet has an inspiration. She asks Heath about a person, dressed totally in white, moving quickly about the course.

"That's a forecaddie. They are essential in helping golfers navigate through this hilly, tree-lined landscape. Forecaddies assist with club selection and have the unique ability to find balls that are seemingly lost forever," Heath explains.

Heath agrees with Jet's plan, and we leave the clubhouse with a bag holding her latest outfit. He leads us to a golf cart, then hands us a course map. "Take a tour of the course, just please keep on the cart paths, stay clear of golfers, and watch for flying balls," directs the pro.

We discover plenty of hiding spots among the bunkers, trees, and fragrant junipers of this golfer's paradise. So many, we realize we need to depart from the original plan of both of us joining Sipes' entourage. As in planning for any battle, one must make the best use of available resources. Bo and Jun will supply adequate close-in protection and Jet will provide supplemental security and communications. We realize to make it all work, we need air support.

A helicopter would allow for quick response, and could land anywhere on the course, but there are two problems. One, most helicopters are very noisy and would be distracting to the golfers. Two, we don't know where to find a chopper quickly. Our inspiration comes from the sky as we drive back to the cabin we'd rented at Hayden Lake. The little yellow Cub seaplane is just touching down on the glassy water.

As we pull up, the Piper docks in front of a log house on the lake. Mike Philips, owner of Mountain Lakes Seaplanes, welcomes us to the beach where he runs his seaplane training school. We discover a connection when he relates he's retired from the Alaska sport-fishing guide business. It's probably more Jet's charm than our common Alaska ground, but after a few minutes of talking, Mike agrees to let the State of Alaska rent his seaplane for the evening.

I grab my pack from the rental truck and Jet and I kiss for good luck. She heads to the cabin to change into the forecaddie outfit and to find a place on her body to conceal her new Kahr Arms pistol. We agree to make radio contact when I fly over the golf course.

Mike gives me a brief checkout in the crisp-performing little seaplane, adds fuel, and reminds me to be safe. His little yellow hopped-up Piper J-3 is a beauty and, as with Super Cubs, the clamshell door opens wide so the tandem-seated occupants have an unobstructed view of the terrain below.

"Oh, and by the way, there's a little 12-gauge shotgun in the back that's part of my survival kit. If it's in your way, I'll grab it," he offers. Barely two feet long, the shotgun takes up little space, so I lay my pack and rifle next to it. After a quick pre-flight and run-up, I quickly lift off sparkling Hayden Lake for the short trip over downtown Coeur d'Alene to the golf course.

Jet and I check in on our Blueberries as the Cub approaches golf course. We learned just yesterday these little technological wonders act as two-way radios on our discreet frequency. Additionally, mine plugs directly into the airplane's communication box, allowing me to talk and receive through my headset.

With only thirty minutes until tee time, Jet is in place wearing the white uniform. She's been teamed with another forecaddie as she scans for our bad guy. Flying a thousand feet above the course, I count eight forecaddies, easily picking out Jet by her blonde hair and graceful walk. She avoids giving herself away by not looking up at the plane, however, she inconspicuously asks me by radio to do a quick overhead recon of the course.

To conduct an aerial search, I first fly the whole vicinity, adjusting to the topography and to the colors. My next sweep is to look for movement, or for anything that does not belong. During this sortie, I note that every fairway or green has golfers. There is nothing out of the ordinary behind the trees, or in the gullies.

Broadening my sweep, I fly along a creek which cuts through the northwest end of the course and flows under a road. As I climb high for a broader view, Jet's voice breaks onto the radio.

"Jack, Sipes has arrived. He will be riding a cart with his playing partner. Bo and Jun will be in a cart in front of them. I'll be running alongside with the other forecaddie. Tee-off is in five minutes."

I acknowledge Jet, then fly out along the Interstate to get some distance from the course. Even though this little plane is quiet, it will still be noticeable, if not disturbing, to the golfers. If there is a killer down there, I would rather not draw unnecessary attention. My goal is to appear as if I'm sightseeing and just playing around.

The conditions are perfect for flying a little open door seaplane, as the water-skiers and sport boats below me make the best of the warm evening. To kill a little time and have fun in the process, I drop down and do a few splash-and-goes a half mile offshore. After lifting off from my fourth landing, I climb to the east, following a flotilla of watercraft to the end of the lake, then make a one hundred-eighty degree turn. The Blueberry's GPS tells me I'm over Beauty Bay, a fitting name for this scenic, mountain surrounded cove. This may be one of those very rare missions where I feel guilty for being paid.

As I follow Interstate 90 westbound, Jet calls with an update. "We're just starting on the twelfth hole. Sipes has already taken four mulligans. Do you see anything yet?" In our planning, Jet and I concluded that it's most likely any attempt on Sipes would be made on the back nine, however, you never know what's in the mind of a killer. I start to ask what a mulligan is, but figure we can discuss that after what hopefully, will be an uneventful golf game. Something interrupts my scan.

It's funny how the brain works. Like after purchasing a new car, you notice all the cars on the road of the same model and color. In this case, we've been looking at big, white motorhomes for the past few days. Now I see another one.

The Blueberry identifies the road under the right side of the plane as "Coeur d'Alene Lake Drive," where I pass lakefront estates with sandy beaches and expensive boats docked in front. Next, a marina full of blue canvass-covered boat slips and an adjacent restaurant passes beneath my open door. Then comes a big parking lot, abutting a lakeside bike trail. The motorhome is in the parking lot. Slowing the Cub to fifty-five miles an hour, I crank into a tight turn. "Big Dog" is written on the cab-over roof of the RV, and the license plates are yellow with blue numbers—like Alaska plates.

Seeing no activity around the motorhome, I tell Jet of my discovery, then continue flying past the five million dollar per-unit high rise condos. The condominium parking lot is full, but one vehicle jumps out at me. It's parked away from the rest of the cars, on the far west end of the lot. It's a silver SUV.

"Jet, this could be nothing, but there's a silver rig parked within a short walk of the course. It looks like the one we've seen on and off for the past few days. Maybe a coincidence, but..."

"Roger, Jack. Wait a minute, speaking of coincidences, there's another one of those RC helicopters flying over the course," Jet interrupts with excitement in her voice.

"What hole are you on, Jet?" This is too much of a coincidence.

"The fourteenth, with the floating green. Sipes made it onto the green in two shots and is walking down to the dock to get into the boat."

"I'm headed there." Slamming the Cub's throttle forward, I dive toward the lake.

"He's on the dock now, Jack. The helicopter is coming at us!"

With the nose pushed over, the airspeed reads one hundred and ten miles an hour—fast for this vintage Piper. The wind blows like a hurricane through the open door as I reach into the back seat. The pack and rifle have slid to the rear of the baggage compartment, but my hand feels wood and metal. I grab it and pull it into the front seat with me. Mike's sawed-off 12-gauge is the perfect size, more compact than the rifle for which I was searching. The shotgun is a single shot, so I'll only have one chance. Breaking the breech open, I feel lucky to find a red shell lodged in the chamber. The pistol grip of the little shotgun feels good in my hand as I rest it on the doorjamb.

"Jack, the chopper is hovering over Sipes and Zach. What do you want me to do?"

"Get everyone clear, NOW!" I yell over the radio.

Pulling the throttle back, I hug the shoreline adjacent to the floating green and trim for the rapid descent. Now only fifty feet above the water, I slow to just above a stall, side-slipping the plane so the open door is away from the wind. My left hand is on the control stick and my right holds the shotgun. Through the windshield, I catch a glimpse of people scurrying from the dock to the shore. Then I spot Jet with her arm on Sipes' back. The mini-helicopter is hovering over them, as I slide the thumb safety forward on the shotgun. I pick a line that will allow the wide pattern of 12-gauge double-ought buck to miss the floats, the wing struts, and the prop of the airplane, while hopefully hitting my target. My mind races to make calculations of wind, speed, and range.

The RC helicopter is just a gray blur as I close in on it rapidly, gripping the shotgun with both hands, and holding the plane's control stick with my knees.

It seems to happen simultaneously—I squeeze the trigger, the helicopter blows into pieces, and Jet and Sipes spring off the dock and into the water. Throwing the shotgun behind me, I grab the stick and crank the Cub around, banking hard back toward the beach for a landing. The Cub splashes down between the floating green and the shoreline and I fast-taxi toward the tee box.

"Stay back! This stuff is caustic!" The forecaddie waves at the crowd to make them stay away from the hissing and boiling debris of the RC helicopter.

My soaking-wet wife has pulled herself onto the dock. Bo and Jun each grab one of Sipes' arms, lifting him from the lake.

"What the hell kind of stunt was that, Blake, your idea of a joke?" Sipes berates me, even before I climb completely out of the Cub.

"Boss, I think you should look at this," Bo points at the steaming pile of RC helicopter.

Sipes and his bodyguards cough and choke as they get closer to what was the helicopter's cargo of toxic acid—a cargo that Sipes knows all too well.

"Who would do this?" Sipes demands, as he rubs his temple.

I want to answer that question, but the list of people who hate Sipes enough to kill him is probably endless. Instead, I just reply, "We plan to find out."

Chapter 31

SUSPICIONS

SIRENS CAN'T BE GOOD for the golfers' concentration. An ambulance and fire truck are holding at the guardhouse, and two police cars race along the usually serene driveway to the clubhouse.

"This is the second time in a couple of days I've been dunked in the water, Blake. I've been popping aspirins for a migraine since yesterday, now I'm again drenched and cold. Why in the hell did your wife push me?" I point out that being tossed in the lake is better than being sprayed with acid.

Sipes' face turns pale. He swallows hard before asking, "Do you really think that was meant for me?" Surprised that Sipes is just now getting it, I tell him that someone is trying to even things up in the name of what they see as justice. I can see he doesn't like my answer, but he doesn't argue either.

"Whatever you two are getting paid, I'll double it if you'll quit your jobs and come to work for me," Sipes offers, then vomits into the clear waters of Lake Coeur d' Alene.

"Thanks, Mr. Sipes, but our place is in Alaska. You are leaving tomorrow for Europe and should be safer overseas. You have good bodyguards, just let them do their jobs," I reply, nodding at the smiling Bo and Jun. Sipes shakes his head with a look of pained disgust.

Dripping wet, Jet uses her digital camera to take photos of the acid-drenched plastic, as a Coeur d'Alene police officer runs onto the scene. After I show her my badge, explain our mission, and assure her there is not a firearms threat, she authorizes the fire department to approach. A firefighter takes a quick look at the former RC helicopter, now a steaming pile of junk, then radios for "HAZMAT." This means that a crew trained in handling hazardous materials will soon arrive, giving us little time for our own examination.

Introducing herself as Dallas Lennon, the police officer advises the evidence will be secured after the HAZMAT specialist contains the spill and bags the pieces. We trade business cards and agree to discuss the case later. Meanwhile, Jet and I need to tie up some loose ends.

While Jet runs to the pro shop for dry clothes, I climb back in the Cub. After a quick take-off, I fly over the condo parking lot, learning the silver SUV has left. Continuing along the road, I find the motorhome still parked where I last saw it.

"Jack, are you on?" Jet calls me on the Blueberry radio to tell me she's dressed and ready to get to work. We agree to meet near the motorhome and to approach it with caution.

As the rental pickup cruises down Lake Coeur d'Alene Drive with Jet at the wheel, I cut the power in the floatplane, landing in the still waters in front of the parking lot. After tying the floats to stake on the beach, I scramble up the bank. Jet pulls the truck in behind the motorhome and eases out of the driver's door, pistol at her side. This isn't the time to lose focus, but her attire sets me back for a second. She wears a short madras skirt, a white sleeveless shirt with a pink collar, and tan and white golf shoes. Her still-damp hair is pulled through the opening in the back of a white golf logo cap. This presentation is very un-Jet-like, although I must admit the image is sensually appealing in a country-club sort of way. I refocus, as we need to approach cautiously. The motorhome occupant could be our man.

The cab of the motorhome is empty, so we move around to the living quarter's entry. I knock on the door as we both stand to the side.

"Who is it?" A gruff voice says from inside.

"State troopers," I answer, leaving out the "Alaska" part to avoid confusion.

The burly camper with heavily tattooed flabby arms steps out onto the first step, squints into the setting sun, demanding, "What do you need?"

Jet explains that we are looking for someone from Alaska who is driving a motorhome resembling this one.

"Well, that's not me. I'm from Portland," the camper explains, belching softly.

Excusing myself, I nod to Jet, who continues to converse with the camper as I walk to the front of the motorhome. The bottom part of the license plate is covered by a metal frame, which I pry back to find it's from Oregon. I've now learned that older editions of Oregon license plates have the same color scheme as do older Alaska plates.

The camper produces an Oregon driver's license. That's when I have conclusive evidence this couldn't be our suspect, as we're surprised to find we are talking to a woman. Jet and I apologize for the interruption, retreating to a park bench overlooking the lake.

It's a safe bet the prime suspect is driving the silver SUV. However, since there are so many similar rigs, and we never identified the make, neither an air search on the busy roadways, nor a law enforcement bulletin, would be productive. Jet scrolls through the photos she took at the golf course, then connects her camera to her Blueberry so they can be displayed on the larger color screen.

"This helicopter looks a lot like the one in Palmer." I agree with Jet, noting that a model number can be seen on one of the parts. Then I see something else—pieces of what appears to be a balloon hang from the bottom of the helicopter. In another shot, red wires dangle from the bottom, terminating in what could be a miniature receiver.

"Jet, we need to get some expert advice on this. First, I'll call Officer Lennon and advise her what we've discovered in your photos, so safety precautions can be taken. Next, we need to call someone who knows about these helicopters," I say, as I dial the officer's number.

"I'll call Dewey." Jet punches numbers into her Blueberry. I hate to admit it, but that strange character does know about RC aircraft, and he's our only source.

"No answer at his home or on his cell. Ted Herlihy is working with the task force this week in Anchorage. I'll give him a call and see if he can track down Dewey," Jet reports, as she dials Ted with the speakerphone feature activated.

"Trooper Herlihy." There's a lot of background noise, but it's definitely Ted on the other end. We ask questions.

"Nope, haven't seen the amazing Mr. Dewey for the past couple of days, but I have bad news. Standby." The background noise comes to the foreground, drowning out everything else.

Ted continues with a clearer signal, "Hayden and I are in the helicopter. I just investigated a set of bones found up on the Knik River. I'll fill you in later, but it's the same M.O. as the others. I know Dewey's place. It's sort of a compound, off the Old Glenn Highway. Big house on about twenty acres. It's on the way home, so we'll swing by there. I'll call you back in ten minutes."

AS A SAILBOAT plies the waters behind the Cub, we drift into thoughtful silence. Then we decide our next moves.

Still without a firm suspect, we send emails to Turbo's former supervisor and to Ace's current one. Maybe one or both of them will have an update on the travels of these men.

Surprisingly, I receive an immediate email response from Turbo's sergeant. "Turbulenski is in Mexico. He called earlier in the day and left a phone number for a hotel in Mazatlan. I just called him back, so I know that's on the up and up. He sounded more stoned than angry. Hope that helps." That does help, as we now have only one trooper as a suspect—Ace Trujillo.

Jet's Blueberry alerts her to a call from Titanium Ted. "Jet, we landed on Dewey's property. No one came out, so Hayden kept the blades turning while I beat on the door. It looks like he's gone and so is his truck. Standby. I want to show you something pretty cool."

Ted's back on in a couple of minutes. "Okay, I think this is hooked up. You should be getting a picture on your Blueberry screen. We're sending you a high definition uplink. Do you see it?"

Jet acknowledges Ted as an image appears on her screen, showing the outline of a house as the camera moves around.

"Good. Hayden has been instructing me to use the new FLIR thermal imager in the helicopter. We're trying it out on Dewey's house, just to get some practice," Ted advises. The house is shown in an outline and the roof is a little lighter, due to escaping heat. "See that hot spot? Let me zoom in." We can see clearly that he's focusing on a hot water heater. This generation of FLIR is much more advanced than the one on which I was trained. Rather than just fuzzy white "hot" images, you can actually tell what they are.

"Hey, wait a minute. Do you see that?" Ted asks.

The FLIR has picked up a source of heat in a room off the main living quarters. It's far from the kitchen and other sources of artificial heat. The camera adjusts in and out and re-focuses. There are definitely three separate objects putting out heat and moving slowly.

"Are those cats, or maybe little dogs?" Jet asks.

"I don't think so. You probably can't tell on your little screen, but they are not in the shape of cats or dogs. They're smaller and thinner. By their limited movement, it appears they are in some type of container, with light bulbs being used for heat. Maybe a kennel, I can't tell for sure. My first guess was that Dewey has an aquarium with big fish, but Hayden says they're putting out too much heat to be in water. Oh well, we can ask Dewey about that later. I'll keep trying to reach him. We're running low on fuel, so we have to head back. Let me know if you need anything else." We thank Ted and sign off.

An email alert pops up on my Blueberry. It's from Ace's supervisor, advising me that Ace returned early from his trip, claiming one day was enough of California. Ace reported for work this morning.

Jet and I suddenly feel lost in our investigation. Both of our suspects have been eliminated.

Coeur d'Alene Police Officer Dallas Lennon's email comes next. "Trooper Blake, I wanted to let you know that our explosives expert examined the remains of the RC helicopter. As you guessed, it did have a small explosive device attached to those wires. After rendering it safe, he examined it thoroughly. He found that the device's purpose was to detonate inside the balloon, apparently to spray the acid below the helicopter. I'll keep you posted on our investigation, and trust you will do the same for us."

Sipes is leaving for Europe tomorrow, our two prime suspects have been eliminated, and both the FBI and the local police department are investigating the golf course case. Jet and I concur that at least for now, our work is done in the Lower 48. Our need to get home quickly is reinforced by a call from Ronnie Torgy.

With his usual excitement, Ronnie converses through the speakerphone on Jet's Blueberry. "Greetings Blakes, how's your vacation in America?"

"Fine, Ronnie, how's it going up there?" Jet responds.

"Great! I met with Dewey McDougall at his house the other day. Taking the tour of his place confirms my earlier feelings that he's a strange dude, but he sure seems to be on our side and I guess you could say we've become buds. The good news is that, after plugging all the facts of the marmot man case into his matrix, he has come up with a plan. He gave it to me on a flash drive for showing at the next task force meeting. Dewey won't be able to make it. He left on a trip into the backcountry."

"Do you know where in the backcountry?" I ask.

"He said he's running his airboat to his fishing camp. You should see the lab in his house where he makes computers, other electronic gizmos, and tinkers with RC helicopters—it's state-of-the-art and filled with of all kinds of equipment and tools. He made two very tiny transmitters and a mini-cam for us to use on the investigation. He also gave me a couple of tracking receivers. It's all high tech and very cool," Ronnie says.

"That's great. Ronnie, we should be in Anchorage tomorrow," Jet says.

"Oh yeah, another thing. Dewey has monitors everywhere in his house. It looks like they are connected to cameras, which are set up all around Alaska, maybe even around the world. Some appear to be way out in the Bush. I don't know how he powers them, and there's something even stranger," Ronnie adds.

"You have us on the edge of our chairs, Ronnie, WHAT is even stranger?" Jet deadpans and smiles at me. So far, all that Ronnie has reported just confirms our guess that Dewey is a computer and technology geek, who'd like to be a cop, and who plays with toy aircraft.

"Jet, maybe you should hold your ears while I tell Jack, 'cause I know how you feel about these things," Ronnie continues.

Jet chuckles while shaking her head and motions for me to answer Ronnie.

"Okay Ronnie, Jet's in the 'cone of silence,' go ahead with the strange-but-true fact on Dewey," I ask.

"Snakes! It's the snakes. He has two big glass containers with rattlesnakes in them. They were in a little side room that I wandered into, when I was looking for the bathroom. They really freaked me out," Ronnie said.

Jet and I stare at each other for a second, then say our goodbyes to Ronnie. We need to get back to Alaska. Quickly.

We flight-plan for twenty hours in the Cessna 185. With Jet and I trading flying duties, one of us will nap while the other flies. The governor's office again arranges smooth passage through Canada, this time through Customs in Calgary. Weather along the Alaska Highway is favorable, with the exception of moderate turbulence, and fifty-knot winds between Calgary and Red Deer, low ceilings and fog around Watson Lake, and thunderstorms near Whitehorse. We don't have the time to stop and smell the flowers on this trip, but the endless June daylight allows us make it to Anchorage in one very long day. With two fuel stops and two very sore rear-ends, we're happy to be back on our own turf.

Part Four

Chapter 32

CONFESSIONS OF THE SOUL

AN EMERGENCY MEETING of the task force has been called. To jump-start our systems, Jet and I grab double-lattes on the way to the Anchorage troopers' office. Yesterday's long flight from Coeur d'Alene to Anchorage left us fatigued, but we need to focus, so we give in to paying way too much for coffee. All but one of the task force members is present.

"I knew there was something strange about that Dewey guy," Trooper Ted Herlihy exclaims, as he bangs his titanium hand on the table.

"I hate to admit it, but he had me fooled," admits Investigator Dave Daniels.

"I should have seen it sooner, but I was focused on the obvious. If there's a good side to all this, it's that our killer isn't a trooper, or even a former trooper," I reflect.

"No one should feel bad, he surprised us all," Jet empathizes.

"Snakes! What's up with the snakes?" Ronnie Torgy wonders.

"We've all been updated with latest developments in Jack's case down in the Lower 48. Before we decide on a course of action with Dewey McDougall, we have some unfinished business. Standby. I need to call the attorney general. He asked to be a part of this discussion." Dave punches numbers on the conference phone and brings Cyrus Webster into the conversation.

"Welcome to our meeting, Mr. Webster," Dave says.

"Ted, what can you tell us about the latest case?" Dave motions for Ted to speak up so his voice carries to the speakerphone.

"Bones were found by bear hunters up on the Knik River. I'm guessing the shallow grave is from last season. The skull had a hole in it, but no bullets were found. We found another sheep pin, but no other evidence," Ted reports.

Dave provides a quick synopsis of where we stand. "We'll probably never know for sure how many bodies of missing girls are out there. There's still nothing from the lab on DNA tests from the ski pole blood. I wish it was like TV, where the lab turned around conclusive results overnight. A few days ago, we thought time was on our side. That's all changed, thanks to a poor salmon run in Bristol Bay, resulting in a temporary closure of the fishery. A wildlife trooper called two days ago to report Homocker got on an Alaska Airlines jet to Anchorage. He's probably already on the prowl for more victims."

"What about pushing forward with a search warrant on his house?" Ted asks.

Cyrus' voice booms over the speakerphone. "From what I've reviewed on the case, it's my opinion that a judge would certainly issue search warrants for Mr. Homocker's house, hangar, and airplane. I imagine you would find a significant amount of physical evidence. However, that might not help much, the way the justice system functions. We need to tie him directly to a scene, or better yet, catch him in the act of kidnapping."

"So, are you saying we have to let this sicko continue with his killing?" Ted pulls at his collar as he barks the question to the attorney general.

"Not at all, trooper. I'm just saying that there's still more work to be done. Jet, I understand you had some luck speaking with him. Do you think you can draw any more out of him in a conversation?" Cyrus asks.

"It might be a little difficult to draw information from him about his extracurricular activities, since my cover is a magazine reporter. Boasting about hunting is one thing, murder is another. But sure, I'm willing to talk to him more." Jet looks at me tentatively.

"Well, you troopers discuss it and let me know when you need my help. I'll make certain you have an assistant district attorney on your team when you're ready. I have to run to a meeting with the governor. Please keep me in the loop and be safe," Cyrus signs off.

"Any suggestions to what we should be doing while Jet develops more on Homocker?" Dave asks the other four troopers.

"Let's get a warrant for McDougall's house and see what we can dig up there," Ted suggests.

"Oh yeah, that reminds me. I have a flash drive Dewey gave me. He said we should watch it during this meeting." Ronnie lays a one-inch long black piece of plastic on the table.

Dave turns on the projector and plugs the flash drive into the attached laptop. A media presentation begins.

A photo of a very skinny, pimple-faced teenager with big glasses and a silly grin fills the screen. Then Dewey's voice narrates, "That's me when I was fifteen. Yep, total geek. The kids in my school would sometimes force me into my locker. I'd be stuck in there throughout chemistry class, which, besides physics, was my favorite. And that's when they were being kind. I pretty much got my tail kicked on a daily basis. But that's in the past. Most of them are probably losers today and I'm worth more than ten million at last count. Maybe because of all the torment in school, I had a strong desire to get involved in the justice business, like you guys. But, my ticker disqualified me from law enforcement work.

"My luck turned when I developed a little device in my lab which allows computers to communicate with satellite technology. That earned me my first million. Sorry Jack, I had to muffle a laugh when you asked me that on-point question about the Sat-Go system, since I helped design it." A photo of Dewey in his mid-twenties now appears on the screen. He's filled out, his complexion has cleared, and he no longer wears glasses. "This photo was taken after I'd been on a health kick for a while and after Lasik surgery—now I only need glasses for close-up work.

"By the way, there's no need to race out to my house. I'll be long gone by the time you see this. Now, before we get into the nitty-gritty, let's have some fun. I made this short music video. It shows some of the stuff that really annoys me, and how I get even for the little guys." Dewey speaks as the video starts rolling.

To the music of "Another One Bites The Dust," the video shows Dewey pointing to a metallic blue sports sedan racing into a clearly marked handicap parking space. An able-bodied young man jumps out and runs into the store. Air hisses loudly as Dewey explains, "Here I am tapping into the tire pressure monitoring system that some new cars have. A few key strokes on my custom remote control, and all four tires are deflated. Then I make a call to the police department and the violator gets tagged with a two hundred dollar ticket." Ronnie laughs with the video.

"Do you guys hate to see those drivers going up and down parking lots, looking for a space that's maybe fifty feet closer to the store, when there are many vacant spots a little farther away? They pull into a tight spot and then wiggle out, while smashing their door into the adjacent vehicle. They don't even flinch at the obvious dent they've caused." The video shows Dewey next to a car whose owner just caused such damage. He continues, "Let me introduce you to the 'Dewey Dinger.'" Dewey sticks what looks like clear wads of Silly Putty on the violator's door. "When the driver gets back in his car and starts the engine, tiny explosives are detonated, causing a series of dings in his door." "Bites The Dust," fades as Dewey continues his narration.

"The Anchorage Police Department should have hired him for parking enforcement," Ted chuckles.

"Oops! I Did It Again," plays for the next sequence. "Anybody hate tailgaters as much as I do?" Dewey asks, as he glances up to a camera mounted on the ceiling of his car. The camera switches to a rear outside view as a car rapidly closes in. "Okay, I'm going the speed limit and that guy is within ten feet of my bumper. Now he's flashing his lights, like I'm supposed to bust the speed limit for him." The car creeps closer, now just a few feet away. "Okay, you asked for it. 'BOMBS AWAY!'" Erratically, the tailgater swerves back and forth, and then abruptly skids off the roadway onto the shoulder. "Some of you may have used 'Stop Sticks' to flatten the tires of a suspect during a high-speed chase. Same theory here, only I can drop mine remotely.

"Cell phone abuse drives me crazy. Say you're in a movie, in a store, or even a library, and some idiot is blabbing away loudly on a cell phone. Check this out." "Oops I Did It Again" accompanies a video showing a man in a darkened theater chatting loudly into his cell phone. Abruptly, a woman's high-pitched scream interrupts his conversation, then cusses through the cell phone's external speaker at the maximum volume. With the audience protesting the rudeness, the man slaps his phone shut and sticks it in his pocket. The screaming continues as the man bolts from his seat and runs from the theater. "I call that my 'rude cell phone callus interruptis' program," explains Dewey.

"Maybe our Blueberries can be modified to do that," Dave laughs.

The music stops and the video transitions to Dewey sitting behind a large wooden desk. In front of him are bottles of pills. "Okay, that's some of the fun I have in the name of justice for all. My vice is wanting to get even for the little guy. But, as Honest Abe said, 'It has been my experience that folks who have no vices have very few virtues.' If I were king, I'd have immediate justice in my kingdom. Mine would be like the system in Afghanistan where the hands and feet of thieves are amputated, criminals are publicly beaten, and murderers are executed in brutal and public ways. The punishment would fit the crime. There'd be very few repeat offenders.

"Now I need to get serious with you good troopers who, I hope, are my friends. Life throws us plenty of curve balls. I always thought my bad heart would take me out, but last winter, I had to cut back on my workout routine because I was feeling tired all the time. I lost weight, became easily fatigued, and became anemic. I'd bruise easily and was constantly aching, deep within my bones. Finally giving in, I went to the doctor. After a series of tests, the diagnosis changed my life. Unfortunately, ignoring the warning signs for too long meant the acute lymphoblastic leukemia was at an advanced stage. I was given just four months to live.

"I've suffered through chemotherapy and radiation therapy. Some cancerous cells were probably killed, but the process harms healthy cells as well. I worry those therapies might kill me faster than the cancer will.

"I've tried all the drugs the docs prescribed, but the problem is the drug companies only spend research money on meds that can be patented. I can't blame them, as the FDA-approval process costs hundreds of millions of dollars and years of time—it's just the nature of the pharmaceutical industry. My concern is that any drug which has been altered from its natural form, which it must be to be patentable, might become toxic to your body. Maybe that's why the greatest number of drug deaths in the U.S. is from prescription drugs. Of course, I'm only a computer guy, not a doctor.

"One naturopath suggested natural supplements for fighting the cancer. Another told me those also have the potential to be toxic. A friend now has me on alternative treatments, including Blue-Green Algae and Graviola. None of it's working. The Food and Drug Administration approved a pilot study to see if Ecstasy helps terminal cancer patients with anxiety and depression. Locally, some use 'Mat-Su Gold' marijuana for cancer pain and appetite issues related to chemo. One or both of those may be my next step, as the cancer is spreading quickly. I don't want to be a wimp, but it can be rather painful." The room has fallen silent. No one knows what to say.

"Okay Jack, I want to make it easier for you, so all the task force's energy can be put to solving the murders of the young women. I confess to taking out that cop-killing rapper in Hollywood. That was my first use of my Sat-Go remote control device in the field. It worked flawlessly. Once I remotely disabled his SUV, it was simple to take him out with his own gun.

"The Phoenix mission was my favorite. Not only did that scum have it coming for what he did to that family with the cancer-stricken little boy, but using the snakes for the execution was such perfect justice. I sent the family a cashier's check so they can buy another home and get the care they need for their child.

"Salt Lake required me to do a little research on explosives, but the rest was easy. I was disappointed that Sipes wasn't on the chair lift, but his partner was equally guilty in the murder of Sipes' wife, so it worked out okay.

"Jet, I must apologize for getting a little sloppy at the golf course. I really wanted to douse Sipes with solid sodium hydroxide, which is even more deadly than the acid he used on his wife. I've always been careful to avoid any collateral damage. When I saw you next to him, there was no way I could even consider dropping the load. I was hovering, waiting for my chance, when you pushed him into the lake. Then here comes Jack out of nowhere in the floatplane—that was a heck of a shot you made! I figure Sipes will screw up again someday. Maybe not enough to put him away for life, but I have a feeling he will again end up in the courts. Hopefully, he won't be lucky enough to get an incompetent, star-struck jury again. Plus, there's always the afterlife—I hope and pray there's a special place waiting for B.B. Sipes. For some reason, I have a sense it won't take too much longer for him to get there.

Dewey holds up a document. "I know this video might not be enough to convince everyone, so I'm leaving this signed and notarized confession. My house is unlocked, and I herby give you my consent to search it as you wish. You will find all the evidence you need to tie me to the Sat-Go modifications. I've left video copies of each of the case scenes, clearly showing me as the executioner. Seattle left with me with regrets of having to sacrifice creativity for a fast job, but it still avenges the deaths of two innocent people.

"I've also left a copy of my will on my desk. I'm leaving most of my estate to Kids Village, as they do wonderful work, and this money will allow them to expand their operation and care for more children. Jet, don't worry if you go into my house—the snakes are gone.

"Okay, enough about me. As you know, Homocker is back from Bristol Bay. I've been monitoring him since his return, as you can see by the next videos." Clips of the marmot man show him entering and exiting his house and hangar, driving away in his truck, and conversing several times with the bartender in Wasilla.

"You can find Homocker every day at the bar around 5 P.M. That is, unless he's out trying to pick up women from the streets of Anchorage. Here is some footage of his plane up on the Knik Glacier, and more of him flying the river flats." The marmot man's Cub is shown flying at low level over a milky-looking river littered with gravel bars.

"I plugged everything into my matrix. Homocker will strike again and again, until he is stopped. My analysis indicates that he usually kills a woman wherever he happens to be hunting. He likes to stay on his turf in the Mat-Su Valley, but occasionally ventures to the Brooks Range, or to the Wrangell Mountains near Glennallen—wherever the critters are. Since the bears are still roaming around the upper Knik, I'm betting that's where his next hunt will be—hunting for a woman he's picked up in town and set free in the Bush, so he can chase her down and kill her. He's made two flights up there since he got back, doing touch-and-goes on the gravel bars and searching for good places for his 'hunts.' Unfortunately, there is no way to conceal a stakeout in those open flats. The only possible way to catch him is to have a female trooper go undercover. That's where those transmitters I made for you come in. I trust you've shown them to everyone already, Ronnie."

Ronnie's face flushes red as he scrounges two radio receivers from his flight bag. Digging deeper, he pulls out a small jewelry case and opens it to show two small earrings. Another case houses a necklace.

"The earrings contain miniature GPS devices, which constantly transmit the wearer's location. Little buttons are concealed within them. Push either button, and a loud squeal and a flashing red light will be transmitted to the receivers, alerting that an immediate response is needed. My suggestion is to have the undercover agent push the alarm as soon as she has enough evidence to convict him.

"Now to the necklace. That contains a miniature video camera which transmits images from anywhere. What's cool about the design, is you can just swing the chain around from your chest to your back, depending on what video coverage you want.

"Try the gadgets, review my findings on the rest of this disc, and decide for yourself. My plan calls for ground and aerial support, allowing for minimal response time to the scene if things get dicey. "Let me leave you with a quote from Winston Churchill, 'All the great things are simple, and many can be expressed in a single word: freedom, justice, honor, duty, mercy, hope.'

"Okay, one more quote. Sir Winston also said, 'A man does what he must—in spite of personal consequences, in spite of obstacles and dangers and pressures—and that is the basis of all human morality.' As always, best of luck, and know that I've always just wanted to help."

Ronnie rubs his red and runny eyes. I must look as disoriented as the rest of the group as we try to sort through confusing emotions. The silence is broken, by probably the funniest thing I've ever heard from the usually stoic Titanium Ted, "If you think the marmot would hit on a cross-dresser, I'm willing." We all laugh, trying to imagine the already lofty Ted in high heels and a skirt, his titanium hand brightly shined for the occasion.

"It's sad about Dewey's illness, but it looks like he has chosen his way to go, whatever that might be. I've thought long and hard about how we can bring this case to a resolution, and put Homocker away for life. I have to admit that Dewey's plan is better than anything I came up with. Anybody else have a better idea?" Dave says.

"I kinda like Dewey's taste in 'bling bling.' How about you, Jack?" Jet's eyes gaze intently into my mine. She doesn't need fancy jewelry to look beautiful. She's beautiful in her heart and that's the kind of beauty that lasts. I know what she's suggesting. I don't want to answer.

Chapter 33

PLANS

DEWEY MUST HAVE KNOWN Jet would volunteer to go under-cover. The transmitter-equipped earrings he made match her teal eyes, and the gold nugget locket blends with her hair. Most importantly, the jewelry allows us to constantly monitor her location.

Dave, Jet, and I hash out possible scenarios. Even with the ever-present risk of another murder, we consider delaying, with hopes of catching the suspect in the act. Dave presents two possible problems with that approach. First, if we catch him with what turns out to be a prostitute, she—in order to keep from being busted in what she believes is a vice case—might claim the encounter was a "date." Second, if she does cooperate, the most we'd have is a kidnapping charge. The way the justice system often works, Homocker could end up with just a brief stay in a cozy cell while dreaming up more ways to kill.

If, through an undercover operation, we catch Homocker in the act of flying a victim to remote location—then hunting her like an animal—we can nail him for attempted murder, kidnapping, and other charges. Bringing together evidence from the other cases, and what we hope to seize with warrants, he could be convicted of multiple counts of first-degree murder.

My pleas to Jet are impassioned, but I know she's right—the only way for us to catch this killer is an undercover operation. Dave and I discuss recruiting another female trooper, but Jet points out that she's built some sort of trust with Homocker. I'm finding it difficult to get onboard with a plan involving my wife being taking prisoner by a madman. Sure, she's very capable and can defend herself. Yes, I will be close and ready to respond as soon as she pushes the button. But, will that be good enough?

To field-test the equipment, Ronnie Torgy left in a patrol car and Ted departed in a Cessna 185 an hour before our meeting at the Palmer trooper post. Ronnie is now in Chickaloon Pass on the Glenn Highway. Ted is airborne, north of Willow. Both report strong, constant signals from the transmitters embedded in Jet's earrings.

"Sound the alarm," Dave says to Jet.

Jet pushes the button on her right earring.

"Okay, a red light is flashing on the receiver and the heading indicator shows a course of one hundred-twenty-four degrees and fifty-eight miles," Ted transmits on the airplane's radio.

"I've got a red light as well, showing a course of two hundred-twenty-one degrees and fifty-three miles," reports Ronnie. The alarm screeches in the background.

Jet pushes the button on her left earring, which also produces alarms on the receivers.

"Okay, that's a roger, guys. Now let's see if you can pick up the video transmission on your Blueberries," Dave says as he nods to Jet to activate her camera.

"Got it," reports Ted.

"Me too," Ronnie acknowledges.

I was hoping the systems would fail and we could stop this insanity. I'm ready to turn the case over to someone else. But, there's so much riding on this. First, and most important, we can put a murderer out of business. Second, when this is over we can start our lives together in Lone Wolf. Jet senses my concern.

She holds my hands and speaks softly, "Jack, don't worry. You know I can take care of myself. This is the way to catch this maniac and stop him before he kills more innocent women. Soon, we'll be back in Lone Wolf, sitting on the dock with Piper, catching fish. I need your total support, not your worry."

"I wish it was me instead of you," I say the only thing that comes to mind.

"Sorry Jack, but I'm cuter," Jet smiles, momentarily breaking the tension.

"When should we do this?" I ask, hoping someone will say "Never."

"I have no plans this evening. How about you, Dave?" Jet asks.

IT LOOKS LIKE THE MODERN VERSION OF AN OLD WEST POSSE, as the aircraft and troopers gather on a grassy patch at the Palmer Airport. Hayden Bensen, in his navy-blue flightsuit and bushy blonde mustache, stands in front of the A-Star trooper helicopter. Towering next to him is Dave Daniels, wearing blue jeans, a flannel shirt, and Kevlar vest. Dene Jones, a member of the Special Emergency Response Team—Alaska's answer to SWAT—stands in front of the chopper's bubble nose. The stern, powerfully built man wears a black tactical uniform and an expression indicating he'd love to use the sniper rifle he holds. He might come in handy.

Tucked in between the red and white Cessna 185 and the gleaming helicopter, sits Jet's green and white Super Cub. His hand resting on the big prop of the Cessna 185, Ted Herlihy intently studies the gathering. Next to him stands Ronnie, dressed in trooper blues, holding his absurd red backpack-parachute.

Jet wears a pink chamois shirt, jeans, hiking boots and a yellow cap. She looks the part of the innocent reporter, ripe for the picking by the killer.

"Let's make sure we have a fail-safe plan with backups. Then let's catch this killer and put him away." Usually willing to let others do the talking, it's different now that Jet's life's at stake. I step up and address the group, hoping to appear confident, although inside, my apprehension grows.

"Ronnie, I want you in the Cub with me." Ronnie beams and nods at me.

"Ted, you'll be up high in a Cessna 185. You'll be our communications platform and can call in the cavalry as needed," I say.

"Whatever you say, Jack." I know Ted would rather have his finger on a gun trigger than on a radio button, but he agrees.

"Dave, you'll be in the helicopter with Hayden Bensen and Jones."

My focus turns to Jet. "And you, Trooper Blake, don't be shy about activating that button. As soon as he makes his move, push it. Don't let him lay a hand on you."

"Yes sir, Trooper Blake, and I will be streaming video—as battery power allows," Jet gives me her crooked grin, meaning she's as nervous as the rest of us.

"Let's test the panic button again," I suggest.

Jet presses her left earring and a loud screech breaks from the receiver. The unit I hold flashes her coordinates in red digits. "Good, now let's all see if we can get Jet's video feed on our Blueberries," I ask.

Dave, Ted, Ronnie, and I watch Jet as she walks around with her camera activated, cracking us up with her joking observations of the serious troopers surrounding her. Jet's humor helps lighten the mood. For a bit, anyway.

As we continue our briefing on the sunny, fifty-five degree day, several airplanes in the pattern practice landings and take-offs. We'd selected a quiet spot off the departure end of the runway, where the traffic is a thousand feet above us. Our concentration is broken by an interloper who taxis a Cessna 182 in our direction. The pilot pulls his plane in front of the helicopter, kills the engine, and kicks his door open. *"Alaska Bush Ministries"* is boldly scrolled across the white and purple tail of the airplane.

"I thought you guys looked familiar!" The pilot strides toward me with his hand extended.

"Rich Emery, it's great to see you," Although not the best timing, I greet my former supervisor, who exchanged his badge for the cloth of the church. Jet hugs Rich, as the rest of the guys stand by to shake his hand.

"Sorry to barge in. It looks like there's something big going on. It's not my business anymore, so I won't ask." Rich served as a state trooper for eighteen years and knows there are times when the fewer people who know about an investigation, the better.

"As far as this mission is concerned, be glad you took an early retirement. By the way, Jet and I have been meaning to thank you for coming all the way out to Nishlik Lake for our wedding," I offer.

"I'm just sorry I had to leave before I performed the ceremony, but I hear it turned out well," Pastor Rich says, then exuberantly briefs us about becoming a flying minister.

The pastor smiles as Jet gives him the details of the wedding ceremony. Then he seems to notice the worry on our faces. He studies each of us individually, spending a little extra time on the trooper with the sniper rifle, then scans our little air force. "I can tell something weighs heavily on all of your minds. I'm sensing that you face special danger today. Do you mind if I say a prayer with you?"

"We need all the help we can get, Pastor," I say.

Rich asks us to bow our heads, then prays for guidance and for our safety. He shakes everyone's hand again and wishes us good luck. We watch as he takes off into the northern skies.

It seems we've been over the plan a hundred times. We've discussed every contingency the assembled troopers and pilots could throw out. We have a "back out" point for Jet if things get too crazy in the beginning. We have backup plans in case something goes wrong. We have comfort in our readiness, but I have a nagging feeling that we're missing something.

We rented a compact, nondescript car for Jet. Instead of a trooper log, she carries a notebook full of scribbling, to appear to be a freelance writer. She hands me her badge, all her official identification, and her Blueberry. Instead of a gun in her purse, she now carries the same essentials any woman totes. Nothing marks her as a state trooper. I realize the need to distance herself from her true identity, but the thought of the killer finding her personal items suddenly brings into focus how real this is.

With my arm around her shoulders, I walk Jet to her car as the troopers silently watch. We hug tighter than we ever have, then kiss. I tell her to be careful. She tells me to be safe. I close the door after she slides in behind the wheel and we both mouth, "I love you." Her white rental car disappears in a cloud of dust as she drives toward the unknown.

WE GO OVER THE PLAN ONE MORE TIME, after Ronnie asks "What do we do now?"

"We wait," I tell the usually happy, now nervous trooper. The men seem to be feeling the gravity of all this just as I am.

Ted Herlihy will be flying at high altitude in the Cessna 185. He will have the unobstructed range to track Jet, pass on communications, and to keep an eye out for the suspect. We test his receiver, which shows a green dot representing Jet's progress on the Parks Highway toward Wasilla.

Dene, the S.E.R.T. trooper, checks his .223 sniper rifle as Dave and Hayden check over the FLIR equipment in the helicopter. They will be standing by, high on the glacier.

Ronnie and I test the receiver we will be monitoring while flying the Super Cub. The screen shows Jet a mile away from the bar. I ask Ronnie to climb into the front seat and show him how the controls work on this tandem-seat airplane.

"The little Cessna I've been flying has a steering wheel instead of a stick, Jack, but the view sure is better in a Cub. Why do you want me to sit in the front?" Ronnie asks.

I explain to Ronnie that I'm able to fly the plane just as easily from the rear seat, and the extra space allows for more room to operate the tracking receiver. If necessary, I can shoot from the Cub's big door opening. The only hitch is the lack of a control stick in the back. That's quickly resolved in true Alaskan Bush pilot-style, using the fuel checker that's stored in the seat pouch. Taking silver duct tape from the baggage compartment, I wrap one end of the slim clear-plastic cylinder until it fits perfectly into the socket for the rear control stick. Now I can move the ailerons for turning, and the elevators for climbing and descending. I also have my own set of rudder pedals and a throttle control.

"This is going to be great, getting some stick-time in a Super Cub! Mind if I toss my chute in the back?" Ronnie swings out of the Cub and hands me his red parachute.

"Fine, Ronnie," I humor him, wondering how he plans to climb over me to get to his security blanket. Ronnie's concern is we don't crash. My concern is, if the red light flashes, we get to Jet in time. I cram the parachute next to my rifle pack.

My Blueberry beeps to announce a grainy video coming onto the screen. The camera jostles around, then Jet's face comes into view. She smiles, then mouths, "I love you" into the camera. The necklace drops to her chest and the camera again moves erratically as she walks. We don't have voice with this miniature camera system, but seeing live TV on our Blueberries, fed by a little wireless camera miles away, is impressive. I hope this silent movie has a happy ending.

Jet appears as a distant image, reflected in the mirror behind the bar. She lays her notebook on the counter and begins scribbling. The bartender walks over to her, grinning as he speaks. He nods down the bar and the camera turns that way. The pasty face of the man with the heavy black-framed glasses comes into focus. The marmot man moves closer, close enough that he must be sitting next to Jet. He smiles, not a friendly smile, but more of an evil sneer, as he lights a cigarette. The camera turns again to the mirror as a bottle of beer and a glass of wine are set on the bar.

The camera moves back to marmot man as he takes a swig of beer. The wine glass comes toward Jet's face. Marmot man looks at Jet the way a trapper might size up a glossy-coated black wolf caught in his Manning #9 trap. His close-set dark eyes bore through his thick glasses like muzzles of a double-barreled shotgun. They aim at the bartender, then back to Jet.

Jet writes something in her notebook, as Homocker motions with his hands in the air and speaks. The camera swings around, showing big game animal heads on the walls. Then the focus moves back to the marmot man. Silent words flow from his repulsive mouth.

The Blueberry goes blank. I reassure the troopers around me that it is to be expected. Jet said she'd turn the camera off to save its battery if there was nothing of interest to broadcast. I hope that's what she's done now.

The team reviews our plan once more. Then we engage in small talk, pre-flight our aircraft, check our weapons, anything to keep from looking at our watches. Twelve minutes and thirty-two seconds after the camera went blank, it comes back on. The suspect must still be bragging about all the big game he's killed, as he continues to speak animatedly.

The camera swings toward the mirror behind the bar. The bartender bends over and pulls a bottle of beer from ice. He grabs a wine glass from a shelf and sets it on the counter, then reaches for an open bottle of wine. He shuffles around, as if he's concealing something. He watches in the mirror as his left hand reaches forward. I can't tell what he has, but his left hand quickly moves over the wine glass. His right hand pours wine into the glass at the same time.

Did Jet see this, too? The grinning bartender places the glass and another bottle of beer in front of his customers. Homocker's hand raises the bottle to his mouth and he takes a drink. He nods toward Jet's glass. The camera focuses on the wine. Jet's hand reaches for the glass and it's lifted up and out of view.

Suddenly, the screen goes blank.

Chapter 34

HUNTING SEASON

A SUDDEN CHILL FILLS THE AIR. As light rain falls from the heavens, I grab my jacket from the Super Cub and join the other troopers under the wing of the Cessna 185. This is one of those unexpected storms which seems to race in from nowhere, surprising even the weather prognosticators. The light rain turns into a downpour, followed by a short, but vigorous dumping of pea-sized hail. Hayden checks the airport's automatic weather broadcast, finding the temperature has dropped from the mid-fifties to the low forties.

"She's on the move!" Ted holds up his receiver. Gathering around, we watch the illuminated dot indicating Jet is exiting the bar. The light on the receiver pauses, then continues in a northerly direction on the Parks Highway.

"Where are they headed?" Ronnie asks, his voice almost drowned out by the sound of hail pounding on the Cessna's wings like a snare drum.

"Probably toward Homocker's place," the wind rocks the airplane as I try to guess the madman's next move.

Hayden updates us on the weather. The FAA Flight Service station reports the freak storm should blow through in a few minutes and move off to the west.

"Once the weather breaks, what's next?" Dave Daniels asks.

"Do you want me to fly up to his airstrip and bust him?" Ted asks.

"Just get me within five hundred yards and I'll take him out," offers Dene Jones, as he cradles his scoped sniper rifle.

"Let's stick with the plan. Unless they stay too long at Homocker's place," I say.

"Why isn't Jet transmitting video?" Ronnie asks.

242

"Probably still trying to save battery power," I say hopefully, as we watch the green light moving toward Homocker's airstrip.

As if choreographed, we all simultaneously check our wristwatches when the light stops at Homocker's hanger. As suddenly as they began, the rain and hail end and the sun peeks through the clouds.

"Hayden, why don't you guys head up to the glacier and get into position? Monitor the radio and we'll feed you updates," I request.

"You've got it, Jack. I'll let you know what we see on the way up. By the way, the weather report shows there's only a four-point spread between air temperature and dew point. We're lucky we didn't get fogged in," Hayden offers.

"Do you want me in the air now, Jack?" Ted is itching to do something besides pacing up and down the airstrip. We quickly review a map and decide to have him fly a high pattern over the river flats.

Six minutes and twenty-two seconds have elapsed since the green light stopped at the marmot man's house. That's long enough for a hasty pre-flight of an airplane. It's long enough for many things.

The A-Star helicopter lifts from the grass, its gold trooper badge reflecting the evening sun. Dave gives final thumbs up, Dene adjusts his door for shooting, and Hayden's voice cracks over the radio with a simple, "See ya." The sleek chopper streaks off to the east.

Nine minutes and forty-three seconds have elapsed since the green light's movement stopped at the suspect's house. That's plenty of time to load gear and a passenger into the back of a Super Cub. It's ample time to do much more.

Crunching along on top of the hail pellets, Ted taxis the Cessna 185 to the far end of the Palmer runway. Announced with the ear-splitting sound from the propeller, the powerful engine responds as he advances the throttle. I check my watch as the red and white Cessna quickly becomes airborne, turning toward the river flats.

"Jack, it's been almost fifteen minutes since they got to Homocker's house. Shouldn't we be doing something?" Ronnie asks. It's actually only been fourteen minutes and twenty-two seconds, and I'd decided twenty minutes will be my breaking point. If there's no video—

or movement of the green light by then—we're going in. I'm keeping that plan to myself for now.

"Let's go over the controls of the Super Cub again. I may need you to fly while I'm tracking." Ronnie leaps onto the big tundra tire, then grabs the overhead bars in the cockpit to pull himself into the front seat. He follows me through as I show him the switches, buttons, and control knobs, explaining the function of each.

Sixteen-minutes and fourteen seconds have elapsed since the green light stopped moving.

"So, is there anything different about landing a tailwheel airplane?" Maybe Ronnie really cares, or maybe he's just trying to keep me from constantly checking my watch. Regardless, I give him a quick lesson on the differences between landing the Cub and a placid Cessna 150. Resembling a pitch hitter course—which teaches basic skills to passengers in small planes in case their pilot becomes incapacitated—I explain to Ronnie the fundamentals of landing. This reminds me of the woman whose husband died suddenly of a heart attack in the front seat of a Cub. Although she'd never flown before, she was able to call the tower in Fairbanks and a flight instructor talked her down to a rough, but non-injury landing.

Asking for a review on using the Cub's radios, Ronnie flips on the avionics switch just in time to hear an air-to-air conservation between Hayden and Ted.

"It's considerably colder up here on the glacier, and there's a slight wind blowing off the ice toward the river. I guess it must be from the rain shower, but there's steam coming from the river's gravel bars," Hayden reports.

"Is there any activity on the river?" Ted asks.

"We saw some wheel tracks on a couple of the gravel bars, and an airboat beached way up the river, but that's it," Hayden answers.

"Isn't it about time we should be getting worried about Jet?" Ted asks Hayden.

A smile comes over my face as I remember Jet gifting me with the aviator's watch now on my wrist. The smile quickly wanes as the timepiece urgently reminds twenty-one minutes and eleven seconds have elapsed. I ask Ronnie to hand me a headset from the plane so I can call in the troops. Forget the mission, it's time to go in.

"Jack, look at this. The green dot is moving again!" Ronnie holds the receiver up and, he's right, the Jet-dot is moving at twelve miles per hour.

"Ted, check your receiver," I radio to the Cessna.

"I was just going to call you. I see the movement," Ted acknowledges.

"Copy that," Hayden checks in.

The speed of the green dot picks up: 15, 18, 23, 35, 48, now 57 miles per hour. I push the zoom feature on the receiver to get a fix, as it quickly transects roads at seventy-five miles an hour. The altitude is eight hundred feet and increasing.

"It appears they are headed toward the Knik River. I'm going to keep making sweeps at six-thousand feet," Ted reports.

"Roger, we're going to hang tight until he passes the airport," I transmit. The GPS receiver indicates the plane is level at two thousand feet, and the speed stabilizes at eighty-five miles an hour.

I've been checking the Blueberry every few minutes, hoping to see an image from Jet's camera. My hopes are now answered.

Grainier than before, the image jumps in sync with the airplane's motions. I see the back of a man's head. The camera swings to show a river, then a view of the Palmer Airport. Now I see the Cub's metal baggage compartment. A rifle with a laser sight lies on one side. On the other side is a compound crossbow. Between the weapons is the paddle antenna photographed by Ronnie when we visited the suspect's hangar. The next image is of a heavily braided silty river, with steep mountains on both sides.

This next image disturbs me—I recognize the hands secured in plastic zip ties.

The Blueberry screen goes blank and I turn my attention to the receiver.

The green dot moves at eighty-seven miles an hour as it winds up the narrowing Knik River valley.

"Jack, this is Ted. I have a visual on a white Cub below me. By the transmitter, I'm sure Jet is in it." I acknowledge Ted and ask him to keep the Cub in sight.

The green dot passes to the right of Inner Lake George. The kidnapper will be forced to either turn around, or to land, as his flight path is taking him directly into high terrain cumulating in a landscape of glaciers and fjords.

"Jack, Hayden here. The temperature dropped another couple of degrees. The wind always comes off the glaciers in the evening and that's what it's doing right now. That steam we saw on the way up on the gravel bars is turning into fog. Unusual for this time of the year, but it looks like it may sock in the whole valley."

I acknowledge Hayden and hope Homocker has the skills to get out of the canyon, and not become trapped in the lowering conditions. Too many Alaska pilots crash under the same circumstances.

This isn't the best time for giving instruction, but when Ronnie asks if he can try a takeoff, I agree. Every little bit of practice he can get will help him. Knowing he may be needed on the controls—so I can use the electronics—I guide him through the takeoff roll.

Abruptly, Ronnie shoves the throttle forward. The Cub lurches to the right, then he stomps on the left rudder pedal so hard that we veer violently toward the edge of the runway.

"Easy, Ronnie, easy. Don't kick the rudders like you're trying to kill a snake." I get the plane back on a straight course, then Ronnie tries again. Fortunately, Super Cubs don't need much runway to get airborne. After meandering like a drunken driver for a few hundred feet, Ronnie yanks the stick back and we climb away from the airport. Stabilizing at fifteen hundred feet, we set a course to the glacier.

After trimming the airplane for level flight, Ronnie keeps the Cub steady while I monitor the transmitter screen. Jet's green dot is now stationary at the base of Lake George Glacier, about twenty miles from us. They must have landed on a gravel bar.

"Jack, this is Ted. I've got you below me. Be careful, it's getting a little foggy down there. My receiver indicates they've landed, but I can't see anything through the soup."

"It's foggy below the glacier as well, Jack. Do you want us to relocate?" Hayden asks.

"Unless you are worried about getting fogged in, how about staying put, Hayden? How's it looking upriver?" I ask.

"The fog seems to be packing in the further up you go. We will probably be above it here on the Knik," Hayden answers.

Taking over the controls, I add power to climb up to the glacier where we wag our wings at the helicopter. Making a series of climbing turns, we wait, hoping Jet will communicate soon.

"This is beautiful. I've never been this close to Dall sheep and I can't believe all the glaciers," Ronnie comments as we fly along the Chugach Mountain Range, and cross the five-mile-wide glacier. "When I last saw Dewey, he told me they filmed scenes for *Star Trek VI: The Undiscovered Country,* on this ice. It's here where Captain Kirk and Doctor McCoy were rescued from the Klingon Ice Planet Prison," Ronnie adds. I envision Dewey and Ronnie animatedly discussing the nuances of *Star Trek,* as I glance up at the 10,500 foot peak of Mount Gannett. The fields of ice, with their bottomless blue crevasses are daunting. But, Ronnie is right, the unique landscape does offer its own type of peaceful splendor.

"*SCREECH, SCREECH!*" The alert on the receiver penetrates the noisy cockpit. The green dot on the screen transforms to a red flash.

"Jack, I've got an alert!" Ted yells over the radio.

"Roger, same here. We're headed that way." My words break over the radio as I shove the throttle forward, diving toward the signal. A band of fog covers the entire valley below us, running from the base of Lake George Glacier for about five miles beyond Knik Glacier, concealing the river.

"Jack, I heard your transmissions. Do you want us in the air?" Hayden asks.

"Are your capable of landing in this stuff?" I question Hayden as we close in on the position indicated by the screeching, red-flashing signal. I hope the helicopter has some sort of high-tech, all-weather instruments, allowing him to "see" through the fog.

"Even with our radar-altimeter, it's an emergency maneuver at best. You never know what's below you in a whiteout. Sorry Jack, if the fog is thick, it's a no-go for us," Hayden delivers the bad news.

"Roger. Stand by where you are and I'll see if we can find a hole for you to drop through. Otherwise, I'd just as soon you not alert the suspect with the helo." We fly over the signal at fifteen hundred feet. It's been one minute and thirty seconds since the alarm.

"Jack, it's solid down there. I can't see anything but white," Ronnie looks over his shoulder and yells through the headset.

"Take the controls Ronnie, and keep her steady," I say, working the zoom function of the receiver and tapping the Blueberry.

The flashing red dot now travels at eleven miles an hour. Then something begins to appear like a ghost on the Blueberry screen.

The image is jumpy. Visibility is very limited in the dense fog. An image appears on the screen, then moves closer.

It's Homocker. He's carrying a rifle.

I've got to get down, somehow. Landing an airplane in this mess would be totally in the blind. At best, we'd crash land, being of little help to Jet with the clamor we'd make. The same outcome would be probable with the helicopter. Somehow, though, I have to get down there.

The blinking red dot is stationary.

The Blueberry screen again flashes a fuzzy image of Homocker. His gun comes up to his shoulder. Abruptly, the gunman swings away from the camera. The rifle appears to recoil from a shot. The red dot moves—now at ten miles per hour, now twelve. Jet is on the run. I've got to do something!

Looking up through the skylight, I seek inspiration. Whatever it takes, I need to get down to Jet. My life means nothing without her.

Closing my eyes, I say a "Church of the Woods" silent prayer, asking for inspiration and guidance. As I open my eyes, my prayer is answered.

Yanking my seatbelt open, I twist around to the baggage compartment, grab the red backpack, and lift it onto my lap. I pull the shoulder straps over me and snap them across my chest. I've never jumped from an airplane. It's almost beyond my comprehension why anyone would purposely sail through the air without wings. Crunching over, I half-stand to pull the leg straps between my thighs, securing the entire harness tightly about me. Using a piece of cord I'd found in the back, I fasten the receiver to the horizontal chest strap.

The red light still blinks.

Sensing my movement, Ronnie jerks his head around.

"Jack, you're not planning on doing what I'm thinking you are, are you?" Ronnie hysterically blurts.

Focused, I respond, "Where's the rip cord?"

"On your left shoulder strap, Jack. How am I supposed to land?" Ronnie screams.

"Ronnie, you've had one more ground lesson for landing a Super Cub than I've had for landing with a parachute. Just set up for a landing like the Cessna 150, but keep the stick back when you touch down. Now how does this thing work?"

"I've never bailed out either, Jack. The guy who sold it to me says to pull the cord as soon as you jump, then steer with the toggles on the sides."

Our altitude is fifteen hundred feet above the ground. If the chute doesn't open, I figure I'll hit the ground in about twelve seconds. My math may be a little off one way of the other, but it will be quick and final. Wind is not a factor, so I'm planning on jumping just a little in advance of where Jet's signal pinpoints her. That amount of lead always worked in the airdrops of supplies I've done.

"Ronnie, slow the plane to sixty and keep her steady at this altitude," I ask, as I slip the Blueberry into the leg pocket of my flightsuit.

"Okay, Jack. I'll do my best. And I'll try not to wreck her on landing."

The cold air blasts into the cockpit as I open the clamshell door. Swinging my legs out into the wind, I pull myself over to sit on the doorframe. The fog races beneath me as I check Jet's coordinates one more time. Reaching forward into the gale-force wind, I grab the wing lift struts, then pull myself out onto the big tundra tire. Struggling to hold on, I glance below to the solid layer of "whipped cream." The thought that, if only it had the texture of real whipped cream, it could soften my fall, runs through my head.

Adrenaline courses through me like never before, as Ronnie returns my thumbs-up sign.

Locking my hand into the ripcord handle, I simultaneously push from the struts and kick away from the tire. My hard yank on the ripcord has the desired effect—the parachute canopy pops open, abruptly jerking me upward.

All hell breaks loose—violently tumbling, my descent is out of control. The receiver flops from the chest strap and smashes into my face. This isn't supposed to happen, at least not from what I've seen in the movies, where para-jumpers glide elegantly to a landing. I whip into another tumble, then—not from anything I did—the parachute rights itself and floats me toward earth.

The whipped cream comes up fast. There's no reason to try steering with the toggles, since the visibility below is zero. Suddenly, the silent fog envelopes me. Then I hit. Pain runs up my right leg as I tumble through the brush, rolling forward into an ungraceful heap. Freeing myself from the parachute, I check the receiver. By some miracle, it has survived my clumsy fall from the sky.

The source of Jet's signal is only three hundred and thirty feet away.

With a quick tug, I pull the sharp alder branch from my left calf. Using the cord from the receiver, I tie pages from my trooper notebook around the wound to stanch the bleeding. My gun belt has twisted around, so the holster is at my back, but it still holds my Glock.

The red dot fades. I untangle myself from of the parachute harness and pull myself up with an alder branch.

In a limp-jog, I struggle toward the signal.

Visibility is no more than ten feet. I weave through the brush onto the open gravel bar. The signal is eighty feet away. I stop and slide the Blueberry from my pocket, but the screen is blank.

Then I hear it.

I pull my Glock from its holster. Silently, I move toward the moan. There's a body on the ground.

Relieved beyond words that it's not Jet, I kneel down beside the man. My eyes go first to the purple blood oozing from the chest wound, then to his face.

"Jack, ol' buddy! How did you get down through this fog?" Asks Dewey.

"Take it easy, Dewey," I say, as I wad up my glove and press it on his chest to try to control the blood flow.

"I monitored the suspect's plane on my remote webcam system from my camp upriver. When I saw marmot man's Cub land, I got down here as fast as could in my airboat. I was lucky—Homocker was just about to take his first shot at Jet when he saw me," Dewey says, coughing blood. "I surprised him. He turned the rifle on me as Jet ran. You've got to go find her, Jack."

"I will, Dewey. Hold this glove tight on your chest. We'll get you out of here as soon as we can," I try to reassure him.

"Jack, I'm not sorry for the things I have done, but for what I haven't done in my life. Don't say 'no' when you are offered once-in-a-lifetime chances—whether it's a special fishing trip, or when your lovely wife wants you go on a vacation with her, or just taking some time to kick back. You never think about it until the end, but it's true that life is too short. Don't end up bitter with regret over the life you wished you'd led," Dewey coughs the words out with blood.

"Dewey, thanks for all you've done for us. Hang on and I'll be back shortly with Jet," I say, knowing it will be too late.

"Go get your wife," Dewey whispers, smiling as his eyes close

The fog hangs like a layer of painter's plastic as I track Jet. She's two hundred and twenty-two feet away.

Suddenly, a silhouette appears through the haze. Approaching carefully, I determine that it's not human. Closer now, I begin to see the outline of an airplane. It's Homocker's Super Cub. I peer through the open door. Both the crossbow and the rifle are gone. So is the tracking antenna.

Kneeling down, I study the fresh tracks in the sand. One set belongs to Jet, the other must be his. Something behind me in the fog breaks my concentration.

Rising slowly, I slide my pistol from its holster. It's too late.

"So, the other one wasn't alone. Now I have two troopers to add to my trophy list," the high-pitched voice wafts through the fog. Dewey would have been proud to hear he was mistaken for a trooper, even if it was by marmot man. Maybe he did hear.

The red laser dot from Homocker's rifle dances on my chest, as he seems to be studying my face—probably trying to remember where we'd met.

Homocker can turn that red dot into a bullet before I can raise the pistol from my side, much less pull the trigger. But it's my only hope. I'll draw as fast as I can and hope that's faster than he can react.

I re-grip my Glock, envisioning where my bullet will hit the marmot man. Homocker's finger tightens on the rifle's trigger.

"*SHHH-THHUNK!*" Homocker's shotgun-muzzle eyes bulge. His black-framed glasses fly from his face. Blood gushes from his throat as the crossbow bolt penetrates into the back of his neck and through his larynx. The marmot man's rifle falls from his hands. He drops to his knees, stares at nothing, then flops face down onto the sand.

Like an angel, a vision floats through the fog. She carries a crossbow and glows with a pink-lipped smile.

"Nice of you to drop in, Jack." Jet drops the crossbow, rushes around the body, and wraps her arms around me. I ask her if she's okay.

"Not a scratch on me. The bartender tried to slip me a "Roofie," but I poured the wine onto the floor as he and this monster were pointing out more of their trophies. Pretending like I was drugged, I allowed him to take me to his place and load me in his Cub. His fantasy was ruined when we landed here, and I kicked him where it hurts. If it wasn't for Dewey, I'd be dead. He took a bullet for me, allowing me to get away and circle back to the plane. I dug around and found a pocket survival tool to cut the restraints. Then I grabbed the crossbow. Where is Dewey anyway?"

We follow my tracks back to Dewey's body. Sadly, we confirm he has no vital signs.

"He almost looks happy," Jet says with tears running down her cheeks.

"Dewey died the best way he could imagine," I guess.

As the fog begins to lift, I use the Blueberry to ask the rest of the posse to join us on the gravel bar.

Chapter 35

LONE WOLF CALLS

THE MIDNIGHT SUN blasts through the clouds, burning away the last of the fog. Ted lands first, using most of the length of the gravel bar in the Cessna. Hayden comes in shortly thereafter, with Dene Jones jumping out of the helicopter before the blades have stopped turning. He seems disappointed to have missed the opportunity to use his sniper rifle.

"Jet, don't you know marmot is out of season?" Ted's dry cop-humor is just what we need. Homocker, aka the marmot man, stares blankly as Ted and Dave zip the orange body bag over his face. Dewey's body has already been loaded on the helicopter's litter.

Jet tends to the cut on my leg with the first aid kit from the helicopter, as Dave takes photos of the scene and secures evidence. While the helicopter stood by on the glacier, Dave was busy on his Blueberry communicating with the attorney general. He now has search warrants for Homocker's plane, truck, hangar, and his house.

Joined by the helicopter, Ted flies Homocker's Cub as Jet and I pilot the 185 in a loose formation to the Palmer Airport. Ronnie excitedly greets us with an ear-to-ear grin, standing in front of the state Super Cub, spouting, "Jack, you wouldn't believe my landing. I greased it on!"

"Congratulations, Ronnie, I knew you could do it," I say, although maybe I'm stretching my vote of confidence just a bit. "I've got your parachute in the 185."

"Oh yeah, how did the day turn out for you guys?" Ronnie asks, as if we'd been out for a leisurely hike.

Jet and I glance at each other, then she answers, "All in all, not bad Ronnie, not bad."

We gather at Homocker's house to serve the search warrants. Two hours later we leave with boxes of women's clothing, charts showing probable gravesites, photos, videos, hand restraints, weapons, locks of hair, sheep lapel pins, and three human skulls.

Dewey's house provides all the evidence that he said it would, but we are surprised to see framed photos of each of us on his wall. Hanging next to the photos is a state trooper shoulder patch and a golden anniversary badge. A cuddly-stuffed Safety Bear smiles at us from a bookshelf. Lying on the center of his big oak desk is a manila envelope with Dewey's notation on the outside: There are two smaller envelopes inside. Open '#1' envelope now and follow the instructions. Thanks. Dewey. P.S., if you're reading this, I must be dead. Hope that went well. Dewey always had a way of getting in the last word.

The #1 envelope contains a letter addressed to the task force, as well as to the governor and the attorney general. Dewey explains that he has arranged for a celebration party for all of us this coming Saturday at the Lone Wolf Trading Post, where his will is to be read.

JAMES STEVENS ADDS HIS SECRET SAUCE to Aunt Bee's enchiladas. Steaks and salmon grill on the barbeque and beer flows freely. Ted and Anna are here, as are Ronnie and his wife and kids. Dave traveled from Kodiak, and Hayden dropped in from a fishery patrol with the helicopter. Governor Tinka Hines and Attorney General Cyrus Webster flew up from Juneau in the state King Air. Forrest Canon even showed up from Los Angeles, exclaiming Dewey had sent him a first-class airline ticket with instructions to be here tonight, unless he heard otherwise. To make Forrest's journey worthwhile, Dewey mailed James Stevens a check to take the big city police officer fly-fishing by Bush plane. Having no idea why they were invited, Russ and Barb from Kids Village are enjoying the celebration.

After toasting Dewey and one another—followed by a great meal, and dancing on the sawdust-covered floor—the crowd is silenced when Dave Daniels clinks a dinner fork on his beer mug. "Before I get started with Dewey's message, I have a couple of announcements to make about late-breaking developments.

"The first one proves timing is everything. Just this morning, I received the DNA test results. The blood smear from the ski pole matches samples Homocker was forced to provide three years ago for the state's DNA registry, mandated by his assault conviction. So, if anyone needs any more proof that we got our man, that should do it.

"The second announcement comes from a friend the Blakes made during their recent vacation in the Lower 48. Bo Chan called headquarters just before I left Anchorage today, saying he and his brother, Jun, are out of jobs. Bo sadly reported their boss, B.B. Sipes, was rushed to the hospital in Coeur d' Alene after collapsing in a bar. He died the next morning from what initially has been determined to be a subdural hematoma, probably caused when he fell from a river raft and hit his head on a boulder. The Chan brothers seemed more concerned about their livelihoods than the death of Sipes. Since the department just started their summer recruitment, I sent them both job applications for trooper positions. Now, on to Dewey's message." Jet softly taps her wine glass on mine and we share a smile. It's funny how things have a way of working out.

Pulling a document from an envelope, Dave continues. "I'll dispense with the legal jargon, but just let me say that Attorney General Webster has already reviewed Dewey's will, finding it to be legal and free of any conflicts of interest involving state employees."

Cyrus Webster nods his approval and Dave begins reading Dewey's words. "I hope everyone made it for the party. It's not a memorial to me, but a celebration of the good work that all of you do, especially in putting Mr. Homocker out of business. As I promised before, the majority of my estate is being left to Kids Village. Russ's face flushes in shock, even though he has yet to hear the generous amount his very worthy organization will receive.

"I'm also leaving a hundred thousand dollars to the Fraternal Order of Alaska State Troopers for their charity work. My house and acreage outside of Palmer is to be donated as a public safety training center, or for a wildlife troopers post, if it's needed. Otherwise, it is to be sold with the proceeds going to the Special Olympics fund.

"Next, this is for Trooper Torgy. Ronnie, you are a great guy, and I hope you considered me a friend. Sure, you may stumble more often than some of your comrades, but your heart is in the right place. I don't know if you noticed the pretty Cessna tied down at the Lone Wolf airport. It has low hours, will haul four people, and the Cessna 182 is considered one of the safest planes ever made. You'll find that the registration is in your name. It's all yours, and I've also paid a Bethel flight instructor to get you through the rest of your training. Enjoy it and be safe.

"Ted and Dave, James Stevens has something for you," Dave reads Dewey's words as Stevens presents each of them with a custom-made rifle.

"To Jack and Jet, I thought long and hard about what you could use. With a little research, I think I've found it. I hope Governor Hines is there and is willing do the honors. That will save Dave from reading the legal stuff below."

The governor strides to our table and gives Jet and me one of her famous group hugs. When a hug involves Tinka, it's something special. She hands an envelope to Jet, asking her to open it.

"What's all this?" Jet questions, studying the legal document.

"It's the deed to my cabin and property. Mr. McDougall bought me out. Jack and Jet, it's all yours. Congratulations!" The governor beams.

THE REMAINS OF fifteen women were eventually discovered. Who knows how many Homocker actually killed, but there are Xs on charts where bodies were never found. Alaska's tundra isn't easy to search, but someday a hunter will likely stumble on bones that have been strewn about by bears or other carnivores. Homocker thought of himself as the world's greatest hunter, be it game or women. HOAR—the outlaw hunting group—must have agreed, as he was honored at its annual banquet.

THE RAINBOW TROUT leaps out of Tranquility River, swallowing the dry fly at the end of my line. With the grayling Jet caught earlier, we now have dinner. Tired from romping with his best pal, Annie the moose, Piper nudges in between Jet and me. The three of us sit on the dock as the state trooper floatplane bobs alongside. It is a golden moment, with nothing more pressing right now than to gaze at an eagle diving for its dinner.

"Do you think our lives will finally be normal, now that all this is over?" Jet's lovely eyes meet mine with the question.

"As normal as it can be in this business. I guess we'll just have to accept that this is our life." That's all I can offer my bride, as the eagle lifts his catch to a branch of a scraggly cottonwood tree.

Jet reaches for my hand, saying, "It's a good life, Jack, now that we have each other." I smile in agreement.

I consider casting one more fly, then think of the words of Henry David Thoreau.

"Many men go fishing all of their lives, without knowing that it is not fish they are after."

Help the adventure continue.

If you'd like to help Troopers Jack and Jet Blake, here's what you can do:

• Buy a copy of *Alaska Justice* or *Alaska & Beyond* as a gift for a friend or family member. Quantity discounts are available. The author will be glad to personalize a book upon request.

• Visit the website, www.AdventurousBooks.com to order books and for updates.

• If you have a website or blog, consider sharing what you like about the book, but don't tell how it ends!

• Write a book review for www.Amazon.com, your local paper, a magazine, or a website. Ask a radio show or podcast to have M.D. Kincaid as a guest.

• If you own a business, consider displaying the books and reselling them to customers. Ask about discount rates through our webpage.

• Spread the word by email or word of mouth. If you are a member of a book club, consider *Alaska Justice* and/or *Alaska & Beyond*. Ask about book club discounts.

• If you think this book will make a good movie, feel free to tell your favorite movie star or movie producer.

Thank you for your support!

Printed in the United States
145694LV00003B/3/P

9 780979 669347